Shadows and Masks

Book 1 of The Chessmen series

Averil Reisman

Heartsong Books

Published by Heartsong Books,
Imprint of Novel Interaction, Inc.
Lake in the Hills, IL

ISBN-13: 978-0-9860528-6-6

Please Note
This is a work of fiction. Names, characters, places, and incidents either are the product of the author's imagination or are used fictitiously, and any resemblance to actual persons, living or dead, business establishments, events or locales is entirely coincidental unless specified by the author in her notes.

Cover by Dawn Charles of BookGraphics
Website: www.bookgraphics.net

Story Content edited by Karen Dale Harris
Website: www.karendaleharris.com

Dedication

To Lisa, Marla, Julie, Jason, and Miranda.
You are my pride and joy
---Mom

Chapter 1

"I need a husband in a week's time. Can you help me secure one?"

Emmeline Griffith's request crackled about the investigator's office like heat lightning on a hot summer day, its effect bold and intense. She scrutinized the man sitting opposite her, thankful a veil hid her heated cheeks.

Lordy! To be reduced to needing help to find a husband. She clamped her jaw tight, afraid she would utter a blasphemy as colorful as the ones her father once spouted, and spoil the only course of action she had left. However, she doubted even a curse would have mattered to the man sitting opposite her.

Bartholomew Turner, the professional her uncle had recommended eons ago, might have been a statue for all the response he gave. Not a word. Not an expression. Not even a blink of his penetrating brown eyes that matched the walls of his office.

Well, fine. Two could play at this game of silence, embarrassment be damned. She would just wait him out, make him speak first. Patience was not only a virtue, but the key to the art of negotiating. As president of Chicagoland Electric, she understood negotiating—both winning *and* losing. In this, she would not lose. Too many people's livelihoods depended upon her success.

She surveyed the brownstone home office in the hopes of obtaining some measure of the man she planned to hire. Definitely a male domain. In fact, more like a lion's den—dark and foreboding, remarkably akin to the man himself. Three tall bay windows overlooking Eugenie Street were covered with heavy swag and cascade drapery. Shrouds, really. Walls of carved mahogany paneling added to the gloom. The office occupied the front parlor of a three-story rowhouse in a fashionable but not quite tony residential neighborhood of Chicago.

Emmie straightened, tucked her crossed feet tight to the davenport, and stared at the investigator. His silence was deafening, his gaze intense. It was as if he saw right through to her soul where her darkest desires and most shameful secrets were buried. And that made her uncomfortable. Extremely uncomfortable.

He reminded her of a lion she had seen in one of her father's safari photographs, the animal lying in wait to strike its stalked prey. Even the way he had moved when greeting her—graceful and fluid—bore a strong resemblance to the big cat at the zoo. Unruly curls drifted about his handsome face as though each strand had a mind of its own. A mane. Brown instead of golden. One coil dangled over his eye, begging to be tucked behind his ear if not for the aura of aggression about him. The man's height, width of his shoulders, length of his arms, even the size of his hands spoke of power and command.

A shiver tracked up her spine. He was danger personified. And absolutely fascinating.

Mr. Turner finally moved, shifting his big frame to the edge of the leather chair, which creaked in response. He clasped his hands between his knees as though in prayer. His mouth had turned up a fraction, a half-moon of amused interest. "You can't be serious."

His smooth baritone flowed over her like warm honey, but for some reason, his voice's deep resonance caused her mouth to lose moisture. "I'm quite serious." Dead serious, really.

His mouth curved up even more. "I have to admit, your request is the most... unusual I've had in a long time."

"Unusual, yes. But then, I'm a most unusual woman."

He laughed, the sound as deep and robust as the timbre of his voice. She felt its power move through her, spreading warmth clear out to the ends of her toes. She didn't like the feeling at all—the sense that she was losing her senses.

Pull yourself together, Emmie. Don't let this man affect you.

"I gather that, Miss Griffith. You're quite direct about things, aren't you?"

"I am that, yes. I don't have time for idle conversation." A crease appeared between his eyes and for some reason Emmie didn't like that either. "I'm sorry if my directness offended you, Mr. Turner. Are you going to help me or not?"

The amusement in his eyes returned and she felt herself relax. "Miss Griffith, I wouldn't think you'd need help in finding a husband. In fact, I find your directness quite engaging, and so would a lot of men."

Pleasure tracked through her, but she tamped it down, accrediting his remark to irrelevant small talk. "Thank you, Mr. Turner, but I'm in a pickle and I need your help."

"Why me? Why not someone else?"

Ugh! This man was impossible. Interesting, but annoying nonetheless. "You were the one recommended." She let it go at that.

The amusement leached from his eyes, replaced by a whisper of sadness that, by all rights, shouldn't have been there.

"Recommended as a husband? Me? Come now. We don't even know each other." His tone was light, playful even, but his expression now was more like he tasted something unpleasant.

His comment drew an equally disagreeable taste in her mouth.

Good Lord! Married to this virile being? Never. He was too dark, too intimidating, too utterly engaging. She didn't want a real marriage to a real husband, didn't want to be stifled or set aside as a superfluous bit of womanhood. She sought something else altogether. Freedom, independence, and the ability to direct her own life. This man would never do.

"I... no... I mean... I was hoping you could find someone. . ." Oh, botheration. She sounded like a tongue-tied ninny. If she didn't get hold of herself, she would become a blithering idiot by the time the interview was over.

He raised an eyebrow, and crossed one leg over the other, the motion drawing his suit trousers tight to his skin. Thick thigh muscles rippled beneath the expensive pinstriped fabric. Suddenly overly warm, Emmie inched farther along the davenport under the pretense of settling her skirt.

Of all the investigators in Chicago, why had her uncle given her this man's name for emergencies?

Because he is good at what he does.

His well-tailored clothes, the confident way he carried himself, the quality of his office furnishings, even his address spoke of success and financial accomplishment. Intelligence inhabited his eyes as he studied her, his head cocked to the side. She would have to watch what she said. Divulging too much too soon was not in anyone's interest—least of all, hers.

"Why do you need a husband so urgently?"

She drew in a breath. It wasn't easy to admit she needed help, but she had no choice. "My father's will stipulates that if I'm not married by my twenty-fifth birthday, his estate will revert to my cousin, Paul Harris, my mother's sister's son."

Mr. Turner recrossed his legs. "I suppose every father wants his daughter married off, but why would he put it in his will? You must have done something wild and reckless in the past to justify his concern."

His bald insinuation rankled. She straightened her spine. "I did no such thing, Mr. Turner. My father and I merely disagreed on what would make me happy. He equated happiness with marriage, while I valued my independence more than having a husband. In the end, he got his way, didn't he? He put the stipulation in his will with a deadline, and I'm stuck with it."

"When did he pass?"

She raised her chin. "Five years ago."

He blinked. "Why did you wait so long to find a husband?"

"I did not wait, Mr. Turner. My fiancée, Alex, died in a riding accident two years ago. His loss was devastating, and it took me a long time to recover. After that, and for a variety of other reasons, I decided I didn't want a real marriage. In fact, if it weren't for the will, I wouldn't have sought a husband at all."

"But two years…?"

"It took me a long time, but I finally found a gentleman from Germany who sought an American wife so he could remain in this country. We agreed to marry in a business arrangement, then divorce at the end of a year. I hear it's done all the time. We were to be married two weeks ago, but the day before the ceremony, he wrote that he eloped with another woman. Which leaves me seeking a similar arrangement once again with only a week left. So, you see why I need your help, Mr. Turner?"

The man stroked his chin, his expression thoughtful. "Matchmaking is not one of my usual services, Miss Griffith. I wouldn't know where to begin, let alone be successful in meeting your time limitations."

A whirling eddy invaded her belly, violently churning its contents. She needed a husband. Now. "Couldn't you try? Surely you have more resources available than I." She hated to beg but she knew of no one else to help her. She wished Uncle Reggie still lived in Chicago. He would have known what to do.

Mr. Turner gave her a small polite smile. "Miss Griffith. I'm sorry. This really isn't my area of expertise. I'm sure there are other professionals in this city better suited to meet your needs. I would recommend you contact one of them." He rose.

Her heart sank to her toes. A dismissal. She hadn't planned on that, and had no intention of giving up just yet. Despite the distraction of his virile physicality and her womanly need to be anywhere but in his presence, desperation now pushed her down a different path.

A very dangerous path. At least for her.

"Mr. Turner, might I entice you to join me for dinner tonight? I'd like to further discuss my *needs*, as you so interestingly put it." If her eyes weren't covered by a veil, she would have batted her lids. As it was, she made sure her tone was thick with sugar.

Surprise suffused his chiseled features. "Miss Griffith, I see no need for further discussion on the matter, but if you'd like a companion for dinner, I'd be more than happy to join you."

Relief, as fresh as the brush of a summer breeze on heated flesh, rushed through her. "I would, and thank you. It's rather lonely eating alone. I'm staying at the Palmer House. How about meeting me in the lobby at seven tonight? I'd love to try Henrici's in its new location on Lake Street, if you don't object?"

"I'd like that very much. I'll meet you at seven, then."

She rose and held out her hand. "Thank you, Mr. Turner. I'm looking forward to it."

And just maybe I can convince you to change your mind without playing my ace.

~~~

The din in the cavernous Palmer House second floor lobby quieted to a soft hush. Society matrons and their daughters, eager to be seen in the vast ornate sitting area, all stared at someone entering the far end of the long rectangular room.

Emmie had never cared a whit about society, or people of import for that matter. But she sensed by the prickle at the back of her neck who had arrived. The man she was relying upon to find her a husband.

Seated in the center of the lobby, she turned in her plush, cushioned chair. The imposing, attractive man she had talked into dinner threaded his way down the marble path between groupings of couches and chairs. Dozens of female eyes beside her own followed his progress.

Beneath her veil, her cheeks heated. She willed her pulse, beating a furious tattoo, to slow. This was a business dinner, an extension of their earlier meeting, only more urgent. Was it not?

And then he was before her, his assessing, chocolate brown eyes sweeping her from hat to boots. "Good evening, Miss Griffith. You look lovely tonight."

His tone was polite, his words perfunctory. Yet, tingles raced along her nerve endings. She fought an urge to peer down at her gown. "Thank you, Mr. Turner."

For this crucial evening, she had chosen a simple robin's egg blue silk with small cap sleeves, fitted bodice, and an enticing décolletage. Devoid of adornment, the gown of a single color and material made her appear taller than her limited height of just over five feet. Still, he soared over her like a tower of granite.

He had shaved, the deep cleft in his chin visible in the soft glow of the gold Tiffany chandeliers. He looked splendid in the black three-piece evening suit and white cravat he wore with an air of comfortable casualness, as though he escorted ladies to dinner every night. Maybe he did. She knew nothing about the man's private life, nor did she care to.

He extended his hand. "Ready?"

"I believe I am, Mr. Turner."

He took the lace shawl draped on her arm, and drew it across her shoulders. The warmth of his fingers brushing her skin sent sparks flying to places she dared not acknowledge. She tightened her jaw, willing herself to rein in her unwanted reaction. She had no time for frivolous feminine feelings. As far as she was concerned, this was a business meeting over dinner. Nothing more. But nothing less either. Failure was not an option.

~~~

After seating Miss Griffith at a table in a private corner of Henrici's, Bart stole a glance at his dinner partner over the edge of his menu.

This puzzling woman had uttered her ridiculous request this afternoon with nary an emotion in her voice, her words ripe with all the intrigue and mystery of a dime novel. He had wanted to laugh, and found himself struggling to keep his face neutral. It wasn't every day a potential client expressed an urgent need for a spouse. And from the sound of things, any man would do.

For all the uniqueness of her request, however, her appearance had been a cliché out of the same dime novel. A thick veil—a lacy thing matching the trim on her gray walking suit—had hung over her face from a small pile of feathers, hiding her eyes as thoroughly as her high necked, long-sleeved jacket had concealed her petite form.

Tonight, her elegant understated attire presented a decided shift from her earlier prudish appearance. The provocative bodice of her evening gown hugged her torso like a corset, pushing swells of creamy flesh well above its edge.

However, another veil cloaked her face, a closely woven net which fell from a small hat perched close to her forehead.

He puffed out a breath and let it escape in silent complaint. Though he was a master at assessing character, Miss Griffith wasn't making his task any easier. He had to see her face.

"Miss Griffith, would you do me the honor of removing your veil? I can't see your lovely eyes."

Her breasts heaved on a long intake of breath. She raised her head from the menu. After glancing around, she slowly drew the bottom of the net with both hands up over her hat.

Large blue eyes scrutinized him from a small oval face that was more handsome than pretty. A long curl of raven black hair fell along a high cheekbone from a sleek knot at her crown. Except for her eyes, which contained a trace of sadness, there was nothing particularly remarkable about her rather plain, even features.

Yet, beneath that ordinary appearance, he detected a strength he'd seldom encountered in the women he'd taken on as clients or, for that matter, the women he'd squired about town. Here was a no-nonsense woman who barreled her way through obstacles as though they were made of paper, a woman who had determined what she wanted and had set about getting it. Regal and self-possessed, she had exited his office this afternoon as though she owned it.

Which had left him wondering if she had any vulnerabilities hidden away, like an oyster might hide a priceless pearl. For some reason, he found her steely bearing oddly compelling. A mystery he would have liked to have solved had he taken her case.

"Ah, better. You don't need a veil."

A delicate pink suffused her face, and she went back to perusing the menu without comment. Except, now her hands trembled.

He cleared his throat. "Miss Griffith, since I already turned down your case, I'm curious as to who recommended me."

She sighed, the sound almost like a whisper of wind. "I probably need to give you this." She rummaged in her handbag, and a few seconds later pulled out a small figurine.

A delicate ivory chess piece.

A king.

What the hell? Bart straightened in his chair, his pulse picking up speed. He stretched out his hand. "May I?"

She handed him the piece. He fingered it gently, passing his thumb over the bottom surface. A small indentation in the center proved the chess piece belonged to the secret government crime fighting agency of which he was a part. The king belonged to Reginald, his mentor and supervisor, the man he credited with turning his life around.

Each member of the organization had his own chess piece, a method of handling referrals that eliminated the need for face-to-face contact or revealing letters. Bart could identify no other agent in the service by sight, and no other agent could identify him. Except Reginald, who met with everyone. Each agent had his personal network of aides and assistants, and each had his own area of proficiency.

Bart hunted murderers.

His profession as a private investigator made the perfect cover for the occasional cases Reginald referred to him. The only differences between his work as a private investigator and as a government agent were the people and places he dealt with, and on occasion, they overlapped.

He frowned, his gaze intent upon the small piece. "How did you come by this?" He hadn't meant to sound so harsh, but his gut was now telling him what he didn't want to hear.

At that moment, the four-piece orchestra in the far corner began the familiar strains of Strauss's *Blue Danube*, and the waiter arrived to take their order.

Miss Griffith waited until they were alone to answer. "My uncle gave it to me along with your name shortly after my father died. Uncle Reggie was about to move to Washington and thought someday I might need a champion when he wasn't in town."

Reginald Griffith's niece? Damn! Why hadn't he make the connection in their last names earlier? The woman's bizarre request shifted out of the sphere of the nonsensical into the realm of the serious.

"Why, in God's name, didn't you show me this earlier?"

She scrutinized him with an intensity that almost made him uncomfortable. Almost. "I had hoped to convince you to help me without having to lean on my uncle to do it. I was wrong, Mr. Turner."

Convince him? Ordered was more like it. Bart rarely turned down an agency referral, and never one from his boss. Like it or not, Miss Griffith was now his client, and he was duty-bound to protect all her interests, however strange they might be.

But where the hell was he supposed to start? Matchmaking was as alien to him as creating a lady's hat.

Start with what you know. Reginald's advice drifted through his mind as clear as if he were sitting at the same table.

Protection. He knew about that. A legal marriage to a stranger posed physical dangers too distressing to contemplate. Was she even aware of them? He shuddered as a wave of revulsion rose from his gut. There were many cruel people in the world and he would not have Reginald's niece harmed by one.

Bart looked up into crystal blue eyes burning with hope.

He steepled his fingers and shifted into his role of an investigator. "You have my attention now, Miss Griffith, but if I'm going to help you, I need to ask some questions of a rather delicate nature."

Her eyes narrowed. "Such as?"

"Do you intend to consummate your marriage?"

Her jaw tightened almost imperceptibly, but his trained eye caught the movement. "No. It would be in name only. We would live together for three months, then live separately for a time, and finally divorce after a year."

She had it all thought out, except he doubted she considered the risks, specifically those posed by men who couldn't keep their trousers buttoned. He needed to protect her from those types at all costs.

He twirled the stem of his wine glass. "What if the man wants to exercise his husbandly rights during those three months?"

Another rude question, but necessary under the circumstances. She needed to consider all the scenarios such a marriage could entail.

Miss Griffith fingered the forks near her plate and shifted on her chair. "As part of the bargain, I'd pay the gentleman handsomely for maintaining a platonic relationship. But I don't think there will be a problem, Mr. Turner."

"And why is that?" So naive she was.

"Because of this." She turned her head to the side and pulled the long curly lock of hair away from her cheek. A jagged white scar ran from her temple down a high cheekbone to her jaw.

"And this." She tugged off an odd-shaped glove from her left hand to reveal middle and ring fingers fused together. From the inside of her wrist through her palm and out to the ends of her fingers, mottled, uneven scar tissue covered her hand.

He glanced up, shocked. "Fire?"

She nodded. The corners of her mouth now drooped. Her head bowed, she replaced her glove with stiff, awkward movements. "My scars are repulsive to men, so your concern is misplaced."

Where did she ever get that idea? A scar that could be hidden beneath a curl, or a deformed hand beneath a glove shouldn't deter any suitor, especially if she were an heiress. He doubted they would halt the advances of a randy temporary husband, either.

"Miss Griffith, I don't think your scars would discourage any man."

Incredulity marked her features. "I question that, Mr. Turner, but should I need assistance in that direction, I have staff living in the main house."

Not good enough.

"I know a man, a master forger, who can get you a fake marriage certificate, one indistinguishable from the real one. Then all we'd need is someone to act as your husband. You'd never have to actually live with him." But as he thought the idea through again, he changed his mind. "Never mind. Bad idea. That would be criminal fraud."

She shook her head, tension radiating off her in giant waves. "It wouldn't work anyway. Papa's lawyer is a shrewd man. He'll easily identify the papers as false. The marriage must be legal. I want no one to question whether I'm following the letter of the will."

"You'd rather decimate your reputation, not to mention the man's, with a divorce?" Though she'd be doing just that with a ruse, as well.

She sat back in her chair and folded her arms about her. The motion caused an impressive display of bosom over the edge of her gown. "I don't circulate among Chicago's elite, Mr. Turner. What people think of me is not important. And it shouldn't be for the man I seek either. The right man."

He would challenge her any day. But, something didn't ring right. She seemed too desperate. Too willing to risk her personal safety, too willing to step close to marriage fraud, and too willing to suffer the social consequences of divorce. Was she the type who would do anything for money? Somehow, he doubted that. Or maybe he just wanted to believe she wasn't the money-grubbing type.

His instincts told him she was omitting something important, something he needed to know to help her. On the surface, her story sounded plausible, but.... He set aside his disquiet for a later discussion with Cedric, his assistant. A fresh analysis of her case would help to clarify his thoughts.

"Miss Griffith, I believe you're walking in the wrong direction. I have seen the ugly side of men, and heard of acts unbearably cruel and inhumane. I wouldn't want anything bad to happen to you."

"Why are you so concerned?" Her tone matched the determined set of her jaw and the statue-like way she held herself.

Because trust is a fragile thing, Miss Griffith. Once shattered, it's extremely hard to restore. If ever.

"If your uncle recommended me, he would want me to protect you as well as assist you in finding what you seek."

Slowly an idea formed in his head, an idea that sent his thoughts racing in a direction he never intended.

"Miss Griffith, would you mind coming to my office Monday afternoon at two? I may have some answers for you, but I need to work out a few details before I tell you."

Her face blossomed into a glorious smile, brilliant blue eyes transforming her plain features into a sunny summer day. He basked in her warmth, and found himself wanting to see more of that smile.

"Certainly, Mr. Turner. But can't you give me a hint of what you plan?"

"I can only tell you my plan would give you everything you want. You want a temporary marriage that is platonic in nature, Miss Griffith. I want to protect you from the villainy of a stranger, a man neither of us knows at this point."

And the best way to do both was to marry her himself.

~ ~ ~

Bart slipped the chess piece he had been fingering into his jacket pocket, and moved to the sideboard in his private office later that evening. He needed a drink. Badly.

Lifting the stopper off a crystal decanter with shaking hands, he poured himself a half glass of bourbon, added a few chunks of ice from a silver bucket, and retreated to the comfort of his leather reading chair. Gaslight glowed softly from a single wall sconce, creating the perfect mood for thinking.

Or mental haranguing, if he were truthful.

What the hell was he thinking? How could he possibly offer himself up to a marriage? Even a temporary one.

He had planned to never marry, never subject a woman to the dangers that lurked in the world he inhabited. Both his government work and his cover as a private investigator brought him into contact with the unsavory underbelly of the city, a world of cunning killers, crazed vengeance seekers, prostitutes, gamblers, cutthroats, robbers and thugs. No woman should have to live with the fear of not knowing when or if he would be coming home at night.

Oh, hell. Even now he was hiding from the truth, the remnants of a past that haunted him still—the darkness within, the long sleepless nights, the memories that refused to fade into oblivion. That was the real reason he couldn't ever share his life with a woman.

He had worked hard to keep his bachelorhood intact all these years. Accepted by an odd assortment of sons of Chicago's wealthy, he discovered that many of his friends shared his repulsion of marriage, though for different reasons. Despite squiring debutantes to numerous balls and charity events, he and his friends had avoided countless snares of determined mothers and simpering daughters on the hunt for suitable husbands.

So, why was he considering jumping into what he had scrupulously avoided?

Because Reginald's niece needed a husband, and he owed Reginald more than he could ever repay. Because the marriage would be temporary with a definite end date. Because for him, divorce was not an obstacle. He never intended to seek a wife anyway.

And because it would be platonic. No commitments. No marital intimacy.

The truth of this last hit him in the gut, a truth he didn't want to face, the truth about a scar he carried to this day. A scar too ugly to risk exposure.

All Miss Griffith's stipulations gave him a way out, a way to help her without fear of a physical or emotional relationship which he neither sought nor wanted. It was a perfect plan to help her and at the same time fulfill the obligation he had to Reginald.

Fifteen minutes later, he felt, rather than heard, his assistant's presence near the door. Cedric's unique facility for stealth made him the perfect information gatherer. If he didn't know the older man descended from a long line of English valets, he might have thought him a spy. Pretending to be Bart's butler and dresser provided an excellent cover for the man's unusual activities in the pursuit of justice.

"Will that be all, sir?" Cedric's clipped English accent was unmistakable. In the ten years he had lived in this country, his pronunciation of the King's English hadn't lessened one bit.

Bart's gaze swung to the door.

"Stay a moment, will you, Cedric? I need to discuss something with you."

Cedric stepped into the parlor, pulling a too-snug vest down over his round belly. "Is it about the young lady who was here this afternoon, sir?"

"That and more."

Cedric seated himself on a nearby chair, his eyes lit with curiosity. "Interesting lady. Are you going to take her case?"

Bart swirled the liquor around his glass. The remaining ice clinked softly against its sides. "At first I declined. I thought her request a joke and, in any case, matchmaking is not what we do. This evening she gave me this."

He dug in his pocket and pulled out the chessman.

Cedric pulled in a breath. "Reginald's?"

"She's his niece. He gave it to her years ago in case she needed help when he wasn't around. We have no choice. She's our client now."

Cedric's puzzled look echoed his own thoughts of a few hours before. "But she seeks a husband, sir."

It came as no surprise that his assistant, who hadn't attended the afternoon meeting, was a familiar with Miss Griffith's case as he. The man had an uncanny ability to blend into the woodwork and eavesdrop, materializing when needed.

"I'm planning on volunteering for the job."

"You?" Cedric's tone was incredulous. He was well aware of Bart's desire to remain a bachelor.

Bart swallowed a mouthful of bourbon. Fire flowed down his throat and settled in his stomach. "Yes, me."

Cedric pulled at his left earlobe. "I say sir, don't you think marrying her yourself is a bit drastic?"

"The marriage will be temporary. Three months spent together, then a separation, followed by a divorce at the end of a year. And it's platonic. In short, a marriage in name only. I don't know how else to find her a husband on such short notice and protect her at the same time. Reginald *would* expect me to protect her, wouldn't he?"

"Of course, but...."

"Here's the problem though, Cedric. My instincts tell me Miss Griffith is holding back something that may have considerable bearing on her situation. I need to know what that is."

"Now that you mention it, I had the same impression, sir. Do we know what her father's estate entails? Land? Gold mines? Railroads? Wouldn't it be interesting if her inheritance made her fabulously wealthy?"

"I'm not sure if that is even it, Cedric, but I'm determined to find out. There is a quality of desperation about her that makes me think there is more at stake here than just money. Over the next few days, I intend to find out."

Bart drank the remainder of his bourbon and set the glass on a nearby table. "Will you alert Judge Mahoney? The ceremony should take place as soon as possible."

His assistant rose and whisked the glass off the table. "Yes, sir. Oh, and Mr. Shields stopped by, but since you were out, he said he would come back early tomorrow morning."

Bart snickered. "Tomorrow is Saturday. Nick doesn't ever rise early, especially on a weekend."

"He seemed somewhat upset, sir."

"Now this I have to see. Nothing upsets Nick, except perhaps not being invited to sample Gertie's cooking."

Chapter 2

"You're going to marry her, and then divorce her? Hell, man. Are you out of your damn mind?" Nicholas Shield thrust his fingers through his blond hair the next morning, and pitched his substantial frame against the stone mantel in Bart's private office.

The scowl on his friend's usually imperturbable features revealed more of his opinion of Bart's plan than what came out of his mouth. Raised Catholic, Nick abhorred the idea of divorce and was even more adamant about remaining a bachelor than any of Bart's other friends. His parents' marriage was a notorious sham he didn't care to repeat.

"Miss Griffith doesn't want a forever marriage, Nick, and neither do I. We'll live together a few months until a delicate piece of business is settled, then separate, and ultimately divorce. The woman needs to be legally married in six days, and she is out of time to find someone else."

"What the hell does she need to be married for?" Nick barked.

Bart slumped against the back of his chair. "To meet a stipulation in her father's will. She must be married by her twenty-fifth birthday, or his estate goes to the woman's first cousin. Her father wrote the blasted thing into his damn will and now she's stuck with it."

Nick rubbed the back of his neck, questions forming in his eyes. "Why you? You hate the thought of marriage as much as I. Come on. Don't do this, man."

Bart shook his head. "Too late to back out now. Judge Mahoney agreed this morning to perform the ceremony Tuesday evening. Miss Griffith doesn't even know yet."

"This is crazy, Bart. How can you blithely throw away everything you've always believed about marriage for the sake of some client's problem? This doesn't make any sense."

Bart listened patiently as his closest friend struggled to understand his plan. Nick's usual jovial personality had transformed into an angry bundle of tension and nerves. Not that he blamed the guy. Hell, Bart hardly believed it himself. But Nick's upset appeared out of proportion to the situation at hand. After all, *he* was not the one getting married.

Nick flopped into a chair and thrust his long legs out before him.

"All this anger isn't about my marriage, is it Nick? Why did you come to see me?"

Nick leaned forward, his hands clasped between his knees. "Shit, Bart. Leave it to you to get to the heart of things. It's *my* marriage burning me up."

Bart felt his jaw slide open.

"My parents made arrangements without my knowledge. They'll be releasing the news to the gossip columns by the end of the week. Arranged marriages just aren't done anymore. How could they do this to me?"

His friend's plight garnered Bart's sympathy. "I don't know, Nick. Maybe your parents want to see grandchildren."

"They could have waited for Sabrina to marry."

Bart choked back his response. At twenty-eight, the likelihood of Nick's sister Sabrina marrying and producing grandchildren was slim.

"Do you know this woman they want you to wed?"

"It's Tessa Brownly, of Brownly shoe fame. She just had her come-out. I'm twelve years her senior, for god's sake. I met her twice. My parents think her family is of the highest quality and that she would make me a good wife. Hell, Bart. She's a vacuous idiot with nothing much in her head."

Bart vaguely remembered meeting Miss Brownly at one of the cotillions this past season. The girl was barely eighteen and one of those giggling creatures he and his friends tended to avoid. Nick's assessment of her mental capabilities might be due to her young age, but that was not the only thing bothering his friend.

"Do you think maybe they wanted you to move on with your life instead of mooning over that woman you were rumored to be in love with years back."

Nick straightened, his expression dark and full of pain. Crimson crept into his fair complected cheeks.

"None of your business, *friend*. I don't want to get married, and that's final. But, backing out now will cause a scandal. God knows, I have disgraced my family often enough to last a life time. I don't want to do it again, but I can't see a way out of this. I came here looking for help only to find you falling victim to the same damn thing. And of your own volition."

"My marriage is only temporary. And platonic."

"Hell, I'd rather be in your shoes."

"I'd gladly give them to you, if I could."

They stared at each other for long uncomfortable moments. Nick's regard turned pensive, thoughtful.

Finally, he spoke. "Then do so. I'll marry your Miss Griffith. Then you won't have to, and I'd be permanently saved from the fires of hell."

As much as Bart didn't want to marry, Nick's plan didn't sit well with him. Nick would be using Miss Griffith to avoid his own unwanted situation. Still, Bart owed his friend a chance to explore the idea.

Nick sank back in his chair, a grin working its way across his mouth. "A temporary marriage, you say?"

"To be ended by a divorce."

Nick absorbed this last in quiet contemplation. "As much as I disapprove of divorce, being married for a short time would save me from a lifetime of unhappiness. Nobody wants a divorced man for a husband, but you probably thought that through yourself, didn't you?"

He had, but then he wasn't Catholic. He simply didn't care whether he was divorced or not since he never intended to marry in the first place. But, if Nick was willing to divorce against all dictates of his religion, he must be desperate to remain unwed. Maybe he did still harbor feelings for this woman of his past, a woman nobody in their circle had ever met. Nick had never talked about her, yet rumors of a forbidden relationship had circulated among the gossip mills.

The longer they discussed Nick's absurd proposal, the lighter Bart's burden of marriage seemed to weigh on his shoulders. The truth was marriage to Miss Griffith scared him to death, even a platonic one. Two people living in the same house for three months might eventually share their worlds, produce an intimacy of thought, of remembrances, perhaps even of secrets. As much as he didn't want that to happen, he had been prepared to take the risk for his client's safety.

And now Nick was proposing a way out, a way to fulfill Miss Griffith's needs and gain something in return.

He studied his friend. "Are you sure you want to do this? You called me crazy a little while ago."

Nick nodded. "Yes, definitely. You have no real reason for marrying her other than she's your client and it's the expedient thing to do under the circumstances. I have a more compelling reason."

Yes, but would it be fair to Miss Griffith? But then, she was prepared to marry that German fellow who also had an ulterior motive.

"What's the plan regarding this estate she stands to inherit? I'm assuming everything will remain in her name despite the fact she would be married."

"The property will become hers, and you'd sign an agreement beforehand to keep everything in her name. The agreement would also commit you to a platonic relationship for which you would be handsomely compensated. Touching her is off limits."

Nick placed his chin in his palm and leaned against the chair's arm, interest highlighting his Nordic features. "So, what does she look like?"

"She's small, but lush in all the right places. Lovely blue eyes. Thick hair the color of night. Nice smile. Delightful laugh. She's intelligent and stubborn as hell, and may hide her vulnerabilities inside a hard outer shell. What else do you want to know?"

A corner of Nick's mouth lifted and for the first time this morning, amusement reached his eyes. "I asked you what she looked like, and you gave me that, plus a litany of her character traits."

Bart stared uncomfortably at his friend.

"I see." Grinning now, Nick resettled himself in the chair. "Sounds like more than just a typical client."

"Piss off, Nick." He couldn't disclose that Miss Griffith was his supervisor's niece because he would have to explain his relationship with Reginald. Bart had told Nick he was a private investigator, but not that he also worked for a secret government agency, the head of which was his client's uncle.

"Platonic you say? Too bad." Nick's tone sounded remarkably like goading.

"If you do this, Nick, promise me you'll keep your hands off her."

Nick held up his palms. "All right. All right. I promise. So, when do I get to meet this paragon of womanhood you so vividly describe?"

For some reason, Nick's grin irked the hell out of him. "Monday afternoon. I invited her here for a meeting. Gertie will be serving coffee and dessert."

"Coffee? How about something stronger? I'm to be a *married* man, for God's sake. You owe me at least a glass of that expensive bourbon you hide for taking her off your hands."

"You're to become a *divorced* man, you mean. And you aren't 'taking her off my hands.' I'll be shadowing you as her body guard. And I don't want alcohol on your breath when you meet her either. I don't want her thinking I'm marrying her off to a man she has to be wary of."

Nick's eyes narrowed. "She's not one of those damned White Ribbons, is she?"

Memories flashed in his mind of Miss Griffith clinging to his arm and nattering on about women's suffrage after imbibing two glasses of wine at dinner. No, she might be a suffragette, but never a follower of the Women's Christian Temperance League.

"Hardly. What you drink after you're married is nobody's concern. But before the ink is dry on the license, I'm asking you to do it my way. And if you wish to attend to your... other needs, do it elsewhere, but for God's sake, be discreet."

"I know about being discreet, Bart."

By the clipped tone of Nick's response, Bart realized he had stepped on his friend's toes. He softened his stance. "I know you do. I have utmost faith in you in that direction. It's just that the risks and consequences of discovery are great."

And now Bart had his own role to plan—that of becoming Miss Griffith's invisible bodyguard, the all-too-familiar role of shadows and masks. He should be relieved he wasn't the one marrying Miss Griffith. So why did his belly feel like it was loaded with lead?

~~~

"Well, well. So, this is the little woman who needs a husband on short notice."

At the sound of the unfamiliar male voice Monday afternoon, Emmie spun about. The over-sized book she had been inspecting in Mr. Turner's office slipped from her hands and thudded to the floor.

A tall, handsome man she guessed to be near thirty strode toward her, warmth radiating from his deep blue eyes and broad, friendly smile. His gray double-breasted suit looked expensive, its formality odd compared to the way his honey-colored hair overran its boundaries like a vine in need of pruning.

She glanced behind him at Mr. Turner.

His expression was shuttered. "Miss Griffith, may I present my friend Nicholas Shield. Should you find him suitable, he has agreed to be your temporary husband."

Emmie peered through her net veil at the man again, relief warming her like the sun's rays after a rainstorm. Almost the same height and build as Mr. Turner, he had a more than a pleasant aspect. His square-shaped face possessed a symmetry of features that would cause women to swoon. She was glad to discover she wasn't one of them. She wished her reaction to the man behind him was the same.

She returned Mr. Shield's smile. "I'm pleased to meet you, sir."

He took her hand in both of his and held it tight. "Call me Nick, Miss Griffith. We'll be spending a lot of time in each other's company in the coming months. I'm sure we can proceed to a more... intimate level."

She withdrew her hand immediately.

"Nick." Mr. Turner's voice held a note of warning. A frown had plowed deep ruts across his forehead and irritation flashed in his eyes.

Mr. Shield shot his friend a glance filled with boyish mischievousness. "My dear Miss Griffith. May I ask you to raise your veil?"

Mr. Turner took a step closer, his jaw now tight. *What was going on here?* She glanced from one to the other. Amusement and devilment danced in Mr. Shield's eyes, while the set of Mr. Turner's mouth into a straight line told a different story.

"Oh, for pity sake." She lifted the veil over her head, eager to complete the necessary formalities to becoming a wedded woman. Her entire staff depended upon her actions. If the charming Nicholas Shield wanted to look at the woman he planned to call wife for the next year, she would comply with his request, no matter what Mr. Bartholomew Turner thought.

"Well, now. You're going to make a lovely wife. Won't she, Bart?"

Heat climbed up her neck as tension coiled across her shoulders. A beauty she was not. Mr. Shield hadn't seen her scar. But Mr. Turner had.

The latter's piercing gaze swept her features. "Yes, she will," he muttered.

His friend laughed.

Time to end this nonsense. "If we're going to live together in the same house for three months, we might as well get to know each other."

A muscle twitched in Mr. Turner's jaw. Mr. Shield chuckled and tipped his head her way in silent approval. Of what, she couldn't be certain. Friends, huh? Men were such strange creatures.

"You understand the nature of the arrangement, Mr. Shield?" Fire crawled up her face again.

Mr. Turner stepped to his friend's elbow. "I already explained that, Miss Griffith. He's agreed, haven't you, Nick?"

She bent to retrieve the dropped book. Silence followed.

Mr. Shield cleared his throat. "Unfortunately, I did agree, Emmeline, if I may call you that, but I'd much rather have had it another way." Laughter bubbled in his eyes when her gaze flew to his. "But, I promise I'll be the gentleman you desire in this unusual arrangement."

Mr. Turner emitted a strangled sound that ended in a cough.

She regarded Mr. Shield with new-found appreciation. He had managed to goad his serious friend into near apoplexy. She recognized in him the person she once was. The hellion who had broken rules simply because they were there to break. The twin to her brother's rambunctious spirit she repressed the moment she stepped into her father's shoes.

She resumed her usual formal business demeanor. "Then it's agreed. We'll marry in this house. The less the newspapers know, the better. Mr. Turner, I'm assuming you've arranged things?"

Mr. Turner nodded, his expression neutral once again.

"Good. I'll be staying at the Palmer House. My wedding clothes will be delivered there tomorrow. They're coming on the morning train from my home near Libertyville. So, if you'll excuse me, I need to return to the hotel."

~~~

A thick cloud of doubt drifted through Bart's thoughts like a slowly approaching storm. Everything was going as planned, wasn't it? Then why did it feel so wrong, like he was a party to a grand deception. A deception far grander than the planned marriage in name only. Nick was using Miss Griffith's situation to further his own interests. And that was wrong.

Why in the hell had he agreed to this?

Too late now to change his mind. The plan had been set in motion, and he needed to step back and let the players control the game. And for someone who always had control, relinquishing the reins played havoc with his insides.

Nick held his arm out to Miss Griffith with decidedly more than perfunctory politeness. "I'll take you back to the hotel, my dear. That will give us time to get to know each other before the judge pronounces us man and wife. It will also allow the public to get used to seeing us together."

Nick's smooth-as-cream voice irked the hell out of Bart. He had heard that tone before, directed at brainless debutantes and restless married socialites, but with Miss Griffith, his tone was totally inappropriate.

"Cedric will take her back," he barked.

Miss Griffith gasped, her eyes wide.

Nick's hands flew up in front of him. "Whatever you say. You're in charge." His *friend's* tone was contrite, but his grin communicated something else. Why the hell had he let Nick talk him into this?

As though summoned from the ether, Cedric appeared. "You called, sir?"

"Please see Miss Griffith back to the hotel. And Cedric, make sure Judge Mahoney is here at seven o'clock tomorrow night."

Cedric tugged his vest down. "Very good, sir. I'll hail a hansom. It will be faster than calling for the carriage." He bowed and left.

By the time Bart turned back to Nick and Miss Griffith, they had their heads together in conversation. Nick was slathering on the famous Shield charm like jam on a slice of bread, and Miss Griffith appeared to be eating it up. Bart held the sarcastic remark ready to slide off his tongue.

Five minutes later, Cedric returned. "The carriage is here, sir, Miss Griffith."

His client pulled down her veil. "I'm ready, Cedric. Until later, then." She nodded at both men and left, clutching his butler's arm as if she were the grand dame of a fashionable Astor Street house.

"That went well, don't you think?" Nick grinned, his own problem solved to his satisfaction.

Bart opened his mouth, a caustic reply ready, but gunshots as loud as July Fourth fireworks exploding outside his front door cut him short. Heart pounding, he sprinted toward the door, Nick close behind. As he dashed across the threshold, the rattle of a fast-moving horse and carriage verified his worse fear.

Shit!

Cedric sat on the bottom step, dazed, but otherwise unharmed. Miss Griffith, however, lay slumped against the concrete stair wall, the skirt of her disheveled gown spread about her like a deflated air balloon. A dark spot widened across the lace shawl around her shoulders.

Swallowing hard, he raced down the steps, searching in both directions for signs of the carriage. A fleeing two-wheel hansom cab and its nondescript horse careened around the corner.

The cab was like hundreds of other for-hire conveyances on Chicago's streets. Like the one Cedric had flagged down, waiting one house down, its driver struggling with a nervous animal. Only, the fleeing cabriolet had a broken lantern hanging off its right side. A rather insignificant identifier, but at least it was something. He would find Miss Griffith's assailant if it were the last thing he did.

~~~

A throbbing ache high on her shoulder registered in Emmie's brain as strong arms scooped her off the concrete steps. She felt like she had been hit on the back with a sledge hammer, but she'd only tripped down the stairs. *Clumsy me!* She gritted her teeth and concentrated on the clean scent of citrus, soap and male musk of the man carrying her.

Mr. Turner.

As she pulled his essence deep into her lungs, searing pain hurtling across her shoulder took her breath away. She tensed. The arms about her tightened. Spots appeared before her eyes. *What is happening to me?*

"Nick, help Cedric inside, and ask Mrs. Carstairs to telephone the doctor. When she's done, send her to the front bedroom." Mr. Turner's deep rumble vibrating through the massive chest under her hand rattled her senses.

For a fraction of a moment, she welcomed his commanding attitude. Then his barked order penetrated the thick haze addling her brain. Doctor?

She summoned as much of an air of authority as she could muster. "I don't need a doctor. I fell down the stairs and hurt myself. That's all. Now put me down. I must go back to the hotel." Her demand turned out to be a feeble whisper. Knives dug into her shoulder.

"You're not going anywhere. At least not until after you're tended by a physician. You've been shot." His dark tone brooked no argument.

"Shot?" Shrouded memories of loud pops filtered through her mind.

Vision graying, her head flopped against the softness of Mr. Turner's summer suit. She clung to his lapel and willed herself to stay conscious, but her world blackened.

Chapter 3

Bart laid his unconscious charge on the four-poster bed and pulled out the pin holding her hat in place. He removed the bit of finery and set it on the nearby chest of drawers.

The bullet wound looked high enough to have only grazed her skin, yet her face had paled to chalk. She appeared so small, so delicate on the big bed.

So incredibly vulnerable.

His hands clenched into fists. The bullet was no stray. Who wanted her dead, and why? Or was this a warning, the shot meant to inflict fear rather than kill? Her situation had changed dramatically. Guarding her from the sidelines wouldn't be enough, not with someone wanting to hurt her.

And one thing was certain. Nick wasn't trained to be a bodyguard.

Bart was.

Return to your original plan. Marry her yourself.

The thought came without warning, but its merit couldn't be denied. Being wed to Miss Griffith would be a rational solution to the problem he now faced. She needed a professional bodyguard at all times, someone who knew what to look for, and how to protect her. Becoming her husband would accomplish this task while fulfilling her need to be married. Nick couldn't do it.

At once, something he wanted to discuss with Cedric increased in importance—the coincidence of Miss Griffith's fiancée's death and her arranged husband's elopement with another woman. These two events might, at first, seem unrelated, but when coupled with the need to marry to inherit, and the shooting this afternoon, a dark picture began to emerge.

Someone wanted to keep her from marrying.

Nick could be in danger.

And if Bart married her, he might be setting himself up as a target as well.

Icy fingers of apprehension froze the blood in his veins. If his hunch was correct, grave danger surrounded them all. They were entering his world now—a place where people disappeared, and killers flourished. Who was better equipped to guide Miss Griffith through it than he?

His mind made up, all he needed to do now was tell her.

A soft moan brought Bart's attention back. Without the veil and the tendril of hair about her face, her scar became quite visible. He fought a sudden inexplicable urge to trace his finger down its raised pearly ridge.

"Excuse me, sir. I'll see to the lady now." Gertrude Carstairs pushed him aside with her Rubenesque proportions and bent over the bed. Gertie, his second investigative assistant, doubled as his housekeeper and cook. "Such a wee bird, she is."

He pressed his lips together. "Don't let her size fool you, Gertie. She possesses a backbone of steel beneath all her feathers."

"Let's hope so. She'll need it with all this blood." Gertie removed the soiled shawl from Miss Griffith's shoulder and dropped it on the floor. "Shot on our front steps, was she? Now who'd do that to a tiny little thing like this?"

"I don't know, but I sure as hell intend to find out."

Gertie pulled out a pair of shears and a wad of white cloth from a deep pocket in her apron and cut the soiled dress at the shoulder, then sopped up the blood flow with the cloth. "Now let's see what we have here. Looks worse than it is. Just a graze, but it'll need stitching. Cedric's been telling me all about this one. Yer takin' her case, I heard."

Gertie's validation of his own assessment of Miss Griffith's condition loosened a band hugging his chest. "Looks like it. We've got our work cut out for us, though."

He kept his eyes trained on Miss Griffith's pale face, on the path a lone tear had taken down her cheek in her unconsciousness.

Cedric materialized like a phantom. His gray complexion had pinked a bit. "How is the lady?"

"Still unconscious. Gertie says the bleeding has slowed, though she might need some stitches. In the meantime, I'd like you to set the older boys to finding a two-wheel hansom cab with a broken right lamp. We need to find it before the lamp is repaired."

"Good enough, sir."

His assistant took a step toward the door, but Bart pulled him back with a small tug on his arm. "Would you tell Nick the situation has changed, and I'm marrying her myself. She's going to need professional protection."

"Yes, sir. He's in the hallway, wearing a hole in the carpet. I'll tell him right away."

"And see if Judge Mahoney can postpone the ceremony to Wednesday. She'll need the extra day."

"Very well, sir."

Gertie straightened. "Enough chatterin'. Out with ye. This girl needs tendin', and not by the likes of any of ye. Go on, git."

After shoving them both out of the room, Gertie shut the door square in their faces. And left Bart to wonder what his soon-to-be bride looked like beneath all her fine plumage.

~~~

Emmie woke to the soothing warmth of a sizable body at her side. Alarmed and groggy, she peered into mahogany-brown eyes studying her intently—the eyes of a big dog, its tail creating a breeze that feathered across her cheek. Rays of the setting sun transformed the animal's dark coat to a vibrant blue-black, while light brown markings around its nose and mouth made the dog seem like it was smiling. She found herself smiling back.

"Rafe likes you." Mr. Turner's baritone broke into her fog-filled world.

Pulling her senses together, she turned toward his voice and discovered the man's dark eyes trained on her the same way as the dog's. Mr. Turner had removed his jacket and rolled his shirt sleeves to the elbows. Thick sculpted muscles disappearing beneath fine linen hinted of a strong man given to serious athletic pursuits.

It was then she realized she was in a strange bed, a massive four-poster affair in a strange bedroom. Fear permeated her chest like an ill wind, uninvited and unwelcome. As she struggled to overcome it, intense confusion invaded what little remained of her waning lucidity. She had been on her way to her suite at the Palmer House. So how did she get here in what she could only surmise was a bedroom in Mr. Turner's rowhouse?

The animal raised its broad head and yawned. "Rafe?" she repeated like an idiot.

Mr. Turner sat back, his imposing frame appearing ludicrous in the small upholstered chair drawn close to the foot of the bed. She tried to organize her thoughts, but nothing fell into place. What happened, and why was she here?

"His full name is Rafael Maximilian O'Toole. You should feel honored. He's a Rottweiler, a new breed in this country. They don't take easily to strangers." Amusement may have laced his tone, but his gaze was as dark as a winter morning.

Rafe shifted and placed his head across her stomach. Though its weight was considerable, the pressure wasn't uncomfortable. She always wanted a pet. She had lived on one of the area's largest dairy farms, but her father never allowed any of his prized hunting dogs in the main house. Too many priceless sculptures on pedestals about, or so he claimed.

She lifted her arm to stroke the animal. "Ouch." Her shoulder stung like a thousand bee stings.

"You've taken a few stitches. Fortunately, whoever shot you had bad aim. The bullet just grazed your skin."

Bullet? She was shot? Like pieces of a puzzle, vague memories began to sort themselves. She had fallen on Mr. Turner's front steps. Because she was shot? She remembered being picked up by Mr. Turner, remembered how his arms felt wrapped about her, cocooning her in a world of comfort and safety she hadn't lived in since Eddie's death. Heat settled low in her belly as she remembered Mr. Turner's wonderful scent of citrus and spice. But then she must have fainted, for she remembered nothing more.

"Why would anyone want to shoot me?"

"An interesting question, Miss Griffith. You tell me." Mr. Turner paused, removing his fisted hand from beneath his chin. His sharp tone seemed almost belligerent.

"I don't know." She raised her other arm to pull the long curl about her cheek and found she wore a woman's pink bed jacket of serviceable cotton. Aghast, she slipped a hand beneath the sheet and discovered her lower body covered only by her chemise.

"Mrs. Carstairs, my housekeeper, removed your soiled dress. She said it was quite beyond cleaning. She's seeing to your things at the Palmer House."

"Please thank her for me." She pushed herself to a sitting position with one arm, adjusting the ribbon ties of the bed jacket so nothing beneath peeked through.

The dog stuck out its long tongue and licked her hand, the sensation like wet sandpaper dragged over her skin.

A line deepened on Mr. Turner's forehead. "We have a change of plans. I'm delaying the wedding a day to allow you to heal. And instead of Nick, you'll be marrying me."

Her throat went dry. Blast, and double blast! Marry the man who turned her knees to rubber and her mind to mush? This can't be happening.

She counted to five, her heart thumping loudly against her ribs. "Why? What happened to Mr. Shield?"

"You need professional protection now. He isn't trained. I am." A judge rendering a decision. An arbitrary decision. One he made without consulting her.

"I don't need a bodyguard, just a husband."

"You need both. Especially now that this has happened. It was no random bullet, Miss Griffith. Something's afoot here, and your life is in danger. You told me your fiancée died in a riding accident. Then the man you were supposed to marry ran off with another woman, or so he wrote. Then you get shot. Coincidence? I don't think so. Someone doesn't want you to marry, or worse, wants you dead. Your cousin? You told me he stands to gain if you don't show up with a husband. I'm taking no chances with your safety. You'll marry me so I can protect you."

Without warning, her world grayed. *Don't you faint, Emmeline Griffith.* "You can't be serious. You're putting unrelated circumstances together and drawing conclusions. That's preposterous."

"Is it? We don't know for sure, and until we do, you need to be guarded."

"But... but why can't Mr. Shield protect me?" She could endure close proximity to Mr. Shield for three months, but Mr. Turner?

"He doesn't have the skills. Besides, Nick's reason for marrying you wasn't altogether altruistic, and I'm sorry I was a party to it. He planned to use the marriage to avoid an unwanted arranged marriage to someone else. A divorce would make him undesirable as a husband, and he wants to remain unwed after his marriage to you is over."

"That doesn't sound all that much different from Hans Bormeister, the German man I told you about. And you, Mr. Turner? What reasons, other than protecting me, do you have for volunteering? A divorce would affect you as well. Spoil your chances for the future."

"I have only your safety in mind. Besides, like Nick, I have no intention of marrying anyone. I'd become your husband for the specified time out of professional courtesy to your uncle. It's the job you're hiring me for. A marriage with no commitments, no relationships suits me just fine."

"Logical, but... but you..." A vision of his lips on hers slid unbidden into her brain. She shivered, her emotions, her thoughts in a whirl.

His stern expression returned, his penetrating stare making her heart beat faster.

"Look, Miss Griffith. Someone tried to kill you on my doorstep. The man missed, but he'll be back. We must figure out who he is and catch him before he tries again. You need my protection."

Rafe whined. She glanced at the animal. Maybe it was the harsh tone of his master's voice or the gravity of his glare to which the animal reacted. She threaded her fingers through Rafe's silky coat.

Dang if she hadn't run out of time. It was far too late to come up with another solution. Marrying Mr. Turner would provide her with a legal husband. And that was the most important part of this endeavor, wasn't it? If the price for becoming a married woman included Mr. Turner's close presence as a bodyguard, then she would pay it. Nothing must go wrong now.

But keeping her wits together during this ruse of a marriage would be a challenge as great as any scientific undertaking to date. She was comfortable in a laboratory, and possessed enough business sense to run a growing company, but managing personal relationships with the male species baffled her. Particularly a relationship with a man whose dark gaze made her quiver and whose towering aspect scrambled her brain. A most dangerous man, indeed.

She ruffled the dog's head. "Well, Rafe. Looks like you're going to acquire a mistress. At least for a little while."

Mr. Turner crossed his long legs at the ankles. "I need a few honest answers first. You have more to tell me." A statement, not a question.

She raised her chin. The time had come. Whether she liked it or not, she must reveal the truth. No more dancing around the facts. No more sins of omission. Uncle Reggie would want her to cooperate.

She scrutinized her soon-to-be husband, then sighed, resigned to telling him everything. Well, almost everything. "I sign my name, E.M. Griffith."

He settled back in his chair, his folded fingers resting against his chin. "And why is that significant?"

"It's who I am. You don't recognize the name?"

"The only E.M. Griffith I'm aware of is *the* E.M. Griffith, president of Chicagoland Electric, and you can't possibly be—."

"I am *the* E.M. Griffith, as you say."

His eyes widened. "I thought—"

"You thought E.M. Griffith was a man. Everyone does."

"I have to admit I did." He rubbed his chin, questions palpable in his thoughtful expression.

She busied herself with petting Rafe in long, languid strokes, considering where to start her explanation.

"We lived a quiet life in the country. I had an invalid twin, Edward, who died in a fire five years before my father. After Eddie's death, Papa taught me the business, and when he died, I just stepped into his shoes as president. No one challenged my right to do so, and because the three of us shared the same initials, people outside our small circle of family and friends assumed the company was being run by my brother. Most were unaware of his tragic death. His funeral had been a private family affair, kept out of the press with great care."

Mr. Turner's features softened, his head canted to one side. "Why conceal who you are?"

She regarded him solemnly. "How many companies do you know are run by women?"

He thought for a moment. "Not one."

"Exactly. The business world isn't ready for someone like me. Women aren't taken seriously."

"How did you manage to hide being female for five years?"

"I was not really hiding it. I just didn't go out of my way to acknowledge it. My interest is in the laboratory, the science behind the company. I hired competent male staff to handle the outside work. They blend well into the world of industry where women are excluded. That freed me to do what I love—invent things."

"Then it was you who lost out to Tesla for supplying electricity to the Columbian Exposition." She nodded. "The story was all over the newspapers. The War of the Currents they called it."

Remembering the disappointment, she sighed, her gaze shifting to Rafe. "We lost because Tesla proved his alternating current system was better than our direct current. We're still there though. Edison and I have exhibits in the Electricity Building. I suppose losing the contract to Tesla turned out to be a blessing. It forced me to take a hard look at where the industry might be heading and refocus Chicagoland Electric in a different direction."

His dark brows arched upward. "The company is the *estate* in question?"

She shifted uncomfortably. "Papa left me the house and the acreage free and clear, but the ownership of the electric company is tied to whether I am married by my twenty-fifth birthday. The company's headquarters and laboratory are located on the Libertyville farm I inherited, which complicates matters. I don't need any impediments at this point. Not when we're so close to success."

He angled forward, his face lighting with interest. "Success with what?"

"We've perfected the first small household device to use electricity for something other than light and communication. A prototype is on exhibit in the Electricity Building. The concept of small electrical appliances for the home will change the world forever."

"What's the product?"

"You'll have to see it for yourself. It's something so ordinary, every household will have one because the price will be affordable. It will be the first of many such products. And Chicagoland Electric will soon be manufacturing them."

He blinked. "This product, is it special enough to kill for?"

The blood instantly drained from her head. "Is that what this is about?"

"I don't know. We'll have to find out, won't we?"

She studied him. "If what you say is true, I assure you, I want to catch this person as much as you do. Even more so."

Chapter 4

A commotion at the foot of the stairs the next morning had Bart out his bedroom door and at the railing before he had time to put on his shoes.

Below, a tall dandy struggled against Cedric's grasp. "Unhand me, sir. I must see to Emmeline."

Bart frowned, unease tightening his muscles. The man had used Miss Griffith's given name in front of a stranger, a breach of etiquette of the first order.

His investigator's instincts flared. "And who might you be, sir?"

Cedric's gaze swept upward and his hold on the man loosened. The intruder smoothed the wrinkles from his jacket with precise, even strokes.

"Jonathan Braithwaite, a close friend of Miss Griffith's. She sent for us. The Palmer House said she checked out. The only other address they had for her was this one. Who might you be? Certainly, not the groom." Disdain marked the man's voice, which sounded pinched, almost as though his nostrils were closed.

Bart stiffened, taking an instant dislike to the preening peacock at the bottom of his staircase.

He ignored the man's personal insult for the moment. "Us?"

The rustle of skirts and tap of a woman's heels on the wooden floor preceded the entrance of another well-dressed person—a young woman of medium height and impeccable fashion taste. A pale green gown hugged her quite adequate figure in the hour-glass shape of the day. He grunted. She better not be another damned preening birds. Two such beings in his household would drive him insane.

The woman gazed up at him, her face flushing below her hat. "I'm

Lydia Holmsford, Miss Griffith's personal secretary. Can we see her? We've brought her wedding gown and trousseau."

She waved her hand toward the three trunks crowding the small foyer.

"Trousseau?" He swallowed over the constriction in his throat. A trousseau suggested intimacy, both physical and otherwise, a state he cared not to explore. And certainly, not with Reginald's niece.

Pink cheeks darkened to crimson. The woman's chin lifted. "Yes. Trousseau. Now, where is Miss Griffith? Her wire said she expected to be married soon. We're here to assist her."

He sighed. Just what he needed. Another no-nonsense woman. Chicagoland Electric must be full of them. Perhaps a fluttering goose would have been better.

What was Braithwaite's role in this? Was he also an employee? He said he was Miss Griffith's friend. Funny she made no mention of him and, at this point, no one in her circle had been ruled above suspicion for the shooting.

"Yes, that's true. She was to be married tonight, but there's been an incident, I'm afraid. Miss Griffith has been shot," he said, scrutinizing their reactions.

Braithwaite paled.

Tears filled Miss Holmsford's eyes and she swayed, her hand swinging out to grab the newel post. "She's not—"

"Dead? No, just slightly wounded on her shoulder. With proper rest, she'll be able to stand for the ceremony tomorrow night, but she may need assistance in dressing."

Braithwaite heaved a sigh, his hands closing into fists. "I warned her not to go into the city alone. Too many unsavory types who might do her harm. Who did this?"

"I don't know yet, but I'll find out. You can count on it." Bart caught the man's gaze and held it.

"For heaven's sake, Mr. Turner, let them come up. They're not going to shoot me." Miss Griffith's order steamed out of the nearby bedroom, crisp and direct. She sounded annoyed. With him.

He gritted his teeth and waved the pair up the stairs. "Be my guest, but don't stay too long. She needs her rest."

Miss Holmsford started up the stairs with grim determination. The peacock trailed behind.

She reached the top and readied to pass him. "Who is the groom, if I may ask?"

"I am."

Miss Holmsford stopped as though barred by an invisible wall. "You?"

"Yes. Is something wrong?"

She searched his face, then scanned his body from top to bottom and back up. Her youthful face transformed into an expression of assessing astuteness. She inspected him like a piece of meat in a butcher shop, and he didn't like the sensation.

"You'll do." She raised her chin, turned and swept past him, heading toward the room from where Miss Griffith's voice had come.

Braithwaite reached the head of the stairs and stopped, giving Bart the same measured appraisal as Miss Holmsford.

"We hold Emmeline in high regard, Mr. Turner. She's told Miss Holmsford and me all about her plan to save the company. Emmeline has entrusted her future to you and that is good enough for us. I'm not going to question her choice of husbands, but should you do anything untoward during the year you are married, you will answer to me. She's been through quite enough in the last few years."

Well, well. The peacock had a backbone. The steel in his tone matched the firm set of his determined jaw. Bart took his own measure of the man. Bag of wind he might be, yet the depth of Braithwaite's devotion came through all the fine plumage he displayed. Why hadn't Miss Griffith married this man for real? Or didn't she return his feelings?

Braithwaite turned and trailed after Miss Holmsford. Loath to let anyone set foot near his charge, let alone in her bedroom, Bart followed close behind.

"Jon! Lydia! I'm so glad you're here. Come sit by me." Miss Griffith's glorious smile enveloped both new arrivals with a delight that made Bart feel oddly left out.

Braithwaite leaned over and kissed Miss Griffith on both cheeks and then settled himself on the foot of her bed. Bart clamped his jaw tight at the obvious expression of intimacy, approving when Rafe growled and repositioned himself to watch Braithwaite's every move. *Good dog.* Miss Holmsford busied herself plumping bed pillows.

Miss Griffith reached out for Braithwaite's hand. "I am fine, Jon. No need to worry."

"Oh, but I do, Emmie dear. I don't want to lose you, too."

Bart found himself listening with avid interest.

"You won't lose me. Ever. I'll always be here for you."

The personal nature of the conversation made him feel like an intruder. Obviously, they cared for each other, but not enough for Braithwaite to become her husband. Friends, then. Close enough that divorce might be too much of a sacrifice to ask of him.

Miss Holmsford smoothed Miss Griffith's covers. "Come now, you two. No more sad talk. Miss Griffith, you need to get your rest. Gentlemen, I believe it's time to leave."

Like a seasoned soldier following orders, Braithwaite rose and kissed Miss Griffith on the forehead. "I'll see you later."

She nodded, a grain of fear poking through the mask of steely resolve Bart was beginning to recognize.

"You'll be all right." The man patted her hand and turned to Bart. "Who will oversee this auspicious event?"

"My housekeeper, Mrs. Carstairs, and my butler, Cedric."

Braithwaite's long, narrow face screwed up with distaste. "That will never do. I best get down there and organize this affair before they make a mess of things."

Bart bit back a retort. He was the one making the sacrifice here, giving up his freedom for a year. Who the hell did this guy think he was, barging in and acting like he was in charge? Patience had its limits.

This Braithwaite character rose to the top of his list of people to investigate. Whoever was behind the attack had studied his client's comings and goings.

And Braithwaite was in an excellent position to do so.

~~~

The tempting aroma of freshly baked cake and pastries greeted Bart as he walked into Gertie's kitchen at the back of the house later that afternoon. Fifteen-year-old Jimmy Taylor sat at the table devouring one of her famous desserts, a chocolate affair in a dish with a dollop of whipped cream. The fact he was here and not at the home meant the boys had been successful in finding the cab with the dangling right lantern.

Glancing at Cedric who'd settled on a stool in the corner, Bart pulled out a chair and sat across from the boy. "Where's Braithwaite, Mrs. Carstairs?"

Gertie set a plate of cookies on the table. "In the dining room gussying up my table for tomorrow night's ceremony. He must think I'm incapable of doing it meself. That man! The way I arranged the trays wasn't good enough for the likes of him. No. He had to clear everything off the table, then put everything back just so. You'd think

President Cleveland was coming and bringin' his new missus." She shook her head.

The corner of Bart's mouth twitched. Gertie didn't take kindly to anyone interfering in her domain. "I hate to ask, but would you mind keeping him busy for about ten minutes?"

His housekeeper wiped her hands on her apron. Her opinion of his request showed in the way her mouth pursed into a straight line. Yet she appreciated the reason for it as well as she appreciated her grandmother's secret recipes.

Her expression softened as she studied Jimmy. She loved the boys from the orphanage. A regular mama bear when they visited every Sunday, going from one to the other until she hugged them all. She sighed. "It wouldn't do to have the man barge in here while ye're talkin' to Jimmy here. I'll go, but could ye be quick about it? Me patience with Mr. Fussy is thinnin'."

"Thank you, Mrs. Carstairs. I'll try to be."

When Gertie left, Bart arched across the table and clasped his hands before him. "What have you got for me, Jimmy?"

The tall lanky boy slipped the last bit of dessert into his mouth and licked the spoon before answering.

"The boys found three broken right side lanterns, sir, but only one was on a two-wheel hansom. It went back to a livery on North Halsted Street. Georgie found it. He can't read so well. He only recognized the beginning. Lem something."

Bart sat back in his chair and searched the recesses of his mind. Several liveries existed on the busy street, most in two-story buildings with carriages stored on the ground floor and horses stabled up a ramp on the second.

"Lemky's?" Cedric suggested from the corner.

Jimmy twisted toward Cedric. "Could be. Georgie recognized the letters l e m from where he stood."

"I know the place. Lemky rents both carriages and horses by the hour." Bart extended his hand across the table. "You boys did well. We'll take it from here. Thank you. And tell the rest I thank them also. Mrs. Carstairs and I will be over as usual Sunday afternoon with cookies. You better get home before Mrs. Higgins starts to worry. We wouldn't want you to miss your dinner now, would we?"

He winked at the boy. Like so many of the children he found begging on the streets, Jimmy's appetite was notorious. Food was the most significant expense for the boys' orphanage he founded three years ago.

"Yes, sir." Jimmy grabbed the cookies off the plate, stuffed them in his pocket and darted toward the back door.

"Thank Mrs. Carstairs for me, will ya? Bye, sir." The screened door banged shut behind him.

Buoyed by his first solid lead, Bart rose from the table. Cedric stood at his elbow waiting for instructions.

"I'd like you to find out all you can about her cousin Paul Harris and a Hans Bormeister, a recent German immigrant. Also, can you prepare for the appearance of Lord Wallingshire tomorrow morning? I think he will do fine for a visit to Lemky's."

Cedric grinned. Wallingshire was his favorite. "Certainly, sir. We haven't seen him in several months. I'd be happy to prepare for his *visit.*"

"Good. Also, tell Gertie I'll need her to keep our guests, including Miss Griffith, out of the kitchen for several hours tomorrow morning. Wouldn't want them bumping into Lord Wallingshire now, would we?"

"Goodness no, sir. But how—?

"I'll leave that to Gertie."

"I was asking how do you plan to keep Miss Griffith from discovering your various... gentlemen friends?"

How, indeed. The very astute Miss Griffith would figure out the truth sooner or later. Better from him, than stumbling upon it herself.

"I don't know, Cedric. I suppose I'll have to tell her. Just not yet. The less she knows about my disguises, the better. I don't want her scrutinizing every person with whom she comes in contact to figure out whether it's me. That would be a dead giveaway of the degree of protection she's receiving."

Cedric nodded.

"I'd also like you to dig around a little about Mr. Braithwaite. I want everything you can find—where he lives, what he does, his habits, his comings and goings, who he sees, his family, his finances. Everything."

Cedric, eyeing still warm pastries on a cooling rack, tugged his vest down. "I noticed you didn't take to the man."

"It's not that I don't like him, though I can't truthfully say I do. I don't know how he fits into Miss Griffith's life and whether he would have reason to want her dead. Someone shot her, and no one, friend or stranger, can be overlooked."

"What about Miss Holmsford?"

"Concentrate on Brathwaite for the moment. He poses far more questions than Miss Holmsford. I'll see what I can find out from Miss Griffith. And Cedric, ask Gertie to see if she can find the bullet that grazed Miss Griffith's shoulder. If she looked like she was cleaning the stoop, she won't be noticed by the neighbors. That bullet may tell us some interesting things."

~ ~ ~

Bart jolted awake late that night, his insides burning with despair so deep he couldn't breathe. His sweaty skin felt cold, clammy. His heart raced as though he had run miles through the city.

The sensation was old, familiar, and no less terrifying than when he was a boy. He shoved himself to a sitting position and brushed a hand across his stubbly cheek.

Another nightmare, and with it the panic, the terror, the horror of it all. Will they ever cease?

The vision was always the same—of murky shadows and Stygian darkness, an image of a heinous reality his mind refused to sharpen. Yet, he would never forget. Never outgrow the feeling of helplessness, of hopelessness. His emotions were too alive, his memories too vivid.

He peered at the clock on the nightstand. Two in the morning.

Body shaking, he rose and padded to the open window. Pushing aside the summer curtain, he stared out at the street below. Gaslights flickered, their tiny flames creating small puddles of light in an ocean of darkness. The same darkness he sensed drowning him now.

He pushed himself from the window, reached for his robe and, like a man possessed, crossed the room to the door separating his bedroom from Miss Griffith's. He had to see her, had to assure himself of her safety. That was his job.

He steeled himself and turned the knob. The door gave, opening into the shadows of her room. Like a thief, he stole into her privacy.

Miss Griffith lay sleeping on her back, her hair spread across the pillow in an array of black silk. Who shot her? Who would want to hurt this elfin innocent sleeping so peacefully in the oversized bed, this woman small of stature, yet a giant in determination and grit.

He had seen the shadow of pain reflected in her eyes the day they'd met.

And fear this afternoon.

Was someone from her past haunting her? Someone who wanted her dead? Her past resembled a puzzle with several missing pieces, pieces he needed to find and fit together to see the whole of it. For her sake.

And while he hunted for those pieces, he would protect this tiny creature with every weapon available in his arsenal. Her safety had become important to him, and it had nothing to do with her being Reginald's niece or his client.

Chapter 5

Bart stepped out of the hidden room off the butler pantry the next morning and stroked the beard he had glued to his chin. Lord Wallingshire had arrived, the perfect disguise to use for his visit to Lemky's Livery.

Cedric pushed a stack of breakfast plates to the back of a pantry shelf and turned to inspect Bart with a valet's experienced eye. "Excuse me sir, but your ascot needs adjusting. If you would hold the pin, please."

While Cedric retied the length of patterned silk, Bart's mind wandered to his visit to Miss Griffith's bedroom last night.

What had possessed him? He prided himself on being logical in every aspect of his life, but his middle of the night visit defied comprehension. He shouldn't have gone, shouldn't have been so presumptuous.

Shouldn't have been witness to the woman she was—the mounds of feminine flesh pushing up the blanket, the lush flow of her long midnight hair, the glow of her skin in the moonlight.

Thoughts of her had kept him awake the rest of the night as he pondered the mystery she presented and the tenuous hold she seemed to have on her future. From the beginning, he admired her spirit and the way she worked through problems with logic and intelligence. Few women he knew were as capable as she.

But, if he were truthful, his curiosity had been piqued. Not by Miss Griffith the client, nor by his boss's niece, nor by the head of an innovative business concern.

But by Miss Griffith the woman, the enigmatic part of her that lay buried beneath the plainness of face. He must work hard to stay focused on his job. It wouldn't do to get lost in the mystery of her.

Cedric pulled on the edges of his ascot, bringing him back to consideration of more mundane things. "You seem to be deep in thought, sir. Does it have anything to do with our client?"

"I have questions, Cedric. Lots of them. Like, was Alex's demise an accident as Miss Griffith believes, or something more sinister? And whatever happened to her Mr. Bormeister, the German she was to marry? Did he really elope with someone else, or was his disappearance from Miss Griffith's life also a mystery to be solved?"

"Looks like you'll have plenty to investigate when you both return to her home." A rare pleased-with-himself expression erupted on Cedric's face. "I'll take the stickpin now, sir."

Bart handed him the ostentatious diamond pin he had made of cut glass. An extremely rich man, Lord Wallingshire flaunted his wealth in the clothes he wore.

"By the by, sir, so far I've turned up little on Mr. Braithwaite other than the man is the youngest of five siblings and was raised on a neighboring farm. More interestingly, the man seems to have no visible means of support. I'm of a mind that he could be an employee of Miss Griffith's, or living off an inheritance. I don't know which yet, but I'll try to find out."

"Do we know where he lives?"

"No, but it has to be close to Miss Griffith's Libertyville estate. He is always there."

That bit of information didn't sit well with Bart.

"Has Gertie found that bullet yet?"

"Yes, sir. It's a 45 caliber Schofield, fired by a Smith & Wesson Schofield revolver. Standard issue for the American Army."

Bart let out a huff. "Not much to work with, is there? Those guns are as numerous as ground squirrels. Soldiers often abscond with them when they leave the Army. Will you thank Gertie for me?"

"Yes, sir."

Having finished pushing the pin through the folds of the properly-tied ascot, Cedric brushed his hands across Bart's jacket lapels.

"There you go, sir, now would you mind turning around."

Obeying Cedric's orders, Bart turned slowly for inspection. Cedric had a remarkable eye for men's fashions, a talent he used to create Bart's many disguises.

"Very good, m'lord. Everything's in order, except your hat and cane."

Bart raised an eyebrow at the use of Lord Wallingshire's title, but his valet stepped around him. Disappearing into the hidden room, Cedric returned a moment later with a black silk top hat and a walking stick.

Bart slipped the hat over his gray wig.

"Your cane, sir." Cedric handed Bart a sleek ebony stick with a filigreed silver top, just the thing for a fashionable English lord. "Good luck, your lordship."

"Thank you, Cedric. Let's go find out what this Mr. Lemky has to say."

Cedric bowed, a leftover gesture of his service days in England. As for his assistant's use of titles, Bart found the formality objectionable, but Cedric, stubborn as he was, refused to give up the habit.

Bart left the house through the kitchen door and stepped into the role of an English nobleman. Strolling down the alley to the street, he tapped the walking stick on the ground as though he walked with it every day. Two blocks away, he hailed a passing cab.

"Lemky's Livery on Halsted Street, my good man," he ordered in his best imitation of Cedric's clipped British accent.

~~~

"Look here, sir. I must find that box. It contains an irreplaceable gift for my granddaughter." Bart banged his stick for emphasis on the pigsty of a desk in the cluttered office of Harry Lemky.

The dirt and filth of the place created a stench much worse than the usual odors of a thriving stable. He swallowed hard against the rising contents of his stomach.

Lemky, a scrawny runt of a man, pulled a cap out of the desk's miserable environs and stood. "Sorry, mister. Can't help you. Carriages come in and out of here all day long. Night, too. I inspect them myself when they return, and I tell you I ain't found nothin'."

Bart moved his stick from one hand to the other. Lemky flinched as though he expected to be hit. Good! Perhaps a little more intimidation would work. He waved the staff in the man's face.

"The devil take it, Mr. Lemky. You must be wrong. This cabriolet had a broken lantern on the right side. I hailed it around three o'clock two afternoons ago near Eugenie and Wells."

"Don't know nothing about it, and why do you think it came from here?" The stable owner turned toward the office door.

"I have my ways of finding out things. Rest assured, the rig belongs to your establishment. Now, who rented it? You keep records, don't you?"

The man coughed, then spit into the dirty brass receptacle beside the desk.

Bart wrinkled his nose. Disgusting habit.

"Don't like to disclose my clients. Sometimes they want their privacy, you know what I mean?"

Determined to get information out of the tight-lipped livery owner, Bart rose to his full six foot three inches and peered down his nose.

"Look, my good man. Let me reiterate the consequences of your decision. Come up with the name of the person who rented the rig, or I will assume you confiscated the box yourself. In which case, I will inform the local constabulary immediately."

Lemky's eyes widened. "But I didn't take it, sir."

"Then tell me who rented that carriage and be done with it."

Lemky slumped to his chair and rummaged amid the heap on his desk, eventually pulling out a black ledger book.

He hastily thumbed through the well-worn volume, turning pages with a loud swish. "Two days ago, you say?"

"Yes, in the afternoon, although it might have been rented for the day. In any case, the carriage had a broken right lamp."

Lemky came to a page and stopped. "Yes, yes. I mark all damage in my book. I repaired the lantern this morning and the carriage is out on the street again."

At last! Bart waited patiently as Lemky drew his finger down a column.

"Here it is, sir. A Mr. Smith rented it for the afternoon. Brought it back around four o'clock with the lantern broke."

"Smith, you say? How utterly common." A stone sank to the bottom of Bart's belly. Damn.

Lemky stroked his bristly jaw. "I remember the fella. A bit unsavory, if you ask me. Came with a friend. Two of them were thugs, lowlife as ever I seen 'em. Didn't look to have a pot to piss in, but this here Mr. Smith peeled my fee off a fat roll of cash like he'd robbed a bank. I wasn't going to turn 'em down."

"No, of course not." Paid assassins. Someone remunerated two men to shoot Miss Griffith. "Can you describe them?"

"Not much to tell. Both about medium height, though this Smith guy was heavier than his friend. They wore workmen's clothes. Clean, but tattered. The other fellow had a cap and sandy-colored hair. That's all I remember."

"Did you, perhaps, get an address?"

"Don't collect 'em."

"No, I don't suppose you do," Bart muttered.

He sighed, then reached into his trouser pocket, drew out a sawbuck from a gold money clip and threw it on the desk. "Here, my good man. Something for your time."

Lemky's eyes grew as round as saucers and he grabbed the ten-dollar bill. "Thank you, sir. Oh, I remember one more thing might be of help to ya. This here Mr. Smith called the other one Willy, and Willy was as Irish as the day is long. Best I can do, and that's the God's honest truth."

"Thank you, Mr. Lemky, and good afternoon."

Bart tipped his hat and left, his thoughts off in a thousand directions. Two hired assassins. A stocky *Mr. Smith* with a big wad of cash, and a side-pal called Willy of Irish descent and sandy hair.

Not much to go on. Maybe they're on Gertie's list. He had to find out who employed them, and quickly before someone made another attempt on Miss Griffith's life.

~~~

Clad in her blue robe, Emmie headed down the stairs, determined to locate her soon-to-be husband. He had been gone all morning, and truth be told, she missed his presence.

Confined to her bed by her overbearing bodyguard, and bereft of anything substantive to do, she had Lydia sneak down into the front parlor office and bring up a selection of books. Mr. Turner's personal library seemed chock full of murder mystery novels which she devoured with relish.

But now, her mind was consumed with the man she expected to marry tonight. Those dark, arresting eyes seemed to peer straight into her heart and the loneliness haunting her soul. A quirk of his lips and a flicker of vulnerability in his eyes stirred tendrils of warmth deep in her heart.

Last night she thought she sensed Mr. Turner's presence by her bedside, but the idea turned out to be absurd. She awakened in the dark to an empty room—empty of anyone's existence except her own.

The loud voices of Lydia and Jon in the throes of one of their daily tiffs spilled out of the parlor and up the stairs. She sighed. They often argued over insignificant things, each intent upon winning the verbal sparring.

As Emmie's competent secretary, Lydia liked things organized. She left nothing to chance. Her methods worked well in a business setting, but not for organizing Emmie's personal life. At times, Lydia's efforts made Emmie feel like a bird trapped in a cage.

Likewise, ever since Alex's death, Jon had hovered over her like an overprotective brother. He discouraged her from nearly everything she wanted to do. Most likely, the argument was over what each deemed best for her. It usually was.

Emmie reached the bottom of the stairs and turned in the opposite direction, toward where she assumed Mr. Turner's private study might be located.

Hearing the soft hum of conversation from somewhere at the end of the long hallway, she padded silently along the wooden floor until she reached a half-opened door.

"I'll check my lists, but this is scarcely a decent lead, sir." Gertie's soft tone reflected skepticism and more than a little frustration.

What lists? What lead? Emmie hesitated, unsure whether to intrude.

"We must find who engaged them, Gertie, before they come back to finish the job. I won't put Miss Griffith through that again, and it's the only lead we have."

The fine silk of Mr. Turner's rumbling tones captured her full attention. Goosebumps erupted over her arms.

She pushed the door opened and entered.

"Since you're talking about me, I want to know everything you've found out so far." She sat on an empty chair and awaited their report. It didn't matter she wore only a robe over her nightdress. There were things far more important than womanly modesty.

Gertie and Cedric exchanged startled looks. Mr. Turner turned his dark penetrating scrutiny in her direction, but said nothing.

Well, fine.

"I have every right to be here. This investigation is about the preservation of my life. *My* life," she repeated for emphasis. "So out with it. What have you discovered so far. I want to know everything you know."

Gertie and Cedric looked at Mr. Turner for direction.

Mr. Turner slumped back in his leather chair and steepled his fingers under his chin, a habit she'd noticed whenever he seemed to be contemplating his next words. She leaned forward.

~~~

Bart noted Miss Griffith's stiff posture, the way she carefully positioned her arm to avoid pain. She wanted answers. Okay, he would give her answers, but not all.

"I'll summarize. The carriage racing down the street immediately after the shooting had a broken right lantern. We traced it to Lemky's Livery on Halsted Street. Mr. Lemky identified the persons who rented the rig as a Mr. Smith and a Willy someone. This Mr. Smith flashed a wad of cash, which means he was paid by someone else.

"We need to find Mr. Smith and discover who retained him before that person secures another man to finish the job. Gertie will check her list of henchmen for anyone matching our suspects."

"A list of bad men? How intriguing." Miss Griffith focused on Gertie with wide-eyed curiosity.

His housekeeper beamed. "Oh, I have lots of lists. Our specialty is finding murderers, ye know. We'll get the person who shot ye, don't fret yerself."

A slight rise of her brow was Bart's only clue Miss Griffith caught Gertie's inadvertent slip regarding their specialty. At some point, he would have to tell her, but not now.

As Gertie explained her various lists, Bart studied his soon-to-be bride. A warmth he didn't care to explore any time soon seeped through him. It almost made him uncomfortable. The sooner he resolved Miss Griffith's case, the better. At the end of the three months, they'd go their separate ways until the year was over. And that suited him just fine.

He sighed and stretched one leg out, thankful they'd finished their meeting before Miss Griffith barged in. No way in hell did he want her to know they were investigating Jonathan Braithwaite, and had added Alex's death and the missing Mr. Bormeister to their inquiry. At least not yet.

He leaned forward and clasped his hands on the desk, the argument in another room infiltrating the wall behind him. The less he saw and heard of Miss Griffith's two bickering friends, the better. Besides, he wanted time alone with her to find out about her childhood, among other things.

"Miss Griffith, why don't you send Miss Holmsford and Mr. Braithwaite home on tomorrow's train? We can follow on Sunday. I find no reason for them to stay, and I don't want to leave until after I see the boys."

"Boys?" Her eyebrows shot up again.

Bart inwardly groaned. The woman didn't miss a thing. Why had he brought up the home? He could almost hear the questions forming in her astute little mind. Few people were aware of his interest in the facility, or that he paid most of the home's operating expenses.

Gertie patted Miss Griffith's hand. "Mr. Turner supports a local home for orphaned boys, sometimes finding the lads on the street and taking them over there himself. On Sundays, we bring cookies for everyone. Why don't you come with us, dearie? I'm sure you'll enjoy it."

Bart held his breath. His Sunday excursions were one of his favorite pastimes. He hadn't missed a visit since he founded the home. What would Miss Griffith think? But more important, why did it matter?

Because sharing this activity with her will increase my pleasure a thousandfold. He shuttered his expression.

Miss Griffith's gaze drifted from Gertie to him, catching him feeling quite vulnerable. Heat flowed to his cheeks. Her intense study lengthened, or at least it seemed that way. He squirmed in his seat.

The corner of her mouth soon twitched, and a dimple he hadn't seen before appeared in her left check. The sparkle of devilment brightened her eyes.

"I'm sure a visit to the boys' home will be quite enlightening. A chance to view another side of Mr. Turner's personality besides the scowling, intimidating, commanding, controlling, arrogant—"

Touchè. "Stop. You've made your point."

Laughter burbled out of Gertie's and Cedric's mouths.

"Intimidating? I doubt that. You've been anything but intimidated by me since we met, Miss Griffith. In fact, you plow through my best efforts to be exactly that."

"All right, so you're not intimidating, at least not to me, but the rest…?" She placed her hands on her hips, a challenge if he ever saw one. The dimple deepened.

Did she really think him arrogant, scowling, controlling, and commanding?

Commanding, yes. He needed to be or lose control of the situation.

Controlling? He needed to be that, too.

Which left arrogant and scowling. Well, he was not arrogant, not in the least.

So, he would try to work on his scowling. Unless he needed to scowl to press a point.

Oh, the hell with it. He was not about to change his ways any time soon, so why try.

"Miss Griffith, I'd be pleased to have you accompany us."

If I get through tonight, that is.

Chapter 6

A dazed Bart waited in front of the ornate front parlor fireplace later that evening for his bride to cross the room on Cedric's arm. His skin itched, and despite his frozen hands, beads of sweat rolled down his back beneath his best summer suit.

This marriage is only temporary. Only temporary.

The words kept rolling through his mind. Three months of living together is not forever.

He fought for air as Miss Griffith reached his side and looped her hand under his forearm. Through the layers of his clothing, through the fine fabric of her gloves, he felt her fingers tremble.

She edged closer, the scent of lavender and woman drifting upward like a fine bouquet, her hand working against his arm in fits of hard squeezes. "I'm scared."

Her simple mumbled admission somehow lifted the gloom shrouding his brain. The steel-edged businesswoman at his side, the one who insisted upon a legal marriage, needed reassurance.

He bent toward her. "We'll muddle through this together."

Her hand immediately relaxed against his sleeve. Satisfaction seeped into his core. Pulling her scent into his still-tight lungs, he led her the rest of the distance to Judge Mahoney and turned to face her.

Wrapped in form-fitting pale blue froth, she reminded him of a mouthwatering confection of spun sugar. A treat as sweet as any of Gertie's desserts. A sling of soft material cradled her arm to immobilize her healing shoulder.

Atop a pile of raven hair sat a small pale blue feathered affair with a single layer of material falling demurely over her face. He itched to raise the veil and see her incredible eyes, but he refrained. That time will come soon enough.

He glanced behind him. Braithwaite and Miss Holmsford stood together a few feet behind his bride. Cedric and Mrs. Carstairs hovered behind him. Nick stood to his right as his best man. All witnesses to the charade they knew was about to be perpetrated. All except for the judge.

Bart turned back to face the man, and threaded his fingers through Miss Griffith's. Her gloved hand tightened against his, her touch at once warm and trusting.

It was up to him to protect her, to find her attacker and see that justice is served.

~~~

Emmie barely heard the judge's words. Her mind fixated on the heat radiating up her arm from Mr. Turner's long fingers entwined with hers. For someone who'd insisted upon a platonic marriage, she was enjoying this simple touch far too much.

She should have been standing beside Alex, a man she had known most of her life, one of her dearest and most cherished friends. But in the years she had been with Alex, holding his hand had never affected her like the fire of this man.

This dangerous man who caused her body to flare to life like a struck match.

"And now you may kiss your bride." The judge's pronouncement jolted her out of her reverie.

Her heart banged against her ribs. A part of her—a very small part—welcomed the new experience. She had never been kissed. Not really.

She cast her eyes down as Mr. Turner lifted the veil over her head. Her skin burned where she felt his gaze fall upon her face. Pulling her lower lip between her teeth, she glanced up. His hooded eyes captured hers. She felt naked, vulnerable. She quashed a need to cover her scar, the scar she had been told over and over would repulse all men.

He hesitated, uncertainty dashing across his usual inscrutable features. Dark brown eyes roved over her face. She stopped breathing, her heart bracing for the rejection she expected would follow.

Then his hand slid to her jaw and held her in place, his powerful fingers warm and gentle. He moved to within a hair's breadth of her and covered her mouth with lips that were firm and warm.

And not platonic in the least.

Tingling sensations shot straight through her, incredibly pleasurable sensations that pulsed through her core and settled in her belly.

Startled, she pulled back. She felt him do the same, a surprised gasp falling from his lips as they parted.

The kiss was not supposed to be so... so electric. Like a current sizzling between two opposing poles. Yet it was, and then some. The force twisted her insides, until she opened her eyes and took another step back.

Her temporary husband's face was now shuttered in a mask of blandness.

Which was just as it should be. Her future was Chicagoland Electric. Her path was one of independence. Nothing must detour her now.

Their witnesses surrounded them with well wishes and hugs. The spectacle seemed so natural, their expressions of pleasure engaging, as if they believed the marriage to be real.

From the middle of the fray, she met Mr. Turner's gaze. His enigmatic smile was at once comforting and unsettling, an odd sensation she couldn't decipher. Nor did she really want to.

She straightened her shoulders.

Two hours later, after the cake had been cut and devoured, the trays of pastries decimated, the punch bowl drained, and half a decanter of fine brandy downed, Mr. Shield raised his glass. He directed a sly, but much inebriated grin at her husband sitting by her side. "I think it's time you turn in for the night, don't you think old man?"

Blood rushed to her cheeks. She cast about for Jon and discovered him next to Lydia on a settee, an expression of horror plastered upon his face.

Her friend bounded to his feet. "I don't—"

Mr. Turner rose from his seat and held out his hand. "Come, Emmeline."

He had used her first name, but his frown was a warning, his tone as crisp as a general's.

What was he doing?

She took his hand and rose, her lungs unable to fill. His hand slid to the small of her back, and he guided her toward the stairs.

She shivered, wanted to break from his hold. He propelled her into the foyer, out of earshot of the rest, and turned her to face him.

Outrage loosened her tongue in her desert-like mouth. "What in heaven's name are you doing? We're not—"

"Nick just reminded us if we're to pull this off, we have to look like, act like, sound like we're a happily married couple. I don't like this any more than you do, but we're in it now. They know we're not going to consummate this marriage. Judge Mahoney does not know, however, or he never would have agreed to marry us. Starting now, we must act like we're a love-struck couple."

His manly scent of spice, brandy and maleness made her stomach flutter. What had made her accept him as a husband? All this agitation—fluttering stomachs, infusion of heat, and racing pulses—was not what she wanted or needed. Better put a stop to it now.

"Despite what I said earlier, Mr. Turner, we need only to get past Friday with this charade and then we can go about our lives as we always have. You have this fine house in the city, and I live at Summerhill in the country. After tomorrow, we needn't see each other despite what I'd said earlier. It's done all the time. Marriages exist quite nicely when two unsuited partners live separate lives. And besides, the danger should be over once I leave the city."

His eyes darkened to the color of aged oak. "If you think you're going back to Summerhill without me, Mrs. Turner, think again."

Her mouth fell open. This won't do. "What on earth for?"

He pushed a wayward curl behind her ear. "What makes you think the person who shot you won't take the train out to Libertyville to finish the job? I agreed to be your husband not because you needed one for your lawyer, but because you need protection from whoever wants you dead. That doesn't mean only while you're in the city. So get used to it. I'm going to be stuck to you like glue."

To have this demanding man share her house, her life, wasn't what she wanted. Not after having tasted his kiss. He would stifle her independence, get in her way, tell her what to do, what not to do. She would have to look at him across the breakfast table, across the dinner table. Still her racing heart. Any other man would have been better than this one.

The truth was she liked this man's kiss all too well. And that scared her.

She pulled in a breath, and whisked through her options. There were none. Until the year had passed and a divorce could be obtained, she had no choice but to make the best of it, even if that meant sticking to the original plan. At least she would have the promise of a platonic marriage to guarantee their separation.

"I really don't have a choice, do I? All right. I agree. Goodnight, Mr. Turner."

She turned and headed for the stairs.

"Now that we're man and wife, you may call me Bart. Sweet dreams, *sweetheart.*"

She jolted to a stop, her back still toward him. The endearment sliding off his tongue sizzled down the length of her spine, reeking of humorous sarcasm.

We must look like, act like, sound like we're a love-stuck couple.

Her mouth twitched. She would step into the role, but somewhere deep inside, she almost wished he had said the endearment for real.

Almost.

But, two could play at this game of pretend.

"Don't worry, *dearest.* My dreams will be sweet, indeed. And may yours be... oh so satisfying."

Chapter 7

"Your lawyer sure has expensive tastes, Emmeline. This building commands the highest rents in the city."

The rolling timber of Bartholomew's voice startled Emmie out of her pleasant interlude of wool gathering two days later. Their first day of marriage yesterday passed quickly enough with Bartholomew showing her the sights of the city as though they were real newly-weds on their honeymoon. Away from his professional environment, she found him to be quite witty and more than a little charming.

Today, she added sweet and thoughtful to his traits when he surprised her with a magnificent bouquet of pink roses for her birthday just before they left the rowhouse.

The man in question climbed out of his fashionable brougham and turned to help her. She grasped his hand and the warmth of his gloved fingers sent sparks flying to some most inappropriate places. For an instant, she wished they wore no gloves at all, a scandalous thought she quickly pushed aside as she stepped out of the plush carriage to the street.

The sidewalk fairly pulsed with people going about their business in the heart of Chicago's financial district. The cacophony of sounds deafening, the city bustled like a living, breathing entity. Energizing. Invigorating. Everyone intent upon getting somewhere, doing something, being someone.

She gazed up at the object of Bartholomew's comment. The red stone and glass Rookery Building took up the entire block at Adams and LaSalle Streets. Its twelve stories soared high above the rest of the structures, a behemoth fortress housing some of Chicago's most prosperous businesses.

"Nothing but the best for Papa's lawyer. He was one of the first tenants when the Rookery opened. In my opinion, the building is a bit oppressive, a hunk of cold stone lit by electricity." She shivered, the action more about what she expected to happen in the structure than the edifice itself.

Feeling Bartholomew's assessing eyes on her, she squared her shoulders. The moment she had anticipated with no small degree of trepidation had arrived, and she must somehow come out the victor. Her only two weapons were a signed marriage contract and her husband's presence, a physical entity as imposing as the office structure before her.

Bartholomew wrapped her hand about his forearm and led her through the huge double doors into the sunlight-infused atrium lobby. "Remember, you're married and you have the papers to prove it."

Inside her gloves, her hands had frozen to icicles despite the warmth of the morning sun. "Of course you're right, but I'll be glad when this is over."

"Things will turn out just fine."

He deftly guided her through the crowded lobby, past the impressive wrought iron staircase leading to mezzanine shops, and over to a bank of hydraulic elevators, inventions she considered a necessary evil in a building of such vast heights. She hated heights, hated elevators even more. Particularly the one her father installed in Summerhill. She'd once been trapped in it for several hours before anyone heard her shouts.

"Eight, please," she told the uniformed operator as she stepped into a waiting car.

Preparing herself for what was to dome next, she propped her hip against the car's side for support. The slight man at the controls pulled the doors closed with a bang. The unbearable sensation of being locked in a black hole descended immediately. The car rose amid a grinding and clanking of gears, ropes and pulleys. Beads of sweat formed between her breasts. She lowered her head and scrunched her eyes shut.

She heard Bartholomew step closer, felt the heat of his hand on her back. She opened her eyes and forced herself to focus on the numbered dial over the door.

The elevator came to a lurching halt at the eighth floor, and the operator pulled open the wrought iron gates with a clang.

By the time she reached the corner office at the end of a long hallway, Emmie's racing heart had slowed to normal. She straightened, steeling herself for the visit she had dreaded. A matronly secretary ushered them into the comfortable office of her father's trusted attorney, Augustus Toliver.

The comfortable *empty* office.

After settling in a leather chair facing the desk, Emmie pulled a white cotton glove off her icy hand and laid it neatly across her lap. Bartholomew followed suit, casually resting his straw Panama hat and tan gloves on a nearby end table.

Edging a glance at her new husband, she found his penetrating eyes exploring hers. He reached for her hand. Her gloveless hand. "Remember, we are happily married newlyweds."

Tiny pings of electricity pulsed up her arm and scattered her wits.

Embarrassed, she pulled away and raised her veil. "Newlyweds. Yes, but—"

A door on the side wall opened. "Well, Emmie, my dear. How are—"

Her father's longtime business associate halted, a frown of bewilderment ripening on his high forehead. "And who do we have here?"

Bartholomew stood, extending his hand in polite greeting. "Bartholomew Turner, Emmeline's husband." He emphasized the last word, his answer direct, commanding. He sounded every bit the proud, wedded man. A role he had been hired to play.

"Husband?" The faintly spoken word fell from Mr. Toliver's lips, stiff and disbelieving, yet he shook Bartholomew's hand with his usual professional civility.

Emmie shifted to the edge of her seat. "We were married—"

"This week," Bartholomew shot a fleeting glance at her, a warning in his expression.

Her attorney's complexion leached to the color of paste, and he sank to his chair in an unceremonious heap. She expected him to be surprised, but his apparent shock was not the happy reaction she'd hoped for. Bartholomew returned to his seat and crossed an ankle comfortably over one knee.

"Yes. Well, I suppose congratulations are in order." Mr. Toliver's anemic smile failed to climb to his hazel eyes which had turned cold. Wasn't he happy for her? "I'm assuming everything is legal and—"

"Oh, you can count on that." Bartholomew directed his answer to the lawyer, but his gaze landed on Emmie's mouth and then her hand, which he brought to his lips. The caress heated her frigid fingers to a blazing bonfire. Other parts of her burned as well. He'd sent her body up in smoke with only a vague innuendo.

One most likely intended for your father's lawyer, not you.

Bartholomew grinned wolfishly. "You have business to discuss, I believe?" he asked of Mr. Toliver while his eyes remained on her.

The lawyer coughed. "Yes, yes. Forgive me. I'm surprised, that's all." He picked up a speaking tube hanging by his desk's side. "Miss Simmons, please send in Mr. Harris."

Emmie's head shot up, Bartholomew's effect on her body forgotten. "My cousin! Here?"

Head lowered, Mr. Toliver busied himself shuffling papers on his desk. "Well, uh, yes. I didn't expect you to show up today with a husband."

She shot off her chair, her glove dropping to the floor. "I am legally married just as Papa specified in his will, though for the life of me, I don't know why he did that. The law allows me to own property in my own right."

The man stood as well. "Emmie, dear, your father's will...."

He left the sentence hanging, though she imagined how it would have ended. She flung herself back in her seat, upset by her lawyer's assumption she wouldn't come up with a husband. He'd known her since she and Eddie were small children. How could he so grossly underestimate her?

Miss Simmons showed in the person Emmie had detested for the last ten years. Deafening heartbeats filled her ears. *Paul would inherit Papa's company over my dead body!* On instinct, she grabbed Bartholomew's arm.

"Hello, Emmie. How are you, my dear?" A trim goatee now hiding his weak chin, her tall oily cousin oozed words of sweetness. However, she had experienced the sting of his spider's bite first hand.

Beside her, Bartholomew tensed.

A nasty comment bubbled up her throat, but she infused the same unctuous tone into her voice and answered politely. "Hello, Paul. I didn't expect to see you here today. Have you met my husband?" She turned to Bart and plastered on a smile. "Bartholomew, dear, this is the cousin I told you about, Paul Harris, my mother's sister's son. Paul, my husband, Bartholomew Turner"

Bartholomew grinned at her, approval lighting his eyes. Pleasure seeped deep in her bones, an odd thing she would ponder later.

A menacing scowl emerged on Paul's face, turning it cold, scornful.

A shudder barreled through her with the force of a speeding train.

Despite his sneer, Paul pushed his hand out to Bartholomew in a gentlemanly greeting. Her husband moved to take it, but Emmie pulled him back. Etiquette be dammed. Her cousin didn't deserve even the most common of courtesies.

Paul withdrew his hand. "My dear Emmeline. I had hoped someday you would consent to marrying *me*."

A muscle in Bartholomew's jaw rippled, and he eyed Paul in speculation. "Maybe she didn't want to marry you."

Paul's eyes narrowed, and his head lowered slightly. He reminded her of a bull pawing the ground before charging.

"Gentlemen, gentlemen. We have business to conduct." Mr. Toliver opened the file on his desk and shuffled through some papers until he found what he sought.

Paul retreated to a corner and slumped against the wall, arms folded over his chest.

After retrieving the page from the stack, the lawyer flattened it with a sweep of his hand.

Emmie's air supply abruptly disappeared. Bartholomew's hand stole over hers, its warmth, once again, comforting, reassuring.

Her lawyer cleared his throat, the sound thick with annoying decorum. "Now, according to your father's will, you, Emmeline Griffith, must be married by your twenty-fifth birthday, today, or your father's company, Chicagoland Electric, goes to your cousin, Paul Harris," he intoned in a sing song manner. "May I have your marriage license, please."

Hands trembling, Emmie dug in her clutch bag and handed the folded documents to Mr. Toliver.

"It says here you were married Wednesday by Judge Mahoney, is that correct?"

Behind her, Paul shuffled.

Be confident. "That's right," she answered in a steady voice that surprised her.

Drawn from his corner, Paul slammed his hands on Toliver's desk. "You were married two days ago? How convenient, Emmeline. Toliver, this can't be legal. She pulled this man off the streets. That paper is a forgery, this so-called marriage a sham."

"Rest assured this marriage is legal in every way that counts."

Bartholomew's words fell from his mouth hard, biting, leveled in a tone that ended all argument.

Thwarted, Paul appealed directly to her. "I love you, Emmie. We might have had a happy life together."

"Never, not after—" She stopped, the ugly truth she'd been trying for years to forget ready to fly off her tongue. She tightened her jaw. "The battle is over, Paul. Accept it. Chicagoland Electric is mine as soon as I sign the papers."

Wasting no time, she grabbed the document in question off Mr. Toliver's desk, reached for his fountain pen, and signed her full name with a flourish, remembering to add Turner at the end. Relief flowed through her veins like life-giving water.

Paul slid into a vacant chair, his chin rising. "Don't think for a moment I'm going to keep your dirty little secret quiet."

Her breath hitched.

"I'll expose you for who you are—an impostor. Everyone thinks you're Edward," he continued.

Emmie let out a long, relieved sigh.

She fixed Paul with a hard glare. "It doesn't matter. From now on I'm going to run this company openly under my own name."

The decision rolled off her tongue with little thought. Her pronouncement sounded good. Right. After five long years, no more hiding, no more acting through intermediaries. No more mystery or secrets. She planned to shed her mask, discard the image she had worked hard to establish. Step out of the shadows and take her rightful place in society.

As president of Chicagoland Electric.

In a symbolic gesture, she removed her hat, yanked the veil away, then set the small clutch of material, beads and feathers back on her head with the long hat pin.

For a moment, she felt vulnerable. Exposed. Much the same as when Bartholomew had lifted her veil during the wedding ceremony.

She sought her husband's eyes, and found pride burning in their depths, and the brilliance of it reached clear to her toes. Something inside her opened, and another vow was formed. One which could take her into the depths of the unknown.

Exploration of the world around her—all the sights and sounds, smells and tastes, experiences and adventures she denied herself since Papa had died.

Chapter 8

Sunday afternoon turned out to be glorious, a perfect day for sugar cookies and milk.

The boys home was nothing like Emmie had expected. Sitting on a lot the size of a city block, the structure was an immense clapboard Victorian mansion with an expansive porch circling the front and sides. Glider swings of all heights hung on chains from the veranda ceiling, and a ball yard was visible in the open space behind the house. A play area for smaller children was tucked into a side yard, and new mass-produced bicycles were lined up like ducks in a shooting gallery in front of a carriage house to the back.

This was a place where children lived and played.

And laughed. The raucous sounds of boys amusing themselves drifted out the open windows.

Bartholomew winked at her as he knocked on the door, a picnic basket hanging from his arm. This, she suspected, was one of Bartholomew's greatest pleasures. And she was sharing it with him. Warmth immediately coiled through Emmie's body. What would it be like to have children of her own? Surprised at the thought, she pushed it away. Her world was of science and invention, not messy faces and fingerprint-marred walls.

A boy of about fifteen with the reddest hair Emmie had ever seen opened the door and beamed wide. "They're here," he yelled to a group of boys crowded behind him.

A clatter of running feet echoed off the wooden floor farther back in the hall.

Holding the screen door open, Bartholomew ushered Emmie and Gertie into the foyer and followed close behind.

The red-haired boy stepped forward, his eyes on the basket. "I'll take that, sir."

Mrs. Carstairs tousled the boy's hair until his cheeks were as red as his unruly locks. "I bet you will, Freddy, but don't you touch one of those cookies before we're ready."

Freddy glanced at his shoes with a sheepish grin. Emmie suspected lifting a cookie from the basket must have been precisely the boy's goal.

"I won't, Mrs. Carstairs." Taking the offered basket, he headed toward the kitchen, lifting a towel to inspect its contents. The sweet aroma of freshly baked cookies filled the hall.

A round woman of middling age made her way through the crowd of boys. "Nice to see you, Mrs. Carstairs, Mr. Turner." A welcoming smile highlighted her warm greeting, curiosity filling the woman's eyes when she spied Emmie. "And who is your lovely guest?"

Bartholomew's hand circled her waist and he pulled her against his side. Heat penetrated her clothing. "Mrs. Higgins, I'd like to introduce my wife, Emmeline Turner." Mrs. Higgins' eyes widened the size of saucers, and a grin split her face in two. "Emmeline, Mrs. Higgins is the lady who mothers all these boys and keeps them in line."

"Your wife. My lord! How wonderful." Mrs. Higgins took both of Emmie's hands in hers. "I'm so happy to meet you. Frankly, I never thought this man would ever marry, but I'm pleased he finally did."

A shadow passed over Bartholomew's features and was gone in an instant. An uncomfortable feeling settled in Emmie's belly. She liked this woman instantly, and the thought of having to deceive her was unsettling.

"Let's see what the boys were up to this week, shall we?" Bartholomew moved into the front parlor and the boys lined up.

A youngster of about three rushed up and clutched Gertie's skirts. "I want my cookie now, Mrs. Ca'stairs. Pease!"

Gertie scooped the boy into her arms and hugged him tight even though he wiggled something fierce. "Tommy, I love ye to death, but you have to learn to be patient. You'll get one soon enough."

"But... but I want mine now," he wailed.

As Emmie watched this little drama unfold, Mrs. Higgins nodded toward another slightly older boy in the hallway wielding a wooden toy sword. "You might start with that one. Louie's in desperate need of some motherly attention."

Her heart sank. *I don't know anything about mothering.*

But I do know about sword play.

She moved closer to the silver-haired boy. "Louie, do you have a fair maiden you're fighting for?"

The boy swiveled and stared at her, his blue eyes examining her closely. "No, ma'am."

"Would you like one? I have lots of experience being the lady who needs rescuing."

The boy considered her offer for a long moment. "Okay. You go hide. The bad men will be here soon and will steal you if they find you. But I can save you."

The familiar excitement of playing knights and damsels in distress rose from somewhere long buried. Most times she was the damsel, but sometimes she played a knight as fearless as any of the boys.

Emmie searched for a hiding place where she could keep an eye on her young knight. The hall was devoid of anything breakable, but a wooden ladder-backed chair would serve as a makeshift hidey hole. After pulling the chair away from the wall, she squatted behind it and peered through its slats.

"I'm ready, my knight."

"You stay there and I'll fight off the bad men." The boy swiveled and faced the imaginary attackers she assumed were advancing from the back of the hallway. "They're riding on their horses from the woods now. I see lots of 'em, but don't worry. I'll keep you safe."

Her rescuer assumed a ready stance, or as ready as any five-year-old could be, then thrust his weapon, swinging it more like a mace than a sword.

"Take that. And that. And that, you blackguard. You'll never get the fair maiden."

Emmie stifled a giggle as her young hero lunged and slashed at the imaginary enemy. Glancing across the hall into the parlor, she caught Bartholomew's eye as he formally shook the older boys' hands and listened to their reports of the week. He flashed her an appreciative grin that melted her insides like chocolate on a hot day.

A few minutes later, Gertie and Mrs. Higgins entered the hallway with a tea cart of glasses and platters of cookies.

As they neared her knight, he flattened himself against the wall. "Don't step on the dead guy, Mrs. Higgins, or you'll get blood and gore on your skirt."

"Well, I wouldn't want to do that now, would I?" Mrs. Higgins lifted her skirts and gingerly stepped over an invisible dead body.

Gertie did the same, but the tea cart rolled right through the bloody mess.

As the cart passed Louie, his nose followed the scent of cookies, and his battle was quickly abandoned. Emmie rose from her hiding place and followed the trio in.

What came next was testimony to the orderliness of the household. All the boys, save one, lined up quietly to receive a cookie, a glass of milk and a hug from Gertie. When Emmie offered to help, she, too, received a hug from each of the boys.

Across the room in a corner, Bartholomew took a seat next to a boy of eight or nine who appeared sullen and withdrawn. And alone. They talked quietly for a while, the boy's eyes on his hands in his lap. Then Bartholomew pulled a handkerchief from his pocket and handed it to the boy, who wiped his eyes, and blew his nose. A few minutes later the boy lined up for cookies and milk, the slightest of smiles marking his countenance.

Bartholomew looked up, then, and captured her gaze. A haunted look filled his eyes, and his features reflected a sadness that reached clear to her soul. It was as if the boy had transferred his pain to Bartholomew, profoundly burdening the man who now carried it.

She turned away, his discomfort too great to witness.

And then he was beside her, his emotions hidden beneath a mask of good will, a smile on his face as though nothing had happened. What was he about, this man who obviously loved children and who would make a wonderful father some day? What possessed him to take a small boy's troubles as his own? What mysteries dwelt in this man's heart?

"Ready to go home?" he asked.

Summerhill.

"Yes. I'm ready." *More than you'll ever know.*

~~~

Two long whistle blasts shrieked as the Milwaukee-St. Paul train to Libertyville lurched away from Union Station later that afternoon. Sitting beside Miss Griffith in the near empty car, Bart stretched his long legs under the seat in front of him and settled in for the leisurely ride. He had an hour and a half to maneuver his client into talking about her childhood. He had a shooter to catch and the more he knew about the people surrounding Miss Griffith, the better.

However, having her company at the children's home this afternoon had left him in a peaceful state of contentment. He wanted to savor it in silence a little while longer. Miss Griffith's warmth and compassion had been evident the moment she entered the rambling structure. To his immense delight, the boys had taken to her much as they had to Gertie. Miss Griffith had chatted and played with them as though she had known each child for years.

As though they were her own.

His mind turned to their wedding kiss, to her lips, warm and eager and responsive. Lips he was unlikely to sample again any time soon.

"Now I know why you enjoy it so."

He startled. "Enjoy what?"

"Visiting the children. I had a wonderful time, especially passing out the cookies. Gertie hugged each boy as she gave them one, and I benefited from her largess. I have never had so many hugs at one time in my life."

The movement of the coach as the train picked up speed jostled their shoulders together in a rhythm of warm touching and cool separation. He found himself enjoying the experience.

Miss Griffith unpinned her hat and set the concoction of straw and feathers on her lap before continuing. "They treated you the same way they treated me. They might not have given you hugs, but even the smallest ones lined up to shake your hand."

"Learning gentlemanly manners is part of their education. They just practice on me."

"From what I saw, that was more than practice. They love you."

A gust of unexpected pleasure swept across him, a welcomed guest on the back of the breeze rearranging a few curls atop her head.

Love? Was that what it was between him and his boys? Respect, maybe, but not love. He never let anyone get that close. He stared out the window at the passing city scene—the wooden porches clinging like vines to the backs of brick apartment buildings, the alleys and streets littered with garbage and refuse, the small knots of people whiling away the warm Sunday afternoon on front stoops.

"Yes, well… uh… more familiarity than anything, I would imagine. I've been visiting them for a long time."

"I don't think it's that. You have a way with those boys. It's as though you understood what they've been through and relate to their problems. They want to be near you because they love and trust you."

Tightness gripped his chest. Trust? An elusive if not downright impossible quality for some to achieve. It had been for him. Until Reginald had given him direction and a purpose in life.

"Children have an innate sense of trust until someone destroys it," he mumbled.

Tendrils of panic too reminiscent of his dreams edged into his consciousness. He pushed the uncomfortable and more than inconvenient feeling aside, its ragged edges tearing at his heart.

Miss Griffith twisted slightly to lean against the window. "I'm curious as to what happened to little Timothy, what's his last name... Forsyth? He was the only one sitting alone. I saw you talking to him for the longest time."

He shot her a glance. Her eyes blazed with curiosity. She wanted to know everything about everything, and was not afraid to ask. Which made things difficult for him.

"Timothy is a challenging case. He doesn't relate to others very well, doesn't like anyone to touch him, is moody and gets into trouble. None of the staff can get him to cooperate much."

"He does well with you, though. After your talk, I saw him help a younger boy reach for a glass of milk."

Another gust of wind blew through Miss Griffith's hair. She raised her hands and rearranged the mass of curls herself.

"Here, let me." He curved over her and pushed the grips on the window down. It slammed shut.

He peered down into her face, his arms trapping her, her scent of lavender trapping him. His gaze fell to her eyes. And discovered them fastened on his mouth.

Breath failed him. He sat back on the seat. Miss Griffith turned as well, two spots of pink blooming high on her cheekbones.

The air thickened with awkwardness. He searched for something to say.

"Timothy needs someone to believe in him, to make him feel better about himself." His voice came out husky.

"How do you know that?" Hers came out breathy.

He shrugged. "I listened to him."

She straightened, her attention captured by his answer. "It was more than just listening. Gertie said most of the boys were dumped on the street by parents who couldn't afford them any longer. They fended for themselves until you found them."

"Most of them, yes. Many played in the streets next to the rot of dead horses. But a few...."

He stopped, unable to continue. A stone formed in his throat. He had a special affinity for those who might have been abused. Timothy was one of them, and Miss Griffith had been astute enough to notice.

The landscape out the window changed to farm pastures and planted fields. This was her world—peaceful, ordered, and somewhat boring.

"So, what was your childhood like?"

She stayed silent so long he didn't think she would answer.

Finally, she let out a sigh. "What would you like to know?"

Her tongue slid out to wet her lips. The movement was a tell. Despite her open-ended question, she didn't want to talk, and somehow, he understood her reluctance.

Start easy. "Tell me about your brother."

A mixture of sadness and joy flooded her face. "Edward? I loved Eddie. I told you we were twins, didn't I? We were always together, despite the condition of his legs. There were four of us... Eddie and me, and later Jon and Alex from two neighboring farms."

Her mouth curved up in memory and the sadness disappeared. Her eyes focused somewhere in the distance. She continued, her tone reflective.

"My mother taught Eddie at home, but I went to public school. I met Jon and Alex there and our friendship began when they started walking me home. To protect me, they said. When we weren't in school, the four of us played together. We were lucky. We had the run of three adjacent farms—acres and acres of space in which to roam."

"How did Eddie—"

"Get around? Jon took him everywhere. At first, he pushed him in a wheelbarrow or carried him on his back. Then when Eddie's body grew and his legs didn't, Jon put him on his pony."

"What about Alex? Tell me about him"

She fingered the feathers on her hat. "Jon doted upon Eddie, and Eddie returned the feeling. Alex looked after me. For as long as I can remember, it was Jon and Eddie, and Alex and me."

She gazed out the window in silence, watching the checkerboard landscape of endless planted fields and fenced pastures fly by. He waited, preferring to let her continue at her own pace.

"One summer Papa built us a house in a big oak tree in the meadow. He nailed wood strips to the tree for climbing, then challenged us to figure out a way of getting Eddie up into it." A smug smile of accomplishment graced her face. "After pouring over our school books, we came up with a rope and pulley system that worked just fine.

"Jon would go up the tree first on the strips, then Alex and I would put Eddie in the rope chair we made and pull on the rope. When Eddie reached the platform, Jon helped him off the chair. Then Alex and I climbed up the tree." She gazed at him, her expression now clearly in the present. "We built a rope and pulley system at the swimming hole and in the old barn hayloft, as well."

Emmie's eyes clouded over then, and she slipped back into her memories. From the sadness radiating off her, he guessed those memories were none too pleasant. Something about the hayloft had upset her. He tucked this piece of unspoken information in the back of his mind for later. When had she developed her fear of heights? She climbed trees and played in haylofts, but now feared elevators? Or was she afraid of closed-in spaces?

The train rolled on, its rhythmic clacking mesmerizing and strangely comforting.

Friends. What he wouldn't have given to have had a few at that age. He sighed inwardly. But this conversation was not about his childhood.

"So, it was natural that you and Alex should fall in love and want to marry?" Now why had he asked that? The question had just dribbled off his tongue.

She whipped her head around. Her eyes flashed irritation, and a crease had formed between her eyebrows. "My relationship with Alex is not open to discussion."

She lowered her gaze to her hands and stroked the feathers of her hat. A bone in her jaw moved ceaselessly. Moisture coated her eyes.

Shit! "I didn't mean to pry." He bit his tongue over the blatant lie.

"Oh, but you did. It is what you do, isn't it? Pry. My relationship with Alex is not germane to your investigation, so please don't ask me again." She turned her head and stared out the window.

A fist punched Bart in the belly. Their conversation ended on a bad note. Their first quarrel, and it concerned her dead fiancée. Did she still love him?

Christ! He thrust his fingers through his hair. Why the hell should it matter anyway?

~~~

Emmie slanted forward in the carriage, eager to see if anything had changed. And, of course, it hadn't. She'd been gone only a week. Nothing as solid and as welcoming as Summerhill could change in such a short time.

Yet as their carriage crossed the pond bridge near the estate's front gate and made its way along the short gravel road to Summerhill's circular drive, Emmie sensed something was different.

It wasn't the pink Italianate house glimpsed through the trees, nor the perfectly landscaped grounds her father had loved. *She* had changed. The sameness of the house and the ageless prairie grass meadow that served as its front lawn brought that point into sharp focus.

Swift and profound, her transformation had been multifaceted, each alteration spawning emotions she failed to understand and now must examine.

She left as E.M. Griffith, the reclusive head of Chicagoland Electric, and returned as Emmeline Griffith Turner, president of the company and ready to conduct business out in the open.

She left as a hermit, sheltered from the world, and returned open and eager to explore what lay beyond Summerhill's fences.

She left as a spinster, and returned as a married woman. Expected, yes. But not with such a handsome, virile husband in tow.

And most importantly, she left as a young woman unaware of her womanly needs, and returned with a husband who evoked emotions, wants and desires she neither understood nor could research.

How could she exist in the same house with a man whose touch she was now eager for, whose kisses she now desired? Theirs was a platonic relationship that afforded neither an opportunity to explore, nor a basis for supposition. What happens between a man and a woman in the bedroom must remain unknown.

Or must it? She had vowed to experience new things. Did she have the courage to delve into uncharted territory of a sensual nature? To take a risk for one night of knowledge to sustain her through a lifetime of spinsterhood?

"Interesting house." Bartholomew's baritone beside her cheek startled her out of her musings.

It was an innocuous comment, and she saw right through it—his way of extending an olive branch across the small chasm created between them on the train.

She glanced at him and worked to keep a smile from bursting into the open. His face, his lips, were inches away, but he wasn't looking at her. His attention focused on the unique house her father had built.

"It's a villa, a replica of one Papa saw in Italy with an open center. Only, in the original, the center remains open to the elements. Because of the harsh winters here, my father installed a glass ceiling that can open in the nice weather and close in the bad."

"I can't wait to explore it." Bartholomew grinned, the mischievous boy emerging from somewhere within.

"The bedrooms off the second floor are all connected so we can still go from room to room when the outer doors off the gallery balcony are shut for inclement weather. Our bedrooms are adjacent to each other."

This last tumbled out of her mouth without thought. Fire raced to her face. She could have put him in any of the villa's numerous guest rooms down the hall but, instead, placed him in the master's bedroom.

With a connecting door to hers.

Or at least that's what she had to do now she had blurted her thoughts.

"Are you suggesting...?"

"I'm suggesting nothing."

He studied her for a long moment, his usual penetrating stare reflecting confusion. "Of course you weren't. My apologies." Then he smirked. "However, being close to you makes it that much easier to be of service, my sweet." He spoke with a European accent, fluttering his eyebrows a few times before stroking his hand over an imaginary handlebar mustache.

She burst out laughing, not only at the shameless innuendo so close to her thoughts, but at the way he expressed it with exaggerated malevolence, the tone playful and light.

How much more difficult would it be to seduce this man? All she wanted was one night with him.

One evening of pleasure to savor for a lifetime.

Chapter 9

Early the next morning, mesmerized by the scene before him, Bart lifted his foot to the lowest fence rail and stretched over the top for a better view. Two magnificent black stallions trotted around the spacious corral as though they owned the world.

A perfectly matched pair, the animals' thick, muscular legs churned high in the air, whirling like the wheels of a buggy. The bright, early morning sun played off firm, muscular flanks, turning black coats into shimmering blue-black silk.

Long, flowing manes and tails and feather hair covering fetlocks gave them a feral appearance that appealed to a part of Bart he kept hidden from everyone—the wild, risk-taking nature of his soul, the soul of the boy he once was. Before....

What he wouldn't give to ride one of these exquisite animals. They were the stuff of King Arthur legends, of knights and warhorses, of chivalry and ladyloves.

Ladyloves.

An image of startling blue eyes and an oval face framed with silky black hair slammed into his mind with the ferocity of a Lake Michigan wave in winter. Last night after a sumptuous meal at a table big enough to accommodate seventy-five people, Miss Griffith had shown him to a bedroom adjoining hers on the second floor.

Knowing she was on the other side of the wall, he lay awake half the night wondering what she looked like sleeping in her own bed. Did she let her hair drape across the pillows, or did she plait it in braids? Did she sleep in a gauzy summer gown with her arms bare, or in a more prudish night dress with long sleeves and a high buttoned neck?

Falling asleep just before dawn, he woke a short time later, his imagination still working overtime.

As though sensing Bart's unsettled presence, the horses halted across the enclosure and regarded him warily, their chests heaving, heads raised in curiosity. Bart stared back, fascinated by the intelligence he glimpsed in two sets of dark-as-night eyes. After a moment, one slowly wondered closer to investigate, his ears pulled forward, listening.

"Hello there, boy. Aren't you a beauty," Bart said softly.

The animal's ears twitched, its obsidian eyes assessing him intently. Holding his breath, Bart slid a fisted hand down his leg farthest from the horse and opened it to indicate he was safe to approach. He'd learned the trick tending his father's stock as a boy.

Within seconds, the black beauty walked to the fence, opened his mouth and flapped his jaws up and down.

Bart chuckled. "Sorry, fellow. I didn't bring carrots this time, but I will the next." He slowly raised his other hand and scratched the horse lightly between his eyes.

After a minute, the stallion whinnied, and trotted back to his companion.

"You made a friend." The male voice to his side held an edge of amusement.

Startled, Bart discovered an elderly man in well-worn trousers and work shirt a few feet away, leaning against the fence. How long had the man been there?

"Sure hope so. They're beauts. What are they?" Bart asked.

"Frisians. Mr. Griffith brought these two back from the Netherlands. Meant to breed 'em with his own Suffolk Punch drought stock, but he died before he could get to it. Miss Emmie, she didn't have the heart to dilute their bloodline. They're just saddle horses now, though Miss Emmie loans them to the town for parades and such."

The two men stood in quiet companionship, appreciating blue-black muscles rippling along strong, sturdy shoulders and flanks as the horses cantered about the enclosure.

Finally, the old man stroked his stubbly chin, then adjusted his cap. "You Miss Emmie's new husband?"

"He is." Emmeline's musical tones sailed through the air.

Bart turned to greet the woman who had inserted herself into his nighttime thoughts now striding down the path between the house and the stable. The strong breeze plastered her blue skirts to her body, outlining lush curves and shapely legs.

"I didn't expect you to be up this early or I would have waited for you." He bent and placed a chaste kiss on her forehead. A spurt of heat shot through him. Startled, he peered into her widened eyes before stepping back.

"I didn't see you at breakfast when I came down, so I came out to find you. I'd planned to show you the rest of Summerhill this morning. I see you've already met Patrick Murphy, Summerhill's stable master. Patrick, my husband, Bartholomew Turner."

So, she too, had felt the heat. Her babbling chatter gave away how flustered his kiss had made her. Balancing the need to appear a newly married couple with the need to avoid physical contact was proving to be tougher than he thought.

Bart dipped his head toward the man in acknowledgment. "We've been talking, but I didn't realize he ran things back here. Please call me Bart."

He extended his hand toward the older man, who'd been observing the exchange with more than a little interest. What did he see? Happily married newlyweds, or the farce they were perpetrating?

"Yes sir, Bart. Pleased to meet ya. Miss Em . . . I mean Mrs. Turner, you want me to saddle up Ebony and Midnight. They could do with some exercise."

Ebony and Midnight. The blacks.

With surging excitement, he glanced at Miss Griffith.

Her hands tightened, her complexion turning a ghostly white. "No! I mean… you can saddle Ebony for Mr. Turner, but find another horse for me, Patrick."

Murphy removed his cap and nervously folded it in sections before stepping closer to Miss Griffith. "Pardon my sayin', Mrs., there's nothing wrong with Midnight. Besides, he befriended your husband here before you arrived. I'm sure the two of them will get along just fine."

Miss Griffith straightened her back into the now familiar line of stubbornness. "Midnight threw Alex. I don't trust him with a rider."

"Midnight didn't cause that accident," Murphy said. "I'd bet my last dollar on it."

Over her head, he met Bart's eyes. The man knew something he hadn't told his employer. What had he kept secret?

"You don't know that for sure. That horse is too dangerous. Saddle Dancer for me."

Knowing when to fold, Murphy raised his hands in defeat. "Yes, ma'am, whatever you say."

Miss Griffith brightened, the lines across her forehead disappearing as though they'd never existed.

"Thank you. I'm going to change clothes." She glanced at Bart, her head to foot perusal feeling like a soft caress. "Are you planning to wear that?"

Bart peered down at his white shirt, sleeves rolled to the elbows, brown vest and trousers, and polished lightweight city boots, then gazed back at her. Hiked nearly to her ears, her shoulders were still much too tense. He hated seeing her that way.

"Would you like me to take them off for you?" He grinned, reaching for his loosely tied cravat.

Miss Griffith's cheeks turned tomato red. Just the response he hoped for. She opened her mouth, but no words came out. Then she giggled, a charming sound like the tinkling of crystals in a soft breeze.

The last shreds of tension faded away. Her body softened, then relaxed completely. Her grin widened until her face filled with sunshine.

"Oh, you." She cuffed him on the shoulder.

Then she did something he never anticipated. She stuck out her tongue.

And for the first time since he met her, he glimpsed the imp of a girl who had played with her brother and two friends without a shred of inhibition. The girl who courageously climbed trees, shimmied up ropes, rode ponies bareback and acted on dares as one of the boys. The girl who had viewed the world as a place to explore and experience as her life unfolded.

A loud, deep laugh erupted from his chest. She gaped at him for a second, and then joined in, her laugh melodious and pleasant.

God, he loved to see her like this, not the cloistered shut-away she'd chosen to become.

He took her hand and kissed it. "I'll change in a minute. You go along first. I want to watch these horses for a while longer."

She gazed at him, her eyes still filled with laughter. "Don't be long, then. I need to go back to work this afternoon." Miss Griffith slid her hand away from his and left, taking the sunshine with her.

Waiting until she couldn't overhear, Bart turned to Murphy, who still leaned against the fence, watching them. His face was unreadable. Only his eyes betrayed his amusement.

Yes, well. So much for portraying themselves as happily married newlyweds. Time to get serious. "I am an investigator, Patrick. I gather you have something to tell me."

Murphy regarded him for a moment, nodded, then pushed away from the fence. "Better yet, I'll show you. I showed them sheriff fellas after it happened, but nothing ever came of it."

The older man led him through the stable to a well-organized tack room and straight to a row of saddles resting on long, thick rungs along a wall. Pulling one down from the top row, he placed it on a small table near a window.

"See this stirrup strap? It's been cut. To someone not looking too closely, it might look like ordinary wear, but see this little part of it? It's too clean to have gotten that way by ordinary use. Someone gave it a start. Them sheriff deputies were either blind, or someone paid them to look away."

Blood roared through Bart's head. "You're saying Alex's death was not an accident?"

"Don't know that for sure, sir. Alex knew these horses and they knew him. He was an excellent rider, even in the fog. Knew the land better than anyone. Found him in a low spot. Alex knew to skirt them spots in a fog. He wouldn't have run into one deliberately. Midnight might have thrown him all right, but seems to me there might have been a reason why."

"Can you be a little more specific?"

Murphy rubbed his chin. "A rip in a stirrup strap causes the rider to become unbalanced, so he grips the horse tighter with his thighs to stay seated. But that only tells the horse to go faster. The faster the pace, the more panicked that unbalanced rider gets and the tighter he hangs on, which makes the horse go even faster. Do you see what I'm saying?" Bart nodded.

"Now add a fog as thick as it was that morning and the rider on a galloping horse can hardly see where he's heading. A horse will pick up on the rider's anxiety and buck or rear. If the rider falls off and hits the ground hard, he could be killed. That's what I think might have happened, sir."

"A very plausible theory. You say you told the Sheriff's men. Did you tell Mrs. Turner?"

"No, sir. I didn't. She was in a terrible state when it happened. Didn't want to cause her any more grief. She's had about all the hard times a body can take. Figured someone from the authorities would be out looking things over after I told those deputies, but the coroner ruled the death an accident soon after and the case was closed. That don't sit right with me, though."

Bart clasped Murphy's shoulder. "Thank you for confiding in me. You were right to save the saddle. It looks like tampering to me. I'll take it from here. From the looks of things, somebody might have killed Alex, and I have a possible reason why. I just need to find out who."

Bart left the stable and headed toward the house, determination claiming his every footstep. The same person who killed Alex might have somehow eliminated Mr. Bormeister, then attempted to do the same to Miss Griffith. The situation seemed to be developing into something far more sinister than he original thought. He intended to step up his investigation and find the culprit before anything else bad happened.

~~~

As Dancer drank from the edge of the small lake, Emmie watched Bartholomew guide Ebony down the sloped path behind her. Sitting tall, her husband maneuvered his horse with surprising expertise, holding the reins lose in one hand while communicating to Ebony with his muscular legs. The sculpted thighs she'd noticed rippling beneath his suit trousers the first day they'd met.

Those legs were now clad in beige riding knickers tucked neatly into tall, glossy brown boots. A long brown jacket hung loosely from his broad-shouldered form. Tossed by the wind, his curly, chocolate hair tumbled about his head in sensual disarray, the sun highlighting streaks of auburn it had earlier kissed into being.

Outwardly, he appeared at ease, yet she detected an undercurrent of alertness, an attentiveness to his surroundings honed by years as an investigator.

She waited impatiently until he came up beside her, her curiosity growing by the second. "What are you looking for? Summerhill is five thousand acres of gardens, pastures, and planted fields. What dangers could possibly lurk out here?"

His forehead crinkled into a frown, then smoothed to a mask of cool casualness. "Not what. I'm concerned about a who, and that person might be anywhere."

He swung down from his horse and led Ebony to the water's edge, his gaze sweeping the far side of the lake with a glance of seeming nonchalance.

Sighing, Emmie began to dismount. "But I'm all right, now. I'm home."

Bartholomew's warm hands clasped her waist from behind and lowered her slowly to the ground. A gust of air hit her pantaloon-clad legs. Warmth crept up her neck, caused only in part by the back of her navy riding skirt rucked up against his waist. His clean masculine scent tinged with spicy aftershave teased her senses, made her want to lean into him, wish he'd drawn her into his arms.

She swiveled. Her skirt descended with a swirl. Sandwiched between her husband and Dancer, she tilted her head back. Without thinking, she reached up and pushed an unruly lock of hair behind his ear.

A soft sound escaped his mouth. For a second she thought he would kiss her. He pulled back instead, leaving her with only his scent. And a dull ache of disappointment.

Something flashed through his eyes before they narrowed into the familiar penetrating stare of Bartholomew Turner, the investigator. "You're not all right. I have reason to believe Alex's death was not an accident."

A heartbeat or two passed before his words penetrated. Her world unexpectedly tilted. Blood drained to her feet and her vision blurred. She couldn't, *wouldn't* believe Alex's death was other than an accident. "You're wrong. Midnight threw him in the fog." Her knees buckled, but before she met the dirt, she felt herself steadied by her husband's strong arms. "Alex murdered? Why?" Tears threatened to take a visible path down her face.

Bartholomew pulled her close to his side, guided her to a fallen tree trunk and sat, his arm tight around her shoulder. Before she knew what was happening, her silk top hat disappeared from her head. Swallowing hard, she desperately willed her tears to stay put.

"Midnight might have thrown him, but someone tampered with his saddle. Patrick showed me the cut in the stirrup strap. He told the sheriff deputies at the time, but they didn't seem to pay any heed. There is no mistake, Emmeline. Somebody wanted Alex dead."

Her heart thundered. "But why? Everyone loved Alex."

The arm hugging her close tightened.

"It might have something to do with whoever shot you. Maybe it has to do with your inheriting Chicagoland Electric, or maybe not, but until we can solve this new mystery, you're in danger. Even here."

Alex died because of me? The ugly truth froze the blood in her veins. The pain of Alex's death, of losing everyone who had mattered to her, came rushing back. Her tears spilled over. Tears she had held back for far too long.

Bartholomew tightened his hold on her, offering softly spoken words she barely heard. Years of sorrow, of hurt and anger, and of loneliness surfaced in deep wracking sobs. She cried for Alex, for Eddie, for her mother, and her father. She cried for herself, for the future that would never be, for the past that was too painful to remember.

After what felt like an eternity, the flow of tears finally stopped. Spent, she became aware of Bartholomew's cheek resting atop her head, his strong heartbeat pounding beneath her ear, his arms enveloping her in welcomed comfort. She drew in a deep irregular breath and snuggled against him, grateful for his kindness. His strength.

At last she looked up and caught his hooded gaze.

He lowered his head, his lips meeting hers in the lightest of kisses. Once, twice they landed on her mouth, his touch as sweet as honey. His lips were warm, soft and pliant, and he tasted of coffee and mint. Desire for this man erupted strong and fiery. Emmie stretched to meet him, her hand pulling his face closer to hers, wanting his kiss.

But, beneath her fingers, his jaw tensed. She sensed his withdrawal before he even moved.

He straightened and pulled away. "I'm sorry. I shouldn't have done that." The cold water of his apology splashed upon her burgeoning desire, suffusing her face with shame and mortification. "I took advantage of you while you were upset. I should have been more sensitive." His brown eyes combed hers closely.

She nibbled on her bottom lip, embarrassed he had been the one to bring her to her senses. What was wrong with her? She just learned her fiancée's death had possibly been a murder, and here she was kissing another man, and liking it.

Emmie rose from the log and walked the few feet to the water's edge. "You know, we used to have races to see who could swim across the fastest." She picked up a stone and threw it into the lake. It skipped twice, then sank.

"Eddie, too?" He stood by her side now, his physical presence stoking the flames still blazing in parts of her body she didn't know existed.

"We put him in a canoe and he raced in that. His shoulders were stronger than any of ours and he often won." No sense talking about Alex. Where he was concerned, her emotions ran far too close to the surface to trust. He had been her beloved friend, her confidant, and in the end, he agreed to marry her not because he loved her as a woman, but because she needed him to be her husband.

"You had fun as a child." Bartholomew's statement was as obvious as the sky was blue.

"Yes. We did…."

Too many people she loved had died. Left her with a grief so vast she had difficulty functioning. And yet, some small part of her longed to live, to be part of something larger than herself. To feel what other people feel, know what other people knew.

Her relationship with Bartholomew was different. She didn't love him, nor he her. He was here to act as her bodyguard and her fake husband. It was a business arrangement. So, knowing their emotions weren't engaged, why couldn't she act on her thoughts of yesterday, explore the desire she felt for him, the electricity that seemed to arc between them?

One night would satisfy her curiosity of what goes on between a man and a woman. One night would leave her with memories she would cherish forever. If she could only figure out how to proceed.

~~~

Bart sat uneasily on Ebony, inwardly berating himself for his insensitivity. He had kissed Emmeline on impulse. Couldn't help himself. Done what he promised he wouldn't. And right after blurting out the truth about Alex. Right after her torrent of tears for the man she had loved, and still did. What the hell was wrong with him? Why hadn't he considered her reaction? Murphy certainly had.

Yet, she had a right to know. Their professional relationship demanded honesty.

Bart swiped his palm against the back of his neck. Kissing Emmeline had pushed him into unchartered waters. He'd finally came to his senses, recognized her vulnerability, her fragile state of mind.

He glanced at her profile as she rode Dancer beside him. She held her chin impossibly high, and her back as straight as a metal pipe. She seemed more resolved, more controlled than before. More like the business woman he met on the first afternoon in his office.

Little Miss Prickly working through a problem.

Pity. He rather liked the relaxed playful girl he encountered earlier this morning. Not that he minded Miss Prickly. She presented an interesting challenge. He would have to work harder to get information from her and to whittle his way through the dense wall of thorns protecting her.

Bart heaved a sigh and stared at Ebony's bobbing head.

They rounded a bend and a stately white farmhouse with a wide veranda around two sides appeared between a copse of trees. A long gravel road ran through the grove to the front of the house. Dormer windows covered with awnings gave the building a friendly, informal appearance. Compared to the ramshackle state of several outbuildings to its side, the dwelling stood clean and bright—freshly painted, if he wasn't mistaken.

"We lived there before the villa was built. Summerhill is a collection of three farms, but my father wasn't good at growing things or milking cows. Like other Chicago businessmen who bought property out here, he much preferred raising horses. Gentlemen farmers, they called themselves."

Her steady voice sounded almost prideful, but he detected an undercurrent of tension in the way she held her arms, bent at the elbows and stiff and tight to her torso. She appeared to be holding Dancer in check, reluctant to go closer to the old farmhouse. Why?

Dancer, ears flat against her head, stepped sideways and snorted. Was she taking a cue from the stress of her rider, or was there something about the farmhouse that frightened her?

While Emmeline worked to calm her mare, Bart scanned the property and noticed a pile of charred, weathered lumber partially hidden behind the house.

"What's all that black wood over there?"

Emmeline stiffened, the color draining from her face. Her fingers tightened on the reins. Eyes wide, Dancer reared, her front legs churning.

Bart's gut did a slow somersault. Powerless to do anything, he watched in horror as the scenario of Alex's death unfolded before him. Emmeline slipped sideways in the saddle, then managed to right herself. Moments later she brought Dancer under control with the gentleness of her calm, soothing voice. The horse blew and stomped on the gravel, its sides heaving. Emmeline bent and stroked the animal's neck, her murmured words like the sigh of the wind.

Unable to swallow, Bart guided Ebony close to the quieting Dancer.

Fire. Of course. Where the hell were his brains?

The fire that killed Eddie must have been in that structure, the blackened remains now silent reminders of a beloved life lost and ugly scars gained. With his tactless question, he managed to bring

Emmeline's most wretched memories to the light of day.

Damn. He deserved to be horse-whipped.

Suddenly Dancer bolted. Bart's pulse spurted at the sight of his wife bending low over the horse's neck, galloping down the dirt road, skirts flying across shiny brown flanks. If he hadn't seen her knees squeeze Dancer's sides a second before, he would have sworn the mare had taken off on her own.

Bart kneed Ebony to a trot. Emmeline needed to be alone. Needed time away from her thoughtless husband and his tactless mouth.

Still, the investigator in him wanted to know what happened in that building. His instincts told him it was something more than a fire, more than the death of his wife's cherished twin and her subsequent disfigurement. An evilness had burned its mark deep in her soul, and she carried that wound to this day.

Was this evil connected to Alex's murder and the attempt on Emmeline's life? Or was it something else, something more sinister than he had imagined. He added this latest mystery to his list to investigate, a list that seemed to get longer with each passing day.

Chapter 10

The moment Bart stepped across the threshold of the barn-like structure an hour later he discovered the existence of another world—the future. Light from dozens of electric bulbs lit the cavernous space as if sunlight streamed through walls of glass. Only, the building was windowless. And locked from the inside. Emmeline had used a key to gain entrance.

Hidden by a thick grove of pines on the north side of the property, the green barn blended into the foliage. Inconspicuous. Discreet. Not even a sign to mark its presence.

Beneath the dazzling illumination inside, an army of female workers dressed in white hovered around worktables and desks, intent upon projects in various stages of development.

"You probably didn't even notice the main house had electricity, did you?" Emmeline crowed.

"No, I can't say I did. The bedroom lamp and the one in the bathroom were gas." He glanced her way and caught the slow smile spreading across her face. Little Miss Prickly had disappeared, replaced by Emmeline Griffith, businesswoman.

Now Emmeline Turner.

Spine straight, she surveyed her domain like the general he presumed her to be, though her features had softened considerably. A glow lit her eyes and her face had become more animated. Here was the seat of her greatest pleasure, the element of life she held to be most valuable. Valuable enough to drive her into a marriage in name only.

"Papa installed small turbine generators in one of the outbuildings. He wired the house for the elevator, the gallery roof mechanism and the call bell system, but urged us to conserve the electricity for use in this structure."

"I can understand why." Awed by the bustling activity, he scanned the room more carefully. "Are all your workers female?"

"Most of them, yes. College-educated engineers no one else would hire. I gave them good paying jobs and they've become loyal, hardworking employees as a result. This was one of the reasons I couldn't let Paul inherit the company. He would have dismissed them all. Some nonsense about science not being women's work." She wrinkled her nose.

Heads turned toward them, the din of voices in the laboratory gradually disappearing. After an endless moment of silence, the soft thud of gloved hands clapping filled the air. Though he couldn't see to the back of the room, eyes peering over hospital masks of the closest workers were brimming with joy. Some even with tears.

Emmeline picked up the end of a speaking tube hanging on the wall near the door.

"Thank you so much, ladies. I'm gratified by your continued support over the years. You've all worked hard to get us where we are today. This morning I'm thrilled to tell you I am the proud owner of Chicagoland Electric. I signed the papers Friday in Chicago. And now I'm pleased to introduce the man who made this all possible, my husband, Bartholomew Turner."

More than thirty pairs of eyes measured him. Normally he regarded the attention of females as pleasurable. To a point. But here in Emmeline's domain, where women were prized for their intelligence rather than beauty, their perusal left him feeling more than a little inadequate.

In a heartbeat, the decorum of the laboratory erupted into chaos. A flurry of excited women surrounded them with congratulations. He shuffled his feet.

Emmeline grabbed his hand, her warmth strangely calming. She accepted the well wishes with confidence and a quiet air of professionalism and dignity. More so than he could say about himself.

He never anticipated the fervor of affection this little woman engendered, yet he shouldn't be all that surprised. She had earned their loyalty and respect long ago, and now they would know how much she sacrificed for their continued well-being.

When the time came to announce her divorce, would she lose their good will? He and Emmeline were being congratulated for a fraudulent marriage, for a state of bliss that didn't exist.

He glanced over the heads of those around him to a nearby corner where a woman bent over a contraption of some sort on a work table. Seeming to sense his scrutiny, she looked up.

Irritation blazed in honey-colored eyes peering at him above the woman's mask.

Emmeline lightly pulled his arm. "Want to see the product we're exhibiting at the Exposition?" Excitement lit her face as brightly as any incandescent light. "They tell me it's already generating quite a bit of enthusiasm from the women who've seen it." He smiled, the unhappy worker forgotten for the moment. "You know I do. Lead on."

She pulled him in the direction of the corner work station, toward the person whose negative emotions had piqued his curiosity. The woman pulled down her cloth mask, her enmity now hidden behind a mask of benign deference.

"This is Sarah Graham, my lab assistant. She does things for me here I can't do with my bad hand. I wouldn't know what I'd do without her." Emmeline squeezed the woman's forearm affectionately. "Sarah, this is my husband, Bartholomew."

Cool eyes sharply examined him. Miss Graham was a tall woman with surprisingly small hands and a rather thin angular shape filling her uniform. From the creases on her face, he would guess her to be well into middle age.

Bart nodded and extended his hand, one professional to another. "Nice to meet you, Miss Graham."

"Likewise." Her grip was brief and limp, her tone bordering on the disingenuous.

He tucked his impression in the back of his mind to examine later.

Emmeline rounded the corner of the worktable and pulled the contraption in his direction. "This is it, the small appliance every household will one day own."

A sharp prick of disappointment stabbed through him like a well-aimed arrow. Someone wanted to kill Emmeline over this… this piece of…?

The device resembled any ordinary six-inch, spade-shaped flatiron used to smooth wrinkles out of clothing. Two thin braided cords flowed out of a small bell-shaped structure screwed to the top of the iron and were kept out of the way by a metal loop attached to the wooden handle.

"An iron?" he sputtered, stunned into disbelief.

"An *electric* iron, Bartholomew. Think of it. Not having to waste time swapping out flatirons when the one you're using cools. Not having to stand near a hot stove while doing this chore. It's not just an iron. It represents the beginning of freedom for women. Freedom from the domestic chores that take up so much of a woman's valuable time. Imagine what can be accomplished without the drudgery of ordinary housework soaking up the day. We're working on several other electric labor-saving devices, as well."

Emmeline's face glowed like the light bulbs overhead, the enthusiasm in her voice reflected in her eyes. This, from a woman who most likely never ironed a garment in her life, and had a staff of many to handle every household *drudgery* imaginable.

Miss Graham came up behind Emmeline, her approach silent and disarming.

"Miss Griffith, we have a problem with the toaster. We can't keep the heating element from burning out each time it's used."

Two deep furrows dug into Emmeline's forehead.

"It's Mrs. Turner now, Sarah, and I thought we had that problem solved." She sighed, and pushed a stray hair away from her face. "Looks like we may not be showing it at the Fair, after all. I had hoped we could. Do you have any thoughts on a solution?"

Emmeline pulled her assistant toward a workstation further along the wall, then turned and said over her shoulder, "I'm going to be involved here for quite a while, Bartholomew. Why don't you go back to the house and have lunch? I'll be fine here."

As much as he didn't want to leave Emmeline alone, sitting in a corner watching her work all afternoon instead of investigating the people in her circle was a waste of time. Without Cedric's and Gertie's aid, he had a considerable amount of research ahead of him. Besides, with the adoration of her staff, Emmeline would be safe enough since no one could gain entrance without a key.

He left, heard the lock click behind him, and headed for the house.

~~~

Lunch at Summerhill turned out to be an event of monumental proportions. An enormous buffet sideboard lined one wall while a formally-set table for at least sixty people filled the center of the long, elegant dining room.

The cacophony of conversations between servants, lab workers, gardeners, and stable and farm hands set Bart's ears to ringing. Everyone knew everyone, and the laughter and camaraderie made it hard to imagine someone here might have murdered Alex.

Bart searched over the heads of the diners for a quieter spot to eat, balancing a plate of fixings for a generous roast beef sandwich in one hand and a glass of lemonade in the other. Open doors at the back of the room beckoned him out to a covered loggia facing the south lawn. To the promise of quiet and solitude. He needed to think through his plan of attack.

Finding a table in the shade, he slid into a chair and set about creating his sandwich masterpiece. His stomach had been rumbling for at least a half hour.

"I see you've found the best kept secret in the house. May I join you?" The familiar voice came from behind his left shoulder.

So much for solitude.

Without waiting for a response, Jonathan Braithwaite set a plate of salads and a glass of iced tea on the table and lowered his lanky frame into a seat. What was he doing at Summerhill, and why did he need to pick this spot to eat his lunch?

Reluctantly, Bart passed his hand about in greeting. "Sure, please join me."

Maybe he could use the opportunity to assess the man.

Braithwaite, immaculate in a tan summer wool suit and white shirt, settled a napkin across his lap before scanning Bart's riding attire with a critical eye.

"You've been out with the horses, I see. Did Emmie show you the property this morning?" His open and friendly tone sounded incredibly like pride, as though he had a stake in what Bart thought of Summerhill.

Braithwaite dumped three spoonfuls of sugar from a silver bowl into his drink and stirred it vigorously with a long-handled tea spoon. Bart popped a slice of German black bread on his towering sandwich and surveyed his creation.

"I have been, and she did. Quite a place she owns here."

"Yes. Emmie took what her father started on a small scale and expanded on things." Pride had more than seeped into Braithwaite's words. The man seemed buried alive in the emotion.

Braithwaite dug his fork into one of three mounds on his plate.

Bart lifted his sandwich. "Are you talking about Chicagoland Electric, the lunch service, or the grounds?"

Before answering, Braithwaite shoved the filled fork into his mouth and ate. "All three actually, though she's taken a few things in a different direction than her father might have wanted."

"How so?" Bart bit into his sandwich. Good, but not quite as good as Gertie's. After swallowing, he used his napkin to wipe away the juice of a tomato from the corner of his lips.

"For one thing, Mr. Griffith wouldn't have hired so many women to work in the laboratory. For another, he was more about delivering electricity than in the uses of it. And this lunch buffet? He would never stand for mixing *common folk* with his family and friends. Wasn't his way."

Sarcasm dripped from Braithwaite's mouth, along with a bit of mayonnaise from his salad, making him look less of a dandy than a few days before. But Bart had to agree with his censure. Many of his own social circle held similar beliefs.

"So, what are you doing here, if you don't mind my asking." Bart gulped his lemonade.

"I run the place."

The drink almost didn't make it down Bart's throat. He coughed. "I'm sorry. What did you say?"

Braithwaite settled his fork on his plate and lifted his glass. His mouth, now wiped clean of the offending condiment, turned up in amusement.

"Surprised you, didn't I? After Mr. Griffith died, Emmie told me she couldn't run both the company and Summerhill. She offered me the job of estate manager and, of course, I said yes. I'd do anything for her. I live in the old farm house you passed today."

How convenient. Too convenient. A perfect location for a lover. Or a murderer.

From the corner of his eye, Bart spotted the topic of their conversation strolling slowly toward a round, raised lily pond at the southernmost edge of the lawn. Head bowed, Emmeline appeared deep in thought. She sank to the pond's sitting ledge and dangled her hand under the gently flowing water of a stone fountain.

She looked dejected, forlorn. Should he go to her? He rose, ready to cross the grass, but Braithwaite grabbed his forearm with surprising strength.

"No. Leave her be. Something is not going right in the laboratory and she needs this time alone to think things through."

The toaster. She must not have found a solution. But Bart wasn't about to divulge the source of her problem to the man sitting next to him.

The fact that Braithwaite seemed to know more about Emmeline's moods than he did bothered him, and he didn't like the sensation. But then, why should he be so troubled? Emmeline and Braithwaite had been friends for a long time.

Because you want Emmeline's friendship yourself.

The thought rose unbidden, killing his appetite. He had no use for female friendships. Too dangerous.

Braithwaite shoved his fork into a different mound of salad. "Whenever she has a problem she heads for the fountain to think. Says the sound of the flowing water relaxes her and opens her mind to solutions."

Bart lined up the edges of his silverware with exquisite care, his thoughts charging ahead full speed. His half-eaten sandwich sat unattended on his plate. "Does she go there often?"

"For years. It's been her spot since the old barn burned down a year after the new house was built."

Bart's gaze riveted to Braithwaite "Old barn? You mean the structure behind the white farm house?"

Braithwaite nodded. A muscle in his jaw twitched.

"What happened?"

Braithwaite pursed his lips, and a storm cloud of bleakness crossed his features. The emotion seemed so stark, so real and alive that Bart found it difficult to watch. Much to his chagrin he felt the warm edge of sympathy seep into his chest. Sympathy for one of his prime suspects. The guy had lost two of his best friends to tragic circumstances. No wonder he was so protective of his only remaining childhood friend.

After a long, tense moment, Braithwaite regarded him with shimmering eyes.

"It's Emmie's story to tell, not mine. You'll need to get your answers from her."

~~~

Shadows. Nothing but murky shadows that wove together, then parted like strips of filmy gauze flapping in the breeze. Whispering, wavering in the stifling air. A shape moved out of the shadows toward him. The devil. Fear, then pain. So much pain.

Drenched in sweat, Bart bolted out of bed and swatted at the air about him. The room stank damp and putrid. Or was he smelling his own fear?

A soft cry erupted from his throat. A cry of frustration, of anger, of futility. His breath came fast and labored, as though his chest had been smashed, his ribs broken. And with it came the crushing feeling of powerlessness.

And shame—overwhelming shame.

Completely awake now, he jabbed his fingers through his hair. Damn. Another nightmare. Another dream of the horror that haunted him still.

He needed air.

Clad only in his pajama bottoms, Bart fled through the open double doors to the balcony he shared with Emmeline. The cool night air bathed his sweaty body. Sucking in large gulps, he bowed over the concrete balustrade and willed his pounding heart to slow.

When calm finally returned, he sank into a wooden lounge chair outside his bedroom door and listened to the night. A barn owl hooted in the distance and crickets chirped. A symphony so unlike the jarring noises of the city it almost sounded unreal. Across the south lawn, the faint sound of bubbling water from the fountain quieted his soul, torn asunder by the nightmare that never seemed to leave him.

He tilted forward in the chair, his hands clasped between his knees.

He didn't want to remember, had worked hard to bury the past. Yet, his nightmares worked against him, pulling up emotions better left buried.

Dead and buried.

Will they ever go away?

~~~

Emmie tossed the sheet aside, flipped to her stomach, and wrapped her arm around the pillow beside her. Somewhere she heard a sound not belonging to the night. Stuck between deep sleep and a semi-awake state, she didn't respond to it, sliding into dark oblivion a few minutes later.

Fire! It's coming closer. Oh, God! Eddie! She pulled with every ounce of strength she had, but he wouldn't budge! Smoke filled her lungs. She couldn't breathe, and if she couldn't . . . neither could he!

The fire still held her brother captive. "Eddie!"

Her heart tore as she called his name, but he didn't answer. Only chirping crickets and the rustling of leaves broke the frightful silence.

A scream.

Her own.

She shot off the bed and ran through the open doors to the balcony balustrade, filling her smoke-filled lungs with clean fresh air.

Tears streaked down her face. And she let them fall.

"Emmeline? Are you all right?" The familiar rumble jarred her awake.

Bartholomew. Behind her. She turned and fell into the solid wall of his chest. Sinewy arms wrapped around her, warm and protective. As they had this morning.

"I couldn't save him. Couldn't get him out. Oh God!"

"Save who?"

The words spewed from her mouth. "Eddie. Fire in the barn. Caught under a beam. I couldn't save him."

Her throat constricted. The rest of her nightmare remained trapped inside, curdling her stomach.

Bartholomew led her to the glider between their two rooms, the place where her parents loved to sit and talk. He settled beside her.

She turned into him and willed her tears not to fall, but they had a mind of their own.

"I'm such a watering pot." She sniffled, embarrassed for crying in his presence yet again.

"You're entitled. You've had a bad time of it today. Tell me about this fire. Everything. From the beginning." His tone was soft and encouraging.

Where exactly was the beginning? He squeezed her shoulder, the motion giving her the courage she needed to speak about the unspeakable. She drew in deeply, searching for the right words.

~ ~ ~

Bart tightened his grip around Emmeline. His heart still thundered with the fear her scream had provoked. When she came flying out her bedroom door, he thought she meant to fling herself off the balcony. He sprang from his chair and raced to the balustrade to pull her back. But, she stopped short, and so had he.

Now he held her in his arms. She was safe. He evened his breathing, a rhythm belying the tension gripping his body.

She settled her head against his chest and brought her hand to rest on his bare chest a few inches below her chin. He covered her trembling fingers with his own and waited.

"I was fifteen. We were all fifteen. Paul had turned eighteen."

Paul? What did he have to do with this?

"He and his family were visiting us for the day. Jon and Alex had come over and had gone somewhere with Eddie who wanted to show off his new twin telescope binoculars. I stayed behind to help my mother. Later, Paul asked me to show him the new litter of kittens in the hayloft. I should have known. He had never been interested in animals. We weren't in the loft more than five minutes when... when Paul swung me about and kissed me. I pushed him away. He's my first cousin."

She stiffened, the look in her eyes, lost, confused. She swallowed and glanced down, the thumbs in her clasped hands rubbing against each other.

Bart kissed the top of her head and struggled to tamp down his rising disgust with Paul. "Go on. What happened next?"

"He pinned me with his body against a tall hay bale." A violent shudder ripped through her body. "He told me I was too friendly with Alex, that he was more of a man than Alex would ever be and he was going to show me. I told him I didn't know what he was talking about. He said he would hurt Eddie if I didn't go along with him or if I told anybody. Then he mashed his mouth against mine to keep me from screaming. He put one hand on my... breast and the other... the other up my skirt. I pushed and kicked, but he was too big, too strong."

Agony tore across her face, and she swallowed several times.

Shit! The tension in Bart's stomach tightened.

"He pushed me to the floor and fell on top, trying to... trying to...." She stopped and chewed on her lower lip.

Rage erupted in Bart's heart, and his lungs seized. "Did he hurt you?"

"No. I managed to push him away and run for the ladder. Paul ran after me and in the struggle, we both fell to the ground. I started to get up when Paul pushed me back down and fell on me. I managed to scream. Jon and Alex were there in an instant. Jon held Paul with his hands behind his back while Alex beat him bloody. But things might have been different if nobody had heard me." Her voice trailed off to a bare whisper.

His regard for Alex rose a hundred-fold. He would have done the same. Some of his rage quieted to seething anger.

"While Jon and Alex were busy with Paul, Eddie limped into the barn. We both tried to calm a frightened foal and her mother in the closest stall, but the other horses grew skittish as well. Jon and Alex left my cousin lying in the dirt to tend the animals."

"And the fire?"

"A few minutes later, Jon smelled smoke. We started to move the horses to safety, but there were twenty of them, all frightened and difficult to control. By the time we had four out, flames had climbed one wall and spread to the hayloft. It traveled fast from there and soon the whole barn went up."

She looked off into the distance, her eyes focused on the nightmare of the past, the thick oppressive force of fear edging into her voice. "We went back in for more horses, the ones Eddie was having difficulty quieting. The roof at the far end collapsed first. Alex had just led some of the animals out a side door when a big crossbeam fell on Eddie, trapping him."

She drew in an unsteady breath and continued, her whole body shaking with the memory.

"Jon and I were the only other ones in the barn when the beam fell. I ran to my brother and tried to pull him out. Jon struggled to lift the timber, but it was too heavy."

Her words tumbled out without a pause, the anguish in her voice palpable.

"Smoke filled the barn. I couldn't see anything. I felt for Eddie's hand and held on. He yelled for me to leave. Jon yelled for me to leave, but I couldn't leave my twin brother to die."

She wiped a tear beginning its descent. What he could see of her face chilled his bones. Pain, raw and deep twisted her features as she relived the horror. Why had he put her through this?

"Flames were everywhere, the smoke so thick I could scarcely breathe. Then Eddie screamed. A terrible, wretched cry that I will never forget. His clothes were on fire, he was on fire, and he screamed and screamed."

She sobbed and sagged into Bart again, the wetness of her cheek dampening his bare chest. A door in his heart clicked open and her agony seeped in.

"I screamed with him and clung to his hand, but Jon yanked me up and ran with me out to the open. He saved me. He left Eddie to die a horrible death to save what he knew his best friend loved the most... me."

Horrified, Bart pulled her into his lap and cocooned her in his arms. His eyes were moist with his own tears. Her grim account was more hideous than he ever thought possible. Deep within, he cried for her. He would do anything to ease her pain.

She wept softly against him, her sorrow unfathomable. No wonder she'd recoiled at the sight of the old barn's charred remains. He would like to beat Paul to a bloody pulp. If the bastard hadn't lured Emmeline to the barn, her brother might still be alive today.

Suddenly, he stiffened as a thought flew through his mind. "Where was Paul during the fire?"

"He slipped away. I didn't realize he was gone until we were trying to calm the horses."

Bart's mind raced. Did Paul set the fire hoping to catch Jon and Alex inside with the horses? Was the fire truly an accident, or a crime of opportunity?

~~~

A whip-poor-will sounded in the distance against a symphony of crickets and other night insects. Finally out of tears, Emmie lay quietly within the warm comfort of Bart's arms, enjoying the evening concert and the rhythm of his heartbeat. As she sat on his lap, the smooth texture of bare skin against her palm filtered through her quiet melancholy.

Saints alive! He's naked.

Emmie's eyes popped open and she glanced down.

Well, not exactly naked, but nearly so. How had she not noticed her husband wore only his pajama bottoms?

The sensible part of her urged her to flee to her bedroom, but her curiosity held her in check, as did the peace she felt in his presence.

Snuggled tight against hard muscle, she studied Bart's sculpted torso without moving her head. The hills and valleys of finely-honed flesh, the small hard nipples encircled by swirls of curly brown hair, and the rhythmic rise and fall of his most impressive chest caused heat to coil through her body like tendrils of incoming fog.

She felt a sudden wanton impulse to run her tongue along his smooth skin. Her nipples tightened to peaks against her lawn nightgown. Recalling Eddie's death had created an urgent need to live, to connect with the newly-discovered part of her that made her feel alive—the world of lusty appetites and carnal pleasures she knew nothing about.

Now was a perfect time to reach for what she wanted. Neither she nor Bartholomew were emotionally involved. Neither of them wanted a permanent relationship. Theirs was a business arrangement, the terms of which could be negotiated at will. This might be her only opportunity to understand what other married women knew. For in her heart she knew she would never marry for real, never give up her independence, her work.

She raised her head, her gaze focusing on his full lips. "Thank you for being here for me."

He tucked an errant strand of hair behind her ear. "My pleasure."

"No, I mean it." Without another thought, she pulled his head down and pressed her mouth against his.

At first, he hesitated, his lips stiff and unyielding. But then his arms tightened about her and, with a groan, Bartholomew gave her what she sought. His mouth opened and his tongue met hers in a wild tangle of flavors and tastes. Then he delved deeper, exploring everywhere, leaving no place untouched.

Bands of tightness around her heart loosened. She soared to life, charged with an energy resembling the power of electricity. Her body tingled and every part of her opened to the vibrancy of his embrace.

Then the kiss changed, intensified, and through it all she sensed a desperation in him that mirrored her own, as though he, too, longed to connect to another soul. His hand slid from her cheek, down her throat to her breast, cupping her through the thin fabric of her nightgown as though testing its weight. Shock waves of pleasure radiated through her.

Yes, this was what she wanted. What she craved. But she wanted more. Much more. And the hard evidence of his hunger strained against her bottom.

Suddenly he pulled his hand away and raised his head. His breathing was erratic and a haunted look flooded his dark half-lidded eyes. "We can't do this."

"You can't pretend you didn't want to kiss me."

"Yes, I admit it. I want to kiss you silly. Take your pain away. Make you laugh. But wanting to and doing so are two different things. Especially between us, and I should have remembered that. I'm your hired husband, your body guard. I'm not your lover, nor will I ever be."

His words stung. Wounded, she stared at her hand still on his chest. "I see," she whispered. "I'm sorry."

He sighed, and drew her closer. "This isn't going to be easy for either of us. We must appear the loving couple without the loving part of it. We agreed."

She was silent for a while, mulling over what he'd said. "What if I don't want the agreement anymore?"

Now he was silent. "You do want it, Emmeline."

And then his lips settled on her head, the lingering caress conveying the depth of his desire as much as the hard ridge pushing against her thigh.

Tightly closed petals of hope unfolded.
He was not immune to her. No, not at all.

Chapter 11

Ignoring the lure of her husband at the table, Emmie breezed into the sunny breakfast room and headed straight for the laden sideboard.

Last night, she had taken a bold step in her quest for knowledge of the marriage bed and was thrilled with her progress. Bartholomew's ardent response told her she was headed in the right direction despite how the kiss had ended. Now she had to plan her next move.

Bartholomew's newspaper snapped as he turned the page with a flourish.

Emmie piled scrambled eggs on her plate, careful to avoid soiling her white laboratory uniform. "I take it you slept well?"

He settled his coffee cup on a saucer with a clatter, then turned another page. "Yes, quite. And you?" His voice held an edge of irritation.

Emmie added both a sausage and two slices of bacon for good measure, far more than she usually ate, but she needed more time with her husband. Lowering her plate to the small table, she slid into a chair across from him.

She glanced at Bart as she unfolded her linen napkin. Dark circles framed bloodshot eyes.

Emmie buttered her toast, watching him from beneath her lashes. "I slept quite well, thank you. And, was your night to your satisfaction?"

His forkful of eggs dropped to his plate.

"It depends upon your definition of satisfaction." He concentrated on plying his fork once again.

She swallowed a bite of toast. "Satisfaction, as having a want or need fulfilled." She added a spoonful of sugar to her coffee and stirred, allowing a small smile to play across her lips.

Bartholomew placed his filled fork on his plate and folded his hands beneath his chin. His brown eyes had darkened to near black. "Sweetheart, I have wants and needs that were definitely not satisfied last night. And won't be any time soon."

Emmie choked on her coffee. His husky-throated comment sent shivers racing along her spine. Though he'd not meant it as such, she took his remark as a challenge from which she would not back away. But before she could come up with a tart rejoinder, Everett, her aging butler entered, his slow shuffle painful to watch.

"Excuse me, Mr. Turner," Everett intoned in his best formal butler's accent, the one she often imitated as a child. "This arrived for you on the morning train."

He handed Bart a large tan envelope.

"Thank you, Everett."

Employed by her family for over thirty years, Everett retreated, closing the glass breakfast room doors behind him.

"It's from Cedric." Bart slit the envelope flap with a clean butter knife and pulled out two smaller envelopes.

Opening the cream-colored one first, he skimmed its contents, and then frowning, read it aloud.

My dear Bartholomew,

The gossips are having a field day over the secrecy and haste with which you married last week. All sorts of stories are circulating, and I can't say I blame the talebearers any. Frankly, I wish you had told me of your plans, as I might have been able to stop the awful rumors before they grew to monumental proportions. That being said, I'm thrilled beyond measure that you finally found someone to love, and who loves you in return.

Bart's eyes flicked to her. Emmie felt heat rise to her face. He continued reading.

I hope you and your new wife will accept my invitation to a small dinner party I'm giving in your honor Saturday at seven o'clock in my home. The celebration will go a long way toward sealing those flapping tongues. Please tell me you'll consent to this token of my affection for you and now your lovely wife, whom I am dying to meet.

Your dear friend,
Bertha

"Bertha? As in Bertha Palmer, Potter Palmer's wife? You know her?"

"The one and only. And yes, I know her. She's promoted my services among her circle for years, and now the sons of her friends are some of my closest friends." Bart sighed and crumpled the note into a tight wad.

"You don't want to go?"

"Not really. I'd hoped we'd have more time to adjust to this. Now everyone must know of our marriage. If we don't pass as happy newlyweds we'd fuel a scandal far worse than gossip. It could sully your reputation and that of Chicagoland Electric."

Pass as happy newlyweds.

Doing so should pose no problem at all. In fact, if she played her cards right, this new development might work in her favor. "I don't think we'd have too much difficulty, do you?"

The lines scoring Bart's forehead deepened. He went on as though he hadn't heard her. "And in a crowd that size I'll be hard-pressed to guard you. Bertha's idea of a small party is never in the realm of small."

"Even more reason we should go. The dinner would be the perfect place for my introduction to society, and to announce my ownership of Chicagoland Electric. I might even procure a contract or two. I've heard Bertha Palmer knows just about everybody who is anybody in Chicago. Besides, I'd like to visit the Exposition. I haven't been there since opening day."

She sipped her coffee, watching his reaction to this last over the rim of her cup.

He responded just as she'd hoped. "Not on your life. Too dangerous. Tens of thousands of people will attend the Exposition on the weekend, and I can't protect you in that kind of crowd. You won't be going to the Exposition until we discover who's behind the shooting."

"But I have an exhibit there."

"Send one of your minions to check on it. You're not going. Not while I'm responsible for your well-being." He scowled, the set of his jaw displaying his determination.

"Then at least take me to the party. We're the guests of honor, Bart. We can't turn it down."

He slumped against the chair. "You're asking me to choose between two bad options, but, you're probably right. One doesn't turn down a command appearance from Bertha. I'll have to figure out how to best protect you at her party while you meet these scions of business."

Emmie smiled as she set the cup back in the saucer. "We'll also have to come up with a reason for the quick wedding."

Bart paused, idly fingering the wadded paper. Finally, he spoke. "We could say we were seeing each other secretly for a long time and decided at the spur of the moment to marry. Couldn't keep our hands off each other, etc., etc."

His face turned a deep red while hers burned with the thought. "How long a time? Alex died only two years ago, and I—"

"A year is long enough to mourn, I think."

A year was *not* long enough to mourn the loss of her best friend. She mourned him still, but he would have wanted her to be happy. "All right. That would be fine with me."

Bart opened the second envelope and glanced at the signature at the bottom. "This one's from your cousin Paul, addressed to me."

Emmie stiffened. "Not that I want anything to do with him, but why you?"

Bart perused the short note. "He says he has information on your shooting mishap he wants to discuss with me. Says he's worried about you and wants to meet with me on the north side of the State Street bridge on Saturday at noon."

"How did he know I was shot? I didn't wear my sling to the meeting with Mr. Toliver."

"My thought precisely, and we never told the police. Maybe he does know something."

The room began to whirl, and she flattened her hands on the table to keep herself steady. "I'll go with you."

Bart clenched his teeth. "You will not! We don't know enough about him to rule him out yet. You'll be safe at home with Gertie and Cedric."

"I'll be safer with you. Besides, this is about me. I need to be there. Please." She hated to beg but saw no choice.

"I don't like it, Emmeline. Especially because of what you said he once tried to do."

"That was years ago. I'm your wife now, real or not. I know you'll look after me."

"I'm not infallible. I don't want you anywhere near that man."

Emmie reached across the table and placed her hand on his. "Let's not argue over this. We'll decide when the time comes."

He said nothing. Only stared at their hands. Then ever so slowly he turned his wrist and gripped her hand in his.

And the intimacy of his touch melted her insides.

~ ~ ~

Stepping across the threshold of the study after breakfast, Bart felt transported to the captain's quarters of a ship from another century.

Lined in dark paneling, the masculine space exuded a sense of comfort and tranquility. Every detail—from the large carved teak desk, to the heavy Tudor-style chairs, to the small brown leather sofa—seemed designed with the male of the house in mind.

The room appealed to him in a way he couldn't articulate, in a way that called to him as *mine*.

"You can use it as your office for the time you're here," Emmeline said. "It's called the Ship Room. The paneling came from a seventeenth century ship, and all the things in here, down to the smallest paperweight, were collected by my father on his various trips. Personally, I think the room's much too dark. I seldom came in here."

Bart scanned the study from her perspective. The only natural light came from two slivers of window high on a wall on the north side of the house. The dim glow from a small desk lamp kept the room in a perpetual state of dusk. Just the way he liked it. A place to relax and think.

"I'll leave you here now. It's time for me to go to work." She turned to leave.

"I'll go with you."

She turned back. "I'd prefer you didn't, Bart. I know you want to protect me, but no one is going to harm me in the laboratory. We lock the door from the inside and no one can enter unless they're identified first."

"I won't be intrusive."

"Please. You'll be a distraction."

"To whom?"

"Me. I'd be terribly inattentive to what I'm supposed to be doing."

She stepped closer and placed her hands on his chest. She tilted her head back and her gaze settled on his mouth, her feminine scent wafting to his nostrils.

He stilled, torn between taking what she offered and stepping away. Doing the right thing. Last night's kiss shouldn't have happened, but he'd succumbed to the temptation of his captivating wife snuggled like a waif in his arms. And now it was clear to him that Emmie wanted more than he cared to or wanted to give. He needed to do something to shock her sensibilities, to cut off her pursuit of him before he damn well lost his mind.

But what?

Put physical distance between them? How could he do that and guard her at the same time?

~~~

His thoughts in a muddle, Bart dismounted the Frisian later that morning and led the black around the old farmhouse to the back. Milkweed, prairie grass and thistle poked through the weathered remains of the barn like whiskers on an old man's face.

What did he expect to find after ten years? Most likely nothing, but something compelled him to search the remains anyway.

He'd compromised by accompanying Emmie to the laboratory and seeing her safely inside. Yet, despite her insistence she would be safe, he had a difficult time walking away. Guarding her and undertaking his own investigation was more than he could handle on his own. He needed help. So, after he left Emmeline, he sent a gardener to the railroad station telegraph office with a message summoning Cedric and Gertie early next week.

Bart's gaze shifted to the field behind the barn, to the acres of prime farmland lying fallow. Weeds had reclaimed most of the acreage, but here and there a corn stalk reached to the sky, a stark reminder of the land's once productive state. How long had it been since the soil had been worked?

He tied the black's reins to a low hanging branch of a large maple and set out on foot for the field. If everyone thought the fire an accident, probably no one had searched for anything suspicious.

As he walked, he mentally divided the field into segments and began his hunt in the corner closest to the barn. Walking through the undergrowth in a straight line, he scanned the ground, pushing away the grasses and weeds with a gloved hand as he went. Overhead, the morning sun beat mercilessly on his neck despite the wide rim of his Panama hat. Sweat moistened the hair flowing over his shirt collar, reminding him he needed to see a barber before Bertha's party.

An hour later, disappointed by his lack of success, he straightened and stretched his aching back. As he surveyed the remaining field, the sun glinted off something about twenty yards away.

Hope and the thrill of discovery zinged through his body. His pulse quickened. Thistle plants slowing him down, Bart reached a small open space where he thought he'd seen the reflection.

As he pushed aside some shorter weeds, he spotted something metallic half buried in the dirt. Excitement burbled up from deep in his chest. How many times had he felt that thrill when evidence surfaced to support a theory? Could this be what he sought?

Digging with his gloved forefinger along the edges of the metal, he tugged a small object out of the soil and turned it over. Weathered and badly dented, a flask of the type used for spirits looked as though it had been out in the field for a long time. Only a small corner of the bottom looked new and shiny, washed clean by countless spring rains and dried by the sun.

"Well, well. What have we here?" he said to the insects disturbed in the brush.

Bart wiped the dirt off the object. Did alcohol have anything to do with the fire? He rose from his crouched position and on a hunch, brushed aside nearby weeds. The toe of his shoe caught on something solid, something definitely not the light pull of a weed. Upon investigating, he discovered a half-buried wire of some sort. Digging around it, he uncovered the rusted, battered remains of a kerosene barn lantern minus its glass.

How did a barn lamp get way out here? Why were these two items discovered so close together? What significance did they have? Were they related to the barn fire?

Or were his finds merely coincidence, the remnants of three young boys drinking out in a field by the light of a lantern?

To conclude these items had anything to do with the fire presented a stretch even to his own way of thinking. Yet, the evidence supporting his theory that Paul may have set the fire just might lay in his hands.

Maybe Emmeline could supply some answers.

~~~

Emmie gasped. Though stuffy, the air in the gloomy Ship Room seemed to disappear altogether.

"Someone deliberately started that fire?" Her question slipped out in a scant murmur.

From behind the desk, Bart studied her with the dark intensity of a private investigator. She felt like a bug under a microscope. Again.

She'd been summoned to his office after dinner by Everett who'd intoned Bart's directive in his formal butler's voice. At first, she thought it a joke, but soon discovered otherwise. Her husband's demeanor was professional, as though they hadn't had a personal relationship at all, hadn't joked, or shared their pasts, or kissed, for that matter.

"These items might have started the fire that killed your brother. I found them in the field behind the barn. Judging from the look on your face, you seem to recognize them." A statement, not a question, his tone neither accusatory nor supportive.

She pulled her shawl tight around her shoulders, wishing she were upstairs pulling the covers over her head. Of course she recognized the items. Both were stark reminders of halcyon days long past, days when Eddie and Alex were both alive.

Though dented and black with tarnish, the battered flask's side included an engraving she immediately recognized. At thirteen, Eddie, Alex and Jon often sneaked behind the barn at Paul's invitation to imbibe from his ever-filled canteen, inviting her on occasion to come along. Most of the time she had refused. As much as she wanted to go, she feared her mother would find out and restrict her activities to only those fit for "ladies." Her freedom meant more to her than spirits with the boys.

She declined, except for once when she sneaked out her bedroom window on a dare and grew too muddle-headed to crawl back in without Alex and Jon's assistance.

She sighed. "It's Paul's canteen. And the other is a kerosene lamp from the barn. Papa saw no need to bring electricity to the horse barn after he spent more than he wanted on wiring the laboratory."

As if imitating her heartbeat, the loud rhythmic ticking of her father's antique chronometer cut through the pregnant silence that followed.

Emmie straightened and met Bart's perusal head on. "You can't believe Paul was involved. I may dislike the man intensely, but even he would never do such a thing."

More silence.

Dear lord! Her own cousin might have killed her brother? She swallowed over the lump forming in her throat.

"Please don't judge him yet, not until you talk to him. I'm sure he has an explanation for how his flask got out to the field. Perhaps it was stolen by someone and tossed there. Or maybe the boys were out drinking and they left it by mistake. They usually went behind the barn."

Bart placed his elbows on the desk. "That could be. But what about the lantern?"

"They always brought it back to its hook," she acknowledged to herself more than to Bart.

"If it were in the barn when the fire started, it would have been destroyed with the others. Paul might have used the lantern to start the fire, then ran with it out to the field to drink and watch the results from a safe distance. Nobody would have noticed he was out there because they were too busy saving the horses."

"You're only making a supposition. You don't know for sure." But a niggle of doubt threaded through her thoughts.

"No, I don't. But maybe we should let it be known we found a flask and lantern out in that field and think they might have been used to set the fire. See what happens, see who steps out of the woodwork."

"Or if anyone steps out, you mean."

"That, too. We'll wait until after we're back from the city. I want to be here if anything comes of this. And I definitely want to talk to Paul on Saturday."

Tension grabbed Emmie's shoulders and created knots where there had been none before. "Of course."

She had no choice but to follow Bart's plan. Yet, the thought of Paul causing her brother's death left a hollow feeling in her chest. Despite what had happened between them, Paul was still family, still her mother's nephew.

She raised her arm behind her to work her sore shoulder muscles. Pain now radiated from the middle of her back to around the edges of her shoulders. She would give anything to have her brother's strong hands knead the knots away like he used to when they were younger.

Memories pierced her heart. She shared so much of her life with her twin that sometimes she imagined him still alive, still heard his laughter, his wit and sarcasm. Still witnessed his indomitable spirit despite his physical limitations.

With great reluctance, she turned her thoughts back to the present. Eddie may no longer be here, but another man was. Another man with strong arms and long, potent fingers. A man who could distract her like no other.

She gazed at Bart in speculation. His heavy-lidded eyes followed her every move.

She smiled, summoning the side of her she'd hidden too long. The feminine side. "Be a dear and work these knots out of my shoulders, will you?"

~~~

Startled, Emmeline's request mirrored Bart's own thoughts—his desire to eliminate her tension. Every part of her showed her distress, from her tight jaw, to her thinly compressed lips, and white knuckled clasped hands.

But, if he were truthful, his desire was for more than just driving away her anxiety. He wanted to touch her, to feel her skin, explore its soft texture and delicate curves. All this despite his vow to distance himself.

Blast and damnation. He forked his fingers through his hair. What was he thinking? If he didn't do something drastic to stop her, no telling what might happen. Theirs was a platonic marriage, and that suited him just fine. He dared not want more. And she deserved someone who could give her more. Much more.

Keeping his fingers busy rolling a pencil, he regarded her carefully. "Does it hurt that much?"

She contemplated his question, a small, coy smile playing across her sensuous lips. God, she was so exciting when she did that. "Yes, it does, more so now than before. You do know how to loosen tight muscles, don't you?"

He nearly choked in a fit of coughing. He knew lots of ways, none of which he cared to indulge in. And none of which would have deterred her current course.

However....

An idea swirled in his brain. An audacious and presumptuous one that would stop any respectable woman in her tracks.

If he dared take the risk.

He slipped behind her and placed his fingers on her shoulders. She jumped, but settled against the chair's back with her head lowered, giving him access to her slender neck. Her reaction told him she had this service performed before. By Alex? He paused, surprised by a sudden sense of discomfort. What the hell? The man was dead. Besides, he'd bet she had never experienced the particular service he had in mind before.

Bart gently squeezed, the tips of his fingers encountering taut knots lodged between her shoulder blades. The whisper of a sigh escaped her lips. And the sound of it warmed his insides.

"You're tight as a bow string. I can loosen those knots, if you like," he murmured.

Her head came up. "How?"

"With the gentle art of massage."

"But you're doing it now."

"This massage would be different."

She turned, her neck and back moving as one. "How different?"

"You lie on the floor and I work your muscles with oil."

One eyebrow rose. "And just where did you learn this gentle art?"

He smiled. The city's higher priced bordellos offered a myriad of services, but he needn't tell her that. "It's not important. Let me help you."

"What are you not telling me?"

"Your back is naked."

She sucked in a breath.

He prayed his scandalous image would shock Emmie into abandoning her request, discourage her from further pursuit of a physical relationship.

She bit her lower lip, a sure sign she was considering his proposal. His heart stopped. She wasn't supposed to accept. The idea of being naked in his presence should be enough to send any maidenly creature fleeing.

"I'd like that very much."

Damn, and double damn. She called his bluff! His throat closed like a slammed door.

Dear Lord, help me now!

He had no choice but to follow through on what he so unwisely suggested. "Thirty minutes. At your bedroom door."

Chapter 12

A half hour later, arms and legs crossed as he balanced against the balcony railing in front of her bedroom, Bart looked the picture of cool nonchalance. Except his expression didn't match his posture. A scowl marked his face, and his dark eyes flashed with displeasure.

Emmie bit her lip, her confidence failing like a downed power line. Even a sky full of stars, visible through the open atrium roof, failed to boost her now jangled nerves.

Had she pushed him too far?

"Ready?" His voice had a hard edge to it. The voice of Bartholomew Turner, private investigator.

Oh Lord! What had she gotten herself into? Where the charming man with whom she'd been sharing her house? She shivered, a warning she heedlessly brushed aside. It was too late to back out now even if she wanted to.

And she didn't.

Words clogging her throat, she nodded.

Bart pushed away from the railing. With a firm hand on her back, he guided her into the empty guest chamber adjacent to hers. For some reason, she found his touch reassuring, even compelling, despite the attitude he seemed to be displaying. Was it all for show? From the kiss they had shared, she knew he'd responded to her.

Inside the room, the steady flicker of scattered thick candles gave off a softened glow of intimacy and provocativeness. Fire raced through her bones and the moisture in her mouth dried. He could have turned up the gaslights, flooded the room with an atmosphere of indifference.

But he hadn't.

Instead, he bared a part of him he'd kept hidden.

The romantic part. The part she wanted to know more about.

He'd pulled the mattress from a narrow daybed to the middle of the floor and covered it with sheets and a thin cotton blanket. The fruity fragrance of orange blossoms, wafting out of a bronze incense burner on a writing table, added a touch of the exotic to the enchanting scene.

Emotions banked, Bart combed her face with impenetrable eyes. "I'll step outside while you take off your robe and gown. When you're done, lie face down under the covers. Call me when you're ready."

The timbre of her husband's deep rumble cascaded over Emmie's skin and weakened her legs.

She should be nervous, yet she wasn't. She relished the adventure, the excitement of once more accepting a risk. An action she hadn't taken since childhood. For the first time in a long while, she felt alive, free, able to let loose of the restraints holding her prisoner in a world she had created. Let loose of the pain she'd endured the last few days as her memories returned to haunt her.

After he left, she quickly shed her clothing and slipped beneath the blanket, feeling more than a bit exposed. The luxurious slide of slippery silk under her pebbly skin sent erotic sparks of anticipation winging to her extremities. She stretched, her body taut, muscles tense. Her hardened nipples rubbing against the satiny sheet provoked feelings of utter femininity, utter decadence. She luxuriated in the sensuality of it all, yet quivered with its impropriety. What would her mother have thought?

A few seconds later, he knocked.

Emmie filled her lungs with the scented air and counted to five.

"Come in." Her face to the wall, her voice came out thin and reedy even to her own ears.

The door opened, and the cool currents of night drifted in. Bart stepped inside and closed the louvered summer doors. Then the inner winter door shut and a lock clicked. Her pulse picked up its pace. Alone. In a locked room. With a man.

"Did you need to do that?"

He didn't mistake the nature of her question. "We don't want to be disturbed."

Pulled by the deep notes of mystery in his tone, she shifted her head toward him. Her breath caught, the air around her suddenly thinning. From his wild curly hair, to the breadth of his shoulders and the trimness of his torso, he exuded masculinity, a virile potency she had come to appreciate.

Bart still wore the black dinner trousers and white dress shirt he'd worn all evening, but he'd rolled the sleeves to his elbows, and removed the studs so the garment gaped to the waist.

Emmie's throat constricted. Brown hair peeked through the opening of his shirt. She had seen him bare chested before, but she hadn't looked her fill. She squelched an impulse to touch him, to let her fingers play in the soft swirls, to stroke the texture of his skin and test the firmness of his well-honed muscles.

His feet bare, he carried a small, etched brass cup which he set beside her head. The vessel contained an oil smelling faintly of almonds. His expression remained masked, but his eyes reflected dark, unfathomable emotion. He didn't seem as irritated as before, nor as calm as he wanted her to believe. There was an aura of tension about him that sent a thrill straight to her heart.

Bart knelt, his knees a few inches from her head. "You'll be more comfortable with your arms down the sides of your body."

Wetting her dry lips with her tongue, Emmie followed his soft-spoken order, rearranging her limbs as he suggested. When she settled, he leaned over and placed both his hands on her covered back, pressing gently, but firmly.

Heat radiated through the layers of sheet and blanket, soaking deep into her tissues, spreading everywhere. She groaned, the pleasure at once erotic and soothing. His scent of citrus, spices and male floated above, easily distinguishable from the incense and oil. She drank in his essence, savoring the tang of him.

"Feel good?"

"Uhmmm." More of an answer became too much of an effort.

"I'm going to fold the blanket down a little so I can work your shoulder muscles," he said several minutes later.

Emmie tensed as cooler air brushed her shoulders.

Bart dipped his fingertips in the brass cup and the rasping sound of rough skin reached her ears as he spread the oil over his hands. Then he wrapped his palms along the ridge of her shoulders.

The shock of Bart's large callused hands on her bare flesh made her insides sizzle, his touch gentle and sure, measured in their slide across her skin. His long fingers soon found the knots he'd discovered earlier and he kneaded them into oblivion. A moan bubbled up from somewhere inside her.

Bart's breath hitched, the sound almost a strangled groan, but his masterful hands continued pressing into her tissues as he glided along in strong, languid sweeps.

When he stopped, a sense of loss ripped through her. She loved every one of his touches, the caress of his magical fingers moving across her skin. She didn't want him to stop. For somewhere deep inside, in places unreachable by his firm strokes, coils of tension tightened into knots of arousal.

"I need to reach your back muscles." His quiet voice asked a question.

Bare her entire back? Did she dare?

The free-spirited girl she had once been wanted to wade in with both feet. He'd told her this was part of it, and she'd accepted, yet faced with the reality of it, she hesitated. Was the hedonism of the moment worth the risk of exhibiting improper and unladylike behavior? Surely, the whole massage bordered on the illicit. But didn't she want to experience new things, to learn about the world both the carnal and the mundane? Ninnies never experienced anything of interest, or so she told herself in answer.

"All right." A squeak.

Bart ran the back of one hand lightly over her shoulders. The feather-like touch sent sparks of something delicious racing to the juncture of her thighs. He folded the blanket and sheet down a little more and paused. Anticipation held her in its grip. She wished she could see his eyes, know what he was feeling at this moment.

A clue of sorts came in his husky rasp. "I'm going to uncover your entire back now."

"All right." Another squeak.

He pulled the covers down more. Cool air flowed over her back as he bared her to her buttocks. She sucked in a breath. Never had she appeared so naked before a man. To appear so in front of her husband—her handsome *temporary* husband—was almost more than she could bear. What was she doing?

She heard him inhale, then air left his lips in a shuddering slide. She glanced up. Despite the slight drift of air from the open windows, his gaze burned her entire back. Need rocketed through her. Desire, hot and wanton. For this man, her husband in name only.

After spreading more oil, Bart glided his hands down the long muscles on either side of her spine, pressing hard with the heels of his palms. The motion sent spirals of electricity surging to her core. Her breath caught, the air in her lungs unable to escape.

When he reached the fleshy part of her bottom, want and need ignited in a hot current that flowed unchecked. Emmie closed her eyes, her senses narrowing to one—the feel of his sensitive hands navigating her curves. Her muscles relaxed. Sculptor's clay couldn't have been more pliant beneath his fingers.

His breathing went from steady to erratic. Even his hands exhibited the slightest of tremors, the same tremors afflicting her now.

He gripped her buttocks for a long second and she heard a strangled moan erupt from his lips. He quickly released her, but his kneading hands descended the length of her back in a slow, even rhythm.

Time ceased to exist.

She imagined his firm pressure heating other, more intimate parts of her, parts now aching for his caress, for the stroke of his fingertips, for the fire of his mouth.

God in heaven, his extraordinary fingers awakened wants and needs she hadn't known existed. She hungered for his touch, her cravings incinerating everything remaining of her more practical side, the part of her that might have stopped this pleasurable insanity.

She had vowed to remain emotionally uninvolved. How wrong she had been. If she gave in to what she craved, she would never be able to give him up when the time came. And worse, the risk of falling in love with a man destined to leave her was far too great. The contents of her heart lay wrapped in confusion, in a blanket of thick fluffy gauze resisting clarity and insight.

With one hand warm on her buttock, he shifted the other one to below her shoulder blade and pushed against both, stretching the long muscle between. Emmie groaned again, unable to keep the evidence of her pleasure inside.

Bart reversed hands and stretched her other side. When the warmth of him disappeared, she waited for his next move, eager to experience more of his adept manipulations, yet fearful of the yearnings each movement now produced.

He dipped his fingertips and spread more oil on his hands. This time he pressed on her lower back, his fingertips reaching the fullest part of her buttocks. With circular motions, he manipulated her deep down—reaching muscles Emmie never realized she had—while his thumbs and the heels of his palms pressed hard against nerves low in her back.

She moaned. She longed to turn over, let him roam along parts of her now aching for his caress. Her lips, her breasts, her—

Emmie opened an eye. Caught sight of the bulge of his arousal. She exhaled in a slow release of air, willing her heart to stop hammering.

Emitting a muffled groan, he rose on his knees, and brushed his lips in a soft caress down the length of her back.

The blood in her veins heated to a boil.

Leaning back, he took in deep gulps of air.

"You can dress now." His terse tone hit her like a slap in the face moments later. "I'll wait outside."

Hard granite sank to the bottom of her belly. Her body burned for him, every nerve alive with want, every part of her screaming for something else. For him.

But Bart only kissed the top of her head and shoved to his feet. After fumbling with the lock in the door, he hurried out as though he couldn't leave fast enough.

Though tense with unfulfilled need, she smiled to herself. His hasty exit proved his defenses weren't as impregnable as he would like her to believe. She resolved to continue her seduction, for she was sure he would eventually succumb.

~~~

Lying in his bed later that night, Bart wondered what in God's name made him think he could give Emmie a massage and not be affected. The encounter was not what he wanted, not what he had anticipated.

Hell, who was he fooling. Truth was, he had wanted to touch her since she first walked into his office. Wanted to feel the slide of his hands along her small delicate body. No woman had ever excited him so.

After she called his bluff regarding a massage, he thought he could hold his own, could explore without becoming involved, but he had been greatly mistaken. His body had overruled all sensible thought and reacted, and that scared him to death.

He'd never had a normal sexual relationship with anyone. Had always avoided intimacy of any kind, begged off when things became too complicated or instead, occupied himself with other hedonistic pursuits.

But tonight, his body had reacted to the sight of Emmie, the feel of her beneath his hands. His gut clenched at the thought, at the apprehension of wanting what he could never have—sexual intimacy. Emmie was a lady, a lovely woman who deserved someone whole and wholesome. He didn't deserve her trust or her regard in any way other than professional. He was too scarred, his wounds carried too deep to be rooted out.

For long hours, Bart tossed in bed, his actions a mirror of the disquiet deep in his belly. Eventually he fell into a fitful sleep.

Only to surge to a sitting position sometime later, his shaking body wrapped in a thick blanket of suffocating terror. Puke barreled up his throat like an exploding volcano. Horrified, he bounded out of his sweat-soaked bed and ran for the bathroom, reaching the toilet not a moment too soon. Sinking to his knees, he gripped the cool sides of the porcelain bowl and spewed his guts.

When he stopped heaving, he gingerly lowered his body to the tile floor, willing himself to stop trembling. Pulling his knees tight to his chest, he rubbed his sleep-filled eyes with the heels of his palms and forced slow, deep breaths. Gradually, the sickness gripping his wretched carcass subsided, and his mind settled into a more rational and sane state.

Shit! When was the last time he'd done that? Bart swept his damp hair off his forehead and sagged against the wall. He felt like an idiot, a bloody cowardly idiot who couldn't even control his innards. He'd puked like a sick school boy, for Christ sake. Now, wrung out and soiled, he felt like a putrid washing cloth.

This time the presence in his horror-filled nightmare coalesced into a shadowy silhouette shape. The big, hulking shape of a man whose body shimmered, sometimes defined, other times blending into the murkiness like an ethereal being. But a man nonetheless.

Murdock!

The terror was real, a bone-deep fear that infiltrated his being, turning his hands to ice while provoking a sweat. Left him unable to move, yet caused him to pant as though he'd raced up a hill. His heart still pounded, as did his head. Like a kettledrum in an orchestra's timpani section.

And the pain! The agony!

He sank his head into the palm of his hand and tried to push his memories away. But they were vivid. And real.

Fifteen minutes later, he scrambled to his feet and padded out to the balcony. The night air of the countryside feathered across his moist skin, while the soft whisper of poplar leaves on the wind sounded like sweet music to his tortured soul.

He had to stop this torment. Had to find a way to make peace with what happened. For if he didn't, he would be forever trapped in the nightmare of a life he was coming to hate.

Chapter 13

Friday turned out to be hot and muggy as Bart and Emmie boarded the train to Chicago for Bertha Palmer's party. Emmie settled near a window in the empty car and inclined her shoulder against Bart's side.

Lavender and Emmie's unique woman's scent drifted to Bart's nose. Despite his best intentions, he found himself filling his lungs with her essence as if it were life giving air. And maybe it was. Her presence lifted him up, made him feel buoyant and light.

Yet, that same physical closeness was also the source of his greatest distress. Since the massage disaster, she migrated to his side every chance she got, her upturned face expressing her desire, her anticipation of something he was not likely to give. Like she was doing now, heaven help him. So young, so fresh, so thoroughly compelling.

Part of him—the part that longed to matter to someone—wanted to cleave to her like a magnet. The other part, his darker side, wanted nothing to do with intimacy of any kind.

For that path led to shame, a hell he'd lived with forever, it seemed.

To maintain any semblance of separateness for the duration of this marriage, he needed to discourage the temptation she so blatantly put in his path. But how? The massage idea had backfired. He thought the shock of what it entailed would send her running. Instead, it whet her appetite for more.

Something had to be done. And soon. For he was beginning to want what could never be.

"We both might be cooler if we sat farther apart."

Startled, she regarded him with all the hurt of a small child in her clear blue eyes. "I'm sorry. I didn't realize I was making you uncomfortable."

She shifted toward the window and gazed at the rolling landscape, her stiff posture expressing her feelings in no uncertain terms.

Damn! He hadn't meant to hurt her.

For the next half hour, the rhythmic clacking of the train on its tracks lulled Bart into a state of semi-consciousness. His gaze fell on Emmie's cheek, on her porcelain complexion now catching the sun's rays through the open window.

She'd been silent the entire time. Hadn't even moved. He would give anything to know what was in that pretty head of hers as she watched the countryside fly by. He'd been most rude. Remorse bound his innards into thickly knotted ropes.

Massage? Hell, he could do with one himself right about now. It was his favorite activity at the various houses he and his friends frequented. Eschewing his friends' customary pursuits at these places, he opted instead for the myriad other services offered, like dining, sampling a fine assortment of imported wines and cognacs, smoking a good Cuban cigar, gambling, and a host of other entertainments resembling a wealthy gentleman's club.

And massages, on occasion.

As he considered when he could fit one into his busy weekend, a service of one establishment in particular came to mind, a service he hadn't the least bit of interest in himself—the exhibition, a peepshow of sorts, renowned for its tasteful presentation. Nick had raved about the show, said it was the best in town. Refined. Elegant. And discreet. It even had a special hidden entrance in the back for arriving with a lady. Bart had passed it off as interesting but not for him.

Could this be his answer? Would suggesting Emmie accompany him to this lewd display of carnal behavior turn her stomach and deter her advances for the rest of their marriage?

With icy fingers, he pulled a handkerchief from his pocket and swiped at the beads of sweat erupting on his forehead.

Was he crazy? The thought of attending such a spectacle made him physically ill. All the fears and terror of his past swirled in his head and took up residence in his gullet. The last thing he wanted to do was something akin to what he'd avoided most of his adult life. He started to tremble, but caught it in time so the movement was just a wiggle of his foot.

As much as he hated to admit, the plan might provide the shock needed to stop her. If… if he could set aside his own fears.

He could. He must.

Without further thought, the idea spilled from his mouth. "There's a place in the city I'd like to take you to, if you're interested."

She turned to him, her forehead puckered, her gaze wary. "Oh? What place?"

Damn and blast! He should have considered it some more. What if his plan failed to achieve its purpose? "You said you'd like to explore new things."

"Yeeesss, I did say that. What do you have in mind?"

The hesitation in her voice gave him pause. How much should he explain? Not much. The jolt to her female sensitivities was what he was after.

"Some place you'd never in your wildest dreams imagine. It's risky, though."

"How risky."

"Very."

She paused, uncertainty settling across her delicate face like one of her lacy veils. She flicked her tongue across her upper lip as she considered his proposal. Then a strange light came into her eyes. "I'll go."

Dread curdled the contents of his stomach.

~~~

"Where are we?" Emmie stared out the window later that evening as their nondescript hansom entered the portico drive at the side of an elegant mansion and continued to the back. Her heart pounded as loud as the raindrops on the conveyance's roof.

"You wanted to do something daring. We're doing it."

Startled by the edge to his voice, Emmie turned sharply. Her lips were inches from his, which were firm and set in a straight line.

"You aren't pleased about coming here?"

He paused, his eyes roaming across her face, his warm mint-scented breath feathering across her forehead. "No, it's not that. I just don't know what to expect. I've never done this."

"Then why did you bring me here?"

"I thought you might like it."

"Based on what?"

"What my friends tell me."

"So, you've brought me to a place you're not sure you want to go to because you think I might like it based on what your friends told you?"

His gaze wandered out the window. "Yes, something like that."

A warmth seeped through her. "You did this all for me? Well, then. I'm sure I'll like it."

Good Lord, she wanted to kiss him right then and there, to lay bare her desire, the contract be damned. Instead, she returned to her scrutiny of their destination, torn between her growing desire to know the secrets of the marriage bed and the truth she refused to acknowledge until now. She was in grave danger of losing her heart to a man who was destined to disappear from her life.

The carriage halted before an arched wrought iron canopy of leaves and flowers, a most fanciful grillwork giving the door a decidedly feminine appearance.

The mansion was no different than any other elaborate, visually eclectic structure of its size in the Lake Shore Drive area—an imposing four-story limestone house decorated with numerous turrets and sculptured stone ornaments.

Except, the back servants' entrance had been adapted for some unknown purpose she couldn't begin to fathom.

"My word, Bart. This is just a house. Well, maybe not just a house. A mansion really. What could possibly be so exciting here?" She couldn't help the disappointment welling inside. He'd promised her an experience she would never forget. This house seemed hardly the place to deliver such an endeavor.

"We'll see soon enough. You can lower your veil. Discretion is the byword here."

Bart descended from the cab and turned to help her out. He didn't smile. His offer of assistance was perfunctory, his mind clearly elsewhere.

"I understand this is the entrance gentlemen use when in the company of a lady," he said, examining his surroundings.

Mulling over that strange bit of information, Emmie arranged her veil before accepting Bart's hand. So, when gentlemen come here without women, they used the side portico. A sudden thought rocketed through her brain, rattling her bones and leaving her breathless.

He wouldn't, would he? Bring her to a bawdy house? Of course he wouldn't. It just was not done. The structure looked too elegant, too refined to be a house of ill repute. Besides, those places were for male pleasure.

Was that what he wanted? To be pleasured? Although she had

expected to do something out of the ordinary, something wild and outrageous, watching Bart make love to another woman was not one of them. A searing pain registered near her heart. As much as she didn't want to admit it, the thought of Bart with someone else made her ill.

She swallowed over the sourness that rose from her stomach. She would pleasure him herself if she knew what to do. But then, there was the risk of falling in love with him. Conflicting emotions played with her mind like two children battling for supremacy, neither coming out the decided winner.

His hands securely around her waist, Bart lifted her out of the hired cab and set her solidly on the driveway.

She peered up at him, her mind caught between the pain of jealousy and her innate curiosity. A flicker of vulnerability flashed through his darkened eyes as he wrapped her hand around his forearm. Heat rolled off him, and the scent of his spicy aftershave and maleness inflamed desire deep in her core.

She hesitated. Where was he leading her?

"Ready?" Beneath his breezy tone lurked a dark note of hesitancy, a reluctance she sensed as though it were her own.

He opened the umbrella tucked under his arm, and sheltered her from the rain. His expression was masked, but his enigmatic gaze burned into her soul. He knew she wanted to explore the world, to experience things she hadn't known about, to step beyond the little box of life in which she'd placed herself. But, what was it about this place that made him think this was it?

Bart led her under the canopy and through the door, opened by a man whose white hair contrasted starkly with a rich dark complexion, and whose sad eyes had witnessed more than he cared to admit. He wore an impeccably tailored black dinner suit with a white shirt and a carefully tied cravat.

"Mr. Turner?"

Bart nodded.

"Your parlor is ready, sir. Follow me." He took Bart's umbrella and folded it.

"Thank you."

Bart's arm now tight around her shoulders, he led her down a long, elegantly appointed hall lit by crystal gas wall sconces on the left wall. The corridor appeared circular, with all doors opening on the right.

The man finally stopped and opened a door marked with the

number five. "Your salon, sir."

Still wrapped around Emmie's shoulders, a slight tremor ran through Bart's arm as he guided her into the room. "Thank you."

He drew a folded bit of currency from his pocket and gave it to the man.

"Thank you, sir. I'm sure you'll find everything to your satisfaction. The window cord is over there." He pointed to the far corner of the room. "If I can be of further service, please ring the bell pull."

"I will, thank you."

The room seemed odd, to say the least. Odd, and private. Instinctively, Emmie folded her arms about her to stifle a rush of apprehension streaking through her body.

In a space eight-foot square marked by a decided lack of furniture, an elaborate crystal chandelier hanging in the middle of the room drew her eye like a beacon. Heavy maroon velvet drapes covered all four walls, and in the center of the enclosure, a maroon brocade couch, flanked by an end table, sat facing a wall that seemed narrower than the others. Behind the couch on the opposite wall, a cut-glass decanter and two matching goblets sat on a high gentleman's sideboard along with a small platter of assorted pastries.

Emmie lifted her veil and removed her hat, placing it neatly on the end table. Under her skirts her knees shook with no small amount of trepidation. *Will he leave me now to go to a whore? Am I to view him from here?*

"Where are we?" she asked again, hoping to be given a clue as to what to expect next.

She settled on the couch, fluffing out her skirts, excitement and apprehension warring with each other. Bart moved to the sideboard and she twisted slightly to keep him in sight, afraid he intended to disappear out the door.

"You'll see soon enough."

Bart's cryptic reply rolled out in his low baritone, marked with mystery and secrets. Tingles skittered along Emmie's nerves. Why did he bring her here?

~~~

"Let me get you a brandy." Bart poured two snifters of amber liquid, and handed one to Emmie before settling on the sofa next to her.

Close to the bell pull. Close to the door.

"To an entertaining evening." He clinked his glass with hers, his breath blocked by a strong force now squeezing his lungs.

His legs shook. He had never been to this house, never cared to. If he hadn't needed to shock Emmie, scare her into abandoning her interest in a physical relationship, he might never have brought her here.

Raising her glass, Emmie smiled, a slow slide of lips and teeth and eyes that transformed her expression into one of playful wickedness. Damn, she was enticing, and she probably didn't even know it.

As he sipped, eyes that glinted of devilishness caught his, and blood surged to where it shouldn't. He jerked his focus back to his glass. He was about to face his worst nightmare, and here he was, hard as a steel girder from a Chicago skyscraper.

His gaze shifted back to her, back to her hooded scrutiny of him. He watched her slowly sip the subtle flavor of the brandy. Her eyes watered, but she never looked away. Shimmering pools of blue held him like a magnet. He imagined the fiery liquid sliding down the smooth interior of her throat, caressing her moist tissues in a slow even progression.

Drops of brandy clung to her lips like morning dew upon a country meadow. Her tongue swept out and wiped them away, and he imagined the taste, the feel of her soft lips as he licked them dry.

Enough! She is my client!

He looked away as she placed the snifter in his outstretched hand, her warm fingers touching his in the brief exchange.

The lights of the gasolier flickered, then darkened, leaving just enough light to discern their surroundings. Dryness stole through his mouth. Following his host's instructions, he crossed to the wall in front of the sofa and pulled the drape open with a jerk.

Emmie gasped.

As did he. Vomit rose to his throat.

A naked man lay sprawled across a round bed of red velvet. It didn't matter that lying next to him was an equally naked woman whose tits were stuffed in his mouth while he stroked the juncture of her thighs.

Terror-filled memories of another naked man flooded his mind. Sweat erupted on his brow.

What the hell am I doing here?

He groaned and sought his seat. Keeping his eyes downcast, he considered how to leave without destroying his purpose for bringing Emmie here.

He hazarded a glance at her.

She stared silently at the tableau before them, her jaw near her chest. He waited, hoping her feminine sensibilities would cause an angry outburst, hoping she would yell at him for having the audacity to bring her here, hoping she would demand he take her home and then keep her distance from him. And he hoped it would happen sooner than later.

Before he lost his dinner.

But nothing happened. If anything, she seemed drawn to the act he assumed was progressing on the other side of the window.

Cold tremors captured his muscles.

For the second time, his plan to quash her interest in a physical relationship had backfired.

The unfolding production served only to sharpen her curiosity. She stared, her eyes round with fascination, her breathing growing more rapid, more irregular by the minute. Her body strained against her clothes. A nipple, now visible from the side, pressed stiff and tempting against the bodice of her satin dress. A delicate flush bloomed on her throat and cheeks. Heat radiated off her body like a stoked fire.

And sweat trickled down his back.

She inched forward on the sofa. Seconds later, she flew to the window and spread her fingers across on the glass.

And then he didn't care about the scene beyond the glass. Only about the woman a few steps away.

Emmie rocked against the window, her movements faint at first, then more forceful. The swish of her skirts merged with the loud and unsteady rasp of her breaths, and suddenly the small room was filled with vibrant electricity, an energy so great it rocked his long-held beliefs, tore apart everything he once thought himself to be.

She embodied life itself, a compelling force of hope and wonder, laughter and joy, success and happiness. And he wanted that for himself. Needed it like the air he breathed.

For the first time in his life, he wanted as a man wants a woman. Needed as a man needs a woman. He wanted Emmie. Only her. Only his wife. And he was willing to risk all to be with her.

In an instant, he was at her back, his torso crowding her small lush form, his hands covering her capable ones against the window. His cock pressed into her, hard and insistent.

She stopped moving, her body rigid.

"Emmie." Her name exploded from his lips on a strangled sigh.

His breathing as labored as hers, he pushed forward and then retreated, encouraging her to return to her rhythm. Beneath him, he felt her tentatively press her softness against him. The rounded globes of her bottom fit snug below his erection. Lavender mixed with brandy and her heavy scent of arousal drew him into a whirling vortex of want and need, of a desire so strong he wanted to turn her right then and kiss her into oblivion.

This felt right. Felt normal. He'd never truly wanted anyone in a sexual way before. Never thought the sensation of want, of need for a woman would be so intense, so consuming. But he wanted Emmie, and he wanted her now. All of her.

As their bodies swayed together, she gasped, and the sound in the quiet room allowed cold, hard reality to intrude.

What he wanted could never happen. Should never happen.

A blackness as endless as death swamped him with despair. His past stood between them.

As did his shame and his nightmares.

As did his work and the inherent dangers it entailed.

As did their contract and his job as her bodyguard.

Bart stilled, his body coiled in knots, adrift in an ocean of unreleased tension. He laid his cheek on her head, let his uneven breaths drift over her ears. His hands still covered hers, though now he intertwined his fingers. She clung to them like a lifeline.

"Christ, Emmie. What was I thinking bringing you here? A little risk, a little adventure. I thought I could do this. I can't." Laced with frustration and anguish, his raw confession came from some deep unexplored part of his soul, from a place hidden even from himself.

She froze beneath him. "Do what?"

"Abide by the contract."

There was more he could have said, things that would more readily explain his conflicted feelings, but he held his tongue, afraid to make himself even more vulnerable than he already was.

An eternity later, she responded. "Then don't."

He tightened his fingers over hers. "Don't what?"

"Abide by the contract."

He sucked in the thickened air. Goose bumps erupted on her neck. He ground his hips against her back, his stiffness trapped between them.

She relaxed and wiggled, inviting him.

And he realized the choice was his.

He swallowed, his conflicted emotions bringing tears to his eyes. Was this the right thing to do? He wanted her and she wanted him. But he was hired to protect her, even from himself. And the contract...? And all the other fears he was afraid to encounter?

She turned within the circle of his arms and searched his face. A myriad of emotions flickered through her eyes. He schooled his features into a mask of blandness as he weighed his decision.

"Emmie?" he whispered, uncertainty pulling at his innards. Part of him wanted desperately. The other part....

"If you're asking me if I'm sure, I have never been more sure of anything in my life." She laid her hand on his chest, the intimacy of her touch firing his blood.

Groaning, he hauled her tight to his body and crushed her mouth with his own. The need to possess, the need to unleash the urgent demands of his body overwhelmed him. He had no patience for tenderness. This was a kiss of domination, of the need to be in control. Of the need to prove to himself that in this aspect of his life, he now had a choice.

And he chose to be a man with a healthy sexual appetite. No more hiding. No more avoidance.

Emmie swept her hands under his jacket and waistcoat and pulled him toward her, taking what she needed.

Moans and sighs were the only sounds in the small room, the scene through the window ignored in a tangle of hands and arms, lips and tongues and teeth. He marveled at the restless passionate woman clinging to his waist, at her ravenous desire as frenzied as his. He slipped one palm to her bottom and dragged her hard against his straining body. He needed her closer. Needed to be inside her.

He lowered his head and grazed the tops of her breasts pushed up by her corset. Her skin felt on fire.

"Now, Bart. Take me now." Her plea drifted out in a quiet moan.

He pulled away and touched his forehead to hers. He could scarcely breathe, scarcely think. Things were happening much too fast. "Not here, Emmie. I never thought...."

No, he had never thought he would want to do the unthinkable.

He turned and reached for the pull, almost invisible in the darkened salon.

Twenty minutes later, Bart grasped Emmie's hand and pulled her up the steps of his house—their house. Crossing the threshold, he carefully closed the door so as not to wake Gertie or Cedric. Shaking with anticipation, he turned her to face him and removed her hat.

Her startled gaze fell to his mouth, a caress that left him fighting for air. Highlighted by moonlight streaming through the door's glass, her eyes darkened and her tongue darted out to wet her bottom lip. His pulse quickened.

The short carriage ride home had been murder, the tension so thick they'd sat beside each other without speaking, their hands on the seat between them close but not touching. And now that they were home, uncertainty crept through his thoughts to feast at his insides. Would she change her mind? Would he?

What he was about to do was sheer madness. He had vowed to never let this happen. Indeed, he never wanted it to happen. Had run from it since he'd come of age. Yet, here he was, about to jump into a sea of unfathomable intimacy.

For he wanted Emmie with the passion of a young buck, a passion every other man of thirty had experienced by now except him.

But taking Emmie to bed was not the tryst of a young buck. She was a woman who deserved the best, deserved to be made love to by an experienced man, to be pleasured and satisfied by someone who knew what he was doing.

Someone other than him.

He swallowed hard against a constriction in his throat. Was he up to it?

"Bart?" Her questioning tone tore him from his tortured thoughts.

And then she made the decision for him by walking straight into his arms.

To hell with experience. The warmth of her soul had captivated his heart.

Letting his instincts guide him, he pulled her small frame tight to his chest and swung her around so her back was against the door. Grinding his body against hers, he took her mouth, prodding deep into its recesses, seeking her response. Needing her encouragement.

Emmie returned his kiss with a fiery want and need of her own, the strength of her ardor the assurance he craved. She forced herself deeper into his frame, rocked her pelvis against his thickening erection, telling him with her body what she wanted, what she desired. Her scent formed an incense of mystery and eroticism that pulled him deeper under her spell. Her taste, of brandy and the sweetness of pastry, invited him to devour her.

Pulling away for air, he inspected her magnificent swollen lips.

"Looks like you've been thoroughly kissed, Mrs. Turner. One of many amusements we might partake of this night. We better go upstairs before we wake the household."

A crooked smile lit her face. "What kind of amusements are you considering, Mr. Turner?"

"Oh, lots of intriguing things." Things he had only heard about in athletic club dressing rooms, but had never done.

Her eyes lit with challenge. "But first you'll have to catch me."

Before he grasped her meaning, she lifted her skirts in both hands and took off running for the stairs. Much to his delight, the capricious girl he had only glimpsed had returned.

He laughed, his spirits soaring. "You little minx. Playing hard to get, are you? Not on your life."

He bounded after her. Halfway up the stairs, he swept her into his arms. "What have you to say now, my fair maiden?"

Her eyes sparkled with laughter. She tightened her arms around his neck and glided her lips across his jaw in small sensual touches. Good God, how he wanted her. Now.

The tinkling sound of her giggle penetrating his defenses. "Oh, Sir Bartholomew. You've rescued me from the dark and ugly dragon, and for your reward you can do with me what you will. I am yours forever."

I am yours forever. The words startled him into immediate sobriety. She had said them in jest, yet their meaning burned into his soul.

He peered into her radiant face. "Then I shall endeavor to please my lady in every possible way."

He only hoped he could.

"Well, kind sir, onward and upward." She flung her hand toward the remaining stairs.

Bart took the steps two at a time, and entered the room she had previously occupied. Tonight would be their real wedding night, and he intended to treat her with all the sensitivity and tenderness she deserved.

Once inside the dark bedroom, he set her on her feet and lit a small lamp. Hands trembling, he struggled to open the tiny buttons on the front of her bodice. Like a stealthy fog, doubt had encroached upon the surety of his actions.

Embarrassed, he glanced up at Emmie.

Her soft skin was suffused with color. She placed her hands on his and said softly, "I'm not going anywhere, Bart. I can unbutton these myself."

"No, I...."

How do you tell your wife you're nervous as hell?

He returned to the fasteners, aware of Emmie's scrutiny. At long last the row of tiny buttons fell open, revealing a white corset trimmed with lace atop a flimsy chemise. His breathing grew ragged. He wanted to see her.

With a frustrated moan, he pushed the opened stomacher aside.

"We're wearing too damn many clothes." Her words, but his opinion as well.

Eyes dancing with amusement, she dug her hands beneath his black suit jacket and worked her way up to his shoulders, finally shoving the offending garment down his arms. His heart hammering, he shrugged it off and flung it over the back of a chair.

"My turn." He twisted her to the side and unbuttoned her skirt, letting it drop to the floor with a whoosh.

They undressed each other, each piece of removed clothing eliciting a groan, a sigh, an intake of breath. Both finally bare, he let his eyes roam over Emmie's small lush body, devouring every perfect inch of her full curves like a man starved for water.

Chapter 14

Mouth dry as sand, Emmie gawked at Bart's strapping bronzed body. At the breadth of his shoulders, the lean muscle rippling down his chest, the flatness of his belly. Lord almighty, he was beautiful. Waves of thunder rolled through her ears.

Bart's exquisite allure, however, also induced familiar pangs of self-consciousness. He possessed a body artists would clamor to sculpt. He was perfection in every way imaginable. By contrast, she was far from a perfect specimen of womanhood. Sarah's honey-coated comments about her flaws were branded across her heart.

Would he want her now that he'd seen her? Would he cringe at the stroke of her damaged hand or recoil at the corruption of her cheek? Oh, why had she encouraged this intimacy? Didn't she realize how vulnerable she would become, how exposed she would be? Since her marriage, she hadn't thought of her scars. Not once. Why should she? She and Bart had agreed to a platonic relationship.

But now, everything had changed.

Despite her anxiety, her eyes drifted to the nest of curls at the juncture of his thighs, her interest drawn to his stiff arousal. Bart's sex was not like the man's in the window. Her husband's erection was thicker, longer, darker. She wanted to reach out and touch it.

But more than anything, she wanted to feel it inside her. Her face heated at the wicked thought. She tried hard to quash her curiosity, but the object of her interest twitched, lengthening even more under her intense scrutiny. Had she caused this reaction? Her tingling nipples hardened into rocks. *Oh Lord! I'm no good at this sensual business.*

He stepped closer, his heat, his body invading her space. Her insecurities escalated. *Don't look at me,* her mind screamed, but her mouth remained closed. If she acted on the urge to cover her exposed body, her scarred hand would become even more visible. Without thinking, she tugged a long curl down over her facial imperfection with her other hand.

Bart's eyes followed the movement, a deep crease forming on his forehead. Reaching out, he tucked the thick strand behind her ear. "You're a beautiful woman, Emmie. Don't hide any part of yourself from me."

His voice flowed over her like sweet maple syrup, soothing her soul. Yet tiny fragments of uncertainty remained embedded in her mind. Before she could ponder further, he lifted her in his strong arms and carried her to the bed. A princess carted off to be ravished by her knight. Her pulse thumped wildly. Her fantasies were about to become reality.

"You can still change your mind." He deposited her gently on the counterpane.

Emmie's mood plummeted, smashed on the rocky shore of her jangled emotions. Did Bart want to back out? Is that why he asked? A dull ache grew near the center of her chest.

Then the logical part of her brain took over. His voice held a sensual huskiness that spoke of desire. Had she read more into what he said than he meant?

She peered into his eyes and saw undeniable yearning blazing like a stoked fire. All remaining apprehension fled as her insides heated with a matching want, with a need to be touched, to be made love to by *this* man.

She'd accepted the inherent risks of their lovemaking, the possibility of opening her heart to him only to lose him when the marriage ended. But this joining was only that—a uniting of bodies by two people who merely desired each other. She would gladly take the risk to experience the joy, the pleasure she knew he could give, even the embarrassment of exposing her imperfections. When this sham of a marriage was over, she planned to never marry again.

But the memory of tonight would fill her dreams for years to come.

Emmie folded her hands in front of her, never more certain of her decision.

"If I wanted to change my mind, I'd have done so before I let you undress me, but your gallantry is noted and much appreciated. Now let's get on with it. I don't know where to begin. I assume you do."

~~~

Bart laughed, but a dark cloud of anxiety spoiled his amusement. Could he give her what she wanted? His experience was limited to a time or two at a fancy bordello to win a bet.

"Always the curious scientist, aren't you?"

"Teach me," she whispered, her mouth drawing his eyes. Then her sweet breasts.

"You don't know how long I've dreamed of doing just that." As the words tumbled out, he recognized the truth in them, a truth he'd been too afraid to admit.

Her breath caught, the sudden inhale pulling her breasts up invitingly.

Bart's anxiety fled in a wave of fascinated lust. He settled next to her and rolled her to face him. The pounding of his heart went from tolerably swift to impossibly brisk in the space of a beat. The heat of her body and her aroused woman scent merged into a heady cloud of carnal potency, inflaming his senses. He wanted to inhale her delicate essence, taste her soft skin, touch her very soul.

His erection pressed hard against her stomach, affirming the irrevocable nature of what they were about to do. He searched her face for signs she changed her mind, but discovered only a longing so intense it shook him to his core.

For it matched his own. It spoke to the awful reality of his chosen lifestyle, the loneliness he often felt, the burden of not sharing his long-buried secrets and desires with anyone.

His flesh heated as her gaze travelled his face and landed on his lips. He pushed her to her back and followed her, his torso pushing her soft body deep into the feather mattress.

Her eyes flashed her excitement. She gasped as he lightly brushed the swirls of his chest hair over her nipples. This is what he needed—his body, naked against hers, decadent, sensual.

In an act as natural as breathing.

Framing her delicate face with both hands, he pressed tiny kisses over her cheeks. She deserved gentleness, infinite tenderness. An emotion he couldn't name lay bare as he touched her, and though he didn't understand it, he warmed to its existence.

He took his time, teased her witless, prepared her for what was to follow. Her hands sifted through his hair and pressed against his scalp to draw his lips toward hers. But he kept them away, nibbling everywhere but where she wanted them. He preferred to go slow, to savor this experience.

Reaching her chin, he shifted her head and her hair fell away to expose her scar. Fear suddenly flooded her eyes and she twisted to avoid his scrutiny.

"Shush, shush. Please don't hide it from me."

His plea, released in a husky raggedness, came from somewhere deep in his soul. He knew about scars and the fear of exposure, the rejection that often followed. His scars were hidden deep inside. Hers were on the surface where they could be healed. And he was dead set upon allaying her fears.

Her eyes closed as he leaned forward. With a racing heart, he brushed his lips across her temple, down the scar tissue's pearly length to her jaw. He poured compassion and understanding, adoration and reverence into his caress, all the emotions that lay jumbled in his heart, the emotions he didn't know how to express in words.

He gazed at her face. Tears leaked from her closed lids, but her body had relaxed, and a muffled sob rose from her lips.

Her eyes opened, and the shining light of gratitude swam among her tears. Another locked door in his heart sprang open.

She pulled his head down and plundered his mouth with the same heated passion of before—hard, demanding, totally consuming. He shuddered atop her. His mind emptied and a well-spring of want, of need crammed the space.

A throaty moan emerged from her lips, a soothing sound like the rush of a heavy wave upon the lake shore. He answered her passion, taking the lead with fervor, plunging into her mouth with a rhythm of things to come. Molten lava seeped through his veins.

Oh, how he wanted his wife, craved her loving, her giving. Everything about her.

Breaking from her hold, he shifted lower, trailing light kisses along her neck and down the valley between her breasts as gentle now as he'd been demanding only seconds before.

She was like a small, but sturdy bird, fragile yet able to live in the harshest of environments. He admired that ability to survive. It resonated with his own sense of survival.

She moaned and thrashed, setting fire to his insides. This woman was no whore experienced in playacting. Emmie was an innocent, her response to him real and true. And so achingly intense that his hands shook with in awe.

She arched her back, sought his questing lips on her rigid nipples.

"Please."

A throaty plea he pursued without pause. Lowering his head, he pulled one erect nipple deep into his mouth and swirled it with his tongue.

A tiny mewling sound burst from her mouth, giving him a deep sense of satisfaction at having pleased her.

The slightly salty taste of her pebbled aureole and surrounding flesh jolted his senses. He wanted to devour her, pour his heart and soul into her. Have her do the same to him.

His erection turned to steel. A loud groan erupted from his throat. He shifted to her other nipple, nibbling on the tip as he covered her flesh.

"So beautiful. So perfect. They fill my hand."

Her breathing seemed to halt as he alternately caressed and nibbled her full breasts, lightly squeezing her with his palm. God in heaven, this was torment. He wanted more. Much more.

Guided by instinct he glided his hand along her torso to her navel where he dipped his finger and circled, then substituted his tongue.

"Ohhhh!" She squirmed, almost levitating off the bed.

He smiled, pleased with his handiwork. Her thighs slid apart, the rich musky scent of her arousal heightening his ardor. He nudged her thighs wider with his knee and she opened with a satisfied sigh.

If he didn't sink inside her soon, he would spend. He needed to be one with her, needed to share with this woman.

Needed to heal himself inside her giving, responsive body.

He glanced at the dark thatch of curly hair at the juncture of her thighs. *Touch her.* Without thought his hand drifted to her opening, a finger sliding inside. Hot, slippery moisture greeted his intrusion. Lust, raw and wild, tore through him.

"You're almost ready."

"Almost? I'm ready now."

"Slowly, Emmie, slowly."

He thrust a finger into her and her back instinctively arched as she begged for more. More of what they were both now ready to receive.

He pulled out and spread moisture about her soft, inner folds, getting her ready. Twice more, he inserted a finger and plied the wetness to her delicate flesh like a soothing salve. How he wanted her. But doubt was fast consuming his emotions.

"Bart, please! Don't tease me. I want you now." Her hands fisted into his hair.

"Soon, sweetheart." Bloody hell. Why was he delaying? "As you command, my lady," he amended.

He shifted into position, his erection brushing her woman's mound. Anticipation seeped into empty places in his heart, places he hadn't realized existed until now.

"This might sting, but the pain will go quickly."

She nodded, her scientist's acknowledgment of consequence registering in her passion-glazed eyes.

He pushed into her, his chest heaving with the effort to keep himself in check, holding back his instincts to move. Old memories crashed into his thoughts, bringing with them no small amount of insecurity.

"It feels odd, but not uncomfortable."

"Hold on."

She tensed.

And he remembered.

Willing himself to continue, his grip on her tightened as he thrust hard. She cried out at the sharp pain spearing her. He stopped instantly, remorse and regret heavy.

"I'm sorry, love. It should ease soon." If only he could be sure.

Body shaking with control, Bart drew her lips into a long, slow kiss. She returned his kiss with the same sweetness, and he savored the exhilarating taste of her, the provocative smell of her.

And then she moved against him.

He lifted his head and stared into passion-filled pools of deep blue. The skin around her eyes and mouth crinkled into a grin.

"What if I want more?"

"Then more you shall have."

She was ready. And willing. His heart swelled, along with his erection. He pulled himself nearly out, then drove forward, his hardened length sliding deep into her body.

Yes! This was what he wanted, what he craved—being one with Emmie. His wife. From the fog of sensuality wrapping his brain, he heard someone moan. Was it him?

He drove in again and this time she met his movement, slipping her arms about his back near his waist, dragging him closer. Her fingers fell on a tiny row of ridges, external scars he forgot were there. She paused, her fingertips grazing against them a second time. He pulled in a breath, hoping she wouldn't ask about their origins.

In the next moment, all thought disappeared as she caught the rhythm he established, taking him to a place where nothing existed except the two of them. Faster and faster they rocked, the rapture intensifying, swelling to heights of boundless sensation.

But shadows of the past suddenly penetrated the thick mist of sensuality.

You don't deserve her. A bleakness crawled through his brain, a thick, dark mass of shame and humiliation he couldn't push aside.

His erection softened. "Damn!"

Frustration and pain slammed into him like a blow to his chest. He'd failed. He pounded his fist into the pillow beside her with a dark rage that rose from deep within.

"What happened? What did I do wrong?" she said, her voice small, plaintive.

Instead of answering, he slowly pulled out of her. "I'm sorry... I.... Damn it all to hell!" His shout filled the large bedroom.

He brushed her shoulder with his lips and rolled off her.

Unfulfilled need blazed on her face, her legs spread, her body quivering. He felt like a cad. He couldn't leave her in this state, not when he'd worked so hard to get her there. Sifting through her folds, he found the erect seat of her pleasure and rolled his forefinger against it. She reached her climax within seconds, her body shuddering violently.

But, this was not the way he had envisioned her first experience. He had failed her.

The burn of embarrassment rose to his cheeks. "Emmie, this isn't your fault. It's mine. I... Christ! I don't know what happened. This never... I've never... wanted you so much, and I... I... failed you. Please forgive me."

His vision blurred through the rush of tears stinging his eyes. Thrusting his fingers through his hair, Bart fled through the connecting bedroom door faster than a strong wind blowing off the lake.

He stalked across his darkened bedroom to the window and flung his hands against the frame. Every part of him shook with barely contained fury—fury at himself. At his inability to give Emmie what she desired most. Release with him inside her.

What the hell happened? She'd asked the same question and deserved an answer. But damned if he had one.

Emotions of every sort pelted him like rocks thrown by a jeering crowd. Anger, guilt, shame, embarrassment, and humiliation. They suffocated him, sucked the air right out of his chest. He wanted to pound his fist into something. Anything. But Emmie would hear him vent his anger, and he didn't want to upset her further. He'd done enough to hurt her already.

In his few previous encounters with high class whores, he'd completed what he started. So why had he failed this time? And why with Emmie, the one woman who mattered the most?

She'd been so receptive, so unfailingly responsive. Helpless in her embrace, he'd lost himself in the wonders of her body, in the scalding pleasure bathing his erection, in the promise of paradise she so freely offered. Never had he been so completely one with a woman, so totally involved in her every sigh, her every moan. Even now his body reacted at the thought of plunging into her.

Should he try again? Risk bringing them both to the brink of release only to fail to complete the act a second time? He swiped his palm down his cheek, his sweat soaked body now cool and clammy. A yawning pit of bleakness opened in his chest.

Bart stared out the window as though answers were to be found on the street below. A small round of light from a gas lamp fell on a man scurrying home. From behind the closed door he heard a muffled sob.

Emmie. Christ!

He'd let her down in the worst way possible—as a lover.

What the hell kind of a man was he? Or was he even a man at all?

Better to keep their relationship strictly business from here on out, to keep to the platonic agreement. She hired him to be her husband in name only and to be her protector. So be it. He stifled any emotion, slamming it deep with the force of a heavy mallet. Their mutual desire wasn't meant to be.

Then another thought struck him.

How would they pass themselves off as loving newly-weds at Bertha's dinner party tomorrow night when he couldn't even bear to face her across the breakfast table?

Chapter 15

Emmie clung to the bedpost with her good hand covering her deformed one as Bart adjust the back laces on her new blue satin corset. She expected Gertie to help her, but Bart appeared in her place.

Since morning, the tension between them had been thicker than an autumn fog. Bart had practically ignored her all day, grunting a small thank you when she handed him a plate of scrambled eggs at breakfast. He'd delivered a reminder about tonight's party in his stern business voice, the one devoid of any emotion. He'd even left to meet Paul without discussing her attendance at the meeting.

Last night she cried herself to sleep, only to wake this morning determined to make sense of what happened. A thoughtful and kind lover, he made her body sing with passion, made her hunger for something she knew naught until she had ultimately reached it. A pleasure so exquisite, her body reacted at the memory of it.

But, she hadn't reached it the way she had imagined—with him inside, spending himself with the same abandoned passion as she had. She hadn't even been allowed the pleasure of seeing to his pleasure. Something had gone wrong. Horribly wrong.

And she feared she knew what it was.

Sarah was right. What on earth made her believe a man as perfect as Bart would want to make love to a woman as imperfect as she? No matter how he had worshiped her scar, in the end he found her so repulsive he couldn't continue inside her even one minute longer. When his erection deflated, he saw to her needs only out of kindness.

Well, no sense dwelling on what would never be. She stuffed her emotions deep inside and considered the practical needs of this evening— the betterment of Chicagoland Electric. She intended to introduce herself as its president, meet some important people, and hopefully obtain the first order for her electric iron.

All she had to do was pretend she and Bart had married for love. But unwanted tears formed to blur her vision. Sheer force of will kept them from escaping.

Glancing about, she caught his reflection in the dressing table mirror, the way his jaw worked when concentrating. The way a stray curl from his tousled mane fell haphazardly across one eye.

He cut a fine figure in his black worsted suit trousers and crisp white shirt with its onyx stud buttons. An image of the body beneath the clothes flew into her mind. Heat flared in places she would rather not acknowledge.

Damned if she didn't wish Gertie stood behind her instead of the man she still wanted, the man she still lusted after.

The man who *didn't* want her.

She pulled a long curl down over her cheek and averted her face, afraid her eyes might reflect the pain she couldn't conceal.

"What happened at your meeting with Paul?"

"I waited an hour and a half, but he never showed."

"Odd. He always keeps his appointments."

Silence. His mouth tightened into a flat line.

"Damn laces. I don't understand why women wear such hare-brained contraptions." Bart's warm breath on her bare shoulders pebbled her skin with goosebumps.

"We don't have a choice. Men made these contraptions so women could get into their hare-brained dress designs. Believe me, if the ladies were in charge, fashions would be different."

He made an indescribable sound and gave one last tug that nearly took her breath away. Literally. But, as he tied off the laces, the feather touch of his fingers against her skin sent electric pulses zinging through her body.

Control yourself, Emmie. He doesn't want you. Not in that way. A lump of disappointment lodged in her throat.

"Thank you," was all she managed to say.

"You're welcome," came the response in an equally polite tone.

Well, hell!

She reached for her blue satin evening dress hanging over the open wardrobe door, but he seized it first, his body crowding her space. An aroma of soap and aftershave wafted over her head, clean and fresh. She breathed in the smell of him, the faint musky essence of maleness uniquely his own.

She tamped down an urge to snuggle into his warmth, find comfort in his arms. Prudence seemed the more appropriate action. Better to move forward without embarrassing herself further. Folding her slim-fitting petticoat about her, Emmie stepped into the gown's opening, and wiggled the dress into place.

An emotion remarkably like longing filtered through Bart's eyes but disappeared so fast she thought she imagined it. His expression remained shuttered, the only telling sign a slight twitch of a facial muscle near his temple. With a sigh, she turned, seeking his assistance with the row of small buttons running down the garment's back.

Pushing aside the gown's short train, he stepped close and drew the two halves together.

A tense stillness filled the room.

Emmie bit her lip as he deftly maneuvered the buttons under the gown's placket. His hands ended up at the fleshy part of her bottom where they lingered longer than necessary. Her mouth went dry.

Hands on her hips, he rotated her to face him, the gown's train rustling across his legs.

"We have to talk." Contrition wove through his soft tones like a fine thread, but she chose to ignore it.

"About what? You don't want me that way, and now I know it. We're back to a platonic marriage, and that's fine with me. We have nothing to discuss."

His eyes blazed. "You believe that?"

To what did he refer—the fact he didn't want her, or that they had nothing to say to each other?

She answered with care. "Should I believe any other way?"

"Yes, damn it. I owe you an explanation." A frown creased his forehead.

Emmie's sense of self-preservation took over. She didn't wish to be told he found her wanting. "Not now. I need to finish dressing."

She gave him her back, her dismissal clear, but her eyes sought his in the mirror above the small table.

Regret flooding his features, he hesitated, then pivoted and left, but not before something flickered through his eyes. Pain? For an instant, she wanted to run after him, tell him everything would be all right, they'd work things through, but pride kept her rooted. She would not chase after a man who clearly did not want her.

After removing her mother's sapphire and diamond necklace from its case, Emmie fastened her most prized possession securely around her neck.

This evening was her come-out of sorts, and she intended to enjoy the event.

For the sake of the company.

And if she happened to meet a man to her liking... so be it. Now that she had a taste of what she'd be missing, she was more open to marriage than before.

But it had to be with the right man.

~~~

Fingers gripping tight around the snifter's stem, Bart gulped his brandy in a fast swig. Fire flew down his throat. Across Bertha Palmer's three-story main hall, his best friend played court to Emmie in a shadowed corner of the octagonal room. From her smiles and how she tilted toward Nick, she seemed to be enjoying his company. Enjoying him.

Had Nick extracted himself from his arranged marriage? Mr. and Mrs. Brownly were in attendance, but not Tessa. Damn, he should have stayed by Emmie's side and put a stop to Nick's play before it began. With his rugged blond looks and even disposition, Nick was a formidable competitor for the attention of any desirable woman. *Any woman except my wife.*

From the moment they'd arrived at Bertha's Gothic mansion occupying an entire city block, they'd been inundated by Chicago's elite. He knew nearly all the party-goers by name, but no one knew Emmie, who confided to Bertha at the outset she was the president of Chicagoland Electric.

With the social aplomb for which she was noted, Bertha embraced Emmie with enthusiasm and a twinkle in her eye. Always the woman's advocate, Chicago's best known socialite seemed to have found in Emmie a prized example of the future to sponsor and promote.

For the past hour, a virtual army of the city's most successful businessmen surrounded his wife. Some seemed eager to learn about a manufacturing company run by a woman. Others seemed to be examining her as they would an interesting insect. He'd been left to fend for himself all evening, content in knowing Emmie had been well-received. Content, that is, until Nick started sniffing around.

"Where's your lovely wife, Bartholomew?" Bertha's low musical tones came from his right.

"Across the room," he answered, nodding in the general direction of his less than loyal friend.

Fifteen years his senior, Bertha Honore Palmer, the scion of Chicago's society and the power behind the city's numerous charity and cultural events, still presented impressive competition for any ingénue trolling for a rich husband. A few inches taller than Emmie, Bertha's tiny waist and soft intelligent eyes set her beauty apart from most of the women in attendance. As did her ever present trademarks—ropes of pearls about her throat and a diamond tiara fixed in her hair.

But, Bertha already possessed a rich husband, and by all accounts was quite happy with him. Millionaire Potter Palmer, twenty-three years her senior, built the original Palmer House hotel for her, however, it, along with most of his other real estate holdings, burned in the Great Fire. His fortune in near ruins, Palmer managed to rebuild a more impressive hotel in a new location, this one of quarried stone.

Bart switched glasses with a passing waiter, and continued his watch. What was Nick telling Emmie that claimed her rapt attention? The bodice of her blue gown seemed lower than when he first buttoned her into it. Soft mounds of delectable flesh peeked over the bodice's edge, giving any man who cared to look a view beyond compare. Christ! The jerk seemed to be reveling in the sights. Brandy burned down Bart's throat again.

Bertha studied the pair for the longest time, then chuckled. "Nicky seems quite taken with her."

Bart's jaw tightened. "It would seem so, yes." He lifted the glass to his lips only to discover it empty.

"Do I detect a note of jealousy?"

"Me, jealous? Of course not. I'm just guarding her." But an unfamiliar emotion had his stomach tied in knots.

Bertha's amused gaze caused his cheeks to heat. "Guarding? I wouldn't call what you're doing *guarding*."

"Someone shot at her recently and we haven't caught the guy. She needs guarding." Why he felt the need to explain himself, he didn't know.

Bertha's eyebrows rose, then her eyes narrowed. "*Humph!* I'd take a wager from any man here about your motivation and win big. I wouldn't worry, though. The way she looks at you when you're attending someone else? The same way you're looking at her now. Like you can't get enough of her."

She fanned her rosy face with a gloved hand. "I've a mind to suggest you two lovebirds retreat to one of my upstairs bedrooms for a while, but as my guests of honor, I need you down here."

But it's all an act. How could Emmie want him after what happened? God knows he wanted her. Fast, and with a passion he found difficult to control. A bedroom sounded like a great idea, except he'd vowed to return to their platonic relationship. Yet, the fact Emmie gave others the impression she wanted him pleased him greatly.

Bertha swung her astute gaze to him. He struggled to hide his thoughts, but he sensed she detected more than he cared to reveal.

"Since Potter's well settled in his room for the evening, I'll ask our friend there to escort me to dinner. You should have enough time to collect your beautiful bride from any throng of admirers."

Her husband Potter preferred the quiet of a room in the mansion's prominent tower than the gaiety of one of Bertha's parties. He frequently disappeared after a short appearance, or failed to show up at all.

"Thank you, and Bertha, thank you for throwing this party. It means a lot to both of us. Emmeline has never been out formally."

"Well, then. She managed to accomplish her entry on a grand scale, didn't she? None of the other young ladies made their debut owning the title of president of a manufacturing company. She's garnered the attention and respect of some of the most forward-thinking businessmen here, though I'm afraid quite a few dolts still believe a woman's place is in the home. As for their wives, many wish her well, but others are envious of her ability to walk in a man's world."

"If they only realized how Emmeline struggled. She would tell you walking that path isn't easy."

"I imagine not." Her eyes followed another servant with a silver tray overloaded with filled glasses. "I'd best visit with some of my other guests, dear. Dinner is sharply at nine."

With a sweep of her shimmering beige gown, the queen of society left.

Bart cast about for his wife and found her surrounded by an interesting assortment of men—his friend Bill Sears, Nick's father, Benjamin Shield, and Aaron Ward. Shield ran a large mercantile store on State Street he'd purchased long ago from Palmer. Sears, who'd recently returned to Chicago from Minnesota with his new business, Sears, Roebuck and Company, and Ward competed as catalog merchants.

Of the three, thirty-year-old Bill made Bart's skin twitch. In contrast to the rest of his friends, Sears made no bones about his desire to marry and raise a family. And he did present a fine appearance, one a woman might find pleasing. Hell, Emmie might find Sears more than suitable as a husband, once she received her divorce from him. A dull ache seeped into his chest and began to throb like the beat of a drum.

"She's quite the bee tonight, isn't she?"

Recognizing Nick's voice, Bart grit his teeth. "And what pollen did she gather from you, Nick?"

His friend chuckled. "Nothing, old boy. Not a damn thing."

"Let's keep it that way."

"Still harping on that old saw? And what pollen has she gathered from you?"

The innuendo struck home. Bart felt a rush of blood flow to his cheeks.

"So, it's like that." The big oaf nearly crowed with delight.

If he only knew! However, Bart kept his mouth shut. His marriage was none of Nick's damn business.

Nick picked some speck of something off his jacket sleeve. "Well, in any case, Bill is fawning over her, all smiles and charm. Whatever those four are talking about, Emmie sure seems pleased. You should be glad you have her all tied up or she might walk into the arms of someone else."

"Like you?"

Nick's chest swelled visibly. "Well now that you mention it...."

"Bugger off, man. She's married."

"Only for the moment."

"By the way, whatever happened between you and Miss Brownly? I expected you to be tied up in your own little marriage knot."

A smug smile broke across Nick's face. "It turned out Miss Brownly didn't like the match any better than I. Her parents approached my parents without her knowledge. She had her heart set on someone else, someone with whom her parents weren't too happy. She broke off with me to elope with him. So, I'm free to do as I please."

"Well, I hope your freedom doesn't include sniffing around Emmie because—"

In the space of a heartbeat, Nick's countenance changed from playful to serious. "Listen, Bart, I have more problems than I can handle to even contemplate ruining your fun. Rina's run away, and I need your help to find her."

Getting over his shock at the revelation, Bart scrutinized his friend's face. Worry etched deep lines in Nick's forehead. The man's younger sister Sabrina seemed the least likely person to run off anywhere. Always the shy wallflower, she stayed close to their mother and avoided the limelight. At twenty-eight, Rina had earned the title of spinster among Chicago's elite.

"Without going into detail here, what happened?"

"She went missing about a month ago, and we've tracked her to some god forsaken gold rush mud heap in Colorado. Dad's Pinkerton man took ill from the altitude. I need to find someone already in the town or nearby who can help me find her and bring her home."

Bart studied his friend's careworn face. "Come to my house tomorrow morning around eleven, and I'll see what I can do."

A relieved grin stretched across Nick's face, erasing the furrows. "Thanks, old pal. I thought you'd be able to recommend someone." He extended his hand.

Bart took it, the warmth of his friend's smile a boon to his professional ego, but he couldn't keep his next words from flying from his mouth. "Uh, Nick? Stay away from my wife."

Nick's lips twitched. "You bet, unless, of course, she comes to me first. In which case, may the best man win."

Hands in his pockets, his friend sauntered off in the direction of one of the unescorted ladies invited to the party, a statuesque widow rumored to be a German countess.

Bart searched the hall once more for Emmie. An orchid among drab flowers, Emmie in her blue gown stood out from the rest. She'd piled her ebony hair atop her head in a simple knot, her long curl creating a dramatic punctuation down the side of her face.

His body stirred, and pride puffed out his chest. He wanted her more than anything he ever wanted before. Damned if he would let anyone else take what was his.

He pushed off, ready to stake his claim.

~~~

Acute awareness swept through Emmie and made her body thrum. Glancing away from the attentive Mr. Sears, she glimpsed her husband elbowing his way toward her through the throng in the large Italianate hall.

His jaw was set in determination. His smoldering eyes burned in the soft gaslight.

She shivered, unsure if she welcomed his attention or feared it. She'd done nothing to provoke him. In fact, she'd gone out of her way to avoid him, hoping no one would detect the note of tension crackling between them.

They'd ignored each other during the carriage ride to the Palmer mansion. The only sound uttered was her gasp when the massive brown and sandstone structure with its turrets and minarets came into view. The house, with crenelations around not one but two towers, resembled a castle in picture books she read as a girl.

Ignoring Bart's approach, she focused on Mr. Sears' engaging smile and twinkling eyes as he described plans for his fledgling catalog business. Nearby, Aaron Montgomery Ward, a vigorous competitor, eagerly soaked up information from the younger upstart with a remarkably bland expression.

Moments later, Bart reached her and slid his arm around her waist. Startled, she controlled an impulse to pull away. Yet his scent of spice and heated masculinity drew her like a magnet. Every nerve came alive with a soul deep lust. She longed to melt against him, to devour his essence. Instead, she waited until Mr. Sears acknowledged Bart's presence before appraising her husband's mood.

His emotions completely open, blatant desire filled his eyes. *Dear lord, he still wants me!* The discovery caused conflicting emotions to feud in her mind. Wanting him was one thing, but risking his disgust again was quite something else. She swallowed hard, pushing her confusion to a corner of her mind.

Amusement broadening his smile, Mr. Sears glanced between them. "Well, Bart, my friend, three is a crowd. Mrs. Turner, I hope we can agree on a contract soon. I would love to carry your electric iron in next year's catalog."

Straight forward words, but the spark of male interest in his eyes begged a totally different meaning. She held her smile through her discomfort. Beside her, Bart shuffled, his movements tense.

"Thank you, Mr. Sears. I'm sure we'll come to an agreement in short order. I look forward to working with you." She extended her hand. He bowed and kissed her fingers instead. She pulled her hand away, bemused by the action.

Bart stiffened, and something sounding like a growl emerged from his lips. "Bill…." His warning couldn't be clearer.

Nor more embarrassing. Her cheeks flamed.

Mr. Sears flashed a knowing grin before turning to Mr. Shield and Mr. Ward who were discussing the state of the economy.

Miffed, Emmie turned to Bart, their bodies merely inches apart.

"What on earth—"

His fiery gaze landed on her mouth like a hot torch. Her lips tingled, burnt by the heat of his silent caress.

"I have come to collect you for dinner."

"Oh? I didn't hear the dinner bell."

"It hasn't sounded."

"Then why—"

"Do I need a reason to talk to my wife?" His tone was brisk.

She dropped her voice to a whisper. "Of course not, but we barely communicate even when we're alone. So why…." Understanding suddenly dawned. Her annoyance vanished at once. "You're jealous."

As he guided her toward the library, his jaw clenched. "I'm no such thing. You still need guarding."

Despite his denial, something blossomed inside her chest, and her heart skipped a beat. He drew her across the threshold of the darkened room, pulled her into his arms, and slammed his mouth down hard on hers. Hot and fevered, his kiss settled rough and raw on her flesh. Brandy spiked the flavors of his mouth, but she didn't mind. He wanted her, and God help her, she wanted him.

Her traitorous body melted into his embrace, her pelvis seeking his. Bart's tongue slipped inside her mouth, and his kiss took on a note of desperation and uncertainty. Her guarded heart opened to his rare show of vulnerability. This poor man. How he must be suffering. She returned his fervor tenfold, her tongue tangling with his as her breathing grew labored.

When they separated, he canted his forehead against hers and took several controlling breaths.

"I never meant to hurt you."

Emmie placed a finger to his lips. "Hush. Don't say another word. I thought you didn't want me, that my scars were as repulsive to you as they were to every other man."

His head jerked back, a scowl marking his handsome face. "Who told you your scars were repulsive?"

Sarah, her insides answered, but she kept the thought to herself.

"Never, ever think along those lines, Emmie. You're the most desirable woman I've ever met, and I want you more than I've ever wanted anyone. The failure was mine, not yours. Can you forgive me?"

Her heart banged against her ribs. The emotion blazing in his eyes couldn't have been fabricated. It was too real, too raw. It shook her to her core.

"I'm willing to try again, Bart, if you want me."

"Want you? By God, Emmie, I want you more than life, but I was afraid you wouldn't want me. I watched you all evening, wondering if Nick, or Bill would capture your interest."

She laughed. "Goodness, Bart. Nick is charming, but he's not you, and Mr. Sears is a business acquaintance, nothing more."

"The way they both looked at you...." He pushed a lock of hair out of the way, his expression haunted.

"Nonsense. You're reading into things that aren't there."

"Perhaps, but still...."

Bart lowered his head and kissed her again, this time with utmost tenderness, his lips moving softly over hers. Steel bands pulled her into the heated circle of his hard body.

She grasped his jacket lapels, needing to press herself closer, needing rigid proof of his desire. It was there.

When the kiss ended, he stroked a finger across her swollen lips, a smile of satisfaction lifting one corner of his mouth. "You... look thoroughly kissed, Mrs. Turner, exactly the way I want you to appear when we enter the dining room."

Emmie quirked an eyebrow. Did she want this? A commitment of sorts?

Yes, if it meant being in his arms.

Dear Lord! How could she possibly sit through dinner when all she wanted was to crawl into bed with her husband?

Chapter 16

Emmie finished the last of her nightly ablutions and slid naked between the sheets to await her husband. A mild lake breeze drifted through the open window and blew wisps of hair across her forehead.

Where was Bart?

Restless, she gazed at the ceiling, daydreaming about the carriage ride home, about the way they fell into each other's arms, mouths and tongues and hands tangling, touching, caressing. About the way Bart's fingers slid under her gown and up her leg, spreading fire where they traveled. About the strength of his erection as she stroked his trousered arousal. Hard. Thick. Reassuring.

When their carriage halted, they raced upstairs at a fevered pace, careful once again to avoid waking Gertie and Cedric. After shedding their clothing as though it burned their skin, Bart left with no explanation other than to say he would return in a few minutes. But, a few minutes flowed into ten, then twenty, and he still hadn't returned.

If he wanted her as much as he said he did, why did he leave her? Doubt drifted through Emmie's mind like an unwanted intruder. Her tense hands grew cold and clammy. Despite his words of reassurance this evening, was she risking rejection again? Last night's pain had been too reminiscent of the wounds she suffered when, one after the other, the people she loved had died, leaving her devastated and alone.

People she loved! Had she let Bart get too close? Would she experience the same sense of loss when their marriage was over? Dear Lord, no. She might share her body with Bart, but never her heart.

The room's air current shifted. Her eyes flew to the opened door between their bedrooms. The dark shape of a clothed man in a top hat loomed in the shadows of the doorway. Fear robbed her of breath.

"Lord Wallingshire at your service." Cedric's clipped English accent delivered in Bart's deep baritone sent waves of relief pulsing through her veins.

The tension ebbed along with her doubts, leaving rivulets of bewilderment behind.

Bart stepped into the room's moonlight and, before she could think, a laugh bubbled up and escaped her lips. He'd glued a trim goatee to his chin, and dressed in a suit of expensive evening wear. A silk striped ascot and a large garish stickpin in his lapel completed the outfit. He rested against the door-jamb, balancing an ebony walking stick on the toe of a polished black shoe. He appeared every bit the English actor in a stage play.

"What in the world...?"

He swaggered across the floor, set the stick against a chair, and removed his hat. With a finger between his neck and the material, he adjusted the ascot as though it were too tight.

"Lord Wallingshire is one of my professional personages, and he's come to my assistance this evening,"

Emmie's mouth twitched.

"How does that work? I mean, will three of us be in bed tonight?" Curious, she sat up, drawing the sheet over her breasts.

Bart followed her movement with eyes full of desire. With a sigh, he came to the side of the bed. Worry dug into his forehead, and his shoulders sagged as if weighed down by a heavy burden. He fingered her hair with a gentle caress. Summoning a modicum of patience within her vast store of restlessness, she waited.

Finally, he spoke. "Bartholomew Turner failed, but Lord Wallingshire won't."

His explanation, whispered in his own voice in a low, pleading tone, tugged at her heart. Without saying it, he had asked her to allow him to become someone else, someone who wouldn't fail, like he thought he had. He'd been truthful after all. It hadn't been her fault. Guilt hung along his frame like a vine growing along a fence.

But why?

Tears welled in her eyes. The cost to his male pride must have been enormous. She ached for him. No matter his outer disguise, inside he was still Bart, still the same man she desired.

Ignoring her nakedness, she reached up and drew him to her. He fell on top of her and kissed her with tenderness, his hands shaking.

Unable to help herself, she giggled. "Uh, Lord Wallingshire?"

He lifted his head. His dark eyes burned with passion. "What?"

"Your beard scratches."

His forehead furled in thought. A scratchy beard on tender skin must not have occurred to him.

She rushed to put him at ease. "If it means that much to you, I could get used to it."

Bart's eyes widened beneath raised eyebrows. "Would you?"

So many emotions locked in those two words. A desire for her comfort conflicted with his need to be someone else. Two opposing wishes with the same goal—pleasing her. Her heart melted.

"Of course I would."

To prove her point, she drew his head down again and kissed him. The hairs of his fake beard brushed over her skin, but this time she didn't mind. Slipping her tongue into his open mouth, she tasted brandy and mint, an intoxicating mix evoking memories of their earlier heated embrace. She pulled him closer.

His lips were soft, eager, opening to allow her to follow her passions. She reveled in the pleasure. Her insides heated and her nipples hardened. Was this what intimacy was about? This intense desire to give and receive, to lay bare one's joy found in the other?

If so, this is what she yearned for. But only with Bart. Only with this man.

Her body tightened, and the long muscles in her torso stretched in anticipation of something more. Something she desperately wanted but couldn't fathom.

He let her lead, let her set her own pace until finally he groaned and pulled away.

"Too damn many clothes," he mumbled.

"Then take them off, my lord." She lay back against the pillow, content to drink in her husband as he slowly unveiled his sculpted, well-toned body to her intense scrutiny.

He shucked off his clothing and dropped the garments to the floor, mindless as to where or how they fell. His staff thick and erect, he stepped close, as though needing her approval, needing to prove his masculinity.

His hard, male part jutted from the dark nest between his thighs. Emmie's mouth dried at his magnificence. She sat up and reached out, her fingers playing in the tufts of hair on his belly. Her hand itched to delve lower, to grab hold of him and stroke, but he tilted her chin up and took her mouth before she could move. She nearly swooned from his naked nearness. Though his kiss remained gentle and tender, the power of his leashed desire radiated through his tense palms as he held her face.

Her core liquefied. Yes, this was what she wanted. Needed.

Her breath coming in short, shallow pants, she opened the sheet. "Welcome to my bed, your lordship."

Lord Wallingshire or Bart, whomever he fancied himself, smiled before accepting.

"Don't mind if I do, madam."

Lord Wallingshire it is.

When he settled beside her, she pulled his head down for another kiss. This time he took the lead, pressing her deep into the mattress, taking her mouth with raw abandon. Her lion had come to mate, and she shivered with the thought. His tongue pulsed in a cadence she hoped he would soon emulate elsewhere. She reveled in the power of him, in the control over her body he obviously needed.

His fingers slipped into her hair, then fastened to the contours of her head, pinning her in place, trapping her beneath his punishing lips. His body straddled her legs. She relished this side of him, of his ardor let loose like newly-opened floodgates on a rain-swollen river.

He spent time at her breasts, the sensations pushing her to new summits. Her control gone, her head flew from side to side as he nibbled and sucked, his fervor firing hers to ever increasing pinnacles. Taking a breath seemed an impossible task. And she loved every bit of it.

He moved down her torso, licking and kissing along the way, shifting his legs to settle between hers. Needing him now, she sighed with relief. He nudged her thighs apart, his hardness coming to rest against her sensitive flesh. She opened for him, eager to feel him pulsing inside her, to be filled by his thickness, his length.

Tonight, Bart's lovemaking felt different, less controlled if not totally wild and feral. At this point she didn't care who shared her bed—Bart or Lord Wallingshire. They were one in the same man. She wanted either one or both, to take her back to where she had once been the night before and push her over the edge to a place her body yearned to be.

~~~

The thrill of possession caught Bart in its cross hairs. Never had he been more certain of his body's next moves, more ardent in his performance. Bart Turner, the shadow of the man he claimed to be, had disappeared. Lord Wallingshire was more vigorous, more eloquent, more manly.

Heart pounding, he positioned himself at her entrance and thrust hard. Buried himself deep inside her slick, wet heat. It was his undoing. Never had he been so ensnared in hot pleasure. Never had he wanted to grind himself into oblivion or propel a woman over a sexual cliff as he did at this moment.

Her groan permeated his haze and seared his insides. She rose to meet him, her unfocused eyes awash in desire.

He wanted her. No, needed her. With Emmie, he could lose himself, escape the world in the confines of her small welcoming body. Within her tight sheath, he became whole, complete. No longer alone.

He pulled out, then plunged hard again, his mind numb with the enjoyment of her scalding fire, of the firmness of her arms hugging his back. She pushed her pelvis against his, seeking what she desired, what he needed to give.

"Now, my lord. Now!"

"As you wish, my lady."

Lord Wallingshire struck up a rhythm. Strong. Demanding. She followed from the start, her eyes closing, the flush of her ardor warming her complexion to a beautiful pink. Her ebony hair fell over the pillow in long waves of lustrous silk. His skin heated, caressed by her cinnamon-scented breath feathering across his chest in irregular bursts. His heart raced with the excitement of being held by her, of being able to give her satisfaction in return.

He pumped into her faster and faster, all awareness of himself disappearing into a conflagration of sensation. Roused by her soft cries that grew into louder moans, his groin tightened. Release was imminent.

"Emmie?" His voice sounded tight, choked even to his own ears.

Her response came in a whisper. "Go!"

He pushed in again. Seconds later, she called out his name, his real name. Her interior muscles contracted with her release, and she milked him, the motion stripping away nearly all of his remaining sanity. At the last minute, he pulled out and spilled himself over her belly, then collapsed beside her, his breath nonexistent, his body singing with release and joy.

He glanced at Emmie. Her eyes were closed and a sweet sheen of sweat coated her body. He leaned forward and tugged a still pebbled nipple into his mouth.

Her eyes flew open, and she arched up as though it were the most natural thing to do. "Ready again?"

"I'll never get enough of you." The God's honest truth.

Mentally discarding the Lord Wallingshire persona, he covered her lips in a gentle kiss before rising for a moistened washing cloth. When both were presentable again, he returned to the bed where she wrapped her arms around his shoulders and nipped his flesh with her teeth. He drew her against his chest, longing to lie with her like this forever, cocooned in the warm afterglow of having made love to Emmie. His wife.

Only now a new thought emerged to dampen his elation.

He didn't deserve her and never would.

~ ~ ~

"Excuse me, sir. Jimmy Taylor is at the back door. Quite agitated, he is. Bobbing from one foot to t'other as though stepping on something hot. He's askin' to see you."

Bart placed his coffee cup in the saucer. "Bring him in, Gertie, and bring Cedric with you."

"Yes, sir."

Bart reclined in his chair, his thumbs hooking the bottom of his suspenders near his waist. There was something special about eating Sunday breakfast across the table from a contented wife. His groin stirred as images of Emmie's small body moving beneath him filtered through his mind. He would never cease wanting her, and he would do anything to make her happy. Even become someone else for her.

Emmie lifted her head from the *Sunday Tribune's* financial pages. "Something wrong?"

"I hope not."

A few seconds later, Gertie ushered Jimmy to the closest chair in the dining room. Cedric followed, but stopped at the sideboard to load a plate for the boy.

"You have something to tell us, Jimmy?"

Jimmy glanced at Emmie, then back at him. "You asked us to keep our eyes and ears peeled for information about Paul Harris?" The boy's eyes lit as Cedric set a full plate before him. "They fished him out of the Chicago River early this morning. Deader than them horses lying in the street."

Emmie's fork clattered to her plate. Shock registered in her widened blue eyes.

Bart carefully settled his own cup in its saucer again as a lead marble careened about his belly.

"Do you have any details?" As much as he hated to burden Emmie with the demise of her cousin, she insisted she be told everything, good or bad. And this was shaping up to be very bad indeed.

"Yes sir. Stinky Smelly Sam—he's one of the street fellas lives in a box near the river—threw pebbles at my window early this morning. When I raised it, he told me the guys on the new Fire Department tugboat, the *Fire Queen,* pulled a man from the river near the State Street bridge about five this morn. They identified him as a Paul Harris, and said the body had been in the river for a few days. Stinky Smelly Sam knew I was lookin' for information on a guy by that name so he ran to tell me. I waited 'till now so's not to disturb your sleep." He looked sheepishly at his plate and jabbed his fork into a mountain of breakfast potatoes.

"Don't know if that's the guy you're interested in, or someone else. Stinky Smelly Sam says they took him to the County morgue. Says he was dressed real nice, like he was goin' somewhere's swell."

Bart swept his hair back with his fingers. If his instincts were right, the man in the river was, indeed, Emmie's cousin. That would explain why he didn't show up for their meeting yesterday, a meeting Harris himself had arranged.

A strange combination of relief and trepidation shook Bart's equilibrium. Relief because his prime suspect no longer presented a threat. Trepidation because now that yet another member of Emmie's family had died, he wasn't sure how she would respond. The man had caused her pain and anxiety, yet he was still a relative.

Bart glanced across the table. A dab of cherry jelly caught at the corner of Emmie's mouth, a dark speck against the stark white of her complexion. She sat motionless, staring ahead with a blank expression.

No one spoke as Jimmy hurriedly ate his breakfast and left, Gertie and Cedric following him to the back door. A dog in a nearby yard barked, answered almost immediately by another canine a few houses down the alley.

Emmie finally spoke, her face an emotionless mask. "They don't know whether he jumped or slipped?"

Or was murdered. The thought screamed to be heard, but he kept it to himself. No sense alarming her any more than necessary. At least not until he had more information. No doubt Cedric had set the network trolling for an answer. Someone was bound to hear something.

"No, they don't."

She sat back in her chair and wrapped her arms around her body as though warding off a chill. Sadness drifted across her features.

"I should be upset. He was a member of my family, but honestly, I don't feel a thing. Isn't that terrible?" She laughed, a nervous twitter that died in an instant. Tears appeared in her eyes, but failed to fall.

"Considering what happened when you were fifteen, and the grief he caused you with Chicagoland Electric, I'm not surprised at all. He didn't deserve your regard."

Gratitude flashed through her shimmering eyes. Then the muscles in her throat moved in a hard swallow. He held his breath, unsure where her emotions were taking her.

A moment later, she rolled her shoulders back and sat up straight. "Paul is dead. He was your prime suspect. The threat is gone, and we needn't worry any more. You don't...." She stopped and glanced away, but not quick enough to hide a note of surprise registering in her widened eyes.

What was she going to say? His curiosity zoomed like a race horse out of a starting gate. "I don't what?"

Her pale cheeks ripened to crimson. "Forget it. I changed my mind."

"About what?"

She gnawed at her lower lip. "I was about to say if you don't need to protect me any longer... if you want to... if you feel the need to, we can live separately in our respective houses. So you can run your business."

Shock punched him in the gut. They had already gone far beyond the mere protection level, and she darn well knew it. But, the more he thought about it, the more he believed she didn't want any such thing. Then why did she say it? Was she thinking out loud?

"You changed your mind because...?"

Her chin rose, and her eyes sparked fire. "Are you going to make me say it?"

He grinned and stretched his hand across the table, certain of her answer. "Yes."

Her features softened. "If you must know, I rather like living in the same house with you."

Like a flower opening in the sun, unexpected joy unfurled inside him. "Oh, you do, do you? Well, I do too." His voice contained an unintended huskiness.

She slid her hand into his and squeezed.

While gazing into her eyes like a love-struck puppy though, he couldn't shake the feeling something about Paul's death stank more than the dirty Chicago River.

~~~

"Where's your lovely wife, Bart? Catching up on her beauty sleep after a long night in the sack?" Hands in his pockets, Nick sauntered into Bart's office later that morning, his jaw flapping inappropriately as usual.

Bart scowled. Nick knew damn well the marriage was supposed to be platonic. The fact it wasn't was none of his damn business.

"Nick, my friend." He added a note of warning to his sarcastic tone. "If you want my help, change the direction of your thoughts."

Nick grinned like an idiot and sprawled out in the usual leather chair he occupied when gracing Bart with his presence. "Sorry, old buddy. I couldn't resist. She's one of the most intriguing ladies I know."

What the hell? Jaw clenched, Bart closed the door and took a seat on the davenport. He didn't like Nick's continued interest in Emmie. Not last night. Not now. Not ever. The strength of his emotion in this regard suddenly hit Bart full force. When had Emmie crawled beneath his skin?

"If you must know, she's upstairs changing clothes. She received some nasty news this morning, so she's probably taking a little longer than normal. We're lunching at the children's home today before we take the train back to Summerhill."

Perhaps appealing to his friend's bottomless belly would distract him from Emmie. "Besides, we wouldn't want to let Gertie's cookies go to waste now, would we?"

A light flickered in Nick's eyes. "Cookies? Gertie baked cookies, and you aren't going to offer any to your guests? Why Bartholomew, how unsociable of you."

"They're for the little boys at the home, not big boys like you."

Nick flicked something off one of the brass buttons on his immaculate blue blazer. "You wound me. I'm a little boy at heart."

"Don't I well know it," Bart muttered.

"You said Emmie received bad news. What happened? I'd hate to see her beautiful smile disappear behind a cloud of unhappiness."

I bet you would. If it were up to Bart, Nick's view of her beautiful smile would disappear for a long time.

"They pulled her cousin's body out of the Chicago River early this morning. Fortunately, there was no love lost between them, so her emotions weren't engaged. Emmie and Paul didn't quite get along. However, Paul was my best suspect for the shooting, and now Emmie thinks the danger is over."

"But you don't."

"I don't know what to think, and that worries me. The coroner's office hasn't announced the cause of death, but it could have been a homicide. In which case, we have to consider someone else for the murders of Emmie's family."

Nick's hand paused in its restless shuffling of Bart's collection of Chinese matchboxes displayed on the side table.

"Murders?"

"I thought I was looking for one shooter, but the investigation widened when I learned the saddle Emmie's fiancée used the day he died had been tampered with. His death might not have been an accident." Hell, her brother and her parents' deaths might have been murders as well. He slumped back on the davenport.

Nick whistled softly. "I had no idea."

Not wanting to discuss Emmie's business any further, Bart changed the subject. "So, tell me more about your sister's disappearance."

Like a rainstorm erupting on a sunny day, Nick's smile changed to a worried frown in an instant. His longtime friend seemed to shrink within himself. Nick never did hold up well under duress.

Nick lifted a matchbox off the table and absently flipped it over. "There's not a whole lot to tell. She's been missing for about a month."

"You told me that, but she could have gone off to visit a friend. Or a man."

"And not tell anyone? That's not like Rina. She never went anywhere without telling someone first, anyone, even her maid. My father hired a Pinkerton agent to track her. The man finally wired back two days ago. He tracked a woman he believed to be Rina to a gold rush town west of Colorado Springs called Cripple Creek. The problem is it's so high in the mountains, the thin air made the man sick. He had to come back without identifying that the woman he was following was really her."

"So, he might have been following the wrong woman, and you need someone to work with you who's used to the higher elevation."

Shoulders slumped, Nick nodded. All the vitality his friend had walked in with had vanished.

"Will _you_ be able to stand the altitude?"

"I don't know, but I need to try. Damn it, Rina's my little sister, and I'm worried about her."

Bart shifted uncomfortably. "She's twenty-eight, Nick, not so little any more, and not so young that she can't take care of herself."

"If she'd written, I'd understand her running off to create a life for herself. But what if she's in some kind of trouble? I have to find out."

As a friend, he'd helped Nick out of many petty scrapes in the past. This time Nick had appealed to him as a professional, and he couldn't let him down. He studied his friend, his mind sorting through his contacts gathered since joining the agency. One name struck him as perfect.

"Colorado Springs, you say?"

"Yeah. The gold camp is on the southwester slope of Pike's Peak."

Bart left the davenport and walked to his desk. Taking a key from his pocket, he unlocked the top drawer and removed a stack of calling cards from an envelope. Finding the one he sought, he lowered himself to the chair and pulled a sheet of paper and a fountain pen from a side drawer.

"I'm not sure if this person can help, but he's the only investigator in the area I can recommend."

He handed the sheet with a name and address to Nick.

"Lee Wilcox. Colorado City? Ever meet this fellow?"

Bart shook his head. "No, but a friend has, or he wouldn't have given me this card." He carefully lifted a white knight from the chess set on his desk and surreptitiously fingered the bottom for the telltale indentation. Satisfied, he gave it to Nick.

"Give this to him. Tell him you got his name from a friend."

Nick folded the paper and slipped it and the chess piece in his jacket pocket. "Appreciate the referral, Bart. Thanks."

He stood and Bart rose with him. "Uh, if there are any cookies left—"

Bart laughed. "Not on your life. They're for the little boys. Remember?"

As he walked Nick to the front door, a disturbing thought crossed his mind. How much of his enthusiasm for helping Nick was based on wanting his best friend as far from Emmie as possible?

Chapter 17

Cedric and Gertie's arrival at Summerhill several days later caused a commotion of sorts.

"Excuse me, Mr. Turner," Everett intoned in the breakfast room. "A man and woman are in the foyer who claim to be from your household. They've brought several steamer trunks and a large crated beast of some sort." His nose wrinkled as though he smelled something vile. "I asked them to go to the servant's entrance in the back, but they refused to leave the animal alone by the front door."

Across from Bart, Emmie covered a smile with her napkin and lowered her coffee cup to its saucer. "Show them to the Ship Room, Everett, and instruct the housemen to move the trunks into the foyer. We'll decide where to put them later. I'll let the *animal* out of the crate in a minute."

Everett's eyes widened. "You're not going to allow that… that beast in the house, are you? Mr. Griffith…." The butler's voice had reverted to its usual flat nasal tone Bart had witnessed upon occasion.

Amused, Bart glanced at Emmie and discovered she near shook with silent laughter.

She rose and placed a hand on the old man's arm. "Dear Everett. I know neither you nor my father liked dogs in the main house, nor the mess they create, but my father is gone now and I'm in charge. This dog is well trained. But if it eases you some, please ask the staff to move the statues to the flower room until a more suitable location can be found. We wouldn't want *the beast* to knock one of Papa's priceless artworks off a pedestal, would we?"

Everett frowned like a thwarted child. "Yes, madam." He rotated slowly and shuffled out of the room.

After a few last quick gulps of coffee, Bart crossed the marble gallery floor to the room he'd taken over as his office, while Emmie saw to emancipating Rafe.

Moving from the bright light of the breakfast room and open gallery to the perennial dimness of the Ship Room had him blinking until his vision returned. He felt Emmie's presence beside him a few seconds later.

"Ahem."

Twisting about, he found Cedric and Gertie standing in a corner, their backs to a Middle Eastern harem screen, a duplicate of one he'd seen in Reginald's home prior to the man's move to Washington.

Before anyone could speak, Rafe bounded into the study dragging a bedraggled length of black cloth. Emmie's shawl, if he wasn't mistaken. The one she'd worn the afternoon of the shooting. At the memory, his fists tightened. He still hadn't found the culprits.

After depositing the material at Emmie's feet, Rafe flattened himself upon it and rolled over for a belly rub.

Emmie laughed, a pleasant sound he hoped to hear more often. "You big baby. Now where did you get this fine bit of lace, Rafael Maximilian?"

Hands twisting, Gertie stepped forward. "Begging' yer pardon, ma'am. The people at the train station said Rafe must travel in a crate in the baggage car with the trunks. Only, Rafe here was havin' none of it. He went in the crate all right, but wouldn't stop barking. Finally, the conductor says he planned to put poor Rafe off at the next station if he didn't quiet down. I had some cheese in my satchel and thought he might calm down with that, but he didn't want it. He smelled yer scarf I was bringin' back to ye and pulled it right out of the bag, he did."

Emmie's eyebrows rose. "Well, did he calm down?"

"Like a babe in his mam's arms, he did. Went right to sleep, but I don't think he's of a mind to give up yer shawl. We took him for a walk this morning by the station, and he dragged the thing everywhere. I'm afraid the lace is quite shredded."

Emmie bent to scratch Rafe's exposed belly. "I suppose it's your shawl now, Rafe. Take good care of it for me."

She straightened, and Rafe rolled upright. Bart swore the expression on his dog's face was of undying love. Emmie would certainly be easy to love by any beast—or man for that matter. Shocked by the thought, he pushed it away.

Remembering his manners, Bart waved his hand at the sofa. "Well, please sit. We have a lot to discuss."

Gertie flung her hand behind her and yanked on Cedric's arm. "Don't mind if I do, thank ye."

Bart's first assistant and most proper valet followed like an obedient child, allowing Gertie to take her seat before lowering himself beside her. Emmie sat in a nearby chair, while Bart leaned against the desk's edge.

"So, what can we do to help ye? That's why we're here, right?" His housekeeper straightened her traveling skirt with a swoosh of both hands down her lap.

Bart crossed his arms. "We can discuss that later. We need to get the two of you settled first. Where do you think they would best fit in, Emmie?"

Emmie drew her finger to her lips as she considered his question. "Let me see. Mrs. Bingham could use you in the kitchen, Gertie. We serve lunch for everyone, so there's plenty to do. Cedric, I'd be grateful if you could help Everett. He's been with us since I was little, and things are becoming quite difficult for him now. I think he's been looking for someone to take over, but no one seems to measure up to his standards."

Cedric puffed out his chest, his vest rising above the waistline of his trousers. "Don't you worry yourself none, Mrs. Turner. I'll be happy to assist him."

Mrs. Turner. The sound of it never failed to send a thrill through Bart.

Returning to Gertie's initial question, Bart leaned back against the desk, gripping it with both hands for balance. "Regarding the investigation, I want you both to listen to the servants' gossip without prying. We'll meet at midnight after everyone is asleep, starting tonight in this room. We have much to discuss."

Before Emmie arrived, he hoped. He needed to explore his disturbing hypothesis with his assistants before burdening Emmie with his beliefs.

That was his plan. However, things didn't turn out quite as he expected.

At half past eleven, a half hour before he told Emmie to arrive, Gertie and Cedric crept into the Ship Room and closed the door. A smile tugged at the corners of Bart's mouth at the sight of them.

His housekeeper's tall generous proportions, wrapped in a heavy pink wool robe despite the summer heat, reminded him of a large stuffed animal a child might take to bed—soft and cuddly. No one would guess she was anything other than a cook and housekeeper. She excelled at information gathering, her astuteness and intelligence guiding her in fruitful directions without detection.

His first assistant, however, appeared the proper English gentleman in a well-tailored smoking jacket, a man the rest of the staff might consider uppity. Bart lifted an eyebrow at the flamboyant, blue paisley silk garment with a gold thread weave, a marked departure from his valet's usual bland conservative attire.

Cedric tightened the jacket's sash with a strong pull, a faint blush rising to his cheeks. "Uh... my sister sent it for Christmas last year. She thought Chicago wouldn't sell proper apparel for a man of my station. Gertie, here, pulled the garment from the back of my wardrobe."

The woman in question beamed. "I thought to meself, this fine jacket would be the perfect thing for a grand place such as this."

The faint flush turned a brighter shade of red. God only knew, Cedric would never purchase such a garment on his own despite the fact Chicago's better men's stores sold similar trappings of wealth. And clearly, Gertie believed him to be putty in her hands, remaking him in the image she envisioned an English gentleman's valet should be.

Though amused, he couldn't help but think he'd discovered another reason to remain a bachelor once his marriage ended. Glancing at the desk clock, he shoved an overwhelming sense of loss the thought caused to a dark corner of his soul reserved for unwanted feelings. Now was not the time to dwell on his complicated mental state. He ushered the pair to the sofa. and returned to his chair behind the desk.

Without preamble, he launched into the subject uppermost on his mind. "I believe someone is systematically killing off Emmie's family and loved ones."

Gertie gasped. Her hand flew up to cover her gaping mouth. "Why would anyone do such a terrible thing?"

"My guess is the motive revolves around Chicagoland Electric, but I'm not sure."

Cedric leaned his elbows on his knees and grasped his hands between them, a frown of drawing his brows together. "Lay out your facts for us, sir."

Bart slouched in his chair, fingering a pencil he pulled off the desk.

"For one thing, someone tampered with the tack Alex used the day of his riding accident. A damaged stirrup strap set off a series of events leading to his death. At least the stable master believes that's what happened, but he couldn't get the sheriff's department to take any interest in his theory. I tend to agree with the man."

He twirled the pencil through his fingers. "For another, the fire in which Emmie's twin brother died may have been deliberately set, with both twins the intended targets. I found a lantern and an old flask belonging to Emmie's cousin Paul in the field behind the barn, but I can't tie them to the fire." He blew out a breath. "Then there's the shooting on our front steps."

Silence descended in the gas-lit room as Cedric and Gertie soaked in his explanation. Bart's hands fisted. He might have lost Emmie in that shooting. Not that he had her to begin with, but she was his wife now, albeit a temporary one, and she'd entrusted her life to him.

"Then there's the mysterious death of Paul Harris this past weekend. He could have been murdered to keep him quiet. Cedric, did you discover anything more about Mr. Harris or Mr. Bormeister?"

"Only that Harris lived beyond his means. He was liked well enough among his friends, but he was financially... constrained. Our people heard that the coroner ruled the man's death a suicide even though he received a blow to the head. They said he hit his head on the bridge girders during the jump."

Bart threw the pencil across the desk. "I don't believe that for a moment."

"Neither do I, sir," Cedric said. "Regarding Mr. Bormeister, he seems to have disappeared. His sister hasn't heard from him in a while, and she didn't know anything about his eloping with another woman. She said both she and her brother had been looking forward to a relationship with a fancy lady, whom I assumed to be Miss Griffith."

After returning the pencil to a cylindrical container, Bart clasped his hands tight. "Bormeister's disappearance is too convenient. He could have gone the same way as Alex and Paul Harris." His throat constricted at the thought his own life might be in danger. "I'm beginning to think Harris was involved in some way, and when he was about to tell me how, someone killed him."

Gertie pulled the sash of her robe tighter. "What would ye like us to do, sir?"

"Probe the servants for information on the deaths of not only Alex and Eddie, but of her parents as well."

"Ach, the poor wee thing."

"My thoughts entirely. This madness is becoming greater than any of us ever suspected, and we can't yet rule out the deaths of anyone as beyond suspect."

He traced the ornate leaf design of a silver rocker blotter with his forefinger, his thoughts charging well ahead of his mouth.

"Start with all employees here for at least ten years, the time of Eddie's death. Mrs. Griffith died a year later, their father five years ago, Alex two years ago. I want to know who is hiding what secrets, who is friends with whom, who hates whom, and anything else seemingly odd, out of place, or the stuff of gossip. Nothing is to be deemed unimportant."

Shifting in his chair, Bart continued. "To solve this mystery, we need to establish motive, means and opportunity, and the more we know, the easier it will be to narrow down the suspects. Nobody is off the list yet. Not even Braithwaite, even though the more I'm with him the less he seems to be a likely suspect."

"How does Chicagoland Electric figure into this?" Gertie, now perched on the edge of the sofa next to Cedric, pulled the front of her robe tight against her throat. Her eyes were bright with interest as she absorbed the details of his logic.

"The line of ownership succession has been virtually wiped out. Upon Mr. Griffith's death, Edward was to have inherited the company. The next in line to inherit was Emmie with the intention of management by her husband with help from Mr. Griffith's attorney. Her husband was to have been Alex."

Bart glanced at the clock, mindful of when Emmie might appear. Only a few more minutes remained.

"Emmie had a contract with Mr. Bormeister excluding him from managing the company. When he disappeared, Emmie was too close to her twenty-fifth birthday to find another suitor. If I hadn't married her—and I have no interest in running her company—her cousin Paul might now be the company's owner. He was our most likely suspect until he turned up dead. What if he was not the one we should be seeking? What if someone else is behind the whole thing?"

Cedric pinched the bridge of his nose with his thumb and forefinger, a sure sign of his difficulty in fitting the pieces together. "Mrs. Griffith doesn't seem to relate to the succession part of your theory. What is her involvement with the company?"

"Nothing Emmie said so far indicates her mother would have been involved in it at all, had she lived. However, she might have retained ownership of everything following her husband's death."

He surveyed the faces of his capable assistants. "Does this line of thinking seem logical to you, or am I trotting off in the wrong direction?"

Before either Cedric or Gertie could answer, the door whooshed open and his lovely wife entered, her eyes flashing first surprise, then annoyance in the space of a heartbeat.

~~~

"Oh, am I late?" Despite an effort to remain neutral, Emmie couldn't keep the sarcasm from leaking into her tone.

Rafe, pushing past her, picked a spot near Gertie's knee and sat as though invited to the meeting.

Drained from yet another day's failure with her toaster, Emmie had looked forward to immersing herself in a mystery not the least bit scientific. She pulled the sides of her blue silk robe closer and plunked herself in a vacant chair.

Her husband stood, chagrin evident in his tight smile.

Though vexed, she couldn't keep her gaze from drifting down Bart's impressive frame. He wore trousers and a white linen shirt with rolled sleeves that exposed the thick corded muscles of his forearms. Remembering the feel of those arms wrapped about her melted her irritation.

Worry gave his eyes a peculiar sheen. "No, Emmie. You're not late. Gertie and Cedric arrived a few minutes early and we've been chatting."

She folded her arms across her chest. "You've been discussing the investigation without me."

Gertie glanced at Cedric, who stared at Bart.

"You're right. We were discussing the investigation. I didn't want to burden you with my thoughts until I'd discussed them first with Cedric and Gertie."

His eyes flashed across the faces of the named pair who nodded in return. Neither revealed any emotion.

She pulled herself straight. "Burden me? I'll decide whether I'm being burdened or not."

He returned to his chair, and despite her frosty reply, swept her body with a heated gaze more like a caress than a perusal. Were his thoughts going in the same direction as hers?

Then his lips pursed and regret flooded his eyes. His chest rose and fell.

Oh, dear.

"I thought about keeping this from you, but you have a right to know."

Her heart fluttered.

"The deaths in your family might not have been accidents. We've already talked about Alex, and the possibility of someone setting the barn on fire, killing Eddie. Now we add the convenient disappearance of Mr. Bormeister and Paul turning up dead. Emmie, we need to widen our investigation and consider the deaths of your entire family."

Emmie's breath caught. Blood drained from her head causing white spots to form at her vision's edges. "Are you suggesting my mother and father were also murdered?"

"I don't have an answer for you, and that's why we need to investigate all these deaths." Bart's gentle baritone ran smoothly across her skin, yet felt far from settling.

"But why?" Tears seeped into her eyes, and she willed them to stay put. She'd been a watering pot for far too long.

"Ownership of Chicagoland Electric sounds like a good enough reason to me."

"To want my entire family, including me, dead?" Something deep inside her balked at accepting Bart's theory. He couldn't be right, could he?

Silence. Her answer given in the lack of one. She swallowed hard as the contents of her belly rose.

"My father died of a stomach ailment that caused him to wither away, and my mother... my mother...." Her throat constricted as horrid memories returned. She forced herself to meet Bart's scrutiny. "My mother took her own life with an overdose of laudanum. My parents weren't murdered by anyone."

Sympathy softened Bart's expression, and she turned away. She didn't want his sympathy. She didn't want.... Oh, curses! At this point she didn't know what she wanted. Certainly, not this.

Rising, he came to her side, fell to one knee and covered her two icy hands with his warm palms. "Emmie, you are a very brave woman, a survivor. We'll figure this out. I promise you."

His steady regard and the set of his jaw spoke of a confidence she didn't share.

"I wish I were as certain as you." She fumbled in her pocket for a handkerchief and blew her nose. The enormity of what he suggested made her head spin with confusion.

"Let's move on to other things." He swept his gaze to Cedric while lowering himself to a nearby chair. "Did you discover anything more about our two shooters?"

For an instant, the man's face appeared pinched, as though sucking a lemon. "Sorry, sir, they've disappeared. None of our people have seen them since the boys spotted the rig. Either they left town, or they're in hiding. Rest assured, though, we will find them."

"Good, but do all your communicating to our friends by wire. Too many unknown ears are attached to the telephone party line. We'll meet again tomorrow night to discuss what you've been able to learn."

~~~

The next evening the remains of a hot sultry day made meeting in the windowless Ship Room impossible. They had moved to the library, where a slight breeze through open windows lifted the summer curtains like flickering fairy wings. No one wore night clothes despite the late hour.

As Emmie settled herself on her favorite reading chair, Bart came right to the point.

"Now, what have you gleaned so far from the staff here?"

Gertie edged forward on the sofa, excitement brightening her eyes. "Begging yer pardon, Mrs. Turner, but your kitchen is ripe with gossip. I asked what yer father was like to work for, and I got all kinds of opinions as to how he died. Most thought his death... unnatural, even though the Sheriff said he died of natural causes."

The hair on the back of Emmie's neck rose. "What do you mean?"

"Mrs. Bingham, now there's an organized woman for ye, she thinks he was poisoned."

Queasiness gripped Emmie's insides for the second time in two days.

"I says to her can ye explain more, and she says she keeps close count in the storeroom, and noticed a gradual disappearance of rat powder she couldn't account for. I says, ye thinks it were put to no good use, and she checks to see who's listenin' before nodding. Says she suspects someone might have dropped small amounts of the stuff into Mr. Griffith's coffee, him drinkin' so much of it every day. She would have told the Sheriff, but yer da had been ailing for months, and she thought no one would believe the ramblin's of an old woman with no proof, and she didn't want to burden ye when ye were grievin' so."

Oh God! She *was* going to be sick. Emmie whipped her handkerchief to her face and swiped her mouth.

Gertie leaned toward her. "Dear me. I'm so sorry. I didn't—"

Bart stood abruptly and strode to a side table where her father kept his best brandy. Selecting an unopened bottle, he struggled with the cork until Cedric nudged him aside.

"Here, let me, sir." Cedric opened a drawer in the table and pulled out a small sommelier knife.

Bart's eyebrows lifted.

"Everett showed me what's what."

The container open, Bart poured half a glass and handed it to Emmie. "Here, drink this. The brandy should settle your stomach."

A sip of the dark-colored liquid burned its way down her tight throat and settled warm in her core. Another sip eased the edge off her physical discomfort, replacing it with the warm afterglow of fruity spirits. But her tortured thoughts remained raw and bleeding.

Pulling herself together, she asked the unthinkable. "And my mother?"

Silence.

Bart's dark calculating gaze met hers. "We don't know yet."

Her jaw tightened. "You don't know, or you won't tell me?"

"A little of both, I'm afraid. Laudanum, as well as the many remedies containing it, is common in most households. How often your mother used the opiate and in what form and quantity needs to be determined. In any case, you've had enough shock for tonight. But there are other things we need to discuss."

Emmie's hand flew to the tense muscles at the back of her neck, now aching something fierce.

Rafe rose from his spot on the rug and padded over to her. She reached for his head, seeking the comfort of his soft, warm coat.

"Tell me about Jon. Would he have wanted to harm anyone in your family?"

She bridled. "Jon adored my family, and spent more time with us than with his own. If you're suggesting he set the barn fire, he had nothing to do with it. He tried to rescue Eddie and me and the horses. He took Eddie's death hard."

Bart's expression didn't change. Looking elsewhere for agreement, Emmie flit her eyes first to Gertie, then to Cedric. Nothing showed on their faces either. Not an emotion, a facial tick or a movement of muscle to reveal their thoughts. *Humph, trained by the best.* Their lack of response spoke volumes.

Emmie drew in another breath. This conversation wasn't going well at all.

Gertie's round face turned soft and gentle. "Sweetie, Mr.

Braithwaite's involved in something, though I'm not sure what yet. I happened upon him and Miss Holmsford arguing in the flower room this afternoon."

"They always argue."

"It's what they argued about that struck me as odd. She says to him, you do as I say or I'll expose yer little secret. Then he says, ye wouldn't do such a thing, and she says, wouldn't I, and then she walks away all starched and uppity. Somethin's not right there. She seems to hold a tight rein on the man. The day he showed up at Mr. Turner's house with your trunks, he appeared to be someone who knew what he was about, and didn't give a fig, if ye pardon me language, what anyone else thought. From what I see here, he's much more tense. Mind me, she's holdin' a secret of some kind over his head to get him to do her bidding."

A chill slithered up Emmie's body like a snake. *Jonathon, what have you gotten yourself into?* "I don't for one minute accept the notion he would harm me or anyone in my family, nor would I suspect Lydia of doing anything so foul. Besides, Lydia has only been employed for two years."

But if Gertie was right, what mystery existed between her trusted secretary and her best friend? And did it have anything to do with Bart's theories, the ones that now wracked her insides.

Bart shifted in his chair, drawing Emmie's attention. His dark eyes now blazed with something alive, something feral, something potent and virile. It heated her insides, made her quiver despite the discomfort of the subject under discussion.

Take me away from all this, my husband. Make me forget.

A tense silence permeated the room as their gazes locked in unspoken communication.

Cedric rose with a yawn and pulled Gertie off the davenport with a not-too-gentle tug. "Well… uh… we can continue another time."

Gertie's mouth twitched. "We'll be gettin' on to bed now. Ye younguns don't want to listen to us jabberin' all night. Besides, I think we're done for the evening."

She eyed Bart who nodded absently, his eyes never leaving Emmie's lips.

Emmie's heart banged against her ribs.

Bart levered his big agile body out of his chair and came toward her, reaching for her hand.

Chapter 18

A brisk breeze rustled through the trees near the fountain at Summerhill three weeks later. Glancing at the thick black clouds racing across the ominous-looking southwestern sky, Emmie shivered, but not because of the approaching storm.

Like the winds, feelings of ambivalence swirled about her, buffeting her one way, then the other. Lethargy and a strange sense of melancholy kept her rooted to the bench.

And her husband had a big part in the reasons why.

For the past few weeks, Bart had been preoccupied, more so than before Paul's death. He left her alone most often, except for their nights together when he made love to her with a passion she'd come to cherish. He'd told her nothing, only that he was investigating the case.

She needed to think, to sort out her mental state, and put her most disquieting thoughts in a box with a tight-fitting lid. She was a scientist. She wasn't supposed to be given to bouts of emotion she didn't know how to handle.

Disturbed by a spray of fine mist, Rafe rose from where he lay at the fountain's base and padded to Emmie's side. She absently scratched the large head he settled on her knee, grateful for the warmth and comfort he silently offered.

The familiar sound of Jon's resonant voice a few feet behind her broke the silence. "You seem so forlorn. What's wrong? I saw you out here oblivious to the weather, so I thought I'd fetch you before the skies opened."

Emmie shifted the white skirts of her laboratory uniform to make room on the seat for her friend. "I'm sorry, Jon. Today was not a good day. In fact, it was a most horrible one."

She sighed when he settled beside her, thankful for his uncanny ability to sense when she needed his keen insight.

"I'm listening."

The warmth of old friendship wrapped itself about her like a familiar robe.

She started with the easiest to explain. "The electric toaster we've been working on will not be ready in time to exhibit at the Chicago Fair. Other scientists are engaged in developing the same product, and I wanted to be the first one on the market with it. It looks like the fair will be over before we can perfect it."

"Why, what seems to be the problem?"

Emmie smiled. It was just like Jon to show interest in everything she did, even the scientific, which he never understood.

"The heating element simply refuses to burn hot enough without melting in the process. I think we're using the wrong metal for the wire, but figuring out which is the right one could take months." She clutched her fingers tight in her lap.

Jon was pensive for a moment. "Look at the bright side. You know what the problem is. Your competition might not even be that far."

"I suppose you're right, but it's so discouraging."

What was left of the late afternoon sun cast eerie beams of light on the ridge of swift moving storm clouds. She should heed Jon's admonition to go inside before it rained, but for some reason she couldn't move off the bench. She breathed in the heavily laden air, content for the moment in the solace of her friend's quiet company, and the somber mood nature provided.

Jon took her hand and squeezed tenderly. His smooth palm, so different from Bart's, was warm and soft, but his touch didn't make her shiver like her husband's did.

"I have never seen you this despondent over a scientific complication. I think there's something else upsetting you." His voice was gentle, encouraging.

Emmie nodded, reluctantly acknowledging the truth of his observation. Her shoulders slumped. "Since Paul's death, I've enjoyed incredible freedom from Bart's constant shadowing. My life is almost as it was before I married—no one to answer to, nor anyone to stand in my way."

"I sense a *but*."

She gazed at him through watery eyes. "Bart's whereabouts these past few weeks baffles me. He goes somewhere during the day and won't tell me where. I miss him, Jon. I miss the quiet, and not-so-quiet companionship I shared with him prior to…." She stopped, shocked at what she almost blurted out. Better not talk about their strange nights of passion. It was none of Jon's business.

Her friend's eyes widened slightly before speculation consumed them. The pregnant silence that followed was excruciating. She focused on the stand of tall blue larkspur bobbing in the stiff breeze, her discomfort all consuming.

"Jon, where does he go every day? And what does he do?"

Oh, botheration. She sounded like a whining child. She wanted a temporary marriage, a platonic arrangement with an end date, didn't she? Well, she'd obtained them, but now that she and Bart were sharing a bed, their marital state was anything but chaste. Nights were the only time Emmie believed she held Bart's attention—or at least the attention of whichever persona happened to show up.

Night after night he donned a disguise and pleasured her well beyond her wildest dreams. One night he was a harbor stevedore, the next a Pullman train porter, a fireman, or a copper. Even a construction worker, a hack driver and a host of others. He said he used them all at one time or another in his investigations.

When he wore a disguise, he acted like a person possessed. His actions, his words, even his manner of speech reflected the character he claimed to be. So authentic were his impersonations, she had begun to wonder who her husband was beneath the personalities he became every night.

Did she even know the real Bartholomew Turner anymore? Had she known him at all?

Spray from the fountain flew in her direction. She shifted closer to Jon. Rafe followed, crowding against her leg.

"Oh, hell's bells, Jon. Why should I care, anyway? Certainly I can muddle through the remaining time of this marriage."

He squeezed her hand again. "Who are you fooling, Emmie. You do care. More than you thought you would. You need to open yourself to all possibilities. Including a future with your *temporary* husband. You can't live your whole life afraid of loving someone because they might leave you."

Startled, Emmie twisted toward him. "I'm doing no such thing, Jonathan."

His observation, however, had some ring of truth to it. Was that the reason she had guarded her heart all these years, why she preferred the shadows to the public glare of the marriage-minded social circuit? To hide her heart? To protect herself from further pain?

"For Pete's sake, Emmeline. You've been living with that fear for years. That's why you've never sought out a suitable husband, why you settled for Alex who was nothing more than a brother to you. I didn't like Bartholomew at first, found him to be rather a bully. But I finally realized he's looking out for your best interests. And he protected you. I'm sure there are good reasons why he's not as attentive at the moment. And now that Paul is out of the picture, there's no reason to guard you as closely."

She opened her mouth to tell him about Bart's theory, then thought better of it. Ridiculous as it seemed to her, Bart, Gertie and Cedric still considered Jon a suspect.

He swiveled to face her. "But my bet is he's as afraid of opening his heart to you as you are to him. I've seen how he looks at you when he thinks you're not looking."

Her hand slid from Jon's, and she let his observations sink into her heart. Was he right? Was Bart as fearful of their growing attraction as she? The idea had never occurred to her—Bart afraid of his feelings.

"He's become part of my life, Jon, a lightning rod for forbidden thoughts."

The admission slipped from her mouth, propelled by a force she couldn't explain. Despite the disguises, she enjoyed herself in her husband's arms, in his bed, his heated flesh singeing her own as he covered her with passion. She tamped down the sudden heat of desire those memories stoked.

"But being with him is like falling into emotional quicksand. I seem to be trapped in a quagmire of conflicting emotions too deep to fathom. Oh Jon, what am I to do?"

"Confront him, Emma. Ask him—"

The loud crack of a gun interrupted him and something whizzed by. Disturbed air slammed against her cheek.

Jon flew against her, knocking her to the ground, his body covering hers.

~~~

Noooo! Fear clawed at Bart's insides as Jon surged against Emmie and toppled them both off the fountain bench to the ground.

From his position across the lawn, Bart's professional instincts pulled his eyes to a small copse of trees, the only vegetation significant enough to provide a hiding place for a shooter. Movement low to the ground caught his eye as something threaded its way through the trees in the opposite direction.

Squelching an investigator's desire to follow the shooter, he sprinted to Emmie, his heart beating hard and fast.

Only moments before, he'd rounded the bend in the path between the stables and the house and had come to a dead stop. The sight of Emmie's forlorn figure sitting alone on a stone bench across the lawn had hit him like a fist to the chest. Her posture personified the gloomy state of the skies—dark and bleak.

She frequently came to the fountain seat to think, but he knew her well enough to note the difference in her bearing this time.

A wave of guilt had tightened his chest and he'd swallowed past the dryness inhabiting his throat. Emmie was too damn desirable. She affected him more than she would ever know. Even sitting opposite her at the table caused his groin to ache. Her passion-filled moans and sighs, her tender touches, and her tight wet sheath consumed his thoughts. He wanted her constantly, and with each passing day he found it increasingly more difficult to hold himself in check.

He'd kept his distance under the pretext of the investigation, coming to her only at night when he had time to become someone else. Someone who wouldn't fail her.

But, seeing her sitting there touched him deeply.

He had started across the lawn until the sight of Jon had brought him up short. The unfolding intimacy of the pair—the way she made room for her friend on the bench, slid close with their shoulders touching, their hands entwined, their heads together—had caused an unwelcome emotion to spread through his chest. The same emotion he experienced when Nick played court to Emmie at Bertha's party. He didn't like the feeling then, and he sure as hell hadn't liked it now.

And then he'd heard the unmistakable crack of a gunshot exploding across the lawn, and dread took the place of his ire.

What seemed like an eternity later, he reached the fountain and found Jon lying on top of Emmie, a pool of blood near her spreading fast. Rafe stood guard, his teeth bared in a snarl as he faced the copse.

Tears clouding his vision, he touched Jon, who immediately shifted off Emmie, bewilderment flooding his eyes. Blood dripped from his arm over the back of Emmie's white uniform.

"Emmie?" Bart whispered, kneeling to examine her. *God, oh, God. Let her be alive.*

She coughed, then sat up.

A warm tide of relief loosened his tense muscles. "Were you hit?"

She shook her head, dazed. Scratches made by the gravel path marred her cheeks and forearms. He passed his hands swiftly down her arms and legs. Her dress was bloody, but other than the paleness of her complexion, she appeared intact.

Her eyes suddenly cleared and she twisted toward Jon.

The gut wrenching scream of anguish that followed pierced Bart's heart.

The man had slumped to the side, unconscious. Blood flowed copiously from his upper arm.

Emmie lifted his head to her lap. "Jon, don't you dare leave me."

Her plaintive plea hung in the thickened air.

Without thought, Bart pulled the suspenders off his groomsman's disguise and tied it tightly around the man's arm above the wound.

Despite his personal feelings for the man, the shooting reinforced Bart's opinion of Jon he'd held since their conversation on the loggia. The man wouldn't harm a hair on his wife's beautiful head.

But it also reinforced the hard fact that Emmie's life was still in danger.

~~~

The gauze curtains fluttered lightly in the welcoming breeze and shafts of soft moonlight flickered in the bedroom. The turbulent nature of the three-day storm had mirrored the wild, unrestrained spirit of Bart's lovemaking during it. Emmie had bent to his need, sensing an undercurrent of some emotion she couldn't readily identify.

The rain had finally stopped, and Jon was healing nicely. Yet, as much as she tried to push it away, even deny its existence, fear penetrated her soul like a shard of glass.

Nobody was safe around her, including Bart who'd doubled his efforts at guarding her since the incident. Except when she was locked in the research laboratory, he was present at her side from morning through the long nights.

Now, boneless and snuggled atop his tranquil body, Emmie watched in fascination as the tiny bit of gold attached to his ear flashed each time he took a breath. Tonight, he dressed as a sailor off a cargo ship docked in Calumet Harbor.

What would he be like if he came to her bed without a disguise? The memory of that first night was beginning to fade with each new personality he donned.

His leg shifted under her, the smooth muscle of his thigh coming to rest against the juncture of her thighs. Desire rekindled, but she tamped it down, her mind sifting through various openings to the discussion she had put off for days.

She opened and closed her mouth several times, surprised she couldn't find the courage to even begin.

"What is it, Emmie? Something is obviously bothering you."

Vibrations from his deep voice rumbled through his sculpted chest. She loved listening to his rich, resonant tones, loved the way they filled the room with vibrancy and excitement.

She hesitated a moment before plunging in. "Before the shooting, where did you go all day, Bart? I hardly saw you these past weeks, and when I did you were distant, occupied with something to which I wasn't privy. Since the shooting, the change in you has been stark. You're like my shadow. You put yourself in danger, and I couldn't bear it if anything happened to you. I don't know what to think any more."

He stilled, his chest muscle tightening. Tension radiated off him in thick sheets. Why?

"Remember what you said after Paul's death? About not needing to be guarded now that our primary suspect was dead? I agreed with you despite the fact my gut told me otherwise. The shooting proved my gut was right."

"That doesn't explain where you went every day before then."

"I'm getting to it." Exasperation edged into his tone. "Paul was killed in the city. My guess was his slayer also lives there."

Her patience ebbed like the outgoing tide while her vexation increased. "How does that affect what happened here?"

"Whoever the murderer is, he has an accomplice at Summerhill, someone close to your family. We need to find out who."

Emmie's mouth dried as the implication of what he was saying set in, but his answer was yet another evasion. She puffed out a gasp of exasperation. "So, what does that have—"

He grabbed her hair, though didn't pull. "Don't for a minute think I was far away from you."

Frustration permeated his loud, terse tones.

Silent a moment, she scrutinized him, her eyes widening when understanding finally dawned. "You were in disguise. That's why you were dressed as a groomsman when Jon was shot. I hardly recognized you with that bushy beard."

Yet she had. And if she was truthful, she saw him far more clearly than he might have liked. Beneath the gruff professional exterior and ingenious disguises existed a vulnerable man given to great tenderness, and possessing a kind, gentle soul. It was *that* man she longed for.

"Yes. I used disguises to fit in with whomever I needed to watch or interview." Something else flashed in his eyes. Guilt? Remorse?

"I never noticed you."

He fingered a strand of her hair. "You weren't supposed to. Rafe became your visible body guard, but I was your silent shadow, blending into the background, watching everyone who came near you. When I wasn't with you, I eased information out of the staff. But I should have been with you that day instead of Jon and Rafe." Regret filtered through his eyes. "After that I changed how I did things. If anything happened to you...." He turned his head, but not quick enough to hide the bleakness that had settled across his features.

"And what did you discover while you wore your disguises?"

"Not enough to suit me, though Sarah's name kept popping up. Nobody likes her. Nobody trusts her. She returns each night to a lover in the city. Maybe to the same person who hired the two thugs to shoot you. She has free rein of the Summerhill grounds. She would make a likely candidate for the murders here. Even the shooting the other day. That bullet was meant for you."

Though she should have been afraid, it was indignation that threatened to escape her tight control. "But most of my staff lives in Chicago. They ride the train out here. I send a carriage to pick them up, and they return in the evening. Their work hours are tied to the train schedule. And they all have access to every part of Summerhill. Sarah's been a part of the Chicagoland family for a long time. My father relied upon her and so do I. Why are you singling her out?"

Her long-time laboratory assistant would never do anything nefarious. Sarah loved her job. She told Emmie so, many times over the years.

"Don't know, but when my gut tells me something, I listen. My city network informed Cedric most of your staff go home to their husbands, but Sarah isn't married. She's been discreet about the identity of her companion, but rest assured, we'll find out who the man is soon enough."

Dismayed, she rolled away and rose to a kneeling position, heedless of her state of undress. Bart's gaze shifted to her chest, then lowered to the juncture between her thighs. Lust flickered in his eyes. The lecher. She pulled the edge of the sheet up to cover her nakedness.

"You've been spying on my staff at their homes? Bartholomew Turner, I can't let you continue. It's a shameful breach of their privacy."

"Do you want to live?"

"Of course I do."

"Then don't question my methods of keeping you alive." His voice was low and quiet. Ominous sounding. Even a dog wouldn't disobey him.

Surprised by his response, she sat back on her heels. The air in the room thickened with tension. Dark pools of resolve met her indignant stare. He was the professional, the man who named himself her body-guard. Yet she expected him to operate within socially acceptable standards. She found this type of surveillance repugnant. He needed to find some other way to do his investigating.

She opened her mouth, ready to continue her dispute, but his expression inexplicably softened. She kept quiet. He sat up, his hand coming to rest against her cheek.

"I care for you a great deal, Emmie, more than you'll ever know. Nothing must happen to you." His whisper was tight, husky.

A parade of emotions drifted through his eyes—sadness, guilt, regret, all mixed with concern and tenderness. Her annoyance fizzled. This man almost never revealed his emotions. Whatever provoked the crack in the wall surrounding them must be causing him great distress.

Wanting to reduce his suffering, she gently pushed him back, stretching beside him as he fell. He wrapped his arm about her shoulders and pulled her close. She sighed, content to lay within his warmth, within the safety of his arms, offering him comfort by just being near.

The night whispers of the wind in the trees and of insects and nocturnal creatures living their lives after the rain, drifted through the window. She listened intently, her fingers toying with Bart's in a woven caress.

The words tumbled out of her mouth. "Bart, why can't you make love to me as yourself?"

~~~

Air failed to fill Bart's lungs. *Because I'm afraid I'll disappoint you.* But he couldn't tell her that, couldn't divulge his deepest fear to anyone, let alone her. He loosened his hold on her hand as cold panic wormed beneath his skin.

What if he couldn't satisfy her? He would fail her a second time, be even less of a man. His humiliation the first time had been unbearable. If he botched it again, she might never want him in her bed, and he would be lost without her.

He desired her all the time—her warmth, her fire, her arms about his waist, her legs behind his knees. Her trusting naivety made him feel whole, wanted. He cherished the feeling, yet feared it. He didn't trust himself to be with her during the day. Becoming someone else at night allowed him to be the man she wanted, the lover she needed. And now that he'd tasted the comfort of marriage, he wanted her forever.

Forever. The realization rocked his mental equilibrium.

He had fallen in love with his wife.

And she'd asked him to strip the defenses he hid behind. Become the man he wasn't and would never be again. Agony, the likes of which he had never experienced, ripped his heart in two.

How could he do what she asked and retain his dignity, his manhood?

The softness of her breasts pressed enticingly against his side. Desire coursed through him again as her finger drew circles around his nipple. Which hardened under her ministration. As did his cock. *Christ.* Emmie had no idea how sensual her movements were, how exciting a creature she was, how much he needed her.

And not just her body.

Without answering her question, he rolled her beneath him and claimed her mouth. Tonight, he was Joaquin, a merchant sailor from Venezuela. Tomorrow? Well, tomorrow was another day.

Chapter 19

Emmie jerked a hairbrush through her tangled ends a week later, and stared at her blurry reflection in the dressing table mirror.

Despite what Bart had said, was it her fault after all? Did he become someone else because he couldn't stand to make love to a woman with her deformities?

Upset by succumbing to insecurities, she threw her brush at the woman in the mirror.

I will not be a weak-livered ninny. I simply will not. Such notions were not the musings of a confident woman, one who headed a soon-to-be-great manufacturing concern. She must find a way to communicate to Bart why she was no longer happy with his disguises in their bed.

He'd come to her only twice since her initial question a week ago, both times still wearing a disguise. Disappointment spoiled the pleasure he tried to give her. She was left profoundly dissatisfied, empty even.

She longed for the man who had honestly and truthfully shared his body with her that first night, not the parade of characters who tramped in and out of his life like visitors on a tour. The never-ending line of players had been fun at first, but Bart's complete immersion into the role made making love to a seemingly different man all the more unbearable as time went on.

This scenario was not what she envisioned when she invited Bart to share her body. Far from it. She had to do something to change the situation. Maybe stronger words were needed. She straightened, her new-found resolve fortifying her spine.

Yet, the question remained. Who would show up tonight? Bart, or one of his assorted minions? She knew the answer only too well.

Her depressing thoughts were interrupted by a strong, determined knock on the connecting door. *Good lord!* A dominant lover tonight. Despite her misgivings, a zap of excitement surged through her, one she quickly subdued. If Bart entered as someone else....

"Come in." On legs of rubber, she stood to face him. Hope stole into the cracks of her soul.

The door opened. Her pulse pounded with unabashed anticipation, then plummeted when she saw who crossed the threshold.

Lord Wallingshire.

The yawning pit of despair deepened, sucking her down to its dark, dank core. Her frustration, however, soared to new heights. She bit her lip, willing her tears to stay put.

"How is my lady fair?" Bart twirled his mustache, amusement creating crow's feet at the sides of his sparkling eyes.

Oh, how she loved those intense brown eyes. She could peer into them all night and never get tired, but as reality set in, Emmie found little cause for merriment. Irritation pricked her heart like a large patch of thistle. Hiding her emotions became an impossible task.

"Why do you insist on being someone you aren't? I want *you*, Bartholomew Turner, my handsome, competent, investigator, bodyguard of a husband. The man who makes me laugh, who understands my failings, who lifts my spirits and warms my heart. Lord Wallingshire, and the many characters you bring to my bed, are not you. I can't relate to these various personae, men as unique from each other as night and day."

The stricken look on his face speared her soul. He stood silent, gaping at her, his shoulders slumped. *Oh, God.* She hated herself at that moment.

In a toneless voice she had to strain to hear, he finally spoke. "I tried, Emmeline. God knows I tried. But I can't. I don't want to fail you again."

Blinking rapidly, he swiped his hand through his pomade-tamed locks, turned on his heel and stalked out. The connecting door snicked closed. A dark, cold stillness froze whatever blood remained within her veins.

Dear Lord! What have I done? I just shot an arrow into the heart of the man I love.

~~~

Damn it all to hell! Bart peeled off the fake mustache and threw it on a table. Forcing air into his lungs, he struggled to remain upright.on legs weakened beyond belief.

He staggered to the chair near the window and fell into it with a thud.

Damn his pride. No matter how hard he tried this past week, he couldn't bring himself to discard his disguises. Fear stood in his way.

He swiped his hand along his jaw, shaved smooth for a long night of lovemaking with Emmie. Why had he failed that first night? Why was he only successful when he wore a disguise?

What kind of man was he?

God, he felt like puking. Curling into himself, he covered his face with his hands, then wiped away a bit of moisture he found there.

A damn coward. That's what he was. He didn't deserve her, would never be the kind of man she wanted or needed. Sharp needles stabbed deep into his heart.

He never realized how much love could hurt. She had become his life, his love, the one woman who could lift him out of the morass of loneliness in which he seemed to be floundering. What a pair they would have made. They matched wits, laughed at the same things, shared common ideas and interests. Even suited in the marriage bed.

Or so he had thought.

And now it was over. Blast the stupid shortcomings of his body. He could never go back to her now, his pride tucked between his legs like the tail of a chastised dog.

Bart rose on unsteady legs, shucked off the rest of Lord Wallingshire's clothes, and dropped them on the floor. Clad in his underclothes, he surveyed the untidy pile with the last bit of sanity remaining in his brain. Slowly, he reached for each article and folded it in a stack on the chair. Wallingshire might be needed again someday.

Just not in Emmie's bed.

The thought of never touching her again, never feeling her hands on his body, never sliding into her welcoming heat ripped his soul apart. He flung back his bed covers and flopped into the four-poster without a care to its antique wooden frame. The bed creaked and groaned.

Bart stared at the ceiling, turning over every word of their short conversation in painstaking detail. He never noticed how unhappy she'd become. Shock had glued his mouth shut. Humiliation had gripped his thoughts. He'd retreated to his room like a scolded schoolboy, silent and sullen.

Could he even consider taking the risk she'd asked of him?

To do so would require courage he wasn't sure he possessed.

Shadows of a lone elm tree waving in the breeze played across the small settling cracks in the ceiling plaster, creating a brief distraction. But his reflections soon returned to the hopelessness of his situation—the impossibility of fulfilling Emmie's request.

He lay awake brooding for hours. Then exhausted and no closer to a solution, he finally drifted into a fitful sleep.

~~~

"What the hell!" Drenched in sweat, Bart flew off the bed later that night, ran to the open window and flung aside the curtains. Cool night air washed over his damp skin.

Memories of degradation and shame, horror and terror—thought to have been relegated long ago to the darkest corners of his soul—lay exposed on a junk pile of emotions impossible to sort.

His mind focused on the man, a giant hulk with a short, trim goatee and the bulging eyes of a toad—his tutor, Mr. Murdock.

The man who did unspeakable things to him. Repeatedly. For two years.

Fury surged through Bart's body, leaving him shaking like a wind-blown leaf. He pounded his fist against the solid frame of the window with the force he would have used had he been strong enough then. A blow that was hard, punishing. That could have bashed in someone's head.

His wobbly legs collapsed. He slid to the floor, his thoughts a mass of confusion and misery. Tears leaked down his cheeks. Tears of pain, of frustration and anger, of hatred. He tried to swallow, but nothing moved beyond the dry ball stuck in his throat.

Arms wrapped around his knees, he rocked and sobbed silently. Time ceased as he relived those years and the horrible things done to him and by him. He hated Murdock, hated his father.

Hated himself.

He cried until he could no longer think, cried until finally the sorrow of a child's agony gave way to the rational thought of the adult he had become.

Gasping for air, he leaned his head back against the wall and fought for control. It was time he faced this thing locked inside him for years. Questions now cycled in his brain, many of them without answers, or at least none he could understand.

Perhaps talking with someone might help sort through his tangled emotions. Someone other than Emmie. What happened all those years ago was too personal, too humiliating to share with a woman. He needed a male perspective, a man he could trust with his innermost thoughts.

He needed Reginald, his boss, his mentor, the only man he loved like a father. The only man who'd recognized the potential of a street punk and given him a chance.

Reginald was in Chicago this week for a series of meetings with the Pinkerton Agency. The meetings were so secret and so sensitive, his boss hadn't even informed Emmie of his arrival. Only agency operatives had known.

But, how could he leave Emmie with the shooting still unresolved?

He twined his fingers, his conflicted mind sifting through his options. Emmie needed to be guarded. Two attempts had been made on her life, and this last one had come just inches away from being successful. He shuddered at how close he came to losing her.

He loved her completely, and wanted more than anything to make her happy.

Happy in bed, as well.

And, if by chance his performance problems had something to do with his dark past, he owed it to her, to himself, to face his pain and move beyond the black terror of his childhood.

Only a few more days remained of Reginald's visit. Bart had to go now. Cedric and Gertie could guard her as well as he. Both were competent, skilled investigators, both nimble and adept with a variety of weapons. He could go tomorrow and return the next morning. Just twenty-four hours away from his beloved wife.

His decision made, hope for the future blossomed like a spring flower, hope tinged at the edges with the darker shades of dread.

Chapter 20

Emmie fashioned a smile and breezed into the breakfast room the next morning, the skirts of her white uniform flapping about her ankles. Bart was not in the room, nor was he on the porch. Her manufactured expression slid from her face.

Well, ninny, what did you expect? The man to be waiting in eager anticipation? Hardly. Besides, what could she say to him after last night? Thick clouds of disappointment joined fluffy billows of relief to unsettle her belly.

She hadn't slept all night, and she imagined Bart hadn't either. How would they get through the remaining weeks of their temporary living arrangement with some semblance of civility? She squelched a sob before it escaped from her throat. She missed his presence already.

With Rafe at her heels, she trudged to the buffet near the opened loggia and spooned cut fruit into a small bowl. Grabbing a slice of toast in her other hand, she retreated to the veranda, to a spot she enjoyed with Bart every morning.

Loneliness greeted her arrival this morning. Tears threatened, but she willed them to stay put. She had every right to want honesty in their relationship. But honesty had come at a terrible price, one she wasn't sure she wanted to pay.

Taking a seat in the sun, she shook out the folded napkin and placed it across her lap. Birds chirped a merry song in the nearby trees, and the morning breeze rustled the leaves in the rhythmic pattern of waves rolling to shore.

She loved Summerhill in its namesake season, yet despite the beauty of her surroundings, the joy was gone. Bart wasn't sharing his presence, and an odd emptiness enveloped her soul.

With a sigh, Emmie opened the small porcelain container by her place setting and spread boysenberry jam, her favorite, over the toast. Only five weeks remained of the three-month period. Certainly, she could get through the rest of the time without his company. After all, she'd been alone for years before he entered her life.

From the corner of her eye, she spotted Gertie spooning scrambled eggs into a chafing dish on the buffet close to the door.

Keeping her voice as casual as possible, she asked, "Have you seen Bart this morning, Gertie?"

"Oh, he ate early so's to catch the eight o'clock train into the city. Said he would be back tomorrow morning."

The knot in Emmie's belly tightened. Why hadn't he told her of his plans last night? Certainly, he must have known at dinner. But then, when would he have done so?

Gertie poked her head through the opened French doors. "He said he needed to meet with someone. Asked Cedric and me to keep an eye on ye. He looked terrible, dark circles under his eyes and all."

Averting her face with its own dark circles, Emmie nibbled on the toast. Guilt spilled over her like a pail of icy water. She knew exactly what disturbed Bart.

But, who had he rushed off to see? A sudden image of her husband in the arms of another woman, their bodies joined in carnal bliss, sent jabs of pain flying to her chest. A faint wave of nausea spread throughout her belly. Her appetite plummeted and the toast slid from her fingers to her plate.

Rafe crawled closer to her chair and whined. Her hand resting on her upset stomach, she glanced at him, then at the toast which he clearly wanted. He had rounded out a bit since coming to Summerhill, no doubt because of her habit of dropping table scraps at his feet.

"I'm sorry, Rafe. Not this time. Let's feed the birds."

The big dog flopped his bulk to the floor, his sad eyes betraying what he thought of her idea.

Her nausea deepening, Emmie tore the bread in half and placed one of the pieces on the balustrade railing a few feet away. Rafe sniffed the air, his eyes following her every move.

Returning to her seat, she picked at her fruit, her mind occupied by the whereabouts of her husband. Her already beleaguered stomach tightened into a cramp.

Two crows swooped down and flanked the toast. Not wanting to scare them away, Emmie stilled, ignoring the beads of sweat popping out on her forehead. Each bird surveyed the feast with decided interest, as did Rafe, who inched his prone body along the wooden porch floor to a place directly beneath the precariously balanced treat.

One crow finally pecked at the bread. The other squawked and grabbed an edge. The first bird seized the other end and fluttered its wings in an attempt to rise. The effort only succeeded in tearing the toast, leaving him with a small fragment of crust. The triumphant crow gobbled his spoils and set about preening his feathers as an after-meal activity.

Emmie smiled, the smallest bit of normalcy intruding into her dejected state of mind. "Well now, Rafe. That was interesting."

Acknowledging his failure, the dog rose and padded to a larger spot in the sun. He turned completely around twice before finally settling into a tight ball.

The victorious bird suddenly shifted awkwardly and toppled off the balustrade, landing on the porch floor near Emmie's table. She rushed to its side.

The crow trembled, every tiny muscle in its body twitching violently. Shocked, Emmie stared at the ailing bird, her stomach reminding her of her own body's frailty. Suddenly, the bird's little legs stiffened. It stopped moving, stopped breathing. Its rival took flight, its departing kaw, kaw cry piercing her ears.

Emmie sucked in a breath. What just happened? The bird was fine one moment and dead the next, while its companion flew away right as rain. What was the difference between them? The dead crow had eaten the toast, while the live one gained only a small bit of crust, a piece without the sweetness of jam.

Jam.

Dear God! Her pulse raced at the implications, and her hand gripped her own beleaguered belly.

She glanced at Rafe. She'd almost given the toast to him. Would he have died, too? As though sensing her concern, he rose to a sitting position and panted.

Gertie popped her head out the door. "Do ye need anything miss? I'm going back to the kitchen."

"Gertie, I think this jam is spoiled. I gave a piece of toast spread with it to the birds, and a crow ate it and died."

Gertie's eyes flew wide. "But Mrs. Turner, I made that jam meself just yesterday. Tis fresh, it is. Fresh as a new-born babe. And I used nothing but the finest berries and the best sugar." The woman's eyes narrowed. "My preserves twern't spoilt."

A nasty thought tickled Emmie's brain. Her pulse began to race. She tried to maintain a modicum of scientific decorum, but it was becoming increasingly more difficult.

She slumped in her chair as the insidious thought took hold, one she was loath to even contemplate. "Gertie, can you describe for me the process of how this jar made it here from the kitchen?"

"Anna, me wee helper, opened the mason jar, scooped some into the pretty little jam jar matching yer china, and brought it out here. She knows where you usually sit, so she set your place and left it there. I was with her the whole time."

Emmie's thoughts galloped along a trail she found most repugnant. "Then it was sitting out here with nobody watching?"

"I suppose so. I was in and out, bringing food to the buffet and you weren't down here yet." Gertie eyed Emmie's half-eaten fruit. "Yer appetite ain't so good. Are ye well?"

Not really. Her throat tightened. "I think someone put poison in the jam cup, and I was the intended victim." Gertie's brows flew up. "I ate a tiny bit of it myself and I'm feeling a little ill. I almost gave my toast to Rafe. He could have died." *I could have died.* "Good lord, Gertie. What do you think?"

Deep lines appeared over Gertie's brows. "How much did you eat of it?"

"Not much. Crust mostly."

The lines disappeared. "Ah, that's good. Now you be sure to drink lots of water, mind ye, and remain quiet today. And don't eat anything unless I serve it to ye meself. Let's have a look." Abandoning the usual master and servant relationship, the woman pulled out a wicker chair and dropped her tall frame into it. The chair creaked in response. She reached for the jam pot and brought it to her nose. "Smells all right." She peered into the container. "Uh, oh. Look here. I think you're right. Someone added something to the jar's contents after Anna set it on the table."

She tilted the jar toward Emmie. "See these wee bits in there? They're no pieces of fruit. I'd recognize them if they were. I'm thinkin' they may be parts of a coarsely crumbled flower or seed pod, and not boysenberry neither, mind ye. Ye'll not find a lick of fruit leaf or stem pieces in the jams I make. Most likely this leaf was added after I made it."

"But what is it, and who would do such a thing?"

Gertie regarded her a moment, her expression unreadable as she reasoned things through. "I'd guess this to be a crime of opportunity. Whoever did this, saw the jam, knew of a poison plant nearby, and crumbled it in the jar in a hurry."

Emmie's hand flew to her lips. "There's something highly poisonous growing nearby?"

Gertie surveyed the small patch of neatly cultivated garden off the porch. "There." She pointed to a tall stalk of blue flowers in the back of the riot of colors.

"The larkspur. Also called delphinium. Every bit of it is poisonous if eaten, at least to cattle, 'tis." She placed the lid on the jam jar. "Me evidence, Mrs. Mr. Turner will want to see for hisself. I'll have Cedric be your companion until he returns."

Emmie nodded mindlessly, terror squeezing her insides like a vice.

This is the second attempt on her life within the last few days. Someone she knew well at Summerhill wanted her dead.

~~~

Bart hesitated outside the ninth-floor suite at the Chicago Athletic Club, questioning his decision for the hundredth time. What man in his right mind would reveal to another he had been… raped? His cold, clammy hands shook, stones jangled in his gut, and his tongue damn near stuck to the roof of his mouth. He needed to get out of here. Fast.

He turned toward the elevator.

Oh hell! He pivoted back. He couldn't go on without sorting through his raw emotions, and he sure as hell couldn't deal with them alone. He needed help. Maybe he should have gone to Emmie after all. He shook his head. The less she knew of his unspeakable past, the better.

With a hand as heavy as metal, he knocked.

"Be right there." Reginald's voice, commanding in tone, yet muffled in volume drifted through the thin hotel door. Footsteps crossed a wooden floor before the door opened to startling blue eyes. Griffith eyes. Bart started. Why hadn't he noticed the family resemblance from the beginning?

"Bartholomew! This is quite a surprise."

Bart leaned his hand against the door post. "I wouldn't have come if I didn't need your help, sir."

A professional inspection swept Bart from head to toe. "Yes, of course. Come in, come in. Sit down, son."

Reginald ushered him inside a small but lavishly appointed sitting room. The newly-opened athletic club with residential suites on the top two floors lived up to its reputation as being one of the finest such establishments in the city.

"Thank you." Bart glanced about as he lowered his large frame to a sturdy leather settee. The furnishings were bold, and solidly masculine.

"You look like hell, my boy. I'll get you something to settle your belly."

Without waiting for a response, the older man moved to an antique gentleman's sideboard sporting a crystal decanter and several glasses. He poured three fingers of whiskey into one and handed it to Bart.

"Thank you, sir."

Though it was far too early to imbibe spirits, Bart graciously accepted the offered hospitality. Maybe a drink *would* help his nerves, now a jumble of tight sailor's knots. Raising his glass, he gulped a healthy portion, the liquor burning its way down his throat to warm his insides.

Reginald settled in a large, overstuffed chair opposite Bart. "Now what brings you here?"

From above his glass, Bart studied his mentor's face, amazed at how similar it was to Emmie's—the color of his eyes, the shape of his jaw, even the dimple in his chin. But then, Reginald was her father's brother. There should be some family resemblance.

The man's white eyebrows knit in a frown. "You're seeking my help because...?"

Bart opened his mouth, but words failed to emerge.

Though Reginald's features softened, concern inhabited his eyes. "Take it slow and easy, boy. Start at the beginning."

The encouraging tone of his boss's voice scraped away some of Bart's reluctance. He rose and ambled to the window overlooking Michigan Avenue. Across the street to his right, the new Art Institute rose like a ghostly specter, its construction scaffolding looking like bones of a skeleton shielding the building's interior treasures. Straight ahead, the sun's rays upon a sparkling lake teeming with yachts, their colorful spinnakers aloft, created a magnificent view.

He shoved his hands in his pockets. So much had happened to him in those two years he didn't know where to begin. "I told you once I was educated by tutors."

"Yes, I remember. Your father didn't like the local school."

"After my mother died, I wasn't the easiest of students. I misbehaved a lot. Putting it nicely, they asked me to leave."

Reginald chuckled. "As I recollect, you were not any easier as a street thug."

Bart continued as though Reginald hadn't spoken. "My father hired a big burly man as a tutor—a Mr. Murdock—more to make me behave than to teach me anything, in my opinion."

"Did he? Make you behave?"

"In a fashion…." Shit. In the beginning, every time Bart had misbehaved, his tutor had done some despicable things to him. But even becoming the perfect little boy hadn't changed things any. His throat tightened with the painful memory.

"Go on, son."

His mentor's voice was so soft, so gentle, that Bart's close-to-the-surface emotions broke.

"God, Reginald. The man did terrible things to me, and I…. I can't deal with those memories anymore. No matter how hard I try to bury them, they keep returning, and they're unbearable." His hands rolled into fists. "I need help to…." He stopped, his thoughts no longer coherent.

He heard Reginald shift in his chair behind him. Bart sagged against the window pane, afraid to face the man who'd saved him from a life of crime, a life he would have led if he'd remained on the streets.

"Tell me how it started." Reginald's even tone contained no hint of judgment. The last of Bart's reluctance disintegrated, replaced by a surge of courage to continue.

In a slow, halting manner, Bart described every sordid detail, choking on the images, the memories, the guilt, the hurts, and the anger that now consumed him, threatened to consume his very sanity.

And when he was done, the control he struggled for snapped. A sob ripped through him, and his vision blurred. He thought after last night he had no tears left, but he was wrong. The sob soon grew into a torrent he couldn't stop. He turned his face into the drape and wept, burying his head in the softness of the material like a child crying into the bosom of its mother.

Sometime later, as he gained a semblance of control, he became aware of the silence in the room. Dreadful silence he could almost taste. He kept his back to Reginald, afraid to see the blame in his mentor's eyes.

Instead, Reginald's voice once again came calm and encouraging.

"Come sit here, son. Let's discuss this."

Bart drew a handkerchief from his pocket, wiped his eyes and blew his nose. Grown men don't cry, yet he had. Like a baby. He trudged to his chair and sat, prepared for the worst. He took another long gulp from his glass and swallowed the fire.

For the next hour and a half Bart answered Reginald's most personal and provocative questions as honestly and as thoroughly as he could.

He told of being whipped by his father with a belt for even suggesting his tutor was capable of such disgusting activities. He told of his plan to kill Murdock with his slingshot, about his decision to run away, about his life on the streets before Reginald had found him.

Reginald stirred, the movement making the chair's springs creak. "You have nothing to be ashamed of or guilty about. You were in a situation you couldn't escape. What happened was not your fault."

Of course it was my fault. I brought it upon myself. I wasn't good enough or smart enough to prevent Murdoch's torment.

Uncomfortable, Bart took another sip of whiskey, and changed the subject. "I ran away when I was ten. Tried to forget, but never could."

Reginald skewered him with intelligent eyes. "Well, that answers many questions bothering me since I found you in that abandoned building years ago. You were leading a bunch of dirty urchins in grace. I asked myself why would a lad with a proper upbringing be living in a hell hole on the streets? Now I understand. Even then I thought I could make something of a fifteen-year-old boy with such organizational skills. You turned into a fine young man, Bartholomew, and on the right side of the law too."

Bart smiled and sank into the memory of the gang of boys he gathered about him when he was but fourteen.

Reginald continued, his thoughts clearly in the past. "The tables in that room were all set with mismatched dishes and silverware most likely filched from unsuspecting merchants. At the station house, we'd been getting reports of food thefts as well. A few apples here, a loaf of bread there, a chicken from somewhere else."

"We needed to eat." Bart said, as though that explanation alone was an excuse for stealing.

They'd stolen anything and everything to make their situation tolerable. Reginald's interest had been a boon. God only knew what Bart and the other boys would have become had Reginald, then a copper, not brought order and purpose to their lives. He trained them to be information gatherers, their livelihoods coming from the largess of the men at the precinct house. Bart modeled his own information gathering network after the one Reginald had built.

Street noise drifted through the open window as loud as if they were on the first floor. Reginald studied him for a moment, then steered the conversation toward a more personal matter, Bart's romantic affairs, a subject most uncomfortable. Bart emptied the remainder of his whiskey and set the glass on a side table.

Through Reginald's unerring probing, Bart admitted intimate relations with women had been practically non-existent, except those few he paid for as a young man. He had no real desire to bed anyone, including men. He even reluctantly admitted he avoided entanglements that might lead to intimacy of any kind. He didn't deserve to be married.

After a long moment of silence, Bart became conscious of Reginald's measured perusal of his face. A curious half smile twisted his mentor's mouth up at the corners. "Have you ever cared about a woman? I mean really cared, enough to even consider marriage?"

Images of Emmie filtered through his mind. Of her warm sunny smile, of the way she unconsciously tugged at the curl near her cheek when deep in thought, of her moving beneath him when lost in passion, her eyes glazed over, her lips swollen, her breasts heavy with arousal.

Bart's jaw tightened. "Yes."

"You're mumbling. Say it louder." Impatience rode on the edge of Reginald's command, but amusement sparkled in his eyes.

Bart raised his voice. "Yes. If you must know, I have fallen in love with your niece, and if it were up to me, I'd stay in this marriage forever if she would have me. I would do anything for her."

Shit. He glared at Reginald as ire of his own making fired his emotions. Emmie's name wasn't supposed to come up, be part of this discussion, but there it was. He had already informed Reginald of their marriage in name only, of the initial shooting and the need to guard her as well as be the legal husband she sought. He'd also told him of their platonic arrangement.

But a second ago, he almost told the man he'd taken his niece to bed and had failed miserably.

Reginald grinned broadly. "You say you'd do anything for her, anything except bare your soul to her. I think you greatly underestimate my niece."

Reginald's softly spoken words flew like an arrow to a dark corner of Bart's tormented heart, to the gaping wound and tortured feelings he had shielded like precious treasure. To the part of him he'd never revealed to another soul until now. Would Emmie want *that* person, the man with the soiled past?

"If you want to find happiness with my niece, you must tell her everything. And you must forgive yourself and the others you blame, as well. What happened to you was not your fault, and I suspect that's exactly what you're doing—blaming yourself."

Reginald shifted in his chair, but remained silent, letting Bart sort through his thoughts without assistance.

Was he right? Was he blaming himself? Maybe it *was* time to demolish the barrier he had unknowingly erected to protect the scared little boy he had been. *But how do I do that?*

Bart could never forgive Murdock, nor his father, and certainly not himself. But there was something else he could do, and he hoped it would be enough. He needed to tell Emmie about his past. Needed to tell her he loved her beyond life itself and wanted to remain married to her. For real.

"Maybe I *should* tell her, Reginald. I'll be taking the train home tomorrow to do just that." He stood, and a mountain lifted off his shoulders. "Thank you for listening. What you asked was painful to answer, but that's why I came, wasn't it?"

Reginald rose as well and held out his hand. "It's always a pleasure to see you, my boy."

Bart shook it, then froze when his mentor, tears in his eyes, pulled him into an embrace. No man had ever held him with genuine warmth. Not even his father. He returned the gesture with awkward stiff movements.

"Glad to have you in the family, son. Glad to have you. You make me proud."

A burst of joy flooded his heart with its delicate sweetness, the kind of joy one experiences when finding an early spring flower amid late winter snows. A promise of a glorious spring to come. He prayed he would receive the same spring warmth from Emmie.

~~~

For the fifth time that morning, yet another experimental wire burned to a glob of molten metal on Emmie's worktable. The heavy burden of failure lay like a mantel about her shoulders. At this rate, her plans for a viable electric toaster seemed beyond the realm of possibility.

Maybe she should have remained in bed, after all. She followed Gertie's orders to rest, but after only an hour, guilt over her unattended work drove her back to the laboratory, Rafe at her side for protection.

Now, several hours later, her head pounded like a mallet, and her spirits were lower than the nearby dry creek.

She slid off her stool, dragged herself to a side table, and poured a glass of water from a white porcelain ewer. She drained her drink quickly, a feat made more difficult by the queasiness still residing in her abdomen.

Bart, I wish you were here.

She never realized how much she relished the profound sense of peace he imparted with just a few well-chosen words. His intuitive logic delivered in low rumbling tones caused her worries to disappear like clouds in the sky, and her insides to melt in a bonfire of desire.

She missed him terribly, and the abruptness of his departure lent itself to conjecture she dare not explore. Only five weeks remained of their three months of living together. Surely Bart was entitled to a life of his own.

Emmie replaced the empty glass on a tray, cognizant of the emptiness now filling her heart.

A long, low sigh a few inches from her ear startled her. Sarah, her assistant, reached around her and grabbed a glass off the table, her approach so silent Emmie hadn't heard her.

Sarah raised the ewer to fill her glass. "I wish I could find your father's notebook. He encountered the same problem with a different invention he tinkered with years ago."

Emmie's jaw flew open. "He did? And he kept notes?"

Of course he kept notes. Any good scientist would. Sarah had been his assistant before he died, so it made sense she would know of the project. But why hadn't he told his own daughter about it when he shared everything else? Why hadn't he trusted her? And why hadn't Sarah mentioned this other project before?

Tears threatening, Emmie turned lest Sarah notice her distress.

Oh botheration. Everyone probably knew she hadn't been herself lately, and now she was close to becoming a blubbering idiot, though she had plenty to cry about. Discovering a project her father never mentioned was the latest in a long line of recent unpleasant events, not the least of which had been her argument with Bart.

With a mental shake, Emmie shoved aside her jangled emotions to focus on the problem at hand. "Where did you search?"

"Everywhere." Sarah swept her arm around the bright windowless laboratory. Shrewd, assessing eyes returned to Emmie with enigmatic intensity. "The project was one of the last things he played with before starting work on his DC current delivery system. I saw his notebook myself."

"It had to be around here somewhere."

"Well, it isn't in the laboratory. He might have taken it to the main house and forgotten it there. He *was* a little absent-minded."

Emmie offered a slight smile at the reminder. "A little more than absent minded, really. Scattered would be a more apt description." A trait he often relied on her to remedy.

When an idea struck, her father played with it until he lost interest. Nothing ever came of these projects. His passion, delivering electricity to the masses, differed from hers, the inventions that would use the power. If she could find the notebook, the experiments might provide a clue to solving her problem with the toaster's heating element.

"You're probably right, Sarah. It may be in the house. I'll hunt for it after lunch."

Her father's office—the Ship Room—would be the perfect place to begin her search. Notes brought in to study could easily be forgotten and lost amid the clutter of treasures from around the world. A glimmer of optimism buoyed her spirits.

"Do you need help?"

Without warning, the hair on Emmie's neck prickled. Something in Sarah's voice didn't seem right. Was it her too anxious tone? The over-excited enthusiasm of her offer? Or the clipped edge to her pronunciation as though spoken through clenched teeth? Whatever it was, it gave Emmie pause. Anybody could have poisoned her jam, even her closest assistant. At the realization, a cold shiver tracked up her spine.

She scanned Sarah's face for signs of duplicity, but the woman's expression was all scientific eagerness, nothing more. From all appearances, she wanted to find the notebook as much as Emmie, yet something about Sarah's offer to help sounded off its mark.

"Thank you, Sarah, but I think I can handle this myself."

If she hadn't been watching closely, she might have missed Sarah's jaw tighten ever so slightly. Disappointment registered in her assistant's eyes, but she accepted the decision without comment.

With more than a bit of trepidation, Emmie pulled her father's watch from a deep pocket sewn into her uniform. "We have time for one more experiment before lunch."

With Sarah trailing, Emmie returned to her work table, no longer certain of her trusted assistant's loyalty.

And that development was the second most troubling event of her morning.

~~~

Two hours later, Emmie sat on the floor in her father's dimly lit study, frustration shredding the last of her hopes. She had looked everywhere—in the large desk, in the credenza behind it, on the bookshelves, even in the whiskey globe. She found nothing.

How would Bart, the investigator, go about this? She pictured his dark penetrating eyes lost in thought as his keen logical mind grappled with the problem. Well, he was not here to impart his wisdom, so the mystery remained hers to solve.

The notebook must be in this room somewhere, or it would have surfaced elsewhere in the house by now. Maybe her father deliberately hid it, but where, and why?

From her position, legs stretched out in front of her, she felt like a child looking for a hidden Christmas present. Dust clung to her yellow day dress as though she'd rolled on the floor. Which she had, trying to determine if there was a concealed compartment within the desk's knee hole. There were none—no mysterious drawers or compartments, and no sliding panels or obscure cubbyholes anywhere. The desk was as solid as it looked.

Defeated, she slouched against the paneling and plopped her head back. A hollow sound emerged from behind her.

Startled, she scrambled to her knees, turned and rubbed her hands over the intricate woodwork seeking the outline of a door. The wall wiggled, instead. Not a door. A movable panel of some type. Heart pounding with discovery, she sprang to her feet as fast as her skirts would allow and fingered the Spanish carvings etched into the wood. No knobs or levers or handholds materialized.

On a hunch, she planted her hands on one side of the panel and pushed in. The board swiveled, the opposite side swinging out with a whoosh.

"Goodness!" She had lived in the house since it was built and never knew the panels opened.

Behind it, valuable books filled floor to ceiling shelves about five feet in width. She pulled out a book. *History and Present Status of*

Electricity by Joseph Priestley, a first edition published in 1767. Thumbing through its delicate yellowed pages, Emmie found an account of Benjamin Franklin's experiment on electricity. How like her father to keep such valuable research sources close to his heart.

She replaced the book, shifted to the next panel and shoved the same way as the first. It, too, opened.

She drew in a sharp breath, her heartbeat quickening.

Notebooks!

A storehouse of them, their spines meticulously dated and arranged in order from before her birth to shortly before her father's death. The one she sought must be among them. The tension between her shoulder blades loosened.

Why did he keep these here while others were stored in the laboratory? Were these notes all ideas he'd tinkered with over the years? There must be hundreds of projects in here. Awe wound through her like a lazy meadow creek, finding its way to her heart. If she was correct, he had been just as interested as she in the products that would use electric power. Their philosophies hadn't been so different after all. He just selected the most urgent as his top priority— getting the energy to the masses. He left the use of that energy to her.

Though she could hardly wait to search this treasure trove for the notes she wanted, her curiosity pulled her to the third and last wall panel.

A true pocket door, this panel disappeared entirely, revealing an extensive collection of exquisite miniature jade and ivory carvings arranged with precision on five of the six shelves.

Curious, Emmie picked one up.

"Oh, my." Heat spiraled through her body, settling low in her belly.

The carving depicted a man and woman in a most provocative position, one she never imagined before, let alone…. Cheeks burning, she returned it to the shelf and examined about fifty similar ones. Slowly. Carefully. Each was equally naughty. And absolutely fascinating. Each figurine featured a different position of sexual intimacy. What wickedness.

Hells, bells! Her father?

Emmie's eyes drifted to the top shelf, to a large rectangular box covered with Mother of Pearl inlay. It possessed a lock, as though any sort of fastening could deter her curiosity. Dragging the desk chair closer, Emmie climbed up and scooped the box into her arms.

The ornate container tucked tight to her bosom, she gingerly descended and set it on the desk. Remembering an odd shaped key in one of the drawers, she retrieved it, wiggled it in the keyhole and turned. The lock snapped open with a soft click.

As she raised the lid, the scent of her father's aftershave sent her reeling. His presence permeated the room. She could almost feel his warmth, hear his raspy voice. Her heartbeat slowed, her breathing quieted. He was here, with her. Calming her. Encouraging her. She was sure of it. She sat in the chair.

On top was the deed to Summerhill, along with its purchase documents marked paid in full. Beneath were ownership papers for the Frisians—Midnight and Ebony. She took each of these documents out and set them in a neat pile, squaring the corners and edges with precision and care.

Next was an engraved invitation to her parents' wedding ceremony and a photograph of the two of them in their wedding clothes. She touched the tintype gently, her finger lovingly caressing first her mother's delicate face, then her father's robust one. She missed them terribly. With the sadness of bereavement, she deposited the invitation and photograph gently on the stack and returned to her exploration of the box's remaining treasures.

The document at the bottom was a thick packet—The Last Will and Testament of Eli Griffith, dated three months before his death.

Emmie lifted the papers out and, as though drawn by an unknown power, read the pages from cover to back. When finished, she stowed them upon the pile with the others.

A profound sense of loss smothered her in a miasma of grief. The will was the last official communication her father left, to be read and dealt with by her—the sole remaining member of his immediate family—and Mr. Toliver, his lawyer. Though five years had passed, tears of grief sprang to her eyes.

A short moment later her head shot up and her spine stiffened. Something about the will was different. But what? She picked up the document from the pile and read it a second time. Nothing came to her.

Until....

Emmie shuffled through the pages to the section describing the transmittal of the company.

Upon my death, Chicagoland Electric will be given to my daughter Emmeline Griffith, with Augustus Toliver retaining ten percent for services rendered or yet to be rendered.

Plain and simply stated.

To be given to her immediately upon his death.

No mention of a delay until she turned twenty-five. Or of the need to marry. Or of Paul inheriting should she fail to marry. In fact... Emmie rifled through the pages again, her confusion growing. Paul's name didn't appear anywhere in the will.

How strange. She remembered seeing it somewhere....

In the papers shown to her by Mr. Toliver. She flipped the document to the last page and recognized her father's bold tilted signature. Was this an earlier will? If so, why would he have changed it so soon after signing this one?

The enormity of her discovery slammed into her consciouness. Had her marriage to Bart been unnecessary? Could she have inherited the company without having to engage in a temporary charade? Avoided the need for an annulment or divorce, or the damage such a thing would do to her reputation? To Bart's?

Memories of her time with Bart flashed through her mind. Memories of his strong arms about her, of his presence across the table, of walking the many paths of Summerhill together, and a thousand other companionable things they'd done since their marriage in name only had begun. Their temporary arrangement had started out platonic, but now she couldn't imagine not kissing him no matter who he disguised himself as, not touching him, not being touched by him.

Despite her criticism of him, she wanted Bart with a passion she couldn't explain. Wanted him both in and out of her bed. A life without Bart was no life at all. She wanted him with her forever.

A small sob escaped her lips. The world as she knew it suddenly collapsed.

She had fallen in love with a man she might never have had to marry in the first place.

Dear, Lord. What a tangle. How was she to bring order to the chaos she now faced?

Three options quickly presented themselves. Dissolve the arrangement immediately, wait until the contract is concluded, or....

Oh, God. Papa, help me. I don't want to end this marriage. Ever!

Yet, she might have brought about its demise all on her own.

She needed to talk to Bart, tell him of her feelings, but first she needed an explanation from Mr. Toliver.

Chapter 21

Damn lock. Bart bent over a valise on his rumpled bed the next morning and struggled with a snap that wouldn't stay shut. Sleep had eluded him all night as his thoughts had cycled over something Reginald had strongly encouraged.

If you want to find happiness in the future, you must forgive yourself as well as those who wronged you.

How did Reginald expect him to accomplish absolution when he couldn't even manage to carry out the simplest of tasks, like locking a small bag?

The animosity Bart harbored toward Murdock, toward his father, and yes, even toward himself, was too powerful a force to rein in, let alone transmute to a pardon for anyone. Now that his emotions had been unleashed, rage consumed him with the need for revenge, or at the very least, the need to hit someone. But who? His father was dead, and Murdock's whereabouts were unknown.

Bart scooped up his still open valise and slammed it across the bed. Clothes flew in all directions. *Shit.* He shuffled to the opposite side of the bed, stuffed the displaced items in the bag, and banged on the snaplock with the side of his fist. The lock held. He grunted his approval and tugged the valise off the bed.

From where was this forgiveness, this pardon of abhorrent acts supposed to come? From his rational thoughts? From his turbulent emotions? From deep in his soul?

Impossible.

He didn't have it in him. To forgive meant to forget, and he would never forget.

Someone banged the front door knocker twice, interrupting his murderous cogitation. What now? He glanced at his pocket watch. Only forty minutes to catch the next train back to Libertyville and to Emmie. He had much to tell her.

Bart hurried down the stairs and peered through the sheer curtain covering the side window. A boy of about twelve danced from one foot to the other, a yellow envelope in his hand.

Bart's heart skipped a beat. Only Gertie and Cedric, and by now, Emmie, knew he was in the city. Something must be terribly wrong for them to wire when he was expected home in only a few hours.

Bart opened the door. The odor of horses and offal met his nostrils.

"Telegram, sir." A knapsack slung over one shoulder, the boy shoved the envelope in his hands and waited expectantly.

Digging into his pocket, Bart produced a shiny new quarter and handed it over. "Now don't spend this too quickly."

The young man's eyes widened, and a pleased smile ripped across his soot-stained face. He flipped the coin, then dropped it in his shoulder bag. "I won't, mister. Thank you. Appreciate it."

Bart closed the door, the warmth of the boy's delight cutting through his foreboding for the briefest of moments. With stiff, tense fingers, he slit the envelope and extracted the message.

EMMIE TO SEE LAWYER STOP GERTIE AND I WITH HER STOP WORRIED STOP MEET US STOP CEDRIC

Bart crumpled the paper in his fist. Why does she want to talk to Toliver, and why today? The meeting struck him as being rushed, as though arranged at the last minute. Had it been made earlier, she would have mentioned it, wouldn't she? And why was Cedric worried?

The whole thing didn't make sense.

Unless....

Breath fled. Panic buffeted him like a rogue wave. Emmie planned to dissolve their marriage. It was the only explanation for why she would seek out Toliver's services on such short notice. Shock rooted him to the spot.

She wouldn't, would she? No. She couldn't. Not without giving him a chance. A fierce pressure squeezed his chest like a vice. *Emmie, don't do this. Don't leave me.*

Even though they were supposed to live together for only three months, he knew he wanted to live with her forever in a marriage that was real. When he was with her he felt alive, wakened from a deadened world devoid of color, of energy, and of vitality. With Emmie, the future beckoned, luring him like a seductress across the barren landscape of his unhappy past. She was the family he never had and didn't know he wanted. In her arms, he was whole, safe from the sea of darkness and loneliness his life had been before she walked into it.

He loved her, loved her with every part of his soul. He would do anything for her. Anything to remain with her.

Even come to her bed as himself, open and vulnerable, risking failure.

Even forgive, if it came to that.

"Emmie, please don't leave me!" His plea, thick with emotion he couldn't hold back, slid from his lips as if she were standing before him.

Bart glanced at his timepiece again. His hand trembled. Too late to meet the incoming train, but if he hurried, he might be able catch them before they met with Toliver. He needed to tell her he loved her.

And beg her for a second chance.

~~~

The hansom cab lurched to a stop before the Rookery Building on the busy downtown street. The noise of horses, carriages, wagons and people crowded Emmie's senses. Even the smells of the city were different. More pungent.

Emmie straightened her shoulders and waited for Cedric to descend the stairs before scooting to the door to accept his waiting hand. Gertie followed close behind.

Emmie had wanted to come alone, but Gertie would have none of it. She and Cedric practically brow-beat her into submitting to their company. They insisted she needed guarding, claimed her husband would have their hides if something happened to her. Especially after the latest attempts on her life.

Once on the sidewalk, Emmie strained her neck to view the tall face of the red stone building through the bright morning haze. Dryness invaded her mouth, and her heart pounded louder than the street noise. She hated this building—hated its height, the closeness of its elevators, its long corridors of nothing but identical office doors. They made her dizzy, set her stomach to churning.

But she would endure it all to discover which of her father's wills was true.

With Gertie and Cedric on either side like bookends, Emmie entered the light-infused atrium lobby and headed for the bank of elevators. "Mr. Toliver is on the eighth floor."

Gertie inspected the row of decorative elevator doors with interest. "Oh, me lord. This is the first of these contraptions I have been in. Does this thing move fast?"

"Not too fast, but then again not fast enough. I don't like them." Emmie's pulse picked up its pace.

Gertie peered at her, excitement filling her eyes. "Sure now, it would be fun."

"I don't see anything enjoyable about them at all." They reminded her of a small water closet in motion, enough to make her stomach revolt.

"Well, let's have a see." The doors opened, and Gertie stepped inside, nodding politely to the elderly man at the controls and several people who followed them in.

The solid steel outer door, followed by the inner wrought iron doors, slammed shut. *Dear Lord, keep us safe.* The elevator started with a lurch, and the walls of the shaft, visible through the flimsy grillwork of the ascending cage, flew by. Emmie shut her eyes and counted silently. Twice the lift car jerked to a halt to let people off. The third time, the operator called, "Eighth floor. Watch your step."

Emmie opened her eyes, gingerly stepped over the sliver of open shaft to the marble floor, and started down the hall.

"I do say, a rather enjoyable experience, that." Cedric's clipped accent came from a few feet behind her. "Can you slow down a might, Mrs. Turner. My poor old bones are not quite what they used to be."

Emmie slowed. "Sorry. I didn't realize I was walking so swiftly. As I said, I want to meet with Mr. Toliver and leave here as soon as I can."

A few slower-paced moments later, they stood before the law offices of Toliver & Company at the end of the hall. Cedric opened the door. Emmie breezed into the tiny, ornate vestibule and came to a sudden stop.

In place of kindly Mrs. Simmons was a younger woman with blonde hair styled in the latest fashion. Heavily rouged cheeks created a somewhat garish, cheap appearance that ruined the effect of her hairstyle. She smiled, her face friendly though her eyes held a vapid, bored expression.

Emmie walked to the desk. "I have an appointment with Mr. Toliver. My name is Emmeline Gri . . . Turner."

The woman shuffled some papers on her desk and pulled a folded note from under a ledger. "Oh, Mr. Toliver asked if you could join him in front of the Women's Building at the Exposition. He had a visit scheduled with another client at the Fair and thought it would be more convenient for you both. He assumed you had an exhibitor's admission pass." She glanced at Cedric and Gertie. "Um, I think he was expecting you to be alone."

Cedric coughed. "Well, now. She is not alone, is she?"

The woman's blue eyes sparked to life as she raked over Cedric's impeccable gentleman's attire. An Englishman through and through, he appeared a man of means and substance, someone who'd garner attention wherever he went.

A coy smile sprang to the woman's face. "No, she certainly isn't."

Before Cedric, or for that matter, Gertie, could respond, Emmie pivoted and grabbed his arm. "Come. Let's go. I need the air, anyway."

Ten minutes later, Cedric handed Emmie and Gertie up to a hailed hansom cab and directed the driver to the Elevated Rail Depot at Congress Street, the fastest way of getting to the Exposition's main gate in Jackson Park.

Gertie settled the skirts of her serviceable blue dress and huffed out a long breath. "Another client or no, Mr. Toliver sure picked a busy place to meet. Too busy, if you ask me."

An unsettling feeling banded around Emmie's chest. She hadn't given the matter of safety much thought. Had she made a mistake in coming to the city without notifying Bart?

~~~

Bart's hansom cab stopped on a corner near the Rookery Building as another left with its passengers.

Eager to find Emmie, he jumped out and handed his fare up to the coachman who had maneuvered his team with expertise through the congested downtown streets. Bart prayed he was in time to stop her from beginning divorce proceedings.

He pushed his way through the crowded doorway into the lobby. After taking the mezzanine stairs two at a time, he stopped and leaned over the balcony railing, hoping to spot Emmie among the throng of people below. When his search proved fruitless, disappointment nearly choked him.

He ran to the elevators and punched the up button with more force than intended. A long, loud call buzzer sounded somewhere behind the closed doors. *Shit man! Hurry up.* He paced outside the row of lift cars until finally one opened at the far end.

What felt like an hour later, he found himself on the eighth floor where he remembered the lawyer's office to be. Dashing down the hall, he reached Toliver and Company in the corner and strode in. A young blonde-haired woman occupied the desk in the outer lobby.

"Is Mrs. Turner here?" he asked.

The lady smiled in interest. "Your name, sir?"

"Mr. Turner."

"Oh." Disappointment filtered through her eyes, but her smile remained, if less genuine.

"No, I'm afraid she's not."

"She came to see Mr. Toliver this morning."

"Oh, *that* lady. Quite in a hurry, that one. Mr. Toliver left a note asking her to meet him by the Women's Building at the Exposition. She left about fifteen minutes ago."

Damn! He missed her. But why the Exposition?

He donned his most seductive smile. "Did she happen to say what the meeting was about?"

"Well, not when I saw her, but when she telephoned yesterday, she mentioned something about seeing his copy of her father's will."

Lightheadedness left him reeling. She *was* considering a way out of the marriage. Forcing the smile to remain frozen on his face, he thanked the woman and dashed out the door.

He had to stop Emmie. Had to tell her he loved her and would do whatever she desired.

He wanted her in his life. Or his life was not worth living.

~~~

Emmie showed the man in the ticket booth her exhibitor's pass, then paid the fifty cent entrance fees for both her companions. This was her first visit to the Exposition since Opening Day.

Cedric placed her hand on his arm and led her away from a particularly noisy family behind them. "Mrs. Turner, we would have purchased our own tickets."

"I wouldn't have it any other way, Cedric. You're not here as a visitor, and this expense is mine. I'm sure it would be what Bart wanted."

Cedric nodded without saying anything, but his eyes were directed behind her. She turned and stared into the face of a young man in his early twenties wearing a red bandanna about his neck. The man nodded and quickly averted his eyes before walking past them.

"Do you know him?"

A slight flush suffused Cedric's cheeks. He withdrew a

handkerchief from his pocket and wiped his forehead. "Thought I did, but it wasn't him. Hot day, isn't it?"

Before she could answer, someone pushed into her from behind. She stumbled. Drat!

Cedric reached out to steady her, then addressed the person at her back. "Here, here, sir. There's no reason to rush."

Emmie turned, peered first at the red-faced man in his Sunday best, and then at the gathering throng cramming the gates behind him. She expected the Columbian Exposition to draw crowds, but the sheer numbers of people waiting to pay their entrance fee was astonishing.

Momentarily trapped by two elderly ladies arranging their pocketbooks, Gertie finally appeared at her side. "Would ye look at all the people. There must be hundreds here."

Cedric reached for Emmie's hand and wrapped it about his arm, concern wrinkling his normally placid features. "More like thousands, Gertie. Which way to the Women's Building, Mrs. Turner?"

Emmie stood on tiptoe to get her bearings, but all she saw were multitudes of people much taller than she. As an exhibitor, however, she visited the fairgrounds many times to set up her displays before opening day. She knew the layout well.

Closing her eyes, she visualized the vast acreage of large white exhibit halls in relation to the front gate. They had entered near the Transportation Building, a colossal structure consisting of three train sheds and acres of space housing entire trains and displays of other forms of conveyance.

"I believe we go north between the Transportation and Mining Buildings, past the Horticulture Building and the lagoon. The Women's Building is just beyond the south entrance to the Midway. Quite the walk, but it's a lovely day."

"If we don't get shoved around in the process," Gertie mumbled behind her.

Ten minutes later, and only halfway there, Emmie headed for a bench along the lagoon's balustrade and lowered herself gingerly.

"Had I known we'd be coming here, I'd have worn different shoes." She wiggled one pointed toe boot.

Gertie plunked down beside her. "Me, too." But her friend's shoes, with their rounded toes and low heels, looked far more comfortable than Emmie's fashionable higher heeled ones.

"Isn't the building we're looking for over there?" Cedric, a guide map in one hand, pointed to a large structure resembling an Italian

Renaissance villa at the end of the walkway.

"That's it. We're almost there." Emmie rose and shook out her skirts. Her toes painfully made their objections known.

As they approached the Midway intersection, a crowd of eastbound visitors pushed across their path, separating Emmie from Cedric and Gertie. Emmie halted, waiting for an opportunity to ford the river of humanity flowing at right angles to her objective.

From out of the mass, a man wearing a bowler grabbed her arm in a vise-like grip and propelled her up the Midway against the human current. Alarmed, she struggled, catching sight of her assailant.

Mr. Toliver!

Instantly, she relaxed. "You're just the person I was coming to see. I thought we were meeting in front of the Women's Building."

He tightened his grip. Pain shot clear to her shoulder. Alarm bells ringing in her head made her dizzy. "Mr. Toliver, I'm afraid we've lost my companions."

"Good."

What? She must have misheard him above the cacophony of sound along the concourse. Her anxiety quickly escalated.

She pulled against his arm. "Where are we going?"

"Someplace where we can talk alone."

"Why couldn't we meet at your office? My friends would have waited in your reception area."

"Not private enough, my dear." Hard and biting, the edge in his voice made the devil's own sound like a squeak.

Her now racing heart beat loud in her ears. Whatever was going on, she knew without a doubt she had to get away. Emmie yanked her arm again. This time it slipped from his grasp, but his other hand immediately flew up near her face. The blade of a jagged-edged knife flashed in the sun.

"You wouldn't want the rest of your face scarred now, would you?" A statement, not a question, spoken in a malevolent murmur that chilled her bones. "You'll do just as I ask, or I won't hesitate to use this."

Her legs turned to rubber, and the world began to spin. She struggled to remain upright.

Mr. Toliver shifted the knife behind her, out of view of nearby onlookers. The sharp point dug through her clothes and into her corset.

A sob seeped from her lips before she collected her wits.

Don't you dare be a ninny.

Straightening she surreptitiously scanned the street. Though surrounded by hundreds of people, nobody paid attention to her plight. No chance of a rescue appeared imminent.

She was on her own.

But... she had played the captive enough times as a child to remember she must wait for the right opportunity to escape, to leave this nightmare behind.

It was the waiting part haunting her now.

Chapter 22

His patience torn to shreds, Bart pushed through the Exposition's crowded main entrance gate, only to be accosted by a young man wearing a red bandanna.

Scanning the entrance grounds for Emmie, Bart pushed the youth aside without a glance in his direction. "Excuse me."

"Mr. Turner?"

Bart stopped in his tracks, his eyes directed at the individual who now had latched on to his jacket sleeve. "Henry. I didn't see you there. Sorry."

Bart's eyes roamed over the tall, well-muscled man his former street friend had become. Henry had been the youngest of the boys to join his gang before he met Reginald. "I heard you were working here."

"I'm a guard at the entrance gate. Make sure nobody gets through without paying. I saw your man here earlier, but didn't know you'd show up."

"Cedric? You've seen him? Where? I have to find them. I think they were headed towards the Women's Building." He turned, distracted. Where the hell was the Women's Building?

"They went that way." Henry pointed north. "I already alerted my network that Cedric was here and gave descriptions of the three of 'em. They've got their eyes peeled for 'em. If you need help, look for the red bandannas." He fingered his own.

"Thanks, Henry. Somehow, I knew you'd have your own group one day." Bart raced off in the direction Henry had indicated.

Breathing hard, Bart shoved his way through the throng crowding the avenue. Before long he spotted Cedric standing on a bench like a beacon, methodically searching the human herd in front of a sign identifying the Women's Building. Gertie stood on the pavement below, doing much the same. When he finally reached them, Bart sat to catch his breath and wipe the sweat off his brow.

He peered up at Cedric and managed to sputter, "Why are you standing up there? Where's Emmie? Is she meeting already with Toliver?"

Was he too late? His aching muscles tensed at the possibility.

Cedric's cheeks bloomed red, and not from the blazing sun. "We lost her in the press of people coming out of the Midway."

"What do you mean lost her?"

Irritation flared. How could Cedric be so careless? Glancing about, Bart soon tempered his opinion. The crush of people at the intersection was so intense it would be easy to be swept along in the flow of pedestrian traffic. If she wasn't nearby, she would be difficult to find.

And she was alone. With a possible killer on the loose. Someone he hadn't yet identified.

A chilling thought. The air Bart had pulled into his lungs disappeared. He should have been with her.

"We turned around and she wasn't behind us, sir. Been more than five minutes and no sign of her."

Concern invaded Cedric's tone, as did a note of contrition, but now was not the time to lay blame. Finding Emmie was far more important. Bart dug his fingers through his hatless hair. "Do you remember what she was wearing, Gertie?"

His beleaguered second assistant rung her hands as her eyes continued to dart among the crowd. "Her emerald green traveling suit."

His mind conjured up the outfit he'd seen her wear on several occasions. It was her favorite. His, too. It hugged her shapely form like skin, highlighting her best attributes, the ones he never tired of admiring both with or without clothing. "Was she wearing a hat?"

Gertie's attention swung to Bart. "Oh, yes, sir. A wide brimmed, straw one, it was. With a green feather like so." Her hand flipped up in the general shape and position of the plume.

A spark of hope ignited in his chest. Bart leaped atop the bench next to Cedric. The six-inch height difference over his first assistant gave him a distinct advantage in seeing over the heads of the crowd.

Unfortunately, every woman in attendance wore a hat, some straw with wide brims, some with feathers and some without.

Which one belonged to Emmie?

Bart scanned north to south, combing the sea of bobbing hats, lingering longer on the lighter colored ones that might be straw. None of the wearers sported a bright green traveling suit.

He turned toward the Midway, a broad avenue about a mile in length connecting Jackson Park to Washington Park, home to the amusements and attractions not part of the Exposition. A veritable haven for pickpockets and other unsavory types he knew to inhabit crowded places. He ground his teeth at the thought of Emmie alone, a vulnerable target to every thief and thug on the prowl.

Let alone killer.

In the distance, he spotted a light-colored hat on a woman walking next to a man wearing a bowler. Though unable to discern the color of her dress, Bart's instincts told him the woman was Emmie. He recognized the way she walked, the way she carried herself. Controlled. Confident. In charge of her surroundings. The Exposition was her arena.

But who was with her? Toliver?

Bart pointed in her direction. "I think she's way down there, perhaps with Toliver."

At least Bart hoped it was him despite the topic he imagined they might be discussing. But why were they walking up the Midway without Gertie or Cedric when the man asked her to meet him at the Women's Building? The sour taste of dread filled his mouth. Something struck him as being off. Way off.

He did another scan of the Midway and found a half dozen or so people wearing red bandannas, all standing and pointing down the Midway in Emmie's direction. A closer inspection showed them to be street sweepers and vendors, cafe waiters, and a variety of seemingly distasteful types, their only commonality, the red bandannas worn about their necks. How clever of Henry to mark his informants.

Heart pounding, Bart jumped to the pavement and threaded his way up the crowded avenue, his assistants close behind.

He had to reach Emmie before... before what? Damn! To hell with the divorce. If it came, it came. He would think about it later. Emmie's safety was his priority now, and his instincts told him she might be in more danger than she realized.

~~~

Thousands of visitors moving in both directions packed the popular Midway, talking, laughing, oohing and aahing over the exotic sights offered by nations around the world. However, no one knew that a knife prodded Emmie's ribs. Struggling against her captor was useless, unless she wanted to end her life amid an oblivious crowd.

Between the hot sun beating down and the lack of a cooling lake breeze, the weather proved oppressive. Removing her hat might have helped, but she feared shifting her arms, feared even moving the upper part of her body lest the blade dig further into her side.

Rivulets of sweat trickled down her face, between her breasts, along the insides of her thighs, but she was powerless to do anything but continue to walk. Her increasing frustration added another hue to the striation of emotions plaguing her now.

With the knife's sharp edge at her waist, Toliver guided her past block after block of foreign and private exhibits she would have found fascinating at any other time. They walked past the Laplander exhibit with its reindeer and sleds, and a German village, and two Irish villages where one could kiss the Blarney stone. The day grew hotter, and the crowds increased. Her throat was parched.

A street sweeper with a red bandanna appeared suddenly out of nowhere, his trashcan directly in Toliver's path. Her captor stumbled, the knife stabbing hard against a corset rib. His hold on her arm loosened. Heart pounding, Emmie twisted away, but before she could run, Toliver righted himself and yanked her arm close.

Defeat annihilated the tiny spark of hope that had flared for an instant, its deadening weight squeezing the breath from her lungs. If she was to escape, she had to react faster when another such opportunity struck, or if.

Open your eyes, Emmie. Surely another chance to escape this nightmare will show itself. Be ready for it.

They passed the bazaars of Algiers, and a Japanese encampment with gardens and teahouses, and a street in Cairo. The exotic smells of the world's foods also filled the Midway, but Emmie's appetite had long since disappeared. They passed Samoans working on grass huts, Central Africans dancing to unfamiliar rhythms, and a thunderous eruption of Kilauea Volcano.

And all the while, Emmie searched for her opportunity, her eyes and ears open to escape, to that one moment when a distraction presented itself.

Ahead was the Old Vienna exhibit as the city appeared in the mid-eighteenth century, with cafes, shops, homes, town hall and exhibitors dressed in folk costumes of the day, some wearing red bandannas like the one the street sweeper had worn.

Suddenly, her heart stopped. Beyond Old Vienna, a monster loomed out of the ground—the Ferris Wheel, a structure rising more than two hundred and sixty feet. As sure as she breathed, she knew this was where they were headed. To one of the thirty-six cars cycling on the giant circle high above the fair grounds.

Control fled as panic seared her insides. She stopped in her tracks. "No. I'm not going."

"Oh, but you will, my dear. To the very top. The view is said to be magnificent." Menace radiated beneath the surface of Toliver's syrupy sweet tone.

Terror's chilling fingers twisted through her brain, freezing her thoughts.

A group of unruly boys jostled past them, all wearing the now familiar red bandanna. Her kidnapper loosened his hold for a fraction of a second.

Emmie pulled away.

Pulse racing, she fled between the buildings, to the back of one of the cafes. To a man in a blood-stained apron emptying a foul-smelling pail of kitchen scraps into a large wagon.

She latched on to his arm as though it were a life ring. "Please, sir, a man kidnapped me. I need somewhere to hide."

The confused kitchen worker shrugged his shoulders as though he didn't understand her. Once again, hope vanished.

"There you are, my dear. I thought I'd lost you." Chest heaving, Toliver slammed into her, his fingers biting into her arm. Though he smiled, anger smoldered in his eyes. "Don't be afraid. You'll see. The experience will be magical."

She shuddered. The only magic she wanted to experience was her escape. She opened her mouth to scream, but Toliver threw one arm around her shoulders and pressed the knife against her side with the other.

"You make one sound and I'll cut you now. No one would know it was me because I'd be swallowed by the crowd."

Tears formed, but she willed them not to fall. *Do what he says, Emmeline.*

She headed in the direction she was pushed—toward the Ferris Wheel. The pavement burned through the thin soles of her tight shoes. She swallowed hard, fighting for control over her ever-present fear.

A few minutes later, he shifted positions. Her arm was now

twisted painfully behind her, and instead of the sharp edge of a knife, she felt the blunt end of a pistol prodding her side.

"Why are you doing this? I have done nothing to you."

"Stop talking and keep walking."

The closer they came to the ticket house at the base of the Ferris Wheel, the more her beleaguered stomach revealed its impending revolt. The bones of her corset now pinched so tight she could barely breathe. Her vision shimmered and waned.

Don't faint. Eyes straight ahead, she avoided gazing upon the object of her panic—Mr. Ferris's revolving steel contraption.

Bartholomew! I have so much to tell you, so many things I kept hidden from you. And now you'll never know.

She prayed like she had never prayed before.

And inspiration soon struck. Not in how to escape, but rather in how to survive. She must conquer her overwhelming fear of heights. The fear she'd acquired when Paul surprised her in the tree house where she'd gone to grieve after her mother's death. Where she would have been violated had she not jumped the thirty feet to the ground, tearing her cheek on a sharp-edged branch as she fell.

She straightened her shoulders, looked directly at the Ferris Wheel, at its top. *Don't let him win, Emmeline.*

The mouth of the gun dug into her lowest rib. "That's right. Control your fear."

Despite her best effort to stop it, the ominous encouragement whispered in her ear only added to her terror.

He pushed her up to the ticket window. The weapon disappeared from her side, but his grip on her arm tightened. He waved four ten dollar bills before the agent's nose. "I want the entire car for myself, without the operator."

Noooo! Emmie's heart sank. Nothing untoward would happen in a crowded car, but with no witnesses....

The startled agent eyed the money, then the person making the request. "Sixty tickets times fifty cents apiece is only thirty dollars, sir."

"The extra ten is for you to make it happen."

The man's eyes lit. "Yes sir." He counted out sixty tickets and handed them over in exchange for the bills.

Toliver hustled her through the wheelhouse, to one of the multi-level platforms where passengers met the cars stopping to reload. He gave the tickets to the ride's operator, who ushered them to an empty car with a smirk. She choked back a startled cry. Did he think they were lovers?

"Get in, my dear." Toliver shoved her inside and pulled the door closed himself. The car rose.

Gritting her teeth to keep from screaming, Emmie turned to face her kidnapper.

~~~

Chest squeezed tight as a vise, Bart ground to a stop in front of an Old Vienna cafe and cast about for the cream-colored straw hat he'd been following or someone from Henry's red bandanna network. He found neither.

"Lost her," he mumbled, venting his upset.

As he bent to catch his breath, Cedric and Gertie drew up beside him, both struggling to fill their lungs in the stifling heat. The usual lake breeze was practically non-existent. The fair's location, originally a marsh at the lake's edge, amplified the already thick humid air.

Still fighting to breathe, he wiped the sweat off his forehead with a handkerchief he pulled from his jacket pocket. He had to find her, but how? The crush of bodies seemed to increase by the minute.

A few seconds later, Gertie pointed. "There."

Hope unfurling, Bart's eyes followed her finger to two young fairgoers sporting Henry's bandannas. Both pointed up at a Ferris Wheel car rising behind Old Vienna, to a man standing close to a woman wearing a cream-colored hat.

Emmie!

The seriousness of her situation hit him with the force that nearly knocked him off his feet.

Emmie was afraid of heights almost to the point of panic.

He forced his mouth to work despite his tongue's dry, thickened state. "Follow me."

Bart shoved his way through the Old Vienna exhibit, his mind working as feverishly as his legs. What would he do once he reached the Wheel? Emmie was already in the air.

Darting this way and that, Bart halted far enough back to study the entire structure. He shaded his eyes with his hand and craned his neck up. Emmie's car was empty, only two people, while the rest of the cars were packed. How had that happened? Long lines of thrill seekers waiting to ride the attraction still snaked in front of the ticket booth.

And who was the man beside her? Though distance separated them, Bart focused hard on the man's features

Toliver.

The bastard damn well knew Emmie was afraid of heights.

Anger ripped through Bart like a summer tornado. Toliver was up to no good, and there was nothing Bart could do to stop him.

A shattering sense of helplessness nearly dropped him to his knees, the emotion familiar yet different, and just as debilitating as when he was a frightened little boy. Only now it was Emmie in danger of being harmed, Emmie, his beautiful, beloved wife for whom he feared. Alone and vulnerable. Just as he had been all those years ago, unable to control the circumstances in which he found himself.

As if the clouds shrouding a part of Bart's mind suddenly lifted, Reginald's words finally made sense. He had been as helpless and as guiltless as Emmie was now. How could he continue to blame himself for what happened when Emmie was not to blame for what was happening to her.

The epiphany should have lifted his spirits, but it didn't. It only added to his anxiety.

"Fire!" The shout came from a man somewhere near the Wheel.

Startled, Bart stepped back as a panicked throng bolted toward him from the wheelhouse. His sweaty fingers turned cold and clammy. First height, and now fire? Jesus, what next?

He pulled a rushing man aside. "Where?"

The man pointed behind him. "In the car exit area. See the smoke?"

Heart in his throat, Bart ran to the back of the wooden building to investigate for himself. Flames shot from a platform where passengers usually disembarked. Metal gears screeched, the sound loud and irritating, like a scratch on a chalkboard. The giant mass of revolving steel lurched to a stop. The Wheel's cars, each the size of a horse-drawn trolley, swayed precariously on massive axles.

Emmie! He craned his neck up again. Emmie and Toliver were trapped in the uppermost car.

~~~

The car stopped with a sudden jerk. Opening her eyes, fangs of terror gripped Emmie's innards.

She was at the top of the world! Below to the right, the Midway stretched to the east, to the Exposition's white palaces, the lagoon and grand basin, and the dome of the Administration Building. Beyond lay the shimmering waves of the lake, and the vague shorelines of Indiana and Michigan.

She swayed. Her vision darkened. *I will not faint!* Arms clasped over her churning stomach, she backed up to one of the car's swivel chairs where she landed with a graceless thud.

"Why?" She glared at her kidnapper.

Toliver's eyes were cold and menacing. Her breath caught.

"Why indeed! You don't deserve Chicagoland Electric. That company should be all mine, not just a measly ten percent. I made all the decisions. I raised all the money. I created all the necessary paperwork."

Indignation penetrated Emmie's thick veil of fear. Fire settled in her cheeks, and not from the heat of the day.

She rose on wobbly legs. The pistol was still in his hand, still trained on her. "What do you mean, you did all the work? My father's genius created it—his dreams, his inventions, his foresight, his knowledge, his view of the future."

Toliver stiffened. His unoccupied hand curled into a fist. "How do you think he got there, my dear? He followed my suggestions, my legal advice, my business acumen. Your father didn't know a damn thing about how to run the company." His voice sounded maniacal, his words spilling out fast, hard and with the venom of a viper. "He was a scientist, a thinker who wrote in notebooks all day long. I made the company what it is today, and I deserved more than just a piece. I'm going to get it all."

"How?" Emmie's heart banged against her ribs.

His eyes grew wild, crazed. He scared her witless, more even than her fear of heights. The man was clearly insane. And he held a gun.

"You're going to sign over ownership to me."

Her eyes widened. "Never."

He stroked his chin, the unhinged expression intensifying. "It's a long way down, Emmie. Especially if you accidentally fall from the car."

She stilled. Memories of hurtling out of the tree house haunted her. The seemingly endless drop through the air, the pain ripping her cheek, the blow to her shoulder as she landed on the leaf-softened ground. The blood! Her hand flew to her scar.

She'd fallen only thirty feet then. But this... the Wheel was.... *Dear Lord! I'm going to die.*

She forced herself to focus on Toliver, forced the terror back into the dark corners of her brain. Logical thinking was needed here. The unthinkable finally solidified into a revelation that tore at her insides. How had she missed it?

"You are the one who tried to kill me." More a question than a statement. She needed to hear the truth.

A flash of pride drifted through Toliver's eyes. "Those men I hired failed, but I knew every step you took, every place you went. There would be another opportunity, and there was. But my plan began long before that."

Dread wormed its way through her chest.

"You were supposed to marry Paul, you know, but you chose Alex, instead. Paul was more pliant than Alex, so I eliminated your first choice and when that German oaf dropped into the picture, I eliminated your second choice as well. Paul would inherit the company, and as his business adviser, I would make sure I eventually owned it."

She drew in a breath. "Wait, wait! You killed Alex and Mr. Bormeister so you could insert Paul in their place?"

The man was pure evil. Alex—her fiancée, her beloved friend—had been a pawn in Toliver's scheme, a pawn used to further this crazy man's ambition. An innocent in all this, Alex had died as a result. And poor Mr. Bormeister. All he ever wanted was to stay in this country. Guilt assailed her already jumbled emotions.

"Alex was a dolt. He knew nothing of Chicagoland Electric, but I soon realized he would never allow me to take over once he gained control. I didn't kill Alex. I manipulated Sarah into cutting his saddle in a strategic spot, then I took care of your German friend."

A knife twisted in her heart. "Sarah was in on this?"

To suspect her of disloyalty was one thing, but to hear her suspicions confirmed was another thing entirely. Betrayal by a dear friend was more than she could bear.

An icy smile slid across Toliver's features. "The woman fancies herself in love with me, you know. I went along with it to have someone on the inside doing my bidding."

Sarah's unknown lover. Bart was right.

"Did you kill Paul as well?"

He waved the gun in her face. "When you turned up married to Turner, Paul lost his usefulness. I simply cleaned house."

Toliver might have been mad as a bedlamite, but he demonstrated more than just a willingness to tell the truth. He even bragged about the cleverness of his plans. Questions bombarded her like hail stones.

Making an assumption about the two wills, she broached the subject she'd come to discuss. "I found a will in Father's study, but it didn't contain the stipulation of marriage to inherit the company. Yet, you showed me a copy saying exactly that. Why did you falsify the document?"

"I had to put roadblocks in your path, or you'd have inherited Chicagoland Electric right after your father died. I needed more time. Unfortunately, after Alex's and Bormeister's deaths, I never figured you'd thwart my plans by actually marrying someone else."

Her knees weakened. Her thoughts swung wildly, disjointed beyond all logical perimeters. Questions flew out of her mouth in no particular order. "The poisoned jam?"

"Sarah spotted an opportunity and took it, believing I would approve. I did. She ground some larkspur leaves she found in your garden and mixed it in your jam. Sadly for me, the effort failed."

Oh, God! "The rest of my family? Bart thinks they were murdered. Were they?" Emmie struggled to remain on her feet.

"Patience, Emmie. I exercised extreme patience. Paul gave me the idea ten years ago. Paul set the fire in the barn out of revenge. Sarah discovered his complicity, told me, and I used it to blackmail the poor sot. With Edward dead, it was simple to terminate the remaining competition. Your mother drank herself into a grave after Edward's death. She routinely put a little laudanum in her tea to dull her senses. It didn't take much for Sarah to add a little more to one of her special brews. Your father was easy also. Sarah used rat poisoning in small amounts in his coffee to make your father sick."

The contents of Emmie's stomach rose. She swallowed hard, willing herself to remain under control. The vile blackguard must not get away with this.

Toliver reached into his jacket pocket and drew out several folded sheets of paper and a fountain pen. "Now, my dear, it's time for you to sign your name."

Emmie backed away and began to pace. *Think, girl, think.* He'd threatened to throw her out of the car, but now that she knew the truth, he'd never let her live even if she signed the document. She was doomed either way.

She examined the car's interior. Broad panes of glass enclosed the two long sides, but doors at both ends allowed fairgoers to enter and exit in an efficient manner.

Images of Bart flooded her mind. Bart laughing, Bart scowling, Bart thrusting his hands through his hair. Bart making love to her, his hard, strong body touching her, arousing her, filling her completely. She wanted him in her life any way she could have him. She loved him.

Would always love him.

Without warning, an epiphany in all its ugly detail occurred to her. The people she had loved hadn't left her. They'd been taken from her. Murdered by a lunatic—the same deranged person standing before her now.

Emmie stopped her pacing, squared her shoulders, and looked Toliver square in the eye. "You're a monster, and you'll never get away with this. I have no intention of signing away my rights to you or to anyone."

Toliver's face turned crimson. His hand tightened on the pistol, his finger on the trigger twitching ever so slightly. He raised the gun to her head.

Her heartbeat stuttered.

"Once again I must take matters into my own hands. Step closer to the door." He indicated the direction with a motion of his head.

She stood her ground. "No."

He jabbed the weapon into her stomach. "Move, or I'll pull the trigger now."

Her heart pounded with a thunderous rhythm. "You won't do that. If you shoot me, there'd be an investigation and you're the only suspect they'll have. The men you bribed saw me enter this car with you."

He grabbed her arm, twisted it behind her, and thrust her toward the door. "I said move."

She had no choice. He shoved her with his body. A few steps from the door, he twisted around her and pulled it open. A light lake breeze rifled the wide brim of her hat. He stepped behind her. She felt his hands settle on her back. Her racing heart roared in her ears.

He pushed her forward.

Now, Emmie. She jerked to the side.

Momentum sent him stumbling toward the yawning abyss. He toppled over the edge.

Chapter 23

Hanging on to the door frame, Emmie hazarded a peek over the edge. Toliver clung by his fingertips to a steel bar about thirty feet below. He struggled wildly, his legs failing to gain purchase on the steel structure. Seconds later, his perilous grip slipped and, screaming he fell to the wheelhouse roof. A burning wheelhouse roof.

Her belly gave up its contents.

Time ceased as she slowly regained control. Though she despised Toliver, no one should meet his end in such an ignoble fashion.

Leaning against the inside railing, she inched her way to the front window and peered below. Her queasiness returned with a vengeance.

Engulfing the wooden wheelhouse, spikes of red and gold flames danced like Valkyries in the increasing breeze gusting off the lake. She could almost hear the crackle and snap of the inferno below, the sound so ingrained in her memory it readily emerged upon the landscape of her current reality.

Blast and damnation!

Another blaze she couldn't control. Another height she couldn't descend.

Memories of the burning barn tumbled through her mind. Of Paul's hands touching her in the hayloft. Of the fire that followed. Of screaming, terrified horses. Of the roar and thud of falling timber.

Of Eddie trapped beneath. Of the anguish of being pulled away as the flames consumed her beloved twin.

A sob escaped her lips and reverberated in the empty car.

Emmeline, that was then. This is now. Think about your future.

A future with Bart.

Despite the terrible things she said to him, things she now

regretted, she needed him in her life. Forever. Needed his children, his body, his soul. Though their marriage was temporary, if she survived this ordeal, she would work her darnedest to ensure it continued, including accepting whoever he chose to be in her bed.

Oh, Bart. Be whomever you need to be, but don't leave me. I love you and will never leave you. Ever!

She needed a plan, a course of action leading to her goal—a life with her husband. And children. Many children.

Emmie breathed in deeply. Smoke, drifting in through the open door, filled her lungs. She coughed, then struggled to slow her rapid, shallow breathing.

Don't panic. Keep your wits about you.

Think logically. Identify the options, decide on one, and then take action.

The Wheel itself was structurally sound. Its web of steel spokes and axle shaft of some forty tons supported the huge structure without fear of toppling over. But the wheelhouse at its base was made of wood, and the amusement ride rotated into its center. It might be hours, perhaps days, before the ride could be safely turned to let passengers off.

She gritted her teeth and studied the scene out the window. Screams from the cars below pierced her ears even through the glass. She cringed, remembering the shriek of her horses, her own yells, and those of Eddie. Emmie shuddered, mentally shucking off the horrifying images.

Struggling to keep her composure, she strode to the opposite bank of windows. The roof of the car behind her swung precariously, most likely from anxious people trying to figure out a way to reach the ground.

Her heart pumping madly, she jammed her face hard against the window and gaped at the scene directly below through the network of girders. A crowd gathered around the structure like pebbles cast upon a sandy shore. Men from the fire department worked feverishly, yet the blaze was far from out. Off to the side, a patch of red bloomed like a flower.

People jumped from the lowest cars into nets held open by a score of firemen and volunteers. Was that her way off this cycling prison as well?

But, Emmie was in the top car. Alone. Below her stretched the Midway and the roofs and spires of the Exposition's five great buildings, tiny specks far in the distance. Certainly, she couldn't jump, nor could anyone climb to her rescue.

Tears flowed from her eyes now irritated by the rising smoke. A spate of coughing temporarily halted her analysis.

A few minutes later, her options soon became clear.

Stay where she was until the fire was out and the car brought low enough for her to jump like the others. Or rescue herself. The first held the risk of being choked by smothering smoke, and marooned if the mechanical parts failed to start. The second left her more than a little unsettled, yet hopeful.

She studied the structure's architecture. A narrow lattice of steel webbing wrapped around the rim near the Wheel's cars like a safety ladder, its cross-slanted bars offering wide-spaced precarious steps to the bottom.

The more she considered the possibility, the louder her pulse sounded in her ears. One slip on the slanted latticework and she would fall to her death.

Images of Bart flew into her mind. She wanted to be with him more than anything, and the only way to attain her goal was to descend to safety. Like she had when she was twelve and had climbed up a tall tree on a dare. The memory of Alex's smiling face, of his shouted words of encouragement, of his boy's frame braced for her weight when she jumped, was as clear as though it were yesterday.

She'd been scared, but the exhilaration of conquering something neither Jon nor Alex had attempted had been more than worth the effort. Only later, when she hurtled from the tree house to avoid Paul, did her fear of heights gain a foothold. It was time to conquer another untried mountain and rid herself of this irrational fear.

But not dressed in billowing skirts and a breath-stealing corset.

She hesitated. *Gods bones, Emmie.* When had she ever let feminine modesty get in the way of climbing a tree?

With trembling fingers, she unbuttoned her skirt and let it slide to the floor. Next, she discarded her petticoats, her hat, the jacket of her traveling suit, and finally, her corset.

Clad only in pantaloons, a cotton chemise, boots and stockings, she said a quick prayer and gripped the door frame. *Now or never.* Emmie leaned forward, grabbed a vertical bar, and swung her body out to the slanted ladder. Her stomach rose to her throat. Panic quickened her breathing.

Her boot heel caught the crosspiece and held her in place, but the breeze whipped away the remainder of her hairpins, leaving her hair to fly about her head.

One step at a time. Don't look beyond the next rung.

But she did. Her world spun.

Dear Lord, what am I doing?

~~~

The crowd around the Ferris Wheel gasped. A few people wearing red bandannas pointed to the top. Bart's gaze followed them to a barely visible crosshatch of steel attached to one of the outside rims.

His heart lurched. *Damn!*

A white clad figure with flying black hair had begun descending the perilous slanted bars from the Wheel's uppermost car.

Emmie!

Christ.

Terror grabbed his innards. Was she daft? Her foolish scheme put her life in jeopardy. He stabbed his fingers through his hair.

She should have stayed in the car, safe from falling to a gruesome death like Toliver. When the man's body landed in the fire, the army of people gaping at the flaming spectacle screamed. For one horrifying moment, Bart's blood froze. He thought Emmie had been the one to fall, and now, ironically, there she was, putting her life at risk all on her own.

Why couldn't she have been more patient? Eventually the flames would be extinguished, the Wheel mechanism started, and she would be brought to safety. *Damn!* What the hell was she doing?

Yet, despite his alarm, a tiny part of him applauded her pluck. Emmie was spunky, fearless of almost everything, and she possessed the formidable reasoning ability of a seasoned scientist. If she saw a path to her goal, she would take it rather than do nothing.

Like he was doing. *Hell.*

Sweat trickled down his face as the conflagration blended with the sultriness of the day. A sense of helplessness overwhelmed him, squeezing dry the very life flowing in his veins. How could he stand around when Emmie needed his help? He should be climbing the rim and guiding her down, making sure she didn't slip.

The thought spurred him to action. Formulating a plan, Bart pushed through the throng to a fireman holding a ladder.

"Excuse me. I need to borrow this." Bart pulled the ladder from the startled man's arms and ran with it to the lowest horizontal spoke on the circular structure.

The crowd cheered, some people even clapped, but he hardly heard them. He focused on the wildest, craziest rescue he'd ever attempted. Heart pumping madly, he propped the ladder against the steel, climbed to its top, grabbed a rung on the crosshatched section and began his ascent.

Several firemen yelled their objections. He ignored them and continued to climb. Nobody was going to interfere with his rescue of his beloved wife.

Dear Lord, don't let Emmie fall! The higher he went, the more he prayed. He needed to tell her he loved her, that he wanted a family with her, that he would do anything for her, including revealing his darkest secrets.

One step, then another, carefully, his pace slow and steady. By contrast, his thoughts flew through his mind fast and frenzied.

Reginald's voice rang in his ears. *You must forgive the past to find your happiness in the future.*

Emmie was his future, but Bart had yet to reconcile his past.

Oh, he had forgiven himself, and he no longer cared about Murdock. Had no feelings for the man any more. His former tutor was an unforgivable non-entity, someone whose existence didn't matter. He was nothing. Dirt on the ground. Not worth a thought or the time of day.

A slight breeze whisked through Bart's hair. He gazed through the metal web and spotted an American flag lifting listlessly on a pole south of the Midway. For some reason, the flag's presence served as encouragement, a sign that some things were worth risking your life for.

Emmie.

He continued his climb.

Forgive his father? Never. Not when the man hadn't thought enough of his own son to rescue him from a living hell. Withholding forgiveness was Bart's way of punishing him, retribution for the man's failure as a father.

But what if his father had never been loved by his own father, never been shown what it was like to be a real father? Bart knew nothing of his grandfather other than he was a stern preacher given to a no-nonsense approach to life. Or so his mother had told him. How could his father be expected to treat a son with love and respect if he never experienced the same himself? The way Reginald had loved and respected him.

The question filled him with uncertainty. What was the right thing to do? Oh, hell! What difference did it make, anyway? His father was dead. What good would forgiving a dead man do?

Not a damn thing.

But, for the living...?

Startled by the thought, his foot slipped on the bar and slid to the tight angled corner of a cross-hatch. His heart skipped a beat. He gripped the side rail with sweaty palms, forcing his attention back to his climb. To Emmie.

Yet his attention soon returned to his tumultuous thoughts.

Was forgiveness good for the person doing the forgiving? Could Bart really change his attitude toward his father?

In the scheme of things, his father was not important. Not really. Hell, he was not even a father. Not in the sense Reginald had been, a man who never had children of his own. Maybe his mentor's suggestion did have merit. Maybe Bart might be able to forgive his father, or at the very least, not allow him to influence his thoughts and actions.

If he wanted to, that is.

Let it go, Bart. Let it go. Concentrate on the future. On Emmie, on their life together. On their children. Suddenly a profound sense of peace pervaded his soul. Weightless, breathless calm and contentment. Serenity. Love.

He had much to tell her.

Bart breathed in deeply, then choked. Smoke, thick and black, filled his lungs.

~~~

Emmie halted her slow descent and wrapped her aching arms around the vertical bars to rest. The breeze had increased, but not enough to drive away the dense smoke that made navigating the slanted lattice work more difficult. Despite the heat, her cold, clammy hands slipped with regularity, and the heels of her boots hindered her foot placement.

She peered through the haze to the distant parts of the Midway, now crammed with people running in her direction. Held briefly at bay, long fingers of panic began creeping along her nerve endings.

Breathe, breathe.

She sucked air into her lungs, then gagged on the smoke. She could almost taste the fire's acrid odor. Thick, dark vapors filled her nostrils and burned her eyes.

Memories of the long-ago barn fire ripped through her mind. She had temporarily dulled her fear of the flames by concentrating on her climb, but now the horrors below reached up to taunt her. She shut her eyes, shutting out the nightmare tramping through her dreams for the past ten years. Yet in her heart, she knew she would never forget Eddie's terror-filled eyes, his screams, the awful smell of burning flesh.

Emmie bit her bottom lip, hoping the pain would return her to the present.

It did. With a wallop. After a smoke-filled breath caused a spate of coughing that rattled her ribcage.

Whatever you do, don't look down!

But the tug of curiosity was far too great. She squinted through the smoke and steel webbing at the commotion below. Firemen poured water on the inferno from a pumper wagon. A ring of people held large nets between the two wheel rims while, one by one, trapped riders jumped more than thirty feet to safety.

Her vision fading at the edges, she swayed. *Noooo! I will not faint.* Tightening her arms around the bars, she balanced her forehead on the closest rung. The steel bar felt cool and strangely comforting.

"I love your choice of climbing clothes. If that's what you wear, we'll have to do this again soon."

Emmie squeezed her eyes shut, sure she imagined the amused deep tones of her husband's voice coming from just beyond her feet.

Heart racing, she twisted to view below.

Bart's dark eyes, filled with anxiety despite his flippant words, gazed back at her. Relief warmed her insides.

Then reality set in.

Dear Lord, he'll fall to his death. "Holy hell, Bart! What are you doing up here?"

~~~

As Bart expected, Emmie's tone was incredulous, and her question ridiculous despite her choice of dramatic cuss words. "Rescuing you. Why else would I be climbing up this contraption like an unholy monkey? Besides, I might ask the same of you."

It was an effort to keep his voice neutral while examining her bloody chemise. The bastard cut her! Feverish flames of fury swept through him. If Toliver weren't already dead, he would kill him.

"I was kidnapped and forced onto this thing. You think I would be up here of my own free will?"

Of course she wouldn't, nor would she descend over two hundred and sixty feet in her unmentionables in front of a crowd if she had a choice. Only a smoke-filled car would have compelled her to shed her modesty, much less cause her to face her fear of heights straight on.

"Are you hurt bad?"

"No." Despite her denial, panic marked her tone.

Damn!

The Wheel jerked suddenly and they began to descend. His heart froze. Without thought, he climbed up behind her, his hands and feet sharing the same rungs with her. He pressed her to the bars, flattening himself against her back.

Please, don't let her fall.

Emmie lowered her head to a rung, exposing the soft skin at the back of her neck, skin he loved to touch, to kiss. Despite the woodsy odor of smoke, her delectable scent of lavender and heated woman drifted up to tease his nose, and the shallow ebb and flow of her breathing pressed against his chest.

The wheel turned slowly, its massive structure groaning in the stiffening breeze. Below, the snap and crackle of the blaze reached his ears. What must his beloved be feeling? Was she reliving the horror of the barn fire? Was she terrified of being brought closer to the fire's leaping flames. His soul reached out to her.

"Emmie, I'd trade places with you any day rather than have you go through this."

Her knuckles whitened on the bar.

His throat constricted. *Speak to me. Don't shut me out.*

Half crazed with fear for her emotional state, he placed his lips close to her ear. "In case you didn't know, I love you, Emmeline Turner. I want to spend the rest of my life with you, and I'll do whatever I must to win your respect. I don't ask that you love me in return. Just being part of your life is enough for me."

Beneath him, he felt her sharp intake of breath. Her hand crept along the length of steel until it covered his and squeezed. Tears formed behind his eyes as hope filled his heart. Struggling to contain his own rampaging emotions, he twined her fingers between his and folded them in. Christ, how he loved her.

"I love you, too, Bart. Up there, I looked into my soul, and all I saw was you. You are part of me, part of who and what I am, and I could no more live without you than I could live without air."

Joy roared through him. "When we reach the bottom, there is so much I need to tell you."

"And I you."

The Wheel jerked to a stop. His instinct to protect her drove him hard against her body. He glanced toward the ground. A ring of people waited expectantly for them to jump the last thirty feet into a large net.

"You first, Emmie."

Her head dropped as she inspected the scene. "I can't, Bart. Please don't make me do this."

"You must. The Wheel can't go any lower without dipping us into the fire."

She shuddered.

"Shut your eyes and let go. They're right below you."

"I can't. Just can't. I once jumped out of the tree house and—"

"Yes, you can." He swung his body to the side and gently pried her fingers from their death grip on the bar. With his heart in his throat, he pushed her back. "I love you."

"I can do this, I can do this, I can do this," Emmie screamed. She dropped through the air with her eyes closed and landed in the net.

Firemen and volunteers holding the bouncing mesh eased it to the ground where several men helped her to her feet. Gertie stepped forward with a woman's long shawl and wrapped it about her exposed shoulders.

Then it was Bart's turn. He peered at the reorganized rescue net and his heartbeat sped to a gallop, his breathing laboring to keep up. The mesh was the only thing separating him from plummeting to the earth beneath. No wonder Emmie balked. Thirty feet was no small jump.

But his wife was down there. Safe. Waiting for him to follow.

~~~

Despite the heat, Emmie clutched the lacy cloak Gertie placed about her and hunted for Bart in the mass of people. When she didn't find him, her eyes swept upward.

He clung to the steel lattice, his dark, curly hair flying about in the steady breeze.

Her throat tightened as the perilous nature of the huge structure hit her full force. Had she actually stepped into the open with nothing below her except the hard ground?

And death?

Now her husband, the man she loved beyond reason, hugged a bar thirty feet above a wide, round net stretched flat by dozens of firemen and volunteers.

Suddenly, he plummeted.

The din of the crowd disappeared as the blood in her veins froze.

He landed in the netting on his back, bouncing twice. Rooted in place and held tight by Gertie and Cedric, she anxiously watched the ring of men lower him to the ground. Chest heaving, Bart scrambled to his feet, alive and safe, and not the least bit worse for his jump.

A loud sigh escaped her lips.

"Bart! Over here." Emmie waved and surged forward, but was restrained by both her guards.

Bart's eyes sifted through the mass of onlookers until he spotted her. Like sunshine breaking through a sky of clouds, the most glorious smile slid across his handsome face. As he hurried toward her, she shook free of her human restraints and ran to greet him, heedless of the shawl slipping off her body.

Barely able to contain her joy, she leapt into his powerful arms. He swung her around, relief flooding his eyes along with something else.

Love.

And naked desire.

Without thought, she tugged his head down and claimed his mouth. Warm and pliable, his lips tasted like heaven. She wanted to stay there, her body tight to his groin, his response hard and hungry. Seconds later, however, the throng's hoots and cheers penetrated her lust-crazed mind.

They broke for air and surveyed their audience, at once aware of the noisy, crowded world about them. Hundreds of people, gathered to watch the fire, now gaped at a spectacle of a different sort.

Dear lord. What was she doing kissing in public? Warmth that had nothing to do with the weather or blaze crawled up her neck.

Bart tipped his head close to her ear. "I'd gawk, too, if I saw a beautiful woman welcoming her lover wearing nothing but her... climbing clothes."

He winked, then slid her to the ground. Stepping away, he scanned her from top to bottom, a lopsided male grin planted on his face.

She looked down. Goodness! Her gauze chemise revealed the tips of her breasts, and her pantaloons bore tiny blue bows and a slit in a most strategic place. Her face flamed anew. "Oh, dear. I hadn't considered...."

Embarrassed, she lowered her forehead to his chest and felt a chuckle rise from within.

Behind her Gertie laughed, and placed the shawl back in place.

"Yer given' 'em just as good a show as the hootchie kootchie girl down the road, ye are. Let's hope no one here recognizes ye."

Bart's chuckle burst into a deep belly laugh. "Gertie! How would you kn—"

Gertie's attention, however, was on someone behind Bart. "Well, now. A copper headin' this way. Pull yer wrap tighter, dearie. From the looks of him, he might not let you go home to dress before wantin' to talk to ye."

Bart straightened and swiveled sharply, placing his body between Emmie and the approaching policeman of middling years. Beside her, Cedric stepped closer. None of them had mentioned Toliver's death though they must have seen him fall.

"What can we do for you, sir?" Bart's greeting took on the direct, commanding aspect of a professional investigator, one familiar with the workings of the Chicago Police Department.

"A man fell, or was pushed, from the Ferris Wheel's upper car. The lady climbed down from up there, then ye climbed up to meet her. Who might ye be?"

The copper's question in a strong Irish lilt was aimed at Bart, but his attention was drawn to Emmie's chest, and lower. She trembled under her wrap, and pulled its edges closer.

Just where the policeman's interest lay wasn't lost on Bart, who frowned. "Bartholomew Turner, sir. And you are...?"

His curt tone drew the man's head up with a jerk. His eyes widened, and crimson flooded his full, round face. "The lad who hunts murderers?"

Emmie's eyes widened. *Hunts murderers?* Gertie had once alluded to the same thing.

"I am he."

A contrite expression swept across the officer's ordinary features. "Sorry, sir. Me name's Thomas O'Malley. I'm just doin' me job here. I have questions for the lady."

Does he think I pushed Toliver off the Ferris Wheel? Murdered him like that monster murdered my entire family?

Pique straightened her spine.

"The lady is Emmeline Turner. My wife. She needs to go home to put on more appropriate clothing after her ordeal."

Emmie placed her hand on her husband's forearm. "Wait, Bart. Officer, the death of that man was an accident. He pointed a gun at my head and planned to push me out. I ducked away and his momentum sent him flying out the open door. That's the crux of it."

A startled expression emerged on Bart's face. He flung his arm around her shoulders and drew her close. His strength was reassuring, but his scent, all smoky and male, inflamed something deep and primal—desire. Dark, raging feral desire. She longed to be alone with him, touch him, reassure herself they both still lived.

A furrow grew between O'Malley's sea green eyes.

She leveled her most authoritative glare. "I can see you don't believe me." Throwing her modesty to the wind, she opened her shawl. "See here on my side, where he held a knife against my ribs while making me walk here. There's probably a fabric tear and maybe some blood. And here...."

She turned her back to him. "The place where the sharp edge slit my jacket, corset and chemise. I didn't go on the Ferris Wheel on my own. I was forced, and the man who did the forcing paid for his treachery with his life."

She faced O'Malley, sure as anything her remaining clothing left nothing to the man's imagination. Gertie handed her the wrap. Disappointment flashed in the policeman's eyes as she covered her body.

Bart stepped forward, his jaw set. "I'm sure you want more details, and my wife can give them to you. But that will have to wait until tomorrow when her nerves are more settled and she's properly clothed. She's told you the gist of what happened, and showed you physical evidence of what she endured. Surely, a good night's rest and a whiskey or two are called for here. You can bank on my reputation with the police she will return for your interrogation tomorrow."

Emmie inched closer to Bart, and slipped her hand in his. Tension radiated through his fingers to hers. Abruptly, the horror of the past two hours caught up with her. The pounding in her ears escalated. Her belly clenched, and lightheadedness sent her vision spinning.

Officer O'Malley glanced at Emmie, then back at Bart and, in a subdued voice, said, "Take yer wife home, sir. She don't look so good."

Blackness engulfed her.

Chapter 24

Bart pressed his shoulder against the window frame in his bedroom and stared unseeing at the gas lamp across the street. A strange mix of fear and joy tumbled in his gut. He inhaled deeply through a tight chest, hoping to quell the anxiety gaining strength as the minutes passed.

Emmie was safe. For now. The mastermind behind the deaths of her family members was dead. However, Sarah, his lackey, was not, her whereabouts in the city unknown. The afternoon newspapers had been filled with reports of the fire and death of a man who fell from the Wheel. Surely, the woman must know by now.

Tomorrow, Emmie would tell O'Malley everything—every sick detail of Toliver's plan to take over Chicagoland Electric—the same way she had told them on the long carriage ride home. Sarah would be apprehended, tried and put away for life, perhaps even hung for the murders she committed.

Tonight, he planned to make his own confession to his wife. Tell her about what happened to him as a child. The thought of opening this part of him to scrutiny scared him to death, but he needed to lay his heart bare. For that was the only way he would be deserving of her love, the love she'd professed to him on the Wheel.

Bart imagined her at her dressing table, her black hair streaming in long waves over her shoulders as she brushed its lengths with slow, languid strokes. His body stirred beneath the folds of his silk robe. His fingers curled, then flattened at his sides. He longed to be the one stroking her silky tresses, enjoying the scent of her nearness, the peace it gave him.

Behind the closed door between their rooms, he heard Emmie

drop what sounded like a hairbrush on the wooden floor. A chair scraped back. He pictured her bending to retrieve the brush, her blue dressing gown parting to expose a delectable display of full, ripe breasts.

"Ooomph!"

Then a scream.

Bart was through the door in a heartbeat.

Sarah stood behind Emmie, one arm wrapped around his wife's torso trapping her arms, the other wielding a knife to her throat.

The air whooshed out of his lungs. He froze. How the hell did she get in?

Sarah's eyes were wild, crazed, her complexion mottled. The inhuman glow of madness inhabited her expression as if a spirit from a maniacal world had taken over her body. A wounded animal wouldn't have been more dangerous.

Bart moistened his dry lips with his tongue. One wrong move would push the woman over the edge, and with the knife at Emmie's throat, he couldn't afford to make a mistake.

Emmie! Her wide expressive eyes painted a picture of disbelief and fear. She had once trusted her assistant implicitly. Toliver's confirmation of the woman's treachery had been devastating, but seeing Sarah in action must be terrifying. Every part of him felt her horror.

But now he had a job to do. This wasn't his first experience at extracting a captive, only the most important. He'd faced this scenario dozens of times when cornering a murdering rat. Reginald's instructions were written on his brain. *Stall for time. Seek your opportunity. Everyone must live.*

He straightened and focused on Emmie's assailant. "Why, Sarah? Why did you kill her family?"

"Why?" The woman's voice was harsh, shrill, its volume filling the room with hatred. He inched forward. "I'll tell you why. Emmie couldn't do anything with that crippled hand of hers. I did it all. I completed the experiments. I wrote the notes. I made the supply lists. I suggested trial alternatives. I should have been given more credit, more money, a share in the profits and the glory."

A modicum of reason apparently still existed in her addled brain. Maybe he could talk her out of what she intended, but first he needed her full confession.

He gritted his teeth, forced his focus to remain on his task. "How did Toliver fit into the picture?"

Sarah's eyes flashed fire. "That old buzzard? I slept with the man to keep him by my side and coming back for more. I never wanted *him*. I wanted Emmie's father, but he didn't want me, not as a lover."

Emmie gasped.

While Sarah spoke, Bart shifted his weight, inching closer. Sarah's hand on the knife tightened and her mouth formed the cruel snarl of a diseased dog. Bart's muscles tightened as well, but he waited, hoping for an opening.

She laughed, the demonic sound making his skin crawl. "So, I got rid of his wife with an overdose of laudanum."

Emmie cried out and sagged against Sarah, her eyes closing. Bart's hands fisted at his sides, and an impotence of another type gained a strangle-hold on his heart.

Don't faint, Emmie!

Sarah's eyes narrowed. "I thought Eli would turn to me for comfort after his wife was out of the picture. He didn't, so I sought revenge. Knowing Toliver wanted the company, I went to him with a plan to get both. Eli would die a slow death by rat poison. Toliver would gain the company, and I would gain my revenge—all the scientific accolades I knew would come from the company's success."

Bart tore his gaze away from the deadly weapon to glance at Emmie. Her eyes remained closed and tears streamed down her blood-leached cheeks. He longed to pull her into his arms, shield her ears from hearing the diabolical rant of a deranged woman, but he held his ground.

Sarah continued as though she had a need to confess. Maybe she did. She was a killer. Maybe somewhere in her rabid heart she yearned for forgiveness.

"When Eli began teaching her the business, I realized the plan had to change. Emmie would inherit the glory that should have been mine. So, I got Augie to add that clause about marriage to his copy of the will. I knew Eli had another copy, but I couldn't find it and I didn't think she would either. I was willing to wait the five years because I never thought she would marry on her own. Who would want a cripple, a woman whose disfigurement would repulse any real man?"

Bart cringed. *He* wanted Emmie, desperately, whatever her physical flaws. Inside and out, she was beautiful, and he wanted her with a passion he never thought possible. But Sarah only laughed, her eyes aflame with an unholy light.

A flush had turned Emmie's pale cheeks crimson. Her hands coiled. Her knuckles whitened

Bart's gut churned with sadness for the whole damned mess, but his love for Emmie soared.

Spittle ran from the corner of Sarah's mouth. "Augie wanted Emmie to marry that sniveling snot Paul in desperation. He could be blackmailed into signing over the company. But Emmie would have none of him. She chose Alex, so I had to kill him, then she chose some German. Augie took care of him. Then I realized the girl needed to die before she could choose another."

"The shooting on my front steps?" He inched forward.

"Augie hired the men, but it was my idea."

He had to hear it all, every last bit of her confession. "The shooting at Summerhill and the poison?"

"I did that."

Bart was only a foot away now. "And Paul? Who killed him?"

"Augie. Paul was a loose end with an even looser tongue."

Bart had heard enough.

~~~

Emmie's eyes flew open. Bart stood so close she had felt his heat with her eyes closed. Concern painted his sun-kissed face. Plus, something else. Something she instantly recognized.

Love. Despite all her imperfections.

Like a soothing balm, his love eased her fears. They would be all right. Bart was a professional. He would save her.

She straightened abruptly, unbalancing Sarah behind.

"Duck!"

Emmie obeyed Bart's command without question. She pulled away from her assistant as Bart lunged.

The knife. Oh, God!

Emmie scrambled away, retrieving the brush from the floor. If necessary, she would bash the woman over the head with the only weapon within reach. Her heart raced again as she turned to her husband, determined to help.

However, much to her surprise, Bart's movements had been swift and precise for a man his size. He straddled a now subdued Sarah, confining her hands behind her back as she lay face down, the knife well out of reach.

"Have Cedric bring the police. Tell him to use the telephone. They'll arrive here faster," he ordered in the authoritative tone of a man used to being obeyed.

Before she could move, Cedric appeared in the doorway, breathing heavily, his rumpled night shirt hanging to his knees.

"You need me, sir?" Cedric inspected his boss's handiwork, but made no effort to assist. Her husband had everything in hand.

"I swear Cedric. You must live in the woodwork. Yes, I need your help. Use the telephone to summon the police, and have Gertie make a pot of coffee. I'm afraid it's going to be a very long night."

He shifted so part of his knee rested atop Sarah's leg. His eyes found Emmie's and held.

A long night, indeed.

Chapter 25

The door behind them closed with a soft click. Bart leaned against its solidness and watched his wife cross to her dressing table and sit in front of the tall mirror. The flickering glow of the oil lamp softened the dark shadows circling her eyes. His hunger to hold her nearly tore him to shreds.

It had been a long night, longer than he expected. The police arrived within ten minutes of Cedric's call, and they'd been thorough. Exhaustingly so. Not too many hours remained before dawn streaked through the edges of the drape.

Emmie changed out of the serviceable day gown she'd donned for the interrogation into the blue silk robe that hugged her curves like a second skin. She reached for the brush and pulled it through the long curl down the side of her face. Her shoulders still showed the tension of the day, her body weary, her energy drained.

Physical need for her coursed through his veins like a raging river, but he held himself in check. More important was the need to confess, to bare himself before his beloved, to show her who and what he was, as she had asked. Maybe then…. He shut his eyes, wishing to temper the hope that bloomed in his heart.

All he wanted was her love. That's all he ever wanted. Her confession under duress didn't really count. It's what she'll say after knowing what happened to him that mattered.

As if sensing his distress, she glanced up into her mirror and caught him watching her.

"What is it?"

Her voice expressed her concern, but the note of fatigue in it captured his ear. He should wait until tomorrow when she had some sleep, but waiting would only postpone the inevitable. The time was now, while his courage lasted.

"Come sit with me." He extended his hand.

Emmie rose and went to him, questions flickering in her large blue eyes.

He led her to an overstuffed chair near the unlit fireplace. Lowering himself, he pulled her across his lap. She went willingly, though weariness might have played a part in her compliance.

"There is something I need to tell you. The reason why I went into the city and left you without a word yesterday."

She murmured something unintelligible and rested her head against his chest. Her fingers played at the edge of his robe's collar, her touch warming his skin beneath. He took her hand and brought it to his lips. His heart raced at an alarming speed.

He inhaled, ready to plunge into the abyss. "Remember my nightmare?"

Emmie's head popped up. Wide startled eyes perused his face. She opened her mouth but before she could say anything, he placed a finger against it.

"Hush, sweetheart. Let me tell you about it."

She frowned. A combination of distress and her incredible curiosity spread across her beautiful face. So unique, his wife. So wonderfully rare. Emmie nodded and rested her head against him, ready to listen.

He pulled her tighter. A tremor ran through him.

"My mother died when I was five. My father was a country doctor. He left me alone with the housekeeper most of the time. I misbehaved in school a lot. I missed my mother terribly. They kicked me out, which made my father mad. He didn't make much money, but he managed to provide me with private tutors who came to our house. One of them...."

Bart swallowed hard, his tongue suddenly thick. "When I was seven, my tutor at the time... did... did things to me."

Emmie gasped. "What things?" Her question, barely a whisper, seared his soul.

"The man violated me."

She gaped at him in horror. *Shit!*

"Like Paul almost did to me. But, you were only a boy. Did you tell your father about what that man did?"

He nodded, despair shutting off his capacity to speak.

"What did he say or do?"

"Nothing. He didn't believe me. I was nine by the time my father changed tutors. He told me I'd learned as much as I was going to from this man, and he hired someone else."

Her eyes widened to saucers. "He didn't believe you, and it went on for two whole years? My God!" Her voice caught.

"The nightmares were the memories I tried to bury. I'd wake up from them in a terrible state. The night before last was particularly bad."

"After I demanded more from you...." she whispered, her shimmering eyes filled with regret.

Christ. No! She shouldn't feel responsible.

He shook his head. Kissed the fingers of the hand he still held. "This isn't your doing. What you asked of me just gave the inevitable a shove. It was time for me to face it head on. But I couldn't make sense of it by myself. Maybe I didn't want to, but I knew I had to talk with someone. Another male. I went to the city to see a friend." A friend who must remain anonymous. He was not free to disclose the true nature of his relationship with Reginald.

"So, what did he tell you?"

From anyone else, the question might have bordered on the presumptuous, but from his curious wife, the query seemed most appropriate.

"He helped me to see how what happened had affected nearly everything I did, everything I believed about myself, and what I wanted or didn't want. How it even altered my ability to be a man."

Tears rolled down her cheeks. "I didn't know."

Bart wiped the moisture with his thumb. "Nor did I. My friend told me that to move on with my life I needed to forgive everyone involved, including myself, and then tell you."

Emmie twisted in his arms to view him straight on. She cupped his cheeks with both hands. Her touch was gentle, caring, the caress for which his heart yearned. He settled his hand on one of hers and squeezed.

"Your boyhood innocence might have been stolen, but whatever makes up Bartholomew Turner, the man, is good and decent—what you believe in, your sense of responsibility, even your over protectiveness. These things are very much a part of who and what you are—the man I love with all my being"

His intake of breath was audible in the quiet bedroom.

Her fingers now twining in the curl down her cheek, Emmie sank against his chest. "I also have a confession to make."

His gut tightened. What could she possibly need to confess?

"I was afraid to love you. Afraid that if I did, I would lose you like everyone else I loved. Afraid that if I opened my heart to you, I would be devastated when our marriage..."

He stopped breathing. What was she saying?

"I didn't realize what I was doing until Jon pointed it out," she continued.

"And since then?"

She sat up and faced him again. "I can't not love you, Bart. On the Ferris Wheel, I realized there were more things in life to fear than being hurt by loving you. You are my life, my destiny. Even if you choose to not stay married to me, the experience of having loved you was worth far more than the pain of losing you in the end."

The sweetness of joy charged through his soul, eviscerating all his doubts. She wanted to remain with him even after everything he told her. The family he never realized he longed for or needed until recently suddenly surfaced within reach. The family he never had as a child.

Bart bent and took her lips, softly, gently, acutely aware of rampant desire galloping to his cock.

Breaking for air, he set his chin atop her head. "I will never leave you, Emmie. I love you more than life itself."

His reward was something he would remember to his dying days—the slide of her arm around his back followed by a tight squeeze of approval. A hug he needed, the approval he never realized he craved.

He kissed the top of her hair. "Come, let me prove how much I love you."

~~~

Mesmerized by the glint in Bart's eyes, Emmie felt herself being lifted as though she weighed nothing more than a feather. Anticipation pulsed through her veins in the staccato beat of a drum. His firm muscles flexed beneath the hand she slipped around his wide powerful shoulders, shoulders she wished to see move unimpeded by clothing, wished to touch skin to skin.

He moved swiftly to the bed, stood her on her feet and slowly removed her robe and nightdress. His long fingers were sure and steady, but as they brushed across her heated skin, fire scorched her flesh. She wanted Bart, wanted him with a fierceness she could no longer contain.

She stood tall, or as tall as her frame would allow, and let him look his fill.

His eyes blazed with desire and an emotion she had come to recognize as love. Love for her. Her heart swelled with the knowledge of it.

His gaze drifted slowly down her exposed body, caressing every square inch of her with the intensity of his want. She had no doubts as to what he saw. Appreciation burned in his eyes, as did hunger, the same wild and wanton appetite that now devoured her.

Reaching up, she tugged the robe off his shoulders. The moisture in her mouth instantly evaporated. Bare skin greeted her effort—corded muscle, the plains and angles of his sculpted body, a light mat of chest hair that arrowed toward his waist and below. He stood like a statue, letting her study him as he had studied her. Eyes black with desire watched her intently, his irregular breaths giving away his eagerness, his intent. He was all she had ever wished for, all she had ever imagined a husband to be.

Emmie lowered her gaze. Flickering tongues of lamp light gave Bart's rippled chest a tawny glow. She wet her lips, eager to kiss, eager to play. Her eyes drifted lower, to the extended state of his arousal, the thick, hard organ jutting from a nest of dark brown curls ready for her. Her breath quickened.

Driven by an overwhelming need to caress him, she stepped closer and wrapped her hands around his erection. He felt soft and hard at the same time, his length increasing at her touch.

A hiss escaped his mouth. Bart drew her within the circle of his arms, allowing her space to do with him as she wished. She sighed with contentment. This big, feral creature was hers to enjoy.

A bead of wetness seeped from the tip of his shaft. And she knew instantly what she wanted to do with it. She swirled her thumb through the wetness and around the crown of his magnificence. In all her nights with him, she'd never taken the initiative, never touched him in such a bold, wanton fashion. Emmie reveled in her action now.

He twitched in her hand. Startled, she withdrew and glanced up, her heart now in her throat. His eyes were closed, and his face knotted in a look of anguish.

"Am I hurting you?"

"Don't stop." His fevered whisper seared her insides, gave her the encouragement she needed.

She leaned against him for support, her hands moving softly, but firmly, caressing him, loving him, until the need to love him with her mouth turned her legs to mush. Still holding him, she sank to her knees, the blood roaring loudly in her ears.

"Wha—?"

"Let me." A demand, not a request. She expected him to obey.

And he did.

Emmie moved one hand to the base of his staff and enveloped its tip with her mouth. The world disappeared. Nothing existed except her and her husband, and the need to possess him driving her forward. Taking him deeper into her mouth, she explored him with her tongue, circling one way, then the other, stroking him, fondling him, tasting the salt of him, savoring the tangy smell of him.

He moaned, or was it a groan? The pleasure of giving him pleasure sent her soul soaring into the beyond, an experience she intended to repeat often in the years to come.

Bart's hips rocked with her strokes, and his hands fisted in her hair. The room filled with the sounds of his passion and the noises of making love to him. Her heart sang, thrilled with the knowledge she could bring this strapping man to the edge of madness.

"Enough." He raised her to her feet. "I'm too close. I need to be inside you."

His heavy-lidded eyes were glazed with desire. Her pulse beat faster. Mixed in his words was a plea. And a promise.

And a hope.

She smiled, a bit of wickedness flaring in her soul. "I am yours, Bartholomew. Yours, and yours alone. Take me where you want to go, however you want to go."

Black eyes bored into hers. The eyes of the jungle king framed by a curly, brown mane, eyes that promised the fierce wildness she desperately craved.

He lifted her with one arm around her waist, drawing one leg around his thigh. "Wrap them around me."

She complied, her heart thumping like a jungle drum. She tightened her arms around his neck.

Before Emmie knew what was happening, her back hit the wall. She tensed.

"I won't hurt you. Just hang on."

And because she loved him, she did as he asked, excitement surging to the ends of her body.

His mouth crashed against her lips, while his fingers deftly probed her nether curls, sliding through the wetness until they found her nub. She moaned her delight, and he grunted with satisfaction. *How did he know this was what I wanted, what I craved?*

"You're ready." His tone held a note of awe.

"Of course I'm ready. How could I no—"

He circled her folds, rubbing with a rhythm that took her breath away.

Oh, God! Wanting more, she rocked against his fingers, her body ascending to a place where her senses blurred and time disappeared. The paradise she sought beckoned, but she refused to go without her husband.

"I want you inside me."

"Exactly where I want to be." His low growl was untamed, primitive. And exactly what she expected from him.

His finger disappeared, replaced by his erection.

"Now." She pushed against his pelvis, telling him in no uncertain terms what she wanted, what she ached for.

The wall helping him to balance, he slipped his strong hands to her hips and slid into her wet opening with the power of a steam piston.

"Yes, like that. Don't hold back." Not now, not ever.

"You're so damned hot, so wet."

He filled her completely, his length reaching clear to the mouth of her womb. This was what she hungered for, what she craved. The whole of him captured within her, touching her core, bringing her peace. Bringing her life. She couldn't imagine living without him, without his touch, without the driving needs deep in this man's soul.

Her husband, both physically and emotionally naked, coming to her as himself with all his hurts and scars exposed. For her to care for. For her to love.

Bart thrust into her again, establishing a powerful rhythm, a frenzied pace that scrambled her brain, consumed her body, shut off everything except the moans and groans coming from him and from her.

~~~

As Emmie's climax neared, moisture formed beneath Bart's eyelids. He had succeeded in bringing her to a peak without the aid of a disguise. He felt free. Gloriously free, and wonderfully alive.

He pleasured her as Bartholomew Turner, and none other. No one else shared his glory, his satisfaction in satisfying his wife.

Tensing as his orgasm came upon him, he poured himself into her scalding heat, gripping her tight, pounding into her with the fervor he had dreamed of, longed for. Life flowed from his body to hers. Her inner muscles gripped him like iron. Gloriously. Generously. Milking him until he could no longer take it.

The next instant, she shattered with a scream, his name flying from her mouth with abandon. *His* name. The sound of it in the throes of her ardor sent a thrill rippling through him.

He loved her. Emmeline. His wife for life. He held her until he felt the last of her shudders die away.

Spent, and still joined, he carried her to their bed, careful to avoid crushing her to the mattress. The terrible loneliness enveloping him since childhood was gone. A shiny new future lay before him, a future of happiness and joy.

And love.

A glorious sheen covered her soft skin and a smile of contentment lit her face. After cleansing them both with moistened washing cloths, he lifted the bed covers, slid her beneath, then crawled in beside her and pulled her close, spoon fashion.

"I love you, Bartholomew Turner," she whispered.

"And I love you, Emmeline Turner."

She was silent a moment, then turned to face him. Laughter flared in her eyes. "You don't suppose one of your personages might show up in our bed from time to time? To spice things up a bit?"

He barked a laugh, grabbed her hand and twined his fingers through. "Not on your life. All the spicing up in this marriage bed will be done by one persona—Mr. Turner."

"If he's as spirited as you, Bartholomew, I'll take him any day."

"I guarantee you'll be taking him every day, and every night, too."

One corner of her mouth tipped up in an impish grin, and a hint of the she-devil child she once was emerged. "I'll hold you to that."

Epilogue

October, 1893

Twirling the stem of her half-filled wine glass, Emmie glanced down Summerhill's dining room table, curiosity causing an itch she desperately needed to scratch.

On her right, Bart and Uncle Reggie exchanged opinions about Chicago's finances after the Fair's close as though they had been lifelong friends. The easy give and take of their conversation reflected mutual respect and deep regard for the other's thoughts. The two most important people in her life gave the impression their relationship went far beyond mere professionalism. A relationship that couldn't have developed in a few short hours.

Across the table, Jon and Lydia argued over the decor of Summerhill's new nursery. Emmie swallowed her wine, letting the burgundy flow smoothly down her throat to warm her insides. Whatever they chose was fine with her. She had plans of her own that didn't include them.

Her hand slid over the tiny bulge as the raw edge of sadness seeped into her thoughts. She wished her parents were alive. They would have enjoyed spending time with their grandchild expected early next spring.

She shoved her wistful thoughts aside. No sense dwelling on something that would never be. But lately, keeping her focus on a future filled with happiness and contentment had become increasingly more difficult. Her emotions seemed far too close to the surface to suit her. She was fast turning into the maudlin ninny she vowed she would never become.

Placing her napkin beside her plate, she rose. "Let's adjourn to the library. We'll have our dessert there."

Jon surged to his feet and helped Lydia rise from her chair. "I think we'll take another look at the nursery and make some decisions. Arguing over the details at the dinner table is most inappropriate, don't you think, Miss Holmsford?"

Her secretary's heightened brows exposed her surprise while the glint in Jon's lively eyes gave away his intent. Emmie had no doubt as to whose opinion would prevail. Jon was a master at wooing people to his way of thinking. Whatever animus had been between them had disappeared.

Emmie grinned. "Of course. Lydia, I'm glad you could join us."

"I am, too, Mrs. Turner. Thank you for inviting me." Lydia latched on to Jon's ready arm, and the two said their goodbyes to Bart and Uncle Reggie before leaving.

Bart reached for Emmie's hand. "Did I tell you you look ravishing tonight, Mrs. Turner?" The husk in his voice sent shivers up her spine.

"You did indeed, but you can say it as many times as you like," she murmured.

His darkened eyes dropped to her lips. Coils of anticipation tightened her pelvis. Her breasts swelled and flames consumed the rest of her body.

"Later," she mouthed, and out loud added, "Well now, that leaves more dessert for us."

She ignored his responding wolfish grin, knowing full well the opening she had handed him.

"Yes, and I have already selected the sweet I want," he mumbled on cue, his gaze moving down to her ripening bosom.

She swatted his arm. "Behave yourself, or you won't get any after dinner treats. We're not alone." She tossed her head and brushed past him.

Behind them, her uncle chuckled and ushered them out with a wave of his hand. "I for one, don't need additional sweets. But I'll gladly accept my own share of Gertie's wonderful apple pie."

Goodness! Had he heard their exchange? The heat in her cheeks flared into a bonfire.

They crossed the gallery, its ceiling now closed for the winter, and entered the quiet family library at the front of the house. The soft hues of the fall north sky, visible through the floor to ceiling windows, swept the horizon in muted mauve and orchid tones.

Emmie loved this room. Its dark walnut paneling and shelves filled with books gave the room a cozy feeling compared to the open expanse of gallery they'd just crossed. Though dark spaces weren't her favorite, this room, above all others, reminded her of her father. She spent more time with him in here than in the Ship Room, his study across the hall.

Emmie took a seat in a comfortable reading chair while Bart walked to a highboy table and poured two glasses of cognac. "Have they set a date for Sarah's trial?"

After handing a glass to Uncle Reggie, Bart lowered himself to a matching seat adjacent to hers and stretched out his long legs.

Her uncle took a sip of his drink. "Not yet, but I understand they're hoping for April. No leads yet on the two who shot Emmie on your front steps either. They seem to have disappeared."

He ambled to the picture window and twirled the contents of his glass, lost in thought. Distracted, perhaps, was a more apt description of her uncle's current demeanor. Emmie had the impression he had something to discuss but was reluctant to bring it up.

Her curiosity engaged, she waited patiently for him to speak. But the silence grew heavy. And long. She started at a loud snap from the season's first fire in Papa's fireplace.

Since her father's death, the fireplace had remained unused, a symbol of tragedy and grief she would rather forget. Bart had suggested a fire this evening to cap off Uncle Reggie's visit. Even now, the memories associated with flames unnerved her. *Don't be a silly ninny*. This blaze, tended by two grown men, was harmless, and completely contained.

She sipped the remains of her dinner wine, impatient to move the conversation along. She had questions she wanted answered.

"Uncle Reggie, at dinner I noticed you and Bart talking as though you've known each other for a long time. Do you two have a relationship that is more than professional?"

Her uncle turned and took a significant swig of cognac, his face puckering as the fiery liquid slid down his throat.

Bart answered first. "When I was ten, I ran away from home and lived on Chicago's streets. I was fourteen when a copper found me. Reginald was that copper. He taught me and the rest of the gang I ran with how to be the eyes and ears of the police. He changed our lives and I'm indebted to him."

A sudden light flicked on in her brain. "Uncle Reggie was the friend you went to see."

Bart's gaze was steady. "Yes."

"If you were in town, Uncle Reggie, then why—"

"Didn't I come see you? Because I was in town for business and...." Reginald's shoulders heaved in a deep intake of breath. "I may as well tell you because you'll find out sooner or later. I moved to Washington to become head of a secret government law enforcement agency." Emmie gasped. "I hired other detective agencies around the country who took on assignments as independent agents. Bart was one of them."

"Bart?" Being hit with a hammer wouldn't have been more shocking.

A look of chagrin passed across Bart's features. "I hunt murderers, remember? I couldn't tell you because the government agency was secret."

Emmie's hand flew to her lips as a memory of Gertie blurting out the same thing came to mind.

Her uncle continued. "When I gave you the chess piece and Bartholomew's name, I only did so in case you needed help and I wasn't in town. I had no idea this young man's special skills would be put to use. Lucky for you, Bart did what he does best—hunt murderers."

Bart swirled the amber spirits around the edge of his glass, a pink flush rising to his neck. "I didn't do anything, really."

"You did enough. Not only did you guard her when it became apparent she needed guarding, you asked questions, raised awareness that someone was looking into things. You got someone rattled enough to make a mistake. Looking back on it, that turned out to be Sarah's telling you about the notebooks, Emmie. You went looking for them, but found the original will and forced the issue."

"Yes, forced myself right into being kidnapped," she murmured. Grim memories of that day on the Ferris Wheel, followed by the terrifying experience with Sarah, remained imprinted on her brain.

"I know. The outcome could have been horrendous." Her uncle emptied his glass.

Emmie shuddered, then squared her shoulders, determined to force the bad memories to the back of her mind. "So, if this agency is supposed to be secret, why are you telling me now?"

"Because the nature of it is about to change. That's why I was in Chicago that week—to meet with the Pinkerton Detective Agency, the biggest contractor affected." He raised his glass and finished off the liquor. "Seems an obscure section of the Sundry Civil Appropriations Act Congress passed in March prohibits the government from hiring detectives employed by other detective agencies. The measure takes effect January first of next year and puts my agency, or at least the way it's organized, out of business."

A sigh escaped her uncle's mouth. He strolled to the highboy table and poured himself another cognac. This one in a bigger glass.

After studying the bottle's label, he chuckled softly. "Nothing but the best for Eli." He raised his glass in salute to his deceased brother and tossed back a swallow.

Bart edged forward, his shoulders hunched. "So, it looks like I might be out of a government job?"

"I wouldn't say that just yet and that's why I haven't said anything to you sooner. No money has been appropriated to form an internal agency, so for the moment, outside contractors are the only investigators our government has. But, things will change. There are plans to form something called the Bureau of Investigation, but no one knows how that might work, when it might happen, or who would head it."

Emmie absorbed Uncle Reggie's seemingly bad news, a spark of excitement blazing to life. "So, my husband. You might have more time to spend with me and our family." She licked her upper lip. "I've been giving our future a lot of thought lately, and this new turn could work out well for us."

Wariness crept across Bart's handsome face. He was about to lose a source of income, and the prospect didn't seem to be sitting well with him. "And how is that?"

"I want to build the company's manufacturing plant in the city, and it would be wise to move the research facility there as well. The scientists all live in the city anyway, transportation for raw materials and finished products would cost less, and the city would offer a larger labor force for manufacturing jobs. We'd live in your city town home and you can work on expanding your agency."

"But what about Summerhill and that magnificent electric research barn?"

Warming to her subject, she set her glass on an end table. "We'd use Summerhill as our weekend and vacation home, but there is something specific I want to do with the barn, if you approve."

"The barn is yours. Why would you need my approval?"

"Because in an indirect way, it has to do with something you value greatly. I want to return the barn to its original use—a place for cows to be milked."

Bart started. "That's the last thing I'd expect you to propose. Go on. Why?"

"While visiting with your boys, I realized they know nothing about the world beyond the city. Do they even know where the milk they drink with their cookies comes from?"

The corners of his mouth tipped. "Other than from a bottle, I don't suppose they do."

"What if Summerhill became a dairy farm opened to visitors from the city, especially children? The train runs to Libertyville, and if we knew how many people were coming in advance, we could arrange to meet them at the station. We could charge adults a small fee to cover the wagons and drivers, but the children would go free."

She squeezed her fingers tight. "We could sell the milk and milk products in the city under the Summerhill name. It would mean adding processing equipment to a dairy farm to make it a dairy company. Jon grew up on a dairy farm and could run the whole thing."

Uncle Reggie chuckled. "Who said women didn't have a mind for business?"

"You've got it all figured out, don't you?" The approval she sought came in the brilliant glow of Bart's sparkling eyes, which soon darkened with blatant desire.

An answering lust exploded in all the private parts of her body, places she wanted his fingers to touch, his lips to explore, his body to fill. "Yes, I do have it all figured out. When there's something I want, I make it happen."

"Yes, you do, don't you?" He rose, the promise of pleasures to come in the deep rich tones of her husband's low murmur.

Yes, life was good. Very good, indeed.

The End

Thanks for reading *Shadows and Masks*. I hope you enjoyed it as much as I enjoyed writing it.

If you liked Emmie and Bart's story, come ride the train to the gold fields of Colorado in *Memories and Moonbeams*, Book 2 of the

Chessmen series, as Nick searches for his missing sister. Discover what else he finds on his journey to the high country of Cripple Creek, Colorado. To give you a peek, I've included the first chapter at the back of this book.

Sign up for my Newsletter to find out when Nick's story becomes available: http://eepurl.com/cTMjqH

I often troll the reviews on Amazon to see what my readers thought of the book. I would love to read your review. Here is the Amazon link:
Http://www.amazon.com/dp/b072qcvdrv

And I'd love a posted comment about the book on Facebook, Twitter, or Goodreads.

Facebook: http://www.facebook.com/averilreismanauthor

Website: http://www.averilreismanauthor.com

Twitter: @avreisman

Goodreads:
www.goodreads.com/author/show/7350608.Averil_Reisman

Email: averil@averilreismanauthor.com

Other titles by the author

The Captain's Temptress
  (originally titled To Cuba With Love)

Author's Notes

The idea for this book came from a field trip my local book club took to architect Frank Lloyd Wright's office and workshop in Oak Park, IL. Wright was a contemporary of those who designed Chicago's 1893 Columbian Exposition fairgrounds.

At the Wright museum gift shop, I spotted a DVD of the Exposition titled *Magic of the White City,* narrated by actors Gene Wilder and Claire Litton. Having read Erik Larson's *Devil in the White City,* I was intrigued enough to buy and view the DVD. I was hooked from the start. No other world's fair since has compared to the Columbian Exposition's size, beauty, or its exuberant acceptance among the nations of the world. It literally put Chicago on the map.

I realized I had to set a romance among the milieu of that Exposition. It was too good a setting to pass up. I imagined my heroine, Emmeline Griffith, as a spunky girl who, after the death of her beloved twin brother, learned the electric business from her father, and ended up exhibiting a new-fangled product at the fair—an electric iron. Emmie had big dreams for the future, like building a company similar to General Electric, a business that would assist in reshaping the role of women everywhere.

For my hero, I fashioned Bartholomew Turner, a strong alpha male with a horrendous past. He had to be a man who fit as easily into Chicago's high society as on the city's streets with the homeless, a man of honesty, integrity and a talent for routing out murderers. I gave him a home/office on Eugenie Street, an avenue of upper middle class brownstones in a not quite tony part of Chicago.

Turner's response to his sexual abuse is a fictional amalgam of several firsthand accounts of victims appearing in books written by therapists. Because the subject of sexual abuse is vast and complicated, I narrowed Turner's reactions to his feelings about himself, his nearly non-existent sex life and subsequent fears, and his mind's subconscious physical manifestation of duress through erectile dysfunction.

Prior to the formation of the (Federal) Bureau of Investigation in 1908, the U.S Justice Department used borrowed federal agents and marshals, and detectives from the Pinkerton Agency and other private investigating firms to fight the growing federal crime rate. In 1893, the Anti-Pinkerton Act limited the Justice Department's ability to hire investigators and mercenaries employed by private firms. Today, the U.S. still uses private security firms and military contractors.

I love researching my story locations, but this one was especially fun. I grew up in Chicago on its far northern edge, and remember visiting many of the locations I've written about.

For Emmie's country estate, Summerhill, I chose the Cuneo mansion of Vernon Hills, IL, as my inspiration. Though built in 1916 and ultimately owned by book printer John F. Cuneo, the house was originally built by Samuel Insull, personal secretary to Thomas Edison, and subsequent founder of Commonwealth Edison, Chicago's major electric company.

Sam Insull had only one son. It was the mansion's connection to electricity, a key new-fangled product demonstrated with brilliance at the Columbian Exposition, that had me wondering what if Insull had a daughter to whom he imparted all his scientific knowledge. Insull provided the inspiration for Eli Griffith, Emmeline's father.

Insull originally bought the 132-acre Hawthorn Farm and expanded it to 2,000 acres before it was sold to Cuneo during the Depression. Cuneo renamed the farm Hawthorn-Melody and sold its dairy products throughout the Chicago North Shore area. He opened his state of the art dairy to visitors and eventually added an amusement park, petting zoo and wild west ghost town.

I remember several summer camp trips to the farm in the mid-'50s to view cows being milked by electric milking machines. The farm park operated until 1970.

The Palmer House Hotel remains in operation to this day, and is one of the more interesting historical sites of the city, as are the Rookery Building and the Art Institute. The only building remaining of the Columbian Exposition is the Fine Arts Building, now known as Chicago's Museum of Science and Industry.

Mr. Ferris's giant wheel, the predecessor of today's smaller ubiquitous ferris wheels, was dismantled and moved several times before finally being sold for scrap after the Louisiana Purchase Exposition in St. Louis in 1904.

Henrici's Restaurant, originally opened in 1868, burned during the Chicago Fire and was relocated several times over the years before opening in downtown Chicago on Randolph Street between Dearborn and Clark streets. The restaurant remained open until 1962 when it was razed to make way for the Daley Civic Center, Chicago's current city hall. I fondly remember attending many birthday parties and Sweet Sixteen luncheons at Henrici's as a young girl.

Though the telephone came to Chicago in the 1870s, it was not widely available locally. Early telephone use was primarily a long-distance service; Chicago to New York service began in the 1890s. Many businesses in the city had telephone service, as did the wealthy, but telephone usage didn't expand to middle class neighborhoods until the later 1890s.

I mentioned several Chicago notables of the era, one of them being Bertha Palmer, who was the acknowledged queen of Chicago society in the later part of the nineteenth century. An actual person, I've fictionalized her character in this story based upon numerous accounts I read of her life. She was instrumental in convincing the Columbian Exposition leadership to include a Woman's Building, which was ultimately designed by a female architect, and contained exhibits of products and services by and for women.

Though the Palmer mansion, completed in 1885 at a cost then of over $1 million, was easily the city's most splendid home, it was torn down in 1950 to make way for two 22-story residential high rises.

I also mentioned Richard Warren Sears and Aaron Montgomery Ward in one of my chapters. Both were actual giants of catalog merchandising, and their account in this book is fictionalized.

Benjamin Shield is a totally fictional character drawn from the existence of Marshall Field who, with his partner Levi Leiter, bought a thriving dry goods business from Potter Palmer in 1867. Field later bought out Leiter in 1881, and renamed the store after himself.

Marshall Field's stores flourished as a major independent national department store chain until it was sold in 1981 to the British-American Tobacco Retail Group. It changed owners several more times before being purchased in 2005 by Federated Department Stores and renamed Macy's in 2006. In April, 2017, Macy's announced the eighth through fourteenth floors of the former Field's flagship State

Street store were for sale.

Nicholas Shield, a friend of my hero Bartholomew Turner in *Shadows and Masks*, is the hero of *Memories and Moonbeams*, Book 2 of the Chessmen series, excerpted at the end of this book. I hope you'll sign up for my Newsletter at http://eepurl.com/cTMjqH to find out when Nick's story will be released.

Acknowledgements

I couldn't have written this book without the wonderful assistance of a whole lot of people.

First are my fantastic editors—Karen Dale Harris, my amazing story content editor who made wonderful suggestions for improving the story, and my husband, Art, a retired high school English teacher, who read my first version and my last version, pointing out things I hadn't noticed as I wrote, edited and rewrote.

I also must thank my former critique partners: Tara Kingston, Kathleen Bitner Roth, Tessy Grillo, Lane McFarland, Barbara Bettis, Renee Ann Miller, Ashlyn Macnamara, Samanthya Wyatt, and Beppie Harrison, who all read early drafts of this book. I can't thank you enough for all your time and effort. And sharp eyes.

A huge thank you also goes to artist D.C. Charles of BookGraphics.net, who developed the spectacular cover design for not only this book, but all the other books scheduled for the Chessmen Series.

I also want to thank my dear friend Janet Lickerman, who accompanied me on a research tour of the Cuneo Museum in Vernon Hills, IL, the inspiration for Summerhill; and to the docent at the museum who tailor-made a tour for us based upon the mansion's original construction by Samuel Insull.

Numerous other resources were invaluable in providing research for my story. Chief among them was a DVD titled *Magic of the White City*, narrated by actors Gene Wilder and Claire Litton. It brought to life the fair that changed Chicago forever and made my job of conjuring up Exposition scenes so much easier.

While working on this book I gathered a ton of research materials to help with the myriad details I found myself seeking. The best of these books were: *City of the Century, The Epic of Chicago and the Making of America* by Donald L. Miller, a folksy history of the growth of Chicago; *The World's Columbian Exposition, the Chicago World's Fair of 1893* by Norman Bolotin and Christine Laing, a wonderful collection of photos and narratives about the Exposition; and *A Parisienne in Chicago, Impressions of the World's Columbian Exposition* by Madame Leon Grandin, an outsider's view of life in Chicago as it was in 1892-93 when her husband worked on a sculptured fountain for the fair grounds.

A huge thank you also goes to all the members of The Boulder Ridge Book Club who were so supportive during the time I worked on this book. Your encouragement helped immensely, especially when my muse took long periods of time off.

A special thank you goes to my daughters, Lisa, Marla and Julie for encouraging me to try my hand at a mystery romance, since I always managed to spoil their television mysteries by guessing who did it and why within the first fifteen minutes of the program.

And finally, hugs and kisses to my husband Art, who saw very little of me during the time I poured my life into historical Chicago. Your support was wonderful, especially all the dinners you suggested we eat out or bring back whenever I emerged from my writing lair too late or too tired to cook. I love you always.

Memories and Moonbeams
(Book 2 of The Chessmen series)

Excerpt

Chapter 1

August, 1893
Colorado City, Colorado

Nicholas Shield shoved his new Stetson hat back off his forehead, and peered at the number hanging cockeyed over the swinging door.

Well, shit!

He had the right address, but the number was a damn saloon, not the professional office of a private investigator. Raucous laughter, tinny piano music, and the stink of stale whiskey drifted out the swinging double doors, deepening his already foul mood.

Where the hell had his friend, Bart, sent him? Nick had asked for the name of a good detective in Colorado to help him find his missing sister. Bart had suggested a Lee Wilcox and given him an address. But, clearly, this wasn't right. Not a saloon in the middle of this sweltering hellhole.

Colorado City was even worse than Chicago's Levee district. The late afternoon sun beat mercilessly upon the bordellos, saloons, and dilapidated cribs lining the streets. There was enough vice and sin here to separate men from their money at a lightning pace. Scores of miners, mill workers, ranchers, and new gold millionaires crowded the streets in pursuit of whiskey, a good game and a roll with one of the town's army of whores. Any other time, he might have joined in the search for hedonistic pleasure, but not today.

Today, he was after his missing sister who had disappeared from their parents' home in Chicago six weeks ago without a word or letter of explanation. A Pinkerton agent tracked her, or someone who looked like her, to some gold camp up the mountains from here. However, the man took sick before positively identifying her. Nick had come to complete the search.

For all he knew, his sister could be huddled cold and miserable somewhere, praying for him to rescue her as he had dozens of times before. But, this time he couldn't do it alone. He needed the help of a local detective, someone who knew the area and was immune to the effects of the high mountain air.

In short, he needed Lee Wilcox.

Maybe someone in the saloon would know where to find him.

Nick adjusted his hat, and pushed open the doors. A smoky haze hung over the room like a dark thundercloud. He squinted, his eyes rapidly adjusting to the noxious gloom. Gamblers around gaming tables added to the din and the stench of unwashed bodies and cheap cigars.

He sauntered up to a long, dark oak bar as ornate as any in Chicago. Two men, who from their smell hadn't bathed in weeks, sat on nearby wooden barstools arguing.

"...titties the size of melons and an ass soft enough to swallow my whole cock and balls," said the one closest to him, his hands cupping the air to indicate the size of those melons.

"So what? Lurine sucks me deep and gets me off in no time, then rides me to beat the band. She earns my coin, and then some, she does," his friend retorted.

Having no interest in their conversation, Nick turned toward the bar.

A big man about his own age wiped something vigorously with a large towel. Spotting Nick, the bartender placed the clean glass on a rack and set the towel on the back shelf. "Whadya have?"

Nick turned his most congenial smile on the man. "Four fingers of your best, my friend." A good cognac would be preferable, but he doubted this place would stock any. He had no idea what to expect.

"Whiskey all right?" The barkeeper grinned, his gaze tracking down Nick's clothing with undisguised amusement.

Nick bristled. Nothing he wore warranted the smirk on the bartender's face. He'd purchased his new western clothes—hat, string tie, jeans, plaid shirt, black vest and boots—in a store near the train station to avoid standing out like the city dweller he was.

"That will do nicely." Nick tossed a coin on the counter, leaned his tall frame against it and scanned the murky surroundings.

The noise from the crowded establishment made his ears ring, which didn't help matters any. His head still ached from not having slept during the long two-day train ride from Chicago.

The bartender slid a drink in front of him, picked up his coin and returned to washing glasses.

Nick took a sip. Fire raced down his throat but, surprisingly, the whiskey was not half bad. He wiped his mouth with the back of his hand. "Hey, barkeep. I'm looking for a Lee Wilcox. You know where I could find him?"

"Sure do." Chuckling, the bartender whispered to a nearby boy of about twelve lugging a box of empty bottles. "He'll get her."

Her? Wilcox was a woman? With offices in a saloon? What respectable woman—

Nick's thoughts took a sudden turn. Bart would never send him to a whore, not even as a joke, would he?

A painted brunette of small stature, barely wearing a gaudy red dress over her considerable assets, ambled up to him a few minutes later. Vaguely familiar green eyes scrutinized him with intensity. His throat dried. Her eyes reminded him of Lilly, the woman he'd tried to forget for the past seven years.

Suddenly she stiffened, and he could have sworn she paled beneath her thick face paint. "I'm Lee Wilcox, and I owe you this." Her hand rose.

Whack! A stinging pain slammed into his cheek.

He staggered back, his hand flying up to cover his wound. What the hell? His pulse jumped track and raced pell mell along some uncharted path. Struggling to recover his wits, he bent to retrieve his hat which had fallen during the encounter.

That's when he reconsidered his misplaced loyalty. Just who had Bart recommended? Surely not this whore.

Had a card floated off a table and landed on the floor, it would have thundered in the sudden quiet of the gambling hall. The silence was eerie, pregnant. He had the distinct impression each man had taken stock of him and judged him to be a menace. The bartender lay flat across the bar top where he'd pitched himself to come to the lady's aid.

"It's all right, Jake. I'll handle this." The woman placed her hands on her hips, her expression as cold as the ocean's depths.

Handle what? He had been the one on the wrong end of the

assault. Who was she, and what did she think he did to warrant such a venomous payback? The floozy had to be mistaken. And his cheek still stung.

"I'm sorry. Do I know you?" Dumb, but the only thing that dribbled out his mouth.

"Try Lee Wilcox. Or better yet, try Lilly Kane." Her voice spit venom.

He pulled in a breath, then stilled, his heartbeat nearly coming to a halt.

Lilly! Lee.

Memories burst into his consciousness. Blood pulsed in his ears like a thousand pounding mallets. Old hurts he'd worked hard to get over resurfaced to cause an unbearable onslaught to his heart. He tamped them back, and assumed a pleasant smile. The hell if he would acknowledge his disquiet in front of this woman.

He studied her features through eyes rooted in the past.

Beneath the makeup, the delicate heart shape of Lilly's face was discernible, though the youthful hollows below her cheekbones had filled in to give it a more rounded shape. Almond shaped eyes of sea green—Lilly's eyes—peered up at him through gobs of shadow and kohl.

Eyes now sparking with ire. He struggled to pump air into strangled lungs.

This woman, older and with more flesh where it counted, looked like every other working girl in the place, and that somehow bothered him. Thick stage makeup covered her face, but her flamboyant gown exposed more of her impressive bosom than Lilly would have dared allow. More than he would have allowed.

Was she the little shop girl he once knew, the young lady with the beautiful eyes and the sweetly beckoning smile? If she was Lilly, what was she doing in a gambling hall in Colorado City dressed as a whore? Or was she...? He cut off his train of thought, refusing to acknowledge the truth of what his eyes were telling him. No, not his Lilly....

The woman glanced about, then without a word, headed for the back of the saloon, her silk skirts swishing behind her. Why he followed like a dog seeking a treat, he would never understand.

They passed table after table filled with gamblers, all attentive to the backside of the woman who called herself Lee Wilcox. From their expressions of adoration, he knew if he took one step to harm her, he would never live to see the sun set.

She led him to a room at the far corner of the establishment and disappeared inside. Nick halted at the threshold, transfixed by the sight before him. The room's appearance, so different from the dark and dingy saloon, was jarring and out of place—like he'd stepped into someone's comfortable front parlor.

Bright afternoon sun streamed through a wide set of open windows, bringing with it a refreshing breeze. The splash of light reached across the room to highlight some strange form of map hanging on the opposite wall. What appeared to be cut-off hat pins marked various locations on the hand-drawn chart. Books, photographs and bric-a-brac were neatly arranged in a dark oak bookcase.

A wooden desk was positioned to allow Miss Wilcox a view of the mountains while conversing with her clients. If she had any clients, that is. Framed tintypes and rock paperweights decorated the oak desktop. Flowered wallpaper and furniture, and a thick carpet made it a woman's office in—of all places—a rowdy gambling hall and whorehouse.

The office of private investigator Lee Wilcox. Known to him as Lilly Kane.

His Lilly.

If indeed, she was the Lilly he knew.

He entered the room as she seated herself. With a sweep of her hand, she invited him to sit in one of the chairs before her desk, but her countenance was far from friendly. The woman was coiled tight as a spring. She fairly shook with effort to contain her emotions.

Was she really Lilly, the lovely woman he knew with the even disposition? The woman who'd been unflappable in the most trying of situations? The woman who never spoke an unkind word to or about anyone?

He chose to stand. "So, how long has it been?"

"Seven years," she bit out without hesitation.

Nick's breathing stopped. Only his Lilly would know that. Their relationship had been clandestine, kept to dark storerooms and walks on the lake shore after his father's dry goods store closed for the night. This woman hadn't even given his question a thought. The answer sprang from her lips as though she had been counting the years.

As had he.

Lilly! No doubt about it.

Conflicting thoughts he cared not to examine tumbled through his mind.

He schooled his voice to be as noncommittal as possible, but the question uppermost in his thoughts all these years flew from his mouth. "Why did you leave me?"

She shot off her chair, her face reddening through the thick mask of cosmetics. Her hands flew to the desk where her knuckles ground into the wood. Her mouth thinned into a straight line. "I didn't leave you, you bastard. You left me."

The volume of her pain-tinged voice had risen, a reaction uncharacteristic of the Lilly he knew. His Lilly never raised her voice, no matter how upset she might have been.

She swung wildly around the edge of the desk and stalked to the window, her back to him, arms wrapped around her middle. A picture frame wobbled as she passed. It fell, the glass shattering into tiny pieces. Without thought, he picked up the tintype.

The face of a small child with blonde hair and cherubic cheeks looked back at him. He scrutinized the photograph for a long moment. The little girl looked remarkably like the painting of his sister hanging in his mother's bedroom.

As he ruminated, a thought punched him in the gut, its sharp edge twisting painfully. No, it couldn't possibly be, could it? The girl was about four years old. When was this photograph taken? His thumb grazed the image as he did a quick calculation. Horrified, his mind wrapped around a reality he'd run from nearly all his life— responsibility. His sister Sabrina's well-being had been the only thing that mattered to him. Until Lilly came into his life.

Was this child his, or someone else's?

"Who is this?" he asked, but somehow he knew.

Lilly turned to face him, her large eyes like ice. "My daughter, Celia. You were her father."

Another punch landed in his gut with a force that took his breath away. "Were?"

"She died of the fever two years ago." She'd said it as though the child's death had been his fault.

Barely contained emotions barreled through him. He'd discovered he'd become a father, and then, within seconds, learned his child had died. A sense of loss so profound made the room spin. Sharp needles pierced his heart, the stabbing pain unbearable. His knees weakened. He grabbed the back of a chair, his fingers holding on as though it were a lifeline.

He'd had a daughter. And she'd died without knowing her father.

Remorse draped his body in leaden nets of chain mail, heavy and cumbersome. Lord knew he hadn't wanted to be a father, but if fate had made him one, he might have stepped up to the challenge. Might have changed the life he now found profoundly lacking.

Might have. He was so young then.

"Why didn't you tell me you carried our child? I would have...." He stopped, the words clogging his throat like cotton batting. No matter how much he tried, he couldn't bring himself to say what she needed to hear.

Her eyes narrowed. "What would you have done, Nick. Tell me."

"I... I would have been there for you."

"Would you? Really? Married me, given your daughter your name, settled into a normal routine, taken on responsibility for once in your life?"

Nick swallowed hard but didn't answer. Like the rest of his friends, he had led a life of hedonistic bachelorhood, shying away from marriage as though it was the plague. His was the life of a *bon vivant*, a dabbler in fun, adventure, and the finer things of life. There was no room for responsibility and commitment.

Then.

After Lilly left, that life no longer satisfied him, yet he couldn't seem to find what would. His days were empty, meaningless, his nights incredibly lonely.

Lilly continued, her voice sounding thin and strangled. "I tried to tell you about the baby. As soon as I was sure, I went to your house, but your father said you'd moved away, that you were managing a new store somewhere far away."

A pipe dream belonging to a father who desired a different life for his son. A life more in his own image. Blast the man. Familiar bands of frustration tightened about his torso.

He shook his head. "Not true. I never moved anywhere. He sent me to New York on a buying trip. When I returned, you were gone."

"Then your father lied to me. For you. To prevent me, as he put it, from 'sinking my teeth' into his precious wealthy son. He assumed correctly I was in a family way. He made me a generous offer to move away and start over." She lowered her head, tightened her arms. "I had no choice but to accept his proposal. My baby's future was at stake. I couldn't continue working at his store, and I could never give my child up to an orphanage."

Nick believed her account. His father frequently meddled in his affairs, having had a heavy hand in his and Sabrina's lives since childhood. Neither could do much of anything without their father offering an opinion and insisting upon their compliance. Nick rebelled by becoming the antithesis of his father's wishes, but Sabrina disappeared into the woodwork of life, afraid to do anything that might draw their father's unwarranted attention.

"He never told me you came."

"Then he lied to both of us. I showed up at the store hoping to see you, but you weren't there. I came around for a week, but you were gone. No one could tell me where you went. I assumed your father told me the truth."

Nick's hands fisted. This time his father's interference had cost everyone dearly.

Especially Lilly. Moisture glistened in her eyes. "I was alone and afraid. I had no one. My parents sa. . .disowned me. I hate you for causing my family to turn against me. You didn't even try to find me."

"I did try, Lilly, but you told me Kane was the Americanized version of your parents' last name. You never told me the name your family was listed under in the Chicago Directory."

He paused to swipe his forehead with his palm. "I should have tried harder, even rifled my father's private employment files for your address. Instead, I wallowed in self-pity and condemned you for walking away from me, for daring to wound my almighty Shield pride. I'm sorry, so very sorry. Had I known—"

"I don't want to hear your 'would haves.' You would have done what you've done your whole life—shirked responsibility. The only good thing to come out of this was Celia. I had her for four wonderful years, and when she died...." Rubbing her arms, Lilly turned slightly to stare out the window, her small figure cloaked in sorrow.

He deserved her caustic barb, but the husk of pain in her voice burned clear through to his soul. He moved to gather her close, but she jerked away.

"Don't touch me, Nicholas. You don't get to touch me ever again."

To learn more about Nick and Lilly's story and when it will be released, sign up for my Newsletter at http://eepurl.com/cTMjqH

Author Biography

Averil Reisman loves to write steamy American-set historical romances of the late Victorian period. During this era, America's aristocracy created by the Industrial Revolution lived like lords and ladies of England. A closet feminist, she greatly admires the brave woman of the era who fought for equal voting rights, and who often broke society's strict rules to bring about social change and women's equality. Averil lives with her own hero, Art, in a far suburb of Chicago where the corn still grows down the road. They see their three grown daughters, respective beloved spouses, and three very bright grandsons as often as possible.

Made in the USA
Middletown, DE
22 March 2024